BELLA VITA

+1

BELLA VITA

A NOVEL

B.M. SIMPSON

BELLA VITA
A NOVEL

bmsimpson@LIVE.com
www.facebook.com/BMSimpson.author

ISBN- 10: 0-9863954-4-7
ISBN – 13: 978-0-9863954-4-4

PRINTED IN THE UNITED STATES OF AMERICA

Book Design by Mads Berg, Mads Berg Illustration

BELLA VITA

"Yesterday is a memory. You can't touch it any more than you can touch tomorrow. And tomorrow is just a dream. We don't even know if we will see tomorrow. Nobody does. So, all we really have is now."

Avis Humphrey

CHAPTER ONE

It was in February when everything unraveled in one fell swoop, like a hawk striking its prey. It didn't take the entire month, or even a week. To be honest it didn't even take up an entire hour of the day. The axe dropped so fast that the beginning and the end of the big crash were almost at the same point in time. Lucy's career engine was running smoothly, then it sputtered for barely a moment, and then stalled out. Within minutes she crashed and burned, and that was that. Yet, it seemed like her corporate death took a long time. It was like being in a car accident that she could see coming, but there was nothing she could do about it. Everything slowed down to super-slow motion as if the few seconds lasted for hours. Strangely enough, when it was all over, all she could say to herself was, "What the hell just happened?"

She slid out of bed that morning at 6:15 and eased into the kitchen without a care. The preset coffeemaker dripped a steady stream into the glass pot and the smell of coffee cleared the fog from her head. She had always been a morning girl and now she was a morning woman. One cup of coffee then it was off to her yoga class in the fitness center on the 17th floor of the building she lived in. That was followed by a shower, getting ready for work, a short stroll to Starbucks for another coffee and a croissant. At 8:15 she walked into one of the many skyscrapers on Wall Street, New York City. After a ride on the crowded elevator to her floor and a couple of short greetings with coworkers, she sat down at her desk and opened her laptop. There was a message from Allison instructing her to come to her office at 9:00 AM. Nothing unusual there. At exactly 9:00 AM sharp, February 6th, her world started slipping. It only slipped momentarily. After that, over the cliff it went.

Allison Lanahan was an enigma to Lucy. She was her

corporate manager who had a firm grasp of short and long-term financial management and a depth of experience in corporate financial modeling, planning and analysis. From what Lucy had seen in the months she had worked for her, Allison was smart, personable and likeable, but that being said, she was not close to anyone in the office. And while nobody said anything particularly negative about her, conversely, they said nothing positive about her either.

Almost a year ago Lucy had earned her Master's in International Business from Columbia and had finished in the top five percent of her class. There were plenty of jobs to choose from. Plenty of companies who were interested. She chose this job with this company in this city for one reason. It was a fantastic place to start an amazing career. According to her mapped out future, three to five years here with this company, and then she would take a step up to an even more affluent company for another five years. From there she would be positioned to make whatever career choice that struck her fancy. Of course, that master plan had not included this conversation.

If she was the type of young woman who used profanities she would have said that February 6th was when everything went to shit. But she wasn't that type. Lucy was reserved, methodical and careful. She was the internalizing type. She always took the good and the bad into her brilliant mind, processed the data thoroughly, analyzed the options, and made the right decision. Above all, she didn't burn bridges. And of course, she also followed her instincts just as many of her professors, mentors, and her father had instructed her to do over the years. That was the caveat they always threw to their wide-eyed sponges after they instructed them to take in, process, analyze, make the right decision, and don't burn bridges. And, oh yeah... trust your instinct. After six years of college her instincts told her to do the first five steps and disregard the last. Genuine instinct had been all but beat out of her by the time all the books and articles and lectures had been drummed deep into her mind.

Lucy sat comfortably, but not slouching, in the black

armless swivel chair in front of Allison's desk. When the conversation began there was a slight, yet sincere smile on Lucy's face. She was the consummate professional. Always positive. Always engaged. Always absorbing what was fed to her. Always searching for ways to keep a conversation going in a positive and constructive direction. It was at about the three-minute mark when the possible sincerity of her smile turned to obvious insincerity, but the smile remained. The speed of Lucy's thought process had doubled and then accelerated. She had become like a mouse scurrying for cheese in a cage full of cats and she was beginning to feel that despite her frantic pace and all the cats, there may have never been any cheese to be had. She was having difficulty processing how quickly her whole life was changing direction, but she didn't doubt for a moment that the course was changing. At almost six minutes to the second, her smile, sincere or otherwise, was gone. At nine o'clock sharp she had taken her seat and awaited her first review since being hired. She held a master's in economics, with a minor in Mandarin. Since being hired, she had done everything asked of her and much more. She came in early and went home late. She was a rising star who only lacked one thing. Experience. But time would take care of that. She expected nothing less than a stellar review. Best case scenario? Her position would be made permanent and her salary would be adjusted accordingly.

"I don't understand," she said as she fought back tears, anger, confusion and pretty much all the negative emotions she could think of, while still emotionally clinging onto a smile that no longer existed. She felt her jaw clenching and the veins were beginning to show in her neck and forehead.

"Look. I know it's a bit of a surprise, but it shouldn't be a complete shock. Not if you've been paying attention." The genuine Allison, the one that Lucy had yet to become familiar with until now, sat behind her desk and glanced back and forth from the papers she was scribbling on and the young woman sitting directly in front of her. Lucy could feel her face beginning to flush as heat began to consume her. Her mind was fibrillating between flashes of absolute clarity and overwhelming confusion. She was off balance and couldn't wrap her head around what was happening. She was always prepared. She always had a back-up plan for everything, but not for this. It had never entered her mind that Allison was a cutthroat bitch. Lucy continued to sit up straight and confident, even after it began being an act. But she caught herself rubbing her tongue on the front of her teeth with her lips tightly closed. It was a tell that she had worked hard to get rid of after her mother laughed at her one day and said, "You know, whenever you get mad you…" It had been at least three years, maybe longer, since she had rubbed her tongue on her teeth.

"You've spent the past five minutes showering me with praise for my work performance, Allison, and now you're firing me?" Lucy asked as if she were not one hundred percent certain she was being fired. It was an accusation as much as a question. She knew enough to be on the offensive even when she was clearly on the defensive.

"Lucy, I gave you a good review. It's probably a bit of an exaggeration to say I showered you with praise. And the truth is, while you did a pretty good job, I just can't fiscally justify your position at the moment." She said it all as if she were saying the dinner was okay, but nothing special. Certainly not worth the price. Lucy bit her bottom lip and momentarily looked down at her lap and saw 9:06 on the face of her phone. She caught herself wavering and quickly looked back up.

"You said my work ethic and professionalism were exceptional. Your exact word was "exceptional." Now you're firing me?" she asked again as if there were any doubt. "I turned down a half dozen fantastic offers to accept this job at Fudo & Fernandez. You made it clear it would turn into a permanent position." Her palms were sweaty and she noticed that she was crushing her right hand with her left.

"Well, then I suppose it's good that others were interested," she answered with the slightest tinge of sarcasm.

"They'll be wondering why this firm fired me. You're not telling me something, Allison. I deserve a better explanation than 'you can't fiscally justify.' You're going to have to do better than that, Allison." She could feel herself emotionally shutting down or exploding. She wasn't sure which. She had processed so many options over the past few minutes with none of them having a positive result that there were only two reasonable options left. She could either blow up and unleash holy hell on Allison and embarrass herself, or she could climb into an emotional shell and wait until this moment in her history passed on by. She was leaning towards the second while wishing to do the first.

"Really, Lucy. You're going to act like a spoiled little girl now? If this is how you handle adversity you make me wonder if perhaps fiscal considerations should be the only reason for not keeping you." Viciously attacking the vulnerable, the kill shot, it all came natural to her. It wasn't like she practiced it or gave it any thought. Some people were naturals at selling. Others were skilled artist or craftsmen. Compassion and kindness flowed like a warm river from the gifted ones. And some people were natural born killers. In Allison's case, driving the metaphoric knife into the heart of those she needed gone, and then twisting it for good measure, came to her as naturally as breathing air in and out of her lungs. Those who knew her well, or perhaps those who had been in Lucy's chair in the past, were quite certain that Allison could use an actual knife with ease if she thought it was the best way to get the job done, and if she thought she could get away with it. The last person who sat in Lucy's chair was a guy who literally cried when the kill shot came. A woman from HR had to console him as she walked with her arm around him and a security guard behind them when they left the death chamber. "I just bought a condo and my wife is pregnant with our first," he said between snivels and sobs. Allison sat behind her desk skimming over some papers and relishing the moment of a job well done. She was not a man crusher, per say. Over the past fifteen years, she had crushed anyone who got in her way. Gender was never really taken into consideration. The ruling factors in her life decisions were pro/con ratios, risk/reward factors and threat level, all related to her and her alone. Anyone who fell into the wrong category was removed. Her husband of seven years slowly but steadily worked his way on to the wrong side of the slash in the pro/con ratio. He became her ex-husband five years ago. He didn't see it coming and was still paying dearly, even though she made twice his income. As far as she was concerned, he should have been prepared for the turn in his marriage and his economy. As it turned out, she had prepared for both. She beat him to the punch on the divorce, and the alimony he paid carried her through any economic bumps in the road, not that she really had any.

Lucy was young and idealistic and had misread Allison from day one. For lack of better words, she bought the act. She had considered her to be her boss, mentor, co-worker and her friend, in that order. The reality was that Allison was Lucy's boss, and sometimes adversary whether Lucy knew it or not. She had never been her friend or coworker. Being a woman didn't make anyone Allison's friend, unless she were somehow using gender to her own advantage. And mentor? Only if it could benefit Allison. Lucy was young and brilliant, but still learning about life. She was smarter than her boss, more attractive than her boss, and worked just as hard or maybe harder. Sooner or later she would draw attention from people higher up the chain. It was a simple decision really, and it was a decision that was made within the first month of her employment. While Allison saw some favorable advantages to holding onto such a brilliant and valuable asset for as long as possible, the truth was that it was the numbers that determined the outcome. The risk/reward factors to her own career didn't work out in Lucy's favor. The threat level in keeping her was simply too high. Letting her go was really quite painless... for Allison.

Lucy stared at the soulless body that sat in front of her to no avail. Allison continued to scan papers and scribble notes and signatures on them as if the insignificant thing sitting in front of her just needed to go away. It was as if she had just assigned Lucy with a new, yet minor project that she should go get started on. She could almost hear her saying, "Move along Lucy. Go put your life back together. Hup. Hup."

"Now what? I mean...." Lucy's words momentarily trailed off while she tried to think of what to ask. "Am I done, you know, today? Or are you giving me a two-week notice, or..." Her words trailed off again.

"HR is waiting for you at your desk. They're gathering your things. Let them know if you have any personal items they may have missed. Security will escort you out," she said in a dull, distant voice without looking up at Lucy.

"Security! You fucking bitch," she quietly hissed, without believing the words came out of her mouth. "You acted like my friend. We went to dinner last week."

Allison finally stopped pretending she was reading what was in front of her and looked up at her latest pathetic victim. It was all so predictable. She had done it so many times that it didn't even wrinkle her conscience any longer, if it ever had in the first place. She took a certain amount of sociopathic pleasure in the entire process, but truth be known, all her victims disgusted her ever so slightly. They were all so predictable, helpless... pathetic.

"Grow up, little girl," was all she said and then glanced past Lucy towards the door. Lucy turned quickly and saw two security officers standing in the doorway. One of them gave her a warm pitiful smile and motioned for her to come with him. Edward had worked at Fudo & Fernandez for twelve years. He was obviously no threat to the assassin and would likely work there for another twelve. She turned back towards Allison who was already pretending to work on her papers again.

Lucy and Edward quietly walked out of the office and down the hall to her desk with the smaller guard momentarily trailing behind until Edward nodded that he could go. HR had come and gone and left a box of miscellaneous items sitting on the desk along with a folder with the dark green Fudo & Fernandez logo stamped on the front. Below the logo was a yellow sticky that said, "Lucy, please review the documents inside and let us know if you have any questions." She stared at the note and her forehead wrinkled. Allison had just fired her as if she were a thief stealing from the company. HR had cowardly left her a folder on her desk without so much as saying, "I'm so sorry Lucy. I'm sure you'll be better off in your next position. Let's get a drink sometime," like she and her friend from HR had just done three nights ago. She slowly looked at Edward, a man she had never met, and he looked down at her like he was looking at his own heartbroken daughter. If the company hadn't forbidden it he would have given her a warm hug and told her she was going to be okay, but he knew better than most that there were cameras everywhere.

"This everything that's yours? You know, any other personal stuff here?" he asked while she stared at him and continued to process and analyze and search for the proper words. HR had already taken every last item that could have possibly been construed as company property and carried it away. Even the phone and laptop were gone from her desk. Lucy glanced in the box that held a picture of her mother, father and little brother. There were a few pens. A couple books on the markets and the economy. And her favorite coffee cup with the Columbia logo on the front and a slight chip at the top. Edward's question was more rhetorical than actual. All the drawers were open and empty. If there was anything else left, it was hidden somewhere. She wasn't sure if the shock was just setting in or beginning to wear off. Or perhaps, she was just moving from shock to a numb fog. Either way, she reached to pick up the box and walk towards the elevator.

"I've got it Lucy," Edward said. He surprised her when he spoke her name. She was pretty certain they had never met and she gave him a puzzled look. "They make sure we know your name before we come down. You know... it's supposed to make things more... hell, I don't know. They just tell us to call you by your first name. Plus, I know most people here because I monitor the cameras a lot."

"Cameras?" she asked and glanced around.

"No big deal. Never saw you do anything foolish or embarrassing," he said, and clearly implied he had seen plenty over the years. They strolled towards the elevator for one last trip down to the lobby. "By the way," he added. "In a little while, maybe later today or maybe in a couple days, you're going to reach the boiling point. You know, you're going to simmer for a while, but then it's all going to hit you and you'll think that coming back here and raising some hell is a good idea." He looked at her and watched her face until he could tell she had taken in his words. "It's not a good idea Lucy. In fact, it's a bad idea."

He stopped talking and they both stood in front of the elevator waiting for the door to open. Lucy had slid into a complete trance and Edward was hoping the elevator was empty. It was always easier if there wasn't some obnoxious moron who couldn't piece together a security guard carrying a box full of personal items standing beside the walking dead. The door opened, and he felt mild relief no one was standing in front of them. He motioned for her to step inside and then followed her in and pushed the L button. They stood in silence as he held the small memorial to the death of her first professional employment.

"Where are you from?" she asked numbly and stared at the stainless-steel door while drifting to the ground. "I heard your accent. Just wondering...." she said without emotion. The question was more of a reflex than actual curiosity. Edward was politely assisting her to the door. It seemed logical that she would talk to him, she guessed. What else could she ask? 'How many people have you tossed out over the years?'

She's nicer than most, Edward thought. A lot of them were complete asses, yelling and swearing and threatening. But those were not the worst. The criers were the ones who he didn't quite know what to do with. Especially the guys. What the hell was a big guy like Edward supposed to do with a full-grown man who was crying? Edward just wasn't the kind of guy who hung out with guys who acted like that. More than once some sniveling *ex*-employee had told him that his wife would probably leave when she found out he'd been fired. Lucy was shocked and numb and hurt and confused, but above all she remained pleasant and asked, "Where are you from?" Edward thought her question was a sign of good character. Her life was, for the moment, shattered and he was certain her thoughts must be on autopilot. In moments like this most people are not really thinking clearly. Hard times were defining moments. More often than not humans are self-absorbed in the moment and asking anything about another person is not typical behavior. He knew she was a good one the moment she said, Where are you from?"

"Anguilla. In the Caribbean."

"Ahh. Yes. Anguilla, I've seen pictures of it. Looks beautiful," she said without emotion and continued to look at the brushed stainless-steel door panel in front of her.

"You should go sometime," he answered without looking at her. "Nice place. Good place to heal. Good people."

Lucy broke her gaze from the door and looked up at Edward. He looked down at her with a sad smile and still wanted to give her a hug, if not for the cameras. "Seems like I've got some time. Maybe I'll go now." They both smiled for a moment, then they slipped back into reality and their gazes returned to the elevator door. It never dawned on her she'd be on a plane to the little Caribbean island in the very near future.

CHAPTER TWO

For his entire adult life Pellet's decisions, both good and bad, were made with little or no forethought. They were made on the spur of the moment, without any plan, and without any consideration of what the fallout of his choices might be. When an urge struck, he acted upon it. If he had the urge for a seventh beer to follow the sixth, he gave no thought of what tomorrow was going to feel like. If he saw a beautiful woman who struck him as, *the one,* his ill-advised pickup lines poured out like promises from a politician. There was no time spent trying to envision her likely response. If he didn't see the long-range impact, he gave no long-range thought. On the flip side, since he rarely gave his decisions any long-term thought, he rarely saw the impact. His favorite worn and tattered t-shirt had, *"SEIZE THE DAY"* written in bright orange letters across his chest. In Pellet's mind, almost anything he did had only short-term rewards or consequences, so seizing the day seemed like the right way to go. *"SEIZE THE MOMENT"* would have been more appropriate. In Pellet's world there was no sliding scale of importance where the weight of his actions grew in direct proportion to their possible positive or negative impact. All non-life changing decisions fell into the "eh, whatever" category, and they all carried the exact same amount of weight. With a few exceptions, he thought all of his decisions were non-life changing. As far as he was concerned, whether or not to buy a new truck, move to another apartment, or have another beer all carried more or less the same weight and all fell on the spur of the moment side of the line. Very few issues made it to the other side of the line.

Oddly enough, when Pellet had a rare but presumably important life decision to be made, he gave it extensive thought and consideration and then made a more or less detailed plan and acted like a real live grownup. Sometimes he gave it months or years of thought without taking the next logical step. Then, once he eventually put the plan into action, he screwed it up. But not before spending an absurd amount of time in the consideration of all the how, why and when details he could wrap his head around. Inevitably, he almost always left out at least one critical factor. It took him three years to plan his escape from Waldoboro, Maine to his *antipodal point*. It turned out that the journey to his antipodal point ended up being in the Antarctic, hundreds of miles from land, and almost all his thinking and planning had been in vain. But it was, once upon a time, an amazing idea. In time, the Antarctic plan landed him in Anguilla, via a couple years in Florida. But all things being what they were, even though his journey was largely a failure by almost any standard, it was still amazing to see Pellet put such thought into anything.

And while buying a nice truck, or quitting a job, or having a serious relationship, not that he ever had any serious relationships, were not what he would consider to be big life decisions, buying a sailboat was going to become one. For reasons that escaped even Pellet, in the sliding life scale inside his head, trucks, jobs and relationships did not make the beam of the life scale tip all that much. The sailboat, on the other hand, would make it drop like a rock. The seed that was about to take root somewhere deep in his psyche was going to have to grow a bit before a decision was made, but there would be no stopping it. The leaves would need to sprout and the flower of his vision would have to bloom before he took what was likely to be a huge step in a direction that he had not yet envisioned. Buying a sailboat was about to become a Pellet quest that paralleled the quest for world peace or to discover the meaning of life. It seemed that Pellet wanted more out of life, and it turned out that more was going to be a sailboat.

The idea began to grow out of a somewhat emotional and painful experience and it slowly grew into a turning point in his life. It was three o'clock on a Saturday afternoon when Pellet wandered in and quietly slid onto a stool at Dez's Bar. Desmund slid a Red Stripe across the bar and opened one for himself. He put them both on Pellet's tab.

Desmund was an island man through and through. He was Anguilla born and raised and never had any desire to have much more than what his small island life offered. And he never felt the urge to emotionally or intellectually grow and become more, or to travel the world or leave his paradise island. By and large, he was a proud and content island man. As life would have it, many years ago, a twist of fate led him to be married to a devious, money grubbing island woman who became the bane of his existence. A few years later another twist of fate led her far away from Anguilla, leaving Desmund and his small meager bar in her rear-view mirror. It was the best day of his life. These days, he tended bar, chatted with tourists and somehow took on the role of being Pellet's advisor of sorts, friend, bar tender and drinking buddy.

"Hot today, mon."

"Umm," was Pellet's slight response. He looked down at his beer, lost in thought.

"Comin to eat tonight? Avis and Savannah said they'd be by. Probably Helmut and Fatisha, too."

"Dunno." He continued looking down at his beer and looked like his puppy had just died.

"Maybe Oscar and Iggy. I'll call em," Dez continued.

"Cool," was all Pellet said, still adrift in thought.

"Any luck with dat woman you were talkin with last night?"

"Naw. Think she's…" He stopped talking. He didn't really think she was anything, one way or the other. It was his auto response kicking in to make an excuse of how an attractive tourist could possibly say no to a scraggly looking thirty-five-year-old wearing tattered cargo shorts and a faded t-shirt.

"Her loss, ey?"

"Umm," he mumbled one more time.

"Good lawd. Gonna jus sit an mope all afternoon?" Desmund was the master at being the bartender/shrink. He could get a mute to spill their woes on him, and figure out how to make them feel better, at least for a while. Then again, he'd gone through a thousand miles of Pellet's insanity. Hangovers. Lost, yet embarrassing memories of the night before. Fights with perfect strangers, which were fights that he typically lost. Dozens of love affairs or would be love affairs that went bad shortly after or shortly before they even began. Whatever tact and encouragement Desmund would spread on a troubled tourist, or maybe a local who didn't call upon his services all that often, were not shared with Pellet anymore. Seven years ago when he first arrived in Anguilla, Pellet got the royal treatment from Desmund. These days all he got was, "Gonna jus sit an mope some more?"

"Nah. Gonna sit and mope, smoke a cigarette, and drink this beer. Then maybe I'll sit and mope and have another." He reached into the pocket of his baggy cargo shorts and pulled out a pack of cigarettes and a lighter.

"Good to know. Just don't drive no customers away."

Pellet looked around and saw no sign of life. "What the hell are you talking about? I'm the only one here."

"See. Bad already."

Pellet lit his cigarette and inhaled deeply then let a long stream of smoke blow into the bar. He looked down at his beer again and acted as if he were trying to say something, but the words just wouldn't come out. Desmund didn't really care if they came out or not. He walked to the other end of the bar and wiped it down and hoped someone else would come in soon. The moping was more bothersome when he was the only customer to talk to.

"Have you ever found out shit that you already more or less knew to be true, but you just kind of dealt with it okay as long as it wasn't confirmed?"

"Mean like da truck needs fixin, but you jus pretend it's okay till it's all mashed up and won't move no more?"

Pellet said nothing for a moment and then turned and looked in the dirt parking lot and realized Desmund's truck wasn't there.

"Truck finally died, huh?"

"Engine's all mashed up. Dead. Watcha gonna do. Nuther beer?"

"Well, yes to the beer. And not really to the truck analogy. Damn thing blew more smoke than a forest fire for at least a year. You knew it was screwed and just drove it until there wasn't one more mile left in it." He took another drag and reached for the beer Desmund had just set down in front of him. "I'm talking about stuff like, you know, relationships and family and shit like that."

"You didn't know you suck at relationships? An I don't know you family."

"I've got to find another bar to hang out at. Don't know why I even bother to come here anymore. Do you?"

"Tink it's jus for da company. Gonna tell me what's buggin you or we jus gonna keep doin this?"

Pellet looked out over the blue water that flowed between Anguilla and St Maarten. The waves were kicking up a bit more than normal and a warm breeze blew through the open-air bar. He tossed his ballcap onto the bar and ran his fingers through his hair and contorted his face, as if he were searching for words.

"My damn sister. I told her to let it go. Leave it alone. Just couldn't help herself." He took another drink of his Red Stripe and looked down at the bar and shook his head back and forth in disbelief.

CHAPTER THREE

The one thing Pellet had in common with his oldest sister was they both seemed to gravitate to extremes. Not that their extremes were necessarily in the same direction. Cheryl Pelletier was six years older than Pellet, and virtually nothing like him other than once she committed to doing something, she was all in. On Saturday afternoons she did laundry and then went to Shop n' Save for groceries. Pellet was usually at a Caribbean bar. More times than not, she spent Saturday evenings sitting with her cats and ate TV dinners while playing Candy Crush and free online slot machines. He was still at the bar. On Sundays she went to the Methodist Church in Waldoboro, Maine and thanked God for all the things that had been provided to her and her cats and then prayed for help with whatever her most recent obsession was. For the past two years that obsession was *The Family Tree*. On those same Sundays, Pellet would have been either recovering from the bar or on his way back to the bar. Over the past few months Cheryl had spent so much time on the final stages of her project she almost never played computer games and even missed church once or twice. After four years of barely contacting Pellet, she reached out one day a couple years ago to let him know she was researching their family origins and resurrecting their history. It didn't seem like a good idea to him.

"You ever think of finding a man?" he mumbled on the phone while smoking a cigarette on his porch and looking out towards the sea. It was a discussion they repeated at least once a month.

"I'm not interested in finding a man Pellet. Tried it once. He was like a man version of smoking three packs of cigarettes non-stop so you'll never smoke again. Three years of living with Cecil cured me of the habit."

"Okay. You ever think about finding a woman?"

"Good Lord, Pellet. What is wrong with you?"

"How about drinking. Maybe you should drink more. Our family seems to have a knack for that," he continued in an effort to help her find something to fill her time with other than pointlessly digging up the family's abysmal history.

"I had a glass of wine at the church supper a couple weeks ago."

"Really? I'm impressed," Pellet responded. He actually was very impressed that she did anything outside her comfort zone which might have ended in social interaction and possible lively conversation.

"Well. It was non-alcoholic grape wine, but it was tasty."

"That's called grape juice, Cheryl." He shook his head and ran out of suggestions on how she should fill her days and nights. What he was really thinking was that she should find something to fill her time enough so she didn't call him every week or so. As it turned out, Cheryl was a woman of habit, and once a habit was formed, there was no breaking it. His big sister had added him to her list of things that needed to be done on a regular weekly basis. That was that.

"So, anyway," she continued, "The family tree thing is just about done. I'll email you a copy soon."

"Not interested. We've already talked about this. No need to send it to me."

"I'll try to get it out to you before next weekend."

"Don't want it."

"I think you'll be quite impressed when you see it."

"Not gonna read it."

"Come on, Pellet. Stop being silly. You know you'll read it. There are some very interesting characters in our past."

"I doubt interesting is the correct word. Besides, I'm really busy at work lately. Send it to..." he thought for a moment about who she could send it to. "Send it to anyone else, Cheryl."

On the following Thursday evening he received the email. Attached to it was an extensive family tree that covered both sides of the family for several hundred years. It was difficult to say how accurate it was, but accurate or not, the whole thing was pretty damn impressive. Pellet thought it looked much more impressive before he began reading it. It was like watching a bad train wreck he didn't want to see but couldn't look away. Cheryl had been correct about two things. Pellet was indeed reading it, and there were some pretty interesting characters in their past, albeit that "interesting" was an overly kind word to use.

Saturday afternoon he sat at the bar drinking a beer while getting chastised by Desmund for moping and possibly driving away all his non-existent customers.

"My damn sister," he grumbled for about the twentieth time, "I told her to just let it go. To leave it alone. Nothing good could come from this. She just couldn't help herself."

He took another drink of his Red Stripe and looked down at the bar and shook his head back and forth in disbelief. Desmund looked puzzled. Over the past few years he'd listened to Pellet bitch, whine, brag, say stupid things, ask pointless questions and carry on conversations that were often best left in his head. But not once had he seen Pellet sincerely distressed. At least not in an actual grownup manner. Even when his infamous infatuation with Fatisha came to a far more catastrophic end than anyone would have imagined, Pellet was only severely damaged on the surface. She was an obsession he had refused to let go of, which was nothing like losing the love of his dysfunctional life. Today, for the first time since they had met over a half decade ago, Desmund saw actual pain on Pellet's face.

"Family. Almost never listen," Desmund said, shifting to a tone of slight concern. He had no idea of what the sister had done, nor did he know her. He'd never met her and Pellet rarely spoke of his family. So, he just left it alone and waited to find out if Pellet was going to share anything else.

"You know, I don't ask much. Never ask for money. Hell, I send money. Never ask for help. Given up on the idea that any of them will ever come and visit. I go on Amazon and send Christmas gifts to the nieces and nephews." He stopped and smiled and took a sip of beer. "Although one of my other sisters got a little pissed when I sent a beer brewing kit to my nephew last year."

"How old?"

"Thirteen."

"Didn't tink dat one out, eh?"

"Suppose not. Think her husband enjoyed it though."

A twenty something year old tourist strolled in and sat at the end of the bar, nowhere near Pellet. Desmund was surprised when his friend didn't even feign interest. She was attractive and looked like she might have a bit of money. At least enough to pay for a few drinks. And the clincher, she was out of Pellet's league. That in itself was normally enough to spur him into giving a go at picking her up. Dez eased to the end of the bar. After a couple minutes of 'Welcome to Dez's' chit chat, that consisted of where you from, how you like da island, where you stayin, and you wanna try da rum punch, he opened a Heineken and set it down in front of her. He worked his way back down to Pellet to see if he could put two more beers on his tab. The woman looked beyond the bar to someplace a thousand miles away. Wherever it was she came from, it appeared she was still focused on it. There are those who come to the islands and forget the rest of the world exist, and then there are those who simply transfer their lives from someplace on the mainland to someplace on the island. Whatever her issues were, she brought them with her. Desmund had read enough tourist that he could figure out most of them within seconds.

"And she couldn't just dabble with it," Pellet started up about his sister again. "She had to dive full in and drag it out for years. Shit!"

"Sounds bad," Dez answered, still having no idea of what was being discussed.

"It's worse than it sounds." He finished his beer and waved for his third Red Stripe. Dez opened two. "Not even sure why it bothers me so much. All I know is that digging up the family past never seemed like a good idea to me."

"Not much use in lookin back," Desmund responded, as if he had the slightest idea where the conversation was going.

"Not much use? There's no god damn use at all. What good could possibly come from it?" The girl at the end of the bar glanced up and wondered if maybe she should sit at a table, a bit further away from the upset scraggly mutt who seemed to be conversing as much to himself as anyone else.

Dez flashed a smile in her direction to put her at ease. "Let me know if I can get you any ting." She smiled back and kind of held her bottle up to show him she'd barely taken more than a couple sips.

"First there was a family tree. Then a family forest. After that she started finding the stories that went with the names. She searched back a couple hundred years, and let me tell you, all in all, it ain't pretty."

"Everybody got family baggage, mon. How bad can it be?" They seemed like pacifying words of encouragement. Bartender words with a bartender question. Answer if you like. Don't answer if you don't want, kind of talk. It was across the bar small talk that sometimes helped, sometimes not. But it never hurt anything. It was an innocent question.

"How bad can it be?" Pellet snapped back. "Let me clue you in on something my island friend." He had his pack of cigarettes in his hand and slammed them down on the bar top. "My father was the only one out of seven kids in his family to actually have a full-time job for most of his adult life. And from what I understand, his generation of Pelletier's was a step in the right direction from the previous generations. Basically, with the exception of dear old dad, being a semi-unemployed deadbeat was pretty much an acceptable career for my relatives going back a long damn way. I know you may find this hard to believe, but it's possible that my family did not come from what you might call, good stock."

"No shit," Dez shot back with a fake look of surprise on his face.

"Yeah. No shit."

"Okay. Okay. So some of dem were deadbeats. How bout da other side? You know… your Mum's family. Dey cool?"

"No, Dez. They were not cool. They were worse than the other side."

"I don't know, mon. Don't see that it could be dat bad. All in the past, heh?"

"Well, let me tell you how bad it could be." And with that, the resurrection of Pellet's ancestry began to be revealed.

"Let's start with my Dad. You know… the only respectable one in the family. My Dad worked at a shoe factory for thirty years. Since before I was born until I was about twenty, he got up every day and went to work. Didn't complain about it much, but you want to know what he dreamed of?"

"Sure. Why not." Dez answered, a bit indifferent to it all. He thought Pellet had an actual problem. Turned out that it was just more Pellet drama.

"For the thirty years of working in the shoe factory, my father dreamed of *not* working in the shoe factory. The rest of my aunts and uncles were in and out of jobs, on and off welfare and unemployment, and were pretty much useless shits."

"So what? Nobody wants to work in a shoe factory. Anyway, behind you now."

"Oh. That's just the beginning of the family tree. You know, that's just one generation away. It goes downhill from there."

Desmund shrugged.

"According to my sister's research, my great uncle Pierre actually got caught and went to jail for stealing candy from a baby." He stopped talking and stared at Desmund, who didn't know what to say. "From a baby, man! Who the fuck would do that?" Pellet said a bit too loud. It was a rhetorical question. No answer required.

"Your great uncle? From a baby?" Both men turned and looked at the woman at the end of the bar. There was an awkward silence and she began to look as though she wasn't sure why she said anything. She wasn't the type that would just blurt something like that out to a perfect stranger. "Sorry," she added, and shrunk as much as she could while sitting on a barstool. Pellet's head tilted to one side and he watched her without saying a word. She looked away and wished there was a way to exit without being awkward.

"Daaamn," Desmund said in a long-extended word, "I like you. You cool," he said to the woman who had pinned the exclamation point on Pellet's great uncle. Then he turned to Pellet and continued. "Da woman don't even know you, but it's like you jus bring it outta dem." Pellet just kept looking at her and tried to figure out why this woman would jump into his conversation without the slightest sign of an invitation. This was one time that he didn't hit on her, didn't make stupid remarks, and didn't ask some stupid question. And he still got zinged. "Let me get you anatta beer... on da house." Desmund set a full Heineken next to her half full beer and stuck out his hand, and made a mental note to put it on Pellet's tab. "Name is Desmund. Welcome to Dez's."

"Lucy," she answered and shook the bartender's hand. Her tiny white hand disappeared in his huge dark grip as Pellet continued to stare in her direction.

"And dis is Pellet. Dis is good as he gets," he said with indifference and a shrug, just in case Lucy might be thinking she was meeting him on an off day.

"Sorry," she said again, not knowing what else to say. "Nice to meet you?"

"You gonna fit right in here, Lucy. An don't be too sorry for dis guy. Brings on most his troubles without help from anybody."

"I gotta find a new bar," Pellet grumbled again. It was a threat/promise that he had made so many times that Desmund didn't even respond any more.

"Come on," Dez said to Lucy. "Come sit down by my friend. You'll get the full affect when you be by him." His smile was so contagious she couldn't refuse the invitation. She picked up her two beers and walked around the bar and sat down next to Pellet. "Lucy," she said and held her hand out to him.

"Yeah. I heard," he answered, without reaching out at first, but she was good looking and he was Pellet. He took her soft hand in his and inhaled a perfume that was new to him. That was about all it took.

"So, what else does your family tree say," she asked as she made herself at home.

"It says that good ole uncle Pierre wasn't the worst of them."

"Dazzle me with facts and I'll let you know how bad it sounds." She took another sip of her beer and fanned Pellet's cigarette smoke away from her face.

"Well, there was another one in the early 1800's who stole a train, just outside of Marseilles. Ended up spending about ten years in the prison in the Bagne de Toulon."

"Where was he going to take a train? I mean, they're on tracks and, well, you know. I think it would be pretty easy to find." She was being sarcastic as much as realistic.

"Guess you're beginning to get my point. And guess what. His name was Pierre, too."

"So he went to the same prison as Jean Valjean?"

"Who?"

"He was.... never mind. It's not important. What else you got?"

"How about Marie Pelletier. Try to guess what she did." Pellet said, as if either of them would have any idea. "Well, good ole Marie was shot for being a Nazi collaborator. Rumor has it she turned in one of her neighbors for hiding Jewish kids."

"Wow. Sounds like your family has something against children," Lucy blurted out. Pellet cringed and gave her a dirty look. "Hey, I wasn't the one who stole candy from a baby," Lucy responded to his disapproving look.

"She's right, mon. She didn't take no candy," Desmund added, as if he were defending an old friend.

"That it?" Lucy prodded. "Doesn't sound that bad."

"No. As a matter of fact, that is not it. It seems that in the late 1600's there was an entire clan of Pelletier vagabonds that were more or less banned from about half of France. They were like Robin Hood, you know. Except they stole from the rich and stole from the poor and from what I have read, they often stole from each other. And the good news is," he added in sarcasm, "when some of these grifters were driven out of France, guess where they went? Canada," he answered his own question.

"So?" Lucy answered.

"The traveling band of gypsies who stole from everybody, including each other, are my direct Canadian ancestors."

"Not cool," Desmund mumbled. "Shouldn't steal from family."

"And a couple of them were hung in Canada."

"For what?"

"One of them killed a cop... during the kidnapping of some rich family's little girl. Apparently another well thought out plan."

"Good lord. What's the deal with your family and children?" Lucy asked.

"Starting to see why I thought this family tree thing was a bad idea?"

"Gotta be some good ones in dat bunch. Can't all be bad." Desmund said.

Pellet took a deep breath and arched his back and looked up at the ceiling. He shook his head back and forth in disgust and dropped his head forward so his chin almost bounced off his chest. "The pickings are pretty slim. There was a priest, but you know... there's the kid thing again. A couple of small-town politicians, but it's a hard stretch to say any politician is what most of us would call good people. Then there were a few sailors. I think a couple of them were even captains or admirals or whatever they're called. The others just drank and sailed and did stuff that sailors do. From what I read, they all seemed pretty harmless and some of them were even, you know, upstanding citizens," he said with a tone of sarcasm, as if it were hard to believe any of his ancestors could have been upstanding citizens.

"Cool," Desmund chimed in. "You come from sailors.

Dats what you tell folks. I'd keep all that children shit to yourself. Don't sound too good."

"I'm with Desmund on both of those things, Lucy chimed in. "Coming from a long line of sailors sounds pretty good. Nobody wants to hear about all that other stuff." She puckered her face and shivered when she said it.

Pellet looked at his empty beer bottle and then turned and looked at Lucy again with a puzzled look on his face. "Who are you? And why are you still talking to me?" She took a sip of her beer and looked back at Pellet and shrugged with a smile on her face.

"Hey. Be nice, mon. She's cool. I tink she's smart. Should listen to her." He winked at Lucy and raised his eyebrows at Pellet. "Probably went to college and every ting."

"You should both stop talking. And get me another beer." Dez got two and put them both on Pellet's tab again. Lucy had no idea that she had just become part of their world. And Pellet didn't realize that the sound of being a sailor sounded appealing to him.

CHAPTER FOUR

Shira sat with her feet hanging over the seawall and looked off into the distance as if she were trying to see the tiny slither of her past life floating somewhere just below the clouds. It was as if she were trying to locate on the horizon the exact moment where it all went wrong. Looking backwards wasn't something she did intentionally, but as her feet hung above the small waves that splashed lightly against the concrete wall she drifted back further and further and scoured the fragments of her life. A left turn here, a different decision there, a dinner date, a conversation that she did or didn't walk away from, a casual cigarette with someone she barely knew, an evening with an old family friend. All of them, or perhaps any one of them could have changed the course of her life. If her father had not kissed her on the side of the face and taken that last trip to Kuwait. If her mother hadn't walked away from them when she was only seven. If this. If that. If. Her search always left her empty and unresolved. *If* that moment in time actually existed, she had never stumbled upon it. And as she reached back and wandered down the long winding road of unanswered questions, she always ended up in the same place. When the blackness passed, her questions remained unresolved. When she finished journeying through the dark alleys of her mind, the questions remained and the answers eluded her. Perhaps that is what drove her to search again and again. At the end of each tormenting and fruitless search for that unfindable moment, her eyes were always closed and an ever so slight smile came to her face as she listened to the sound of her Papa's voice. In her memories, his voice had the softness of the sea and the strength of steel, and it stayed with her. As so many memories faded and disappeared, the sound of his voice comforted and haunted her eternally.

As Shira and Papa walked across the chilly tarmac and climbed into the two-seat Cessna, the morning chill had made her cheeks rosy. Perhaps it was simply the way her mind chose to recall that morning, but she could still envision the crisp air and the clearest bluest sky she had ever seen. The leaves were turning color and rustling in the breeze off in the distance, and her excitement seemed to radiate an already perfect morning. The sky was empty except for the bright sun and an eternal blanket of blue. She didn't see a cloud, a bird or a single plane. There was only Shira and Papa and their plane and the perfect sky. For fourteen years that was how she remembered her twelfth birthday. He had told her she could start her flying lessons when she turned twelve. That was the morning she sat in the copilot's seat and listened through the oversized headphones while Papa and the tower talked about runways and taxiways and visibility and a dozen other details that sounded like part of a dream.

As she sat with her feet hanging over the seawall, reaching down far enough that her toes barely touched the top of the waves, she thought for the hundredth time or more, that was perhaps the moment in time that changed the course of her life. Or maybe not. She saw his face and his smile, heard his voice, and smelled his aftershave. She took in everything there was to take in and then she breathed a deep breath and opened her eyes and he went away one more time. She looked out over the water in Saint Maarten and saw a plane off in the distance on its landing path towards the airport. Below that was a tiny spec of a sailboat that was so far away it looked like nothing more than a miniscule triangle on top of the smooth blue Caribbean water. She wondered where it was coming from. She wondered who was on the plane and how many lives would get better or worse by landing here. She wondered again what decisions put her life on this course. And finally she wondered why she pondered these useless questions so often. She was an intelligent woman. She knew better than living in the past. She knew today and tomorrow are all that really matter. Memory lane is often a beautiful lane, but best if not travelled too often.

The roar of the ferryboat engine broke her from her trance and she looked up as it pulled in and bumped against the dock in Marigot Bay. A local deck hand jumped off with a line in his hand and threw it over the giant cleat. With complete indifference she watched him, she glanced at a few squawking seagulls and she watched a line of locals and tourist meandering off the boat from Anguilla. She vaguely recognized a few faces, but not most of them. She paid no attention to the two scraggly looking white guys in t-shirts and cargo shorts and faded baseball caps.

Looking back out over the horizon, she found herself once again skimming over the moments in her past that may have changed everything. The passengers wandered into the customs office, the deck hand chatted it up with one of the local marina workers and the seagulls circled and squawked and landed in precarious places. Shira looked away, lit a cigarette and closed her eyes again.

CHAPTER FIVE

Four weeks, two days and four hours after Lucy had first met Pellet and learned about his creepy ancestors, she was once again sitting on a bar stool facing nothing but the blue Caribbean Sea and the island bartender. Her first trip down, which she presumed would be her one and only trip to the island, was supposed to clear her head and mentally prepare her to get back into the game. After she returned to NYC, she spent a few more weeks thinking about getting back on track. And then she drew a deep breath and bought another plane ticket so she could look at the aqua blue water and ponder life some more.

"Hey. Good to see you again" Pellet blurted out as he plopped down onto the barstool beside her.

She smiled politely, but not warmly at the scruffy looking guy wearing the orange faded ball cap, the ragged t-shirt and the cargo shorts that looked a hundred years old and two sizes too big. She was pretty sure they were the exact same clothes he was wearing the last time they met. In hopes he would go away, Lucy didn't say anything and looked around at all the seats of the more or less empty bar. In fact, all the seats were empty. Every last one of them, except for the one she was sitting on and the one the weird guy with family issues had just landed on. She looked over at Dez as if he would give her some guidance as to why this character wouldn't have sat across from her, or two stools away, or anywhere else other than sitting so close to her in the empty bar that their elbows were almost touching.

"No worries. He's…" Dez mumbled and then stopped and thought for a second or two before he continued. "He's like our bar mascot or some ting. Not really a good dog, but a harmless one." She turned her head towards the bar's mascot with a look of total indifference. "Probably don't have fleas," Desmund added, pleased with himself for stacking the already unlikely odds, even further against Pellet having any success with this woman.

"Sorry. Forgot your name," Pellet said and stuck his hand out to greet her.

"Lucy. Lucy LaPuenta," she answered and lifted her beer and took a sip of it and left his empty hand dangling in thin air.

"Lucy... Lucy LaPuenta. L-a-P-u-e-n-t-a," Pellet said in a long drawn out word and let the sound roll off his tongue like warm butter running over popcorn. "Now that's a good name." He waved his hand towards Desmund to bring the Red Stripe that was presumed, but not actually ordered. "Lucy LaPuenta. Yup, I like that name," he added as if she were awaiting his approval.

"And you're Pellet, right?" she asked not so much feeling the need to know but more asking out of common courtesy.

"Yep, Pellet it is. Nice to meet you again," he answered and stuck his hand out one more time. She gave it a light shake, but remained a bit weary of him, despite the *harmless and flealess* proclamation by Desmund. "Real name is Wayne Pelletier, but everyone calls me Pellet."

"Good to know," she answered and looked towards Desmund again for help.

"He ain't goin away, Lucy. Ain't no one else for him to bodda," he answered with a shrug.

"You win!" Pellet added with a grin.

"I'm married, by the way," she added, as if it carried some significance.

"Bullshit," Pellet blurted back at her as if they were old friends and implying he had firsthand knowledge about her life.

"Seriously, I'm married," she repeated as she tried to sell her lie to the bar mascot.

"Happily?" Pellet asked suggesting there was a remote chance that if she were unhappily married she would probably be interested in the Caribbean version of Shaggy from Scooby-Doo.

"What chu boddring dis woman for? You can't even get single women. How you gonna get married ones?" Desmund said as he set his beer in front of him.

"Hey. You never know. Maybe I've been shopping in the wrong store. Or maybe she's desperate. I'm just testing the waters," he answered and looked back at Lucy. "Well?" he asked again and looked at her and waited for a response.

She sipped on her beer and foolishly thought the conversation would fade away if she ignored him for long enough. She smiled at Desmund again and scanned all the empty seats at the bar. She gazed out at the sea and watched the small waves lap the shoreline fifty feet away. And then she glanced at all the empty seats once again before looking back at Desmund.

"Well? Are you happily married?" Pellet asked again as if she owed him an answer to his question.

Her forehead wrinkled and she looked at this strange guy who regretfully gave her the feeling he was going to become part of her stay in Anguilla. Their eyes locked while Pellet waited for an answer and she waited for him to disappear. She glanced at Desmund again as if looking to him for a rescue had become some sort of nervous tic, then back at Pellet. "You don't have a girl friend? Really? Hard to believe," Lucy said with no smile on her face. She had come for alone time. For thinking time. For healing time. She saw no useful purpose for this guy.

"I'm working on fixing that," Pellet said, raising his beer to her then taking a gulp.

"How's the family tree thing coming along," she asked. A wave of guilt washed over her, albeit only a small wave, followed by regret that the words had come out of her mouth. She saw him struggling with it the last time they had talked and it wasn't like Lucy to go for a raw nerve. Even if it were someone as irritating as Shaggy Pellet.

Pellet sat up straight and looked away towards the sea as if he was possibly hurt or offended. Lucy's face softened and she almost apologized for being hateful, but Pellet spoke first.

"Wanna go skinny dipping?" he blurted out with a big smile on his face. He glanced down at her breast and raised his eyebrows and smiled even bigger. Lucy was caught completely off guard and this time when she looked to Desmund for help, she was really looking for help.

"Leave da woman alone, mon. She's limin," he mumbled with full understanding that Pellet wasn't going anywhere, and it wasn't likely he was going to leave her alone.

""Well… I can talk to her or I can talk to you." He looked around the bar and motioned towards the empty seats to make sure they both understood that he was going to talk to one or both of them.

"Lucy, dis is Pellet. Harmless," Desmund added with a quick shrug as he walked to the other side of the bar and began rummaging around in the beer cooler. Pellet grinned. Lucy rolled her eyes.

"Well?" Pellet said again.

"Well what?" she snapped back.

"You said you are married. I don't believe you, by the way," he added. "And then I asked if you were happily married." He took a drink and looked at her again and made it clear he was patiently waiting for an answer.

"Okay," she sighed. "I'm not married, but I'm not looking for anyone either."

Desmund finished rummaging and strolled back over and leaned down on the bar in front of Lucy. "Lady, we weren't lookin for a mascot either and having no chance wit chu don't make him go away. Might as well talk to him. Sooner or later I'll put you drinks on his tab. It's all good."

"Don't worry. I'll grow on you," Pellet reassured and waved his beer at her to toast their newfound friendship. Lucy didn't raise hers back and pondered for a second of getting up and leaving. Then again, she was on vacation and had already taken a long walk on the beach and had come down to the bar to get a drink. She came down to relax and had no intention of leaving simply because a pest sat down beside her. She drew a deep breath and turned to Pellet and smiled. "Nice to see you again Pellet."

His eyebrows raised again and he sat back as a smile came to his face. He nodded towards Desmund. "See, she's warming up to me already." Lucy faked a smile. Pellet ranked fake smiles from good looking women only a slight notch below real smiles.

"Good gawd, mon. You gonna be single forever," the dreadlocked bartender said as he shook his head back and forth and popped the top off another beer for Pellet.

Pellet was thirty-five and strictly a minor league player. She was twenty-five-ish and absurdly out of his league, no matter what age either of them were. Desmund had seen him strike out with so many women, almost all of them out of his league, that it had long ago stopped being noteworthy. He just presumed if a good-looking woman came into the bar alone, Pellet was either going to be quickly or slowly shot down.

"Hey, hey," Desmund mumbled to the man who had quietly slipped in and sat down at a table that was in a corner almost by itself. The man smiled and nodded and began to unpack a computer and tablet from his satchel. Lucy watched him and wondered who he might be. He was fortyish and good looking. His motions all looked purposeful. Eyes were sharp, hawkish, fully aware, not clueless. He was not Pellet. He was slim and solid and she presumed he must be a local lawyer or architect or doctor or something along those lines. Desmund delivered a glass of water and set it down in front of him. They exchanged small talk. She could hear their voices, but not their words. They both chuckled, and the doctor or lawyer or architect glanced up at Pellet, and then saw Lucy watching him and he returned to unpacking his satchel.

Helmut had been in the islands a few years longer than Pellet. She was correct that he was an engineer. Or at least he was in his previous life. Life had taken him down some dark roads for a few years before coming to the islands. His heart and soul had been cut and beaten and nearly destroyed before he landed in Dez's bar. He didn't come to drink and didn't really socialize all that much. He came and sat at the table in the corner and breathed in the salt air, listened to the waves from the Caribbean Sea and wrote stories that he sometimes shared, and sometimes didn't. And while he was hiding from all things in life, both good and bad, a Caribbean angel came and saved him from his self-imposed exile from life. Then he became slightly more sociable, but he still sat at his corner table, and he continued to write.

"He's taken," Pellet blurted out.

"Excuse me?" Lucy asked, a bit irritated that the mascot had felt the need to inform her of the relationship status of some guy she'd never even met. "I was just looking at the only other person in the bar. Like I said, I'm not looking for anything."

"Uh-huh," Pellet said and took another sip of his beer. "I've heard that before."

Lucy slid off her stool and walked barefoot over to the railing that overlooked the white beach. The hills of Saint Maarten stood off in the distance separated from Anguilla by eight miles of white capped, aqua blue waves. The palm fronds made a rustling sound and she glanced up and looked at a clump of coconuts. Just as it felt like the moment could not get any more perfect and peaceful, a voice chimed in like a needle skidding across a vinyl record.

"Cool, huh?"

Lucy turned and looked at Pellet and surrendered herself to her fate. "So, Pellet. Anymore thoughts about your ancestors? You know, the sailor ones?"

"Oh... haven't given it much thought today."

"Well, I'm a believer in focusing on the positive. It sounds like you may have slim pickings, so... you know."

"Did I tell you about my great, great-great something or other who challenged a guy to a sword fight?"

"Nope, you didn't share that one with me," Lucy said, presuming Pellet missed the point of her recommending he focus on the positive.

"Yup. Back in the early 1800's, some semi royalty dude apparently insulted the guy's summer squash."

"Like, the vegetable?"

"Yeah, like a vegetable. So, my way back in time relative was so egregiously offended that he challenged the royalty guy to a sword fight. You know. To protect the honor of his squash. The facts are sketchy, but from what my sister found out it sounded like our relative had never actually held a sword. A few minutes after defending his squash, he was dead."

"Sailing. Definitely sounds like sailing is the way to go," she finally just blurted it out since she could see Pellet wasn't moving in the direction she was trying to nudge him over to. Even when she was down and out, Lucy was compelled to help others. Despite how irritating this Pellet guy was, trying to make him feel good about his wacky family seemed like the decent thing to do.

"Kinda makes you wonder how any of us made it from generation to generation, huh?"

Lucy smiled and pointed out at the sea, "Nice sailboat," she said as they both watched a fifty- or sixty-foot catamaran gliding past, a quarter mile offshore. Pellet stopped talking and watched it. The seed was planted.

CHAPTER SIX

Pellet sat on the barstool in Saint Maarten talking to Avis about boats. Then everything went dark. At some point after that, a second, a minute, or maybe longer, Pellet's eyes opened wide, but the world around him was a loud blur. His brain said, "Breathe, man. Breathe." Then it screamed, "Breathe!" But the air was gone and his lungs struggled, but he still did not breathe. He couldn't quite figure out what was happening. His brain gave the breathe-in order and his lungs seemed to receive the order, but no air arrived. Something he couldn't identify pushed down on his throat and his eyes refused to focus as much as his lungs refused to breathe. He was pretty certain he had only blacked out momentarily when his head slammed against something, the ground he presumed, but there wasn't really a way to be sure if it was momentary or a lot longer. For all he knew a half hour could have passed since his lights went out, but it didn't seem like a priority to figure that out at the moment. He needed air, but his lungs felt paralyzed. His eyes darted around, still looking at blurry undefined shapes as he searched for a way to get air into his lungs, as if he'd find it lingering about somewhere in the bar. Avis watched him struggle on the ground until Pellet's eyes widened and looked genuinely panicked. Shira stood over him, with her left foot firmly pressed against his throat while she casually picked up the Red Stripe that had just been set on the bar for Pellet.

"Better ease up or something. You know, before he passes out," Avis mumbled and nodded in Pellet's general direction. There was no real concern in his voice, nor was there any concern on her face. She instinctively knew how long she could continue to press down before any real danger of death set in. It wasn't like Pellet didn't get what he deserved. On the other hand, there was probably no need to kill the poor guy.

Shira sipped the beer and glanced down at the putz below and looked back up at the putz's mate. One more sip and a wink at him, and then she lifted her foot and kicked Pellet's shoulder.

"Breathe, schmendrick," she said to the guy laying on his back. "And thanks for the beer," she added. Then she looked at the other guy who was still sitting upright on a stool and drinking his beer. She took a little sip from the bottle before she turned and effortlessly strolled across the bar and waved to her friends. The bartender was a white guy with scraggly dreads who had been in Saint Maarten so long that he almost believed he was a Rasta mon. He dropped a damp rag on the bar top and gave it a quick wipe while Avis watched her weave her way through the crowded bar. "Mossad," is all the wannabe Rasta mon bartender blurted out without looking up. "Her name is Shira," he added as he turned away.

Avis turned and looked at him as if there was a question to ask. There wasn't. From what he had just witnessed, Mossad seemed to make perfect sense.

As strange as it seemed to Pellet, her command, "Breathe" was all it took for his brain and body to get on the same page. Well, that and lifting her foot off his throat. Air surged into his lungs as if he had just swam to the surface of a deep dark pool of water. He coughed and took a deep breath and then another. For the next thirty seconds he laid on the floor while his breaths transitioned from torrents of air rushing in, to deep quick breaths, to slow deep breaths, and finally to normal breathing. With each gasp of air the room came a bit more into focus. When his eyes were darting around while he was airless, everything in the bar was a blur of colors, shades, and shapes. As disconnected as the air and his lungs had been, his brain had been just as disconnected with his senses in general, including his vision. He heard noises and talking, or at least murmuring that he presumed was talking, but nothing had been processing through his head other than hearing his own silent panicked voice asking, "What's happening?" and screaming, "Breathe!" There were bright colors that he eventually realized were yellow and red t-shirts and blue and pink bikinis. The blurs nearest to him were legs and feet hanging off the bar stools and of those who had walked over to see what the excitement was. When he began processing the conversations around him it became apparent that none of them were concerned about his well-being. Certainly none of them thought he was dying. He alone clung to that possibility. All of them were highly entertained by whatever had just happened. The first bit of conversation he clearly processed was a guy talking to one of the bikini women, "Don't see that every day," he laughed with a strong French accent. She giggled and then the two sets of feet turned and moved away. Within a minute it made sense to him that he was laying on the ground if for no other reason than he was looking at feet around his head and up at the bright yellow paint of the bottom side of the roof of the bar. How he ended up there was still a mystery.

It happened so fast that he didn't even see it. It happened so much quicker than he would have imagined it happening, if by some assault preventing miracle he had imagined it at all. All he knew was that he was sitting on a bar stool. Then he was waking up on the floor, gasping for air, and pretty sure that if his head was not bleeding it was by sheer good fortune. His brain felt as though he had been hit hard enough to cause, if not permanent damage, a headache that would likely be with him for a while. Somewhere in between searching for air and wondering what had happened, Pellet managed to squeeze in a reoccurring thought of late, "I've got to make a change. There has to be more to life than this."

Avis was barely paying attention to him. After the Mossad woman had nudged Pellet with her foot and ordered him to breathe, the minor crisis came to an end for everyone except for Pellet. The confusion was almost worse than whatever cruelty had just stormed into his life, not that he could recall what the cruelty was. As the small crowd of onlooker's feet began to disperse, he remained on the floor and watched the white bladed Big-Ass fan slowly spin in the foreground of the lemon-yellow ceiling with lime green rafters. All that was left to be done was for Pellet to regain his faculties, pick himself up off the floor, try to regain a shred of dignity, and eventually ask Avis, "What the fuck happened?" But he didn't pick himself up. The ceiling fan continued to spin above him and the bottom of the roof still remained in front of his face. He just laid there and searched his memory for the missing moments of his life. The moments between sitting on a stool chewing on a cheeseburger, most of which was now scattered in the sand around him, and then waking up on the floor. He and Avis had come in, sat at the bar, and had a burger and one beer. Pellet was certain of it. One beer. No rum. No shots. No fifteen beers. One beer. And then something happened. Something, but it eluded him, whatever it was. Now he was on the sandy floor searching for a missing slice of his life that somehow magically disappeared from his head. Avis wiped the remaining ketchup off his plate with the last fry from Pellet's plate and popped it into his mouth and then washed it down with a swig of Red Stripe.

"You going to get up or are you taking a nap down there?"

Pellet took a deep breath but didn't move. "What the hell happened?" was all he mumbled and watched the big-ass fan continue to slowly whirl around on low speed. Some guy stepped over him like he was a sleeping dog in the middle of the floor.

"A hurricane, I suppose." He sat with his beer in front of his mouth but hesitated taking a drink as he pondered for a minute. Then added, "Yup. A god damn hurricane. That's pretty much what happened."

Chapter Seven

Pellet took one more lung filling breath just to reassure himself he was alive and then he sat up on the sandy barroom floor. Avis waved to Gerry, the wannabe Rasta mon, to bring two more beers and paid almost no attention to his cousin who continued to sit in the sand as if he were contemplating building a castle or perhaps just rolling over and laying on his stomach for a while. A local guy nudged him on the shoulder and Pellet jumped, as if he thought it might be starting all over again. When he turned, a large black hand was holding a faded Red Sox cap.

"Easy, mon. Jus you hat."

Pellet looked at the hat and then looked up at the smiling face and reached up and took it and brushed the sand off from its visor.

"Thanks."

"Dat was fun to watch, mon. Dat woman.... Whew.... She bad ass." He smiled down at Pellet and shook his head and strolled across the bar and re-ran the events of the past few minutes in his mind. "Bad ass!" he repeated and broke out into a loud laugh as he walked out the doorless entrance of the bar.

Pellet was still at a loss as to what had happened. The last thing he recalled he was sitting on the barstool and explaining to Avis why buying a sailboat was probably an excellent idea. What he couldn't recall was the moment that *she* walked into the bar and he stopped talking in mid-sentence. Avis glanced at him and then looked to see what had caught Pellet's attention. He shook his head and smiled at yet one more unattainable relationship Pellet had in a split second latched onto. That's how it all started less than five minutes earlier, but it was all still a blank to the guy climbing off the sandy floor and back onto his barstool. He snugged his hat onto his head, took a drink of his newly replaced

Red Stripe and stared down at the bar in silence. Avis sat and waited for the question until it was finally blurted out.

"What the fuck happened?"

"It was a thing of beauty to watch. I mean, it was surreal," Avis said like he had witnessed a miracle from god.

Pellet wiped a trickle of blood from the corner of his mouth. "Damn. I bit my tongue." He wiggled his jaw around and scrunched his lip. "Kinda hurts."

"You deserved it." If he was looking for sympathy he would have to look elsewhere because it wasn't coming from Avis.

Avis was Pellet's cousin who had flown down to Anguilla two years ago. He fell in love with the place and decided to stay. And while he liked drinking beer almost as much as Pellet, and he enjoyed fishing ten times more than Pellet ever would, there was a vast difference between the two men. The first being that Avis was a genius measured by any standard. He had read more books than most people would read in five lifetimes and he comprehended and absorbed every word and every message. But the most obvious difference between Avis and his cousin was that Avis rarely, if ever, did anything stupid. Pellet could not make that proclamation.

Pellet was the kind of guy who was good and generous to the core. He would loan a friend a thousand dollars, but then have to tell his landlord he was going to be late with his rent. He was so blatantly honest he would tell you if your tag was sticking up on your collar, or if you had something hanging from your nose, or if you have spectacular breast. They were all just observations to him. And while he typically wasn't intentionally disrespectful to a woman, he often did it out of nothing more than bad judgement. His thoughts were often best described as unfiltered or, "It sounded better in my head." And so began his introduction to the new woman in his life. His unfiltered thoughts just flowed out.

"I'm telling you, I sailed a 45-foot boat halfway to Tortola and back without any lessons or anything. It just comes natural to me. I'd only been on a couple boats and it was like I'd been…. Holy shit. I think this might be the one," he mumbled as he transitioned from one subject to another in midsentence with barely a breath between the two conversations. Avis didn't really need to look, but he did anyway. Pellet fell in love with women he didn't know and who were so far out of his league it was indescribable, on more or less a weekly, sometimes daily basis. The whole island of Anguilla and even a few people from Saint Maarten knew of his raging love for Fatisha a couple years back. The story of how he crashed and burned was a Caribbean legend that was still harsh salt in his wounds. There had been dozens of women since then. Most of those crashes came within minutes of the conception of the so-called relationship. He was not a guy who learned from failure. His unofficial mantra was try, fail, and then try the same thing again, apparently forever.

First there was the sighting of the prey or victim or as Pellet liked to describe them, "the lucky woman." Next there was his ungraceful, often ever so mildly offensive approach. More often than not, there was a bit of friendly chit chat, and then he was quickly shot down and frequently without mercy. His attempts were futile, but it rarely phased him all that much. On the upside, even Pellet had boundaries. His pickup lines were usually weak and often bordered on bad taste but were not particularly crude. "Nice tan, but it looks like you'll need some lotion if you're heading back to the beach tomorrow. I'd be glad to assist," was a line that had failed for him so many times that he lost count. Yet he kept using it with a tinge of optimism. He never got too far outside the boundaries of decency, unless maybe he got too drunk first. He always remained age appropriate and never went after someone a decade younger than himself. And he never, ever… until he saw this woman, touched a woman he didn't know. Pellet was a knucklehead, but he was a kind, somewhat respectful knucklehead.

She eased in through the doorway and smiled at someone who spoke to her as she continued her walk across the bar. Pellet spun around on the barstool and watched her and sadly allowed his brain to search for the perfect line to break the ice.

"Outta your league, chum," Avis chimed, when he glanced in her direction.

"Hey, he says you're out of my league. What do you say?" Shira, who was still a good five strides away when Pellet tossed the question her way, glanced at him and gave a cold, polite smile and said nothing. She lowered her head and continued to walk.

"Awe, come on. I bet him a buck that you'd let me buy you a beer." This time she not only did not accept the invitation, she didn't even look up. A chubby tourist in a Grateful Dead t-shirt passed by and stepped between Shira and Pellet giving her an easy, comfortable escape, but Pellet was not deterred. As the Dead Head slipped past and she was slipping past in the other direction, it happened. Pellet reached out. Avis's eyes got big when he saw what he was about to do. And then it happened. He took ahold of her arm and started to say something. He wasn't rough. He didn't grab her tightly and he didn't hurt her. But he grabbed her. He grabbed a woman, a perfect stranger, in a bar. What possessed him to do it would be something he would not have time to ponder.

The moment, the microsecond, that Pellet's hand made contact on her forearm, all hell broke loose and it broke loose fast. Her arm shot forward and tore away from his grip, but she did not stop there. As she ripped her arm away from this goofy stranger in a ragged t-shirt and faded ball cap, her momentum continued as she began to spin a full 360 degrees. This was not a spin of some chic who was mad. This woman knew what she was doing and she was spinning with purpose and power. Avis watched it in what seemed like slow motion and could see the muscles in her legs thrusting herself all the way around towards where Pellet was sitting. Her arms and shoulders were flexed and she was in full attack mode. She was like a cage fighter going in for the kill. Pellet just sat there with a goofy grin on his face with no idea of what was about to happen. As she spun around and arrived back where she began, her right-hand clutched Pellet's throat. That in itself would have been bad enough, but her momentum did not stop when she reached Pellet. With her hand on his throat, she continued her power lunge and Pellet went airborne with his neck being crushed by a grip that was much stronger than one would have imagined from such a small woman. He was only suspended in air momentarily before she stopped thrusting forward. As his legs and feet shot over the top of the stool, the newest love of his life gave her body a mighty twist and slammed him downward onto the ground. His head slammed against the sandy floor and his body went limp. Without hesitation, she stood up, put her flipflop on his throat, brushed her long hair out of her face, and picked up his beer and winked at the guy who had been sitting with her victim only moments before.

Avis told Pellet the detailed description of what he had witnessed and left no detail out of his story.

"You seem to be enjoying this story just a bit more than what seems appropriate," Pellet grumbled and took a sip of beer.

"It was a thing of beauty. I mean, damn. That might have been the sexiest thing I've ever seen. It was like a half a second and you were finished. What the hell made you think grabbing her arm was a good idea?"

"Don't remember. Hell, I don't remember grabbing her arm. Or hitting on her."

"Gerry says she was Mossad."

"What the hell is a mossad?"

"Mossad? It's like, I guess the CIA and MI-6. She's an Israeli James Bond... except, you know, she's hot and kicked your ass. Good news is she didn't kill you. Bond kills most of them."

"Great. I grabbed Ms. James Bond?"

"You damn sure did."

"Maybe I should go apologize," Pellet mumbled and glanced in her general direction.

"Hold on," Avis said and reached into the pocket of his cargo shorts. "If you're going to go over and talk to her again, I want to get the video."

"So what do you think about the whole boat thing?" Pellet snapped. Changing the subject seemed like the only reasonable solution at the moment. He didn't really think he'd have the nerve to go over to talk to her anyway. He had too much pride to get beat up by the same woman twice in one day.

"A half second, Pellet. It was over in a half a second." Avis still had a look of amazement on his face as if he had just seen color for the first time. "I mean, damn. It was…"

"Hey! I got it. I was there." They both looked down at the bar and sipped on their beers. Avis drank with childlike excitement on his face. Pellet drank like a man who had just been kicked by a horse in the middle of the town square. Then he smiled the slightest smile. "Man. I'm so glad Desmund didn't see it. I'd never hear the end of it."

Avis did not have the slightest inkling that Pellet would be hearing the end of this incident anytime soon. It was a legendary ass kicking given by a beautiful woman wearing a pink razorback shirt, cut-off blue jeans and flipflops.

CHAPTER EIGHT

"I'm telling you, sailing is in my DNA. You can't fight genetics." Pellet had taken what he had not long ago considered a personal plague of sorts, with some suggestions and nurturing from Lucy, and spun the whole family tree nonsense into the fuel behind his new and either absurd or beautiful dream, depending how it all turned out.

The four of them, Pellet, Avis, Savannah and Helmut sat at a round table in the corner. Dez stood next to them with one hand shoved deep into his pocket and the other holding a drink. Lucy was safely back in New York. More often than not, Pellet rattled on and on with only Dez and perhaps an occasional vacationing nay-sayer casting doubt on his latest "What could possibly go wrong?" plan. A couple years ago, Oscar was a constant buffer between Pellet and the gang at Dez's bar, but since Iggy had suggested that he choose between sleeping with her or drinking with Pellet, he was motivated to pay less visits to the bar. After that, the responsibility of "Pellet-sitting" fell on Dez more than he appreciated. Most of the gang was gathered tonight and Desmund was grateful to be in a spectator mode.

"Didn't you say that you were heading to the Antarctic once upon a time, but ended up in the Caribbean?" Helmut barely smiled when he asked the question. It was meant more to irritate than to garner any kind of information.

"Hey. Maybe that's where I went wrong. If I'd gone sailing there, or anywhere else, I probably would have found my calling." Pellet's confidence wasn't initially this strong when Lucy first suggested he should focus on the positive attributes of his ancestors. Since then however, the thought of sailing had taken root. To be honest, Lucy had nothing to base her advice on other than Pellet's own words that some of the distant people down his family tree were said to have been skilled at boating stuff. With most of his bloodline unnaturally terminated or jailed, sailing seemed to be the only acceptable branch to carry on.

On day one, he more or less scoffed at the idea of focusing on the family tree, positively or in any other way. But turning away from his ancestral stories was like trying to not look at an accident he saw on I-95. He couldn't ignore the wreck then, and he couldn't ignore their stories either. After pondering the list of malcontents that were the providers of his DNA, his depression grew ever so slowly and steadily. With each day and each bit of reflection, if for no other reason than sheer desperation, Lucy's suggestion that sailing was the way to go, became more logical. "Did I mention that one of my half-witted dead sperm donors broke into a prison to find out where one of his partners in crime had hid some money they had stolen together? Apparently he was inside for six years before they let him out. His partner, the one who stashed the money, got out a year before he did," Pellet said to the group sitting around the table, and to Dez still standing off to the side.

"Guess he didn't get no gold," Desmund blurted out, surprising himself that he chimed in.

"I think this boat thing might be a good idea to try," Helmut added, with his strong German accent. "If I buy you a boat, how soon are you going to leave?" Everyone around the table, except for Pellet, saw the humor in his question.

"Pellet, you're not really going to do this are you?" Savannah asked.

When she first met Pellet when they arrived in Anguilla, Savannah held him in lower regard than Lucy did when she first met him. But these days, Pellet was her brother-in-law of sorts. He was right when he said, "I grow on people." Savannah loved him as family and worried about where his life was going to end up. It was likely that she was more concerned for him than the others because they simply did not believe he would go through with it. How could running his mouth about something he'd never actually do, be dangerous? But she was paying attention to him, and he seemed committed to this nonsense.

When they met at the airport a couple years earlier, he was exactly what he appeared to be. He was a scraggly white guy in ragged cargo shorts and a worn-out t-shirt. His Red Sox cap was so faded she could barely make out the red "B" on the front of it. Once she got to know him better she realized he was wearing the appropriate attire. For two years he worked hard, he played harder, he drank too much, and he had to have set some sort of record for crashing and burning in more short-term relationships than one would think possible in an entire lifetime, never mind in two years. But just as with his old friend Maddie, Savannah and Pellet bonded into a relationship that lingered somewhere between brother/sister or great friends or a would be couple if not for Avis… and if Savannah hit her head and lost her senses. Emotionally, if in no other way, they were on similar wave lengths. Over the past few months she began to see his subtle changes. The biggest was that he began to mope and feel bad about things in his life. If Pellet was nothing else, he was resilient. Not much of his life had fazed him before the change began. It wasn't like he was falling into a depression or anything like that, but the vast nothingness of his life was finally catching up with him. For the first time in a long time, a few drinks and a joint or two were not enough to fill his void. Wayne "Pellet" Pelletier wanted more out of life. It was like he had hit a crossroad and it was time to pick a direction. He had been working in Anguilla for seven years and it was time to make a change. The family tree was the last bit of motivation he needed, along with some coaxing from Lucy. He couldn't hang out with Desmund at the bar forever. Besides, sailing was in his blood. He was certain of it. The fact that he'd only been on a sailboat twice in his life didn't seem to deter him all that much. Pellet being Pellet, decided that the fifty or sixty ferryboat trips he had taken to Saint Maarten over the past years were somehow hours that should be applied towards his Captains license, even if only unofficially applied.

"Talked to Boatmon yesterday. His sons got a forty-foot Pearson. Said he'd be glad to give me sailing lessons."

"You might want to go take a look at his boat before making any sort of commitment," Avis added. "If it's the one sitting in the yard beside their house, you'll be taking your sailing lessons on his lawn. The rudder is laying in the weeds next to the propeller and a bunch of other boat parts."

"Well, I'll find someone else to teach me then. Dez... you used to be a fisherman. You wanna teach me to sail?"

Dez laughed a bit and took a sip from his glass of rum and then looked at Pellet who was staring at him waiting for a response. "Oh hell no, mon. Ain't takin you out to sea. Ain't gonna get stuck doin all da work while you drink and stand behind da wheel with a beer in your hand. Besides, I got no sailboat." Desmund knew that Pellet had a way of getting people to join into his adventures and he slammed the door closed with, "I got no sailboat." With that said, he turned and went back behind the bar before something regrettable happened.

"Hmmm. Guess I have to start making a list. Sailing lessons. Buying a boat. And whatever else should be on the list."

"A list. I'm impressed," Helmut mumbled. "A bit short, but still, a list. Surprised you didn't ask me to make it for you." Pellet ignored him and reached across the table and picked up one of Helmut's pens and stole a piece of paper.

"Hey, Dez. Who do you know that might want to take me sailing?" Pellet yelled without looking up from the paper.

"Leave me outta dis. Ain't gonna get nobody from da island hating me."

Avis watched and listened and was more amused by Desmund's panic and retreat than he was by Pellet's new plan. Savannah was seriously concerned that Pellet was actually going to do this. And Helmut was not completely kidding when he complimented Pellet for making a list. He also noticed that Pellet wrote four or five additional things on his list, not just the two he first mentioned. Impressed again.

"What was the worst story from your family tree so far?" Avis asked, not giving the boat all that much thought.

"You mean worse than stealing candy from a baby or

breaking into prison and then getting locked up without actually breaking any laws or having a trial?"

"Yeah. I'm thinking that as much as you're moping around and bitching about the tree, there's got to be something you're not telling us. So, I think it's about time to step up and spill the beans."

Pellet put the pen down and folded the paper and slipped it into his t-shirt pocket. He pulled his ragged Red Sox cap off his head and ran his fingers through his long hair and looked down at the table and put his cap back on. His face scrunched as he looked down and searched for the right words while he considered not saying any words at all. He opened his mouth a couple times as if he was going to say something. Then it closed again without so much as a single word coming out. After three attempts, he picked up his cigarettes off the table and put one between his lips and lit it. He took a long drag and then blew an equally long stream of smoke up into the air, before closing his eyes as he searched for the courage to share the story. But he wasn't only searching for courage. It was possible that sharing any shameful story with Desmund and Helmut would be regrettable. Avis was no piece of cake, but those two would immediately call Oscar and the harassment would be eternal. On the other hand, he never wanted this information to start with. He told his sister that nothing good could come from looking back to where their family came from. It wasn't that he had any prior knowledge or heard any stories of their family history. It was just that he had met most of their living relatives and he presumed that the story of their origin, while entertaining, would not be a story that brought forth any pride or warm fuzzy feelings. Whatever tree the family acorns fell out of, was likely a rotten tree. Now that he had the information in his head, he had to do something with it. It's possible that he thought he could sail away and run from it, but for now he needed to unload his burden and his shame onto his friends. A strange silence lingered as, for perhaps the first time ever, they were all waiting to hear what Pellet had to say. He picked up his beer and took a gulp and put it back down, took another drag, and struggled to make a word come out. Dez came back around the bar to make sure he could hear the story. Helmut leaned back in his chair with his arms folded across his chest and waited for the shameful tale to be shared. Avis leaned forward on his elbows in anticipation. Only Savannah felt his pain and embarrassment. She wanted to give him a hug and tell him to forget about whatever it was that he had to reveal. She wanted him to rip up the stupid family tree and toss it into the sea and forget he ever saw it. In some ways, she just wanted the old Pellet back, the irresponsible, fun and carefree guy who seemed to have almost no regard for the grown-up world that the rest of them lived in.

"There's more than a slim chance that my great-grandfather is also my grandfather," he blurted out without making eye contact with anyone.

"Oh shit," Avis mumbled.

"And," he started up.

"Good gawd. There's more?" Desmund added. Helmut didn't so much as blink. He just listened.

"And, it also appears that my great-great-mother on my mother's side, might also be my great-grandmother… if that's even possible."

"Oh, shit!" Dez spit out again and headed back to the bar. Avis's eyes got big but he said nothing. Savannah simply said, "I don't understand." Helmut rubbed his chin and pondered for a moment then simply said, "This explains a lot," and said nothing more. After a few more seconds of awkward silence, Pellet got up from his chair and strolled across the room and plopped himself down on a barstool. Desmund had already poured two full glasses of rum. They drank in silence.

CHAPTER NINE

"She's a beauty, eh?" the old fisherman asked Pellet without looking him in the eye. In fact he didn't look at him at all. He just kept wrestling with his nets on the dock and worked on untangling them and gave a half-hearted sales pitch. He sort of nodded his head in the general direction of the barely floating shipwreck.

"I thought your son was going to come with his dinghy and take us out to see it?"

"Soon come," he mumbled, still not looking up from his nets. "Gonna give em a talkin too when he shows up. Left da nets a mess. Boy gets lazier every day. Anyhow, soon come."

"Damn. I guess I didn't realize how many kinds of sailboats there are." Pellet stood on the shore and gazed out at the 1974 Catalina. It was a thirty-foot sloop that had seen better days. By, "*so many kinds*" he was referring to the boat condition as much as the boat model or brand. If the boat had seen worse days than today, then it had sat on the bottom of the sea at some point in time. He rubbed his three-day old stubble on his face and looked out with amazement at the dilapidated boat gently rocking on the Caribbean waves. Avis stood beside him with his hands linked behind his back as if he were a schoolteacher examining something one of his students had made in shop class. From the look on his face, the shop project had not turned out as well as one might have hoped for.

"It's quite interesting what people who are trying to sell a boat refer to as "in good condition," huh?" Avis added to Pellet's observation.

"Guess "good" is a vague term," Pellet answered and kept looking at the boat as if he expected it to sink at any moment.

The water in Island Harbor was seven different shades of aqua blue. Each shade was more brilliant than the last. The tiny waves, tipped with white caps were so breathtaking that if an artist had painted the harbor, viewers would have imagined that its magnificence had been exaggerated. A warm northward breeze gently pushed soft air to the shore, and Pellet's messy hair tossed around while he gazed out to the perfect sea that held the small burgundy sailboat. The scene was so perfect that even the most time worn weather-beaten sailing vessel would have looked like a thing of beauty. But Pellet had spent enough time around water, even if not on a sailboat, to know that this Catalina was not going to look as sexy up close as she did from where he was standing. Not that she looked that good, even from the shore.

"Looks a bit rough," Avis said, trying to keep the search positive, yet realistic.

"Looks like a piece of shit," Pellet mumbled and slipped his hat back onto his head. "From two hundred yards away," he added.

"Well, we've only looked at five boats. There are plenty more to pick from," Avis answered. "Besides, you only need one."

"Think I might need to think about going up in price." Pellet said.

"I've read that the first thing you need if you want to be a good sailor is patience. Give it some time. You'll find the right one." Avis was telling a half truth. He had read that the first thing you need to be a sailor is to have money to throw into the floating hole in the sea. Patience was a close second, but Pellet was apparently already learning the first lesson. He was going to need to spend more money to get a decent boat. Patience would come later.

They hung out on the dock for another thirty minutes before giving up on their dinghy ride. Chances of the son showing up, even if he hoped to sell the boat, was only fifty-fifty at best. Island time and all that stuff. They had wanted to see the boat up close if for no other reason than to be able to compare it with other boats they had seen, but even Pellet would have been hard pressed to buy a boat with the name "Squirmer" hand painted across the stern. They helped the old fisherman untangle his nets and listened to talk about how he got caught out in a storm a few weeks back. The storm kicked up out of nowhere and eight-foot white caps started rolling with the wind. He turned forty-five degrees to the waves and the wind, and his old wooden fishing boat pounded against the storm for nearly an hour. "Mothah Nature ain't mean though," he said, being philosophical while working on the nets. "No sir. Mothah Nature is all indifferent to every ting. Take life. Give life. No difference to her. And she don't see no difference between a fish, a bird, and a man. All da same to her." He tossed the untangled net into the boat and looked out to the sea and up at the clouds. "Suppose to be nice fishin weather today."

"Looks nice," Avis answered as he looked up at the blue and white skies.

"Dat's exactly what I said when I get caught in da storm." He smiled and nodded and climbed onto the boat to go out for the day by himself. "Good luck with buyin da boat, son," he called out as he turned the key to start the engine. Neither Pellet nor Avis could tell if they were sincere words of encouragement, or polite mockery of anyone foolish enough to buy an old sailboat, especially in the Caribbean. They both nodded without responding and wondered what the old fisherman meant.

Sandy Ground was a twenty-minute drive on winding roads that sat a couple hundred feet above the sea. Along the way there were huge villas and small houses that dotted the landscape. Pellet's truck chugged along at the same slow pace as always with a slight exhaust cloud trailing behind. When they reached their destination, the truck came to a full stop in a dirt driveway. The driveway stretched from the bumpy paved road to the flawless white beach. Once at the beach, they turned right and walked into the sandy floors of Johnno's to grab a beer and a bite to eat. Being that this was not day-one of the boat search, and after starting the day gazing out towards *Squirmer,* Pellet decided that taking a break and refueling the body and soul was the way to go. Over the past two weeks he had looked at an 84 Morgan 40 for forty-three thousand dollars, US. It was worth twenty thousand tops. Then there was a 94 Pearson 36 for thirty thousand. It was worth, perhaps fifteen. And then there was the 1982 Cal 30 for thirteen thousand. It was so rough that they should have offered Pellet five hundred dollars to take it off their hands.

They were at Sandy Ground to look at a 1989 Jeanneau Sun Dance 36 for forty-one thousand dollars. It was twenty-one more than Pellet had committed to spending, and he thought there was little chance of actually buying it. But he had heard good things about it and he was determined to at least look at one good boat for sale before the day was done.

But first, there was grouper, plantains and beer. And then a few more plantains and a couple more beers. A local woman singing a mix of Reggae and jazz filled the sand floor restaurant and spilled onto the beach. Customers came and went while Pellet sat with Avis. More time and beers came and went. Two hours after parking the truck, Avis, who was a couple beers behind Pellet finally waved the waitress off when Pellet signaled for another beer.

"Time to go look at a boat, Captain."

The disheartened Pellet who left Island Harbor had been replaced with a somewhat drunk and optimistic Captain Pellet in Sandy Ground. They stepped out onto the beach and kicked off their flip-flops and left them laying where they landed. They passed local kids playing in the sea, and mum and dads and waitresses milling about. A few boaters, more recreational than fishermen, puttered on their boats that were in shallow water or tied to the pier. The owner of the sailboat had told Pellet there would be a blue dinghy tied up and he could just help himself and go out and take a look. Avis eased into the tiny boat like a natural born sailor. Pellet nearly spilled both of them into the sea before getting situated on the front seat. "Cast off, Captain," Avis shouted and began to paddle. The few locals on the dock paid no attention to the two buffoons who might possibly drown themselves in ten feet of sea.

A small ladder hung over the back of the Jeanneau. Avis pulled up beside it and climbed aboard and turned back towards Pellet who was right behind him. "Hey! You want to hand me the line or are we going to swim back to shore?"

"Oh. Uhhh. Oh, crap." Pellet hopped back down and into the dinghy before it drifted away. He looked around and grabbed the rope and turned back to hand it to Avis, but he was already ten feet away from the sailboat. He sat in the back seat and grabbed the ores, nearly losing one. Once he started paddling he wasn't facing the boat anymore. After three strokes, he was twenty feet further away than when he began. It took him longer to paddle back to the boat than it took them to get to the boat in the first place. He grabbed the ladder and began to step onto it when Avis reminded him again. "The line?"

The two of were in the cockpit, with Avis on one of the side seats and Pellet standing behind the helm. Compared to what they had been looking at, this boat was a Mercedes Benz. The paint was new. Less than three years old. Squirmer's paint looked closer to thirty years. The bimini didn't have any obvious rips and looked to be in good condition. It was connected to the windshield which was still new enough to see through. It had solar panels that may or may not work any longer. There was a radar station next to the helm. According to the Canadian guy selling the boat, "Absolutely. *Almost* everything worked pretty well, with the exception of a couple little issues. A couple of the ports leaked a bit, but that's to be expected in a boat this age. Nothing a bit of work won't take care of. A couple minor electrical issues, but nothing serious. We can talk about them after you look at it." That's what he had told Pellet when they spoke on the phone a couple days ago. That's when he also told him someone would unlock the boat so he could check it out on Saturday. The boating world was still pretty new to Pellet and he didn't yet grasp the flexibility of the meanings of words in the sailing lingo. For instance, in Pellet's mind "a couple of ports leak a bit," meant just that. When it rained on the outside of the boat, it was likely going to drip on the inside of the boat. But in the boating world, what it really meant was when it rains outside the boat, it rains inside the boat too. And in Pellet's mind, "a couple minor electrical issues, but nothing serious" meant there were probably some lights that needed to be replaced, or maybe some outlets. In the boating world it more than likely meant a bunch of hacks had worked on the electrical over the past twenty years. It's a mess. Sometimes stuff works, sometimes it doesn't and will need to be redone if you ever want to count on it working correctly.

The companionway that led into the cabin was unlocked and was waiting for Pellet to make his grand entrance. He opened it and stood in amazement. "Holy…. Look at this place." There was no doubt about it. This guy knew how to sell a boat, and there was a chance he had made a couple calls and did his homework on Pellet.

Pellet climbed down the stairs and looked at the dining table with a horseshoe shaped settee, covered with blue cushions. The polished teak table had an eight-inch brass compass sitting in the center and a set of brass lanterns mounted on each side of the passageway that led to the head and the v-birth which was large enough to "comfortably sleep two adults." There was a brass barometer hanging next to one of the lights. It never entered Pellet's brain that the lanterns, barometer and compass did not go with the boat. Another boat selling trick. Frenchy would be taking those to his new boat, along with the stack of charts, and everything else that gave the boat it's charm. Pellet climbed up into the bed and interlocked his fingers behind his head and gazed at the ceiling and then got up and started milling about again. The bathroom was twelve square feet so the tour was quick. The galley was what would be called a "one butt kitchen". Obviously implying there was no room for two. He sat down at the navigator's station and scanned one of the charts, as if he had any idea of what he was looking at. Then he slid onto the settee and made himself at home.

"I could get used to this," he said just as he saw a note with his name on it lying beside the compass on the table.

"Pellet, I hope you enjoy the tour and like the boat. Grab yourself a beer out of the icebox and get the feel for her. Give me a call and I'll answer any questions you might have."

"Hey. Beer in the icebox. That's cool," Pellet said as he

looked around the cabin to see where the icebox was.

"Hold on a minute. The beers aren't going anywhere. Let's talk about the boat just a bit." Avis, as always, was methodical and pragmatic. Most of the decisions in his life were made through a process. He weighed things. Pondered things. He didn't necessarily distrust, or trust people in general. Information was for gathering, analyzing, and processing. Buying a boat was no different. "So, how much do you know about buying a boat? Especially a sailboat?" he asked Pellet.

"Well. I know that I shouldn't buy a boat that's sunk," he blurted out with a wide grin.

"Funny you should mention that. Did you know that the chances of buying a boat that's been on the bottom of the sea are much higher in the Caribbean than if you were to buy one in the States?"

Pellet looked at him without responding.

"And did you know that a lot of older Jeanneau's are wired per French wiring, not US wiring. That means it's tougher to get replacement parts. At the very least it will probably take more time and will cost a lot more."

"You're kind of a downer, man."

"And when you see water stains like these," he pointed to the tarnished paint and rotting wood around almost all of the ports in the main cabin, "That means these ports are leaking. And unlike what the guy told you, "a little work" is probably a bullshit under-exaggeration of just what it's going to take to get them fixed. Not to mention money."

"How the hell do you know all this stuff?" Pellet snapped, somewhat miffed that Avis had suddenly become a boat expert. And was pretty much ruining the moment.

"It's all out there on the web and in books. There is tons of stuff that you need to know."

"Damn. I was feeling good about this one."

Avis sat down at the other end of the settee and looked around the boat. It felt good. It felt warm. It felt wrong for Pellet. Whether or not Pellet would actually 'sail away' or not was yet to be seen, but that was the plan. There was no point in starting out in the wrong direction right out the gate. He needed something clean. Something with enough bells and whistles to be convenient, but not so many that he would never learn to use them. And he needed something that didn't already have water stains at every port.

"Well, I'd put a couple rules in place for yourself while you're trying to buy your boat," Avis continued with little confidence Pellet would follow his advice. "First, don't buy a boat while you're drunk. And second, be weary of guys who are offering you drinks while they're trying to sell you a boat. He's probably trying to get you drunk. That's my advice."

"Oh. That's right. There's beer in the ice box. Grab me one." Pellet was already past his disappointment. There would be other boats, but for now… free beer.

CHAPTER TEN

Pellet sat on the barstool and played with his beer bottle more than he drank from it. It was quiet for a Friday night and he was struggling to find optimism after looking at over half-a-dozen more boats in the past week. His fingernail pulled on the label of his bottle and he said nothing to the blonde woman on the next stool, or to Dez who stood behind the bar and watched him. Helmut sat at his table and was intrigued that Pellet uncharacteristically ignored the woman, who out of nothing more than sheer ignorance, seemed to be trying to get the attention of the guy sitting beside her.

"Do you live on the island? I mean, you don't look like a tourist," she asked. The schoolteacher from Myrtle Beach had no way of knowing that if she was looking for a Harlequin Romance weekend in the Caribbean, Pellet probably wasn't the guy to make her dreams come true. He looked like a cool guy in an expat islander sort of way. Worn out cargo shorts, a faded ball cap, and a tan darker than most tourist could get in a couple weeks.

"Mmmm," he mumbled, lost in his thoughts, paying her little attention. "No. I work on the island." He didn't add anything more, nor did he seize the moment and blunder the opportunity. In fact, he didn't even seem interested. Helmut didn't know whether to be amazed or concerned. It was like he was watching one of those reality cop shows. If a cop asked him why he thought something was wrong with the situation, he would have answered, "I'm not really sure. Pellet was just acting *different*. Not like himself." Pellet had hit on more unsuspecting tourist over the years than anyone could ever keep track of. And there had not been too many times that he had a beer long enough to play with the label. But on this particular day he was drinking slowly. And the too beautiful for Pellet blonde teacher from Myrtle Beach felt a slight tinge of rejection when he showed absolutely no interest in her.

"So how long have you worked on the island?" she continued.

"Mmmm, bout seven years. Maybe just a bit more," he answered without looking up from his bottle. She looked at him and waited for him to embellish, but again, he didn't say anything more. She glanced up at the bartender and then back at Pellet.

"What do you do?"

"Hmmm?"

"Your job? What do you do?" It still hadn't hit on him that she was pursuing him. In truth, it hadn't really dawned on her either, but she wasn't the type that most men were completely disinterested in. Each time Pellet showed no interest, her determination grew exponentially.

"Oh. Ahh…construction manager. I'm working on a project here on the island." He still barely glanced up at her when he answered. And once again he said nothing more. Desmund shook his head and leaned back against the counter and continued to watch this strange event unfold. He presumed Pellet was still obsessed with the family tree thing. Or maybe the boat search was wearing him down. Either way, Pellet was off his game. Not that being on his game was typically fruitful. Helmut set his pen down and leaned back in his chair and crossed his arms. Pellet was, if nothing else, predictable. This disinterested reaction was something new. Helmut and Dez both watched to see where it would take him. She, the teacher, on the other hand was very on her game. What had started out as an attempt to have a casual conversation with some expat island guy, was quickly turning into a quest of sorts. There were other people, other guys, sitting around the bar, but she didn't take disinterest all that well. She sat up straight and drew a deep breath. That alone would have caught the attention of most guys.

"You don't talk much do you?" She mistakenly presumed that Pellet must be shy or introspective or something much more interesting than he was.

"What?" There was a momentary confused look on his face, just before the light came on in his attic. "Oh. Umm. I, uh." Desmund smiled. Pellet was back. "No. I'm not usually quiet. I was just kind of lost in thought. You know. I was just thinking about something and well... Hi. I'm Pellet," he said and stuck his hand out towards her.

"Ahhhh. So you do talk," she said as she reached up and gently shook his hand. She had a nice handshake. Soft skin. A gentle squeeze, but a squeeze, nonetheless. Pellet held her hand and didn't let go as he realized for the first time that she was his favorite type of women. Out of his league. Her blonde hair was pulled back into a loose ponytail and hung halfway down her bare back. Her shoulders were slightly tanned and her skin was flawless. It was also the first time he noticed her perfume. He didn't know what it was, but it was good. "And what was this thought you were so deeply lost in?" Helmut smiled a bit wider. He didn't know what Pellet had been thinking about, but he knew that this is likely where the conversation was going to go to shit.

"Oh, nothing really. What did you say your name was?"

"I'll tell you what. If you tell me what you were thinking about, I'll tell you my name. Deal?" She smiled and continued to leave her hand lightly clinched in Pellet's.

"Sounds good," he said and took a gulp from his half-peeled bottle.

"Well?" she asked.

"Did you know that a corpse can move for a long time after someone is dead?" Pellet blurted out as if this were possibly a conversation that would get her to take him back to her room. It wasn't. She gave him a puzzled look and unintentionally pulled back just a bit. Her hand slipped out of his and her fingers began to nervously fidget with a napkin. She was speechless.

"No. Really. I read an article that said not only can they move for hours due to muscle spasms and stuff like that, but they can move for days, even weeks, due to gas and fluids doing their thing inside the body. And..." he added as if this whole line of conversation was heading in the right direction, "A dead body can move for months due to tendons and muscles shrinking and drying out and stuff like that."

"Excuse me?" It was the only response she could muster. "What?"

"Is this how you try to impress women? You know. With obscure knowledge about dead people?"

"Well. To be honest, I just read this article that was talking about some research they did on dead people. And it was pretty weird…"

"Lisa," she cut him off as she slipped off the stool and turned to walk away.

"What?"

"I said I'd tell you my name if you told me what you were thinking about. It's Lisa, but I've got to run." Her name was Tiffani.

"Lisa. Cool. Got her name," he said to Dez and raised his beer to him.

"What would make you say some ting like dat to a nice lookin woman like her?" Desumnd asked, shaking his head back and forth.

"What?" is all Pellet blurted out, not grasping how badly the conversation had just gone. Desmund set another beer in front of him.

"Gotta be some ting wrong in dat head of yours."

"What?" Pellet asked again, as if he were on a one-track thought process of trying to figure out where he had gone wrong while conversing with the good-looking woman. He looked across the bar towards Helmut and couldn't help but notice that she had sat down at the table next to him and gave him the same warm smile that Pellet had completely missed. Helmut looked at Pellet and shook his head at him before picking up his pen and returning to writing. Tiffeani wouldn't have any more luck with Helmut than she did with Pellet, but she wouldn't be having nightmares about him either.

"How's da boat search goin?" Desmund asked to change the subject as much as to find out about how it was going. He had no more interest in hearing about dead bodies that continued to move any more than the schoolteacher had.

"Not good, man. Not good. Turns out that just about everyone sails their boats till they're about ready to sink. Some longer than that. Then they clean them up and ask a king's ransom for them." He took a gulp from his new beer. "Hell. There were a few of them that they didn't even bother to clean up."

"Ain't seen nothin decent?"

"Yeah. Seen some great ones. But I didn't win the lottery and Avis ain't the one buying a boat. My budget was twenty-five thousand. It would be a stretch to go above thirty-five. Haven't seen anything decent for less than sixty-five. And keep in mind, those were only the ones that "looked" decent. Probably had all kinds of things wrong with them. Avis did a bunch of reading and made the whole damn process a bummer." He took another drink and pondered why Lisa had told him she had to leave and then sat back down thirty feet away. The thought left him as quick as it had come. "Found one that was beautiful. Low hours on the diesel. Sails were good. Not much wood on it. I hear the less wood, the better. Guess it takes a bunch of work to keep that stuff nice. It was nothing to...." He took another gulp and stopped talking halfway through his story.

"You gonna finish or what?"

"Oh... mmmm," he mumbled and tried to remember where he was going with his story. "Oh. Anyway, everything looked good. Price was too high, but probably reasonable."

"How much?"

"Fifty, but it was worth a lot more. We talked to the guy on the boat for a while and Avis said we should go get a drink. You know... without the guy who was selling it. Avis googled some stuff while we drank. Then he made a couple of calls. Turns out the boat didn't belong to the guy who was selling it. We went back to talk to him, but he was long gone."

"Who was he?"

"I dunno. Nice boat though."

"Nothin else, huh?"

"Looked at two or three that had been sunk during the hurricane a couple years back. They looked good enough but buying a sailboat that's been on the bottom of the sea ain't never a good idea. Looked at a couple more that you really had to wonder how they were still floating."

"Why'd you tell dat woman about dead folks?" Desmund asked, reverting the conversation back to its beginning. "Tink about it. What was your game? If she was normal, no way she'd like talkin bout dat crap. And if she liked it? What da hell. You wanna sleep with a woman who gets turned on talkin bout twitching dead people? Ain't nothin good can come out of dat talk." He shook his head again and folded his arms across his chest.

"Hell. You know me. I don't give all that much thought before talking. I pretty much just say what's on my mind."

"How's dat workin for you?"

"Soon come," Pellet said with a big grin on his face. "My dream girl, soon come, Mr. Dez." He raised his bottle and they both laughed.

"By da way. Some woman, a tourist woman, came lookin for you a couple hours ago. Said she'd be back later."

"Who was it?" he asked with a bit of suspicion. Couldn't imagine what good situation would bring a tourist woman looking for him.

"Donno."

"What was her name?"

"Dunno."

"Well, where's she staying?"

"Dunno."

"What the hell do you know?"

"Some woman, a tourist woman, came lookin for you a couple hours ago. Said she'd be back later," he repeated and then set another beer on the bar and strolled off to talk to a couple locals at the other end of the bar. "Hey!" he yelled when the name came back to him. "Zoe. Dat was her name." The blood flowed from Pellet's face and he grabbed the edge of the bar, trying to not fall off his stool.

"Holy shit," he whispered and picked up his beer and took a long drink. "Holy shit," he said a bit louder. Desmund glanced over to see what he was mumbling about. "Rum. I need a glass of rum," Pellet added.

CHAPTER ELEVEN

Avis stood on the jagged lava rock and threw his line out into the water and smoked a cigarette. It was 7:30 Saturday morning and there were fewer places and fewer things he'd rather be doing, with the exception of possibly sitting on the edge of a trout stream in New Hampshire, doing the exact same thing he was currently doing. Pellet found a piece of an old boat cushion and set it up on top of the jagged lava rock and made himself comfortable. He mindlessly picked up his pole and baited the hook with a piece of fish and tossed the hook into the water. He slowly turned the handle on the expensive reel as he sat and hoped to catch a snapper or two.

On his very first cast out into the waves, something larger than a snapper hit his line and for the next five minutes he fought a fisherman's battle with his unknown foe. Avis sat and watched as Pellet reeled in for a couple minutes, then the fish fought back and took more line. Pellet glanced up at him every once in a while grinning ear to ear. Not once had the fish surfaced and not once had Pellet taken the time to consider what might be on the end of the line. His pole was nearly bent in half and Avis was just about to tell him he'd better give some extra slack line before the pole broke. Just as the words started coming out of his mouth, the line went slack and Pellet momentarily thought he'd lost his fish. But the fish hadn't gotten away, nor had it given up its fight. What the five-foot-long, black tip shark did do was to speed straight towards the shore until it was less than ten feet from where Pellet was standing. At that point it was still a few feet beneath the surface and, more importantly, still out of site. A split second later it soared straight into the air, flipped and landed on its side in the waves near the shore. Water splashed onto Pellet as he stumbled backwards on the rocks and in a sheer panic reaction, threw the expensive pole and reel at his foe. He stared at the spot in the air where only moments ago was filled by the shark. Avis looked at the spot in the water where his pole and reel landed and shook his head in amazement of the entire event.

"Was that what it looked like?" Pellet asked as blood began to seep through his shorts from a cut that the lava-rocks had sliced into his rear-end when he landed on top of them.

"You owe me a new pole," was all Avis mumbled. Then he turned and looked at his own line floating in the water.

"Holy shit," was all Pellet said. He sat on the cushion for the next half hour and watched the water as if he believed the shark might return to resume the battle. Of course, for that to happen it would need to first return the pole.

Eventually Pellet regained his composure enough to stop awaiting the return of the shark. He sat with a beer and cigarette and no pole, perfectly content to not have a hook and line in the water. The adrenaline rush of seeing the shark seemed to have slowly followed the fishing pole, wherever it had headed to. He gave no thought to any of the other fish. The current flowed between the shoreline where he was sitting and a tiny island about a quarter mile off the northeast tip of Anguilla. A sailboat passed between the two shores and he felt a tinge of envy. He watched it sail away. He watched a few clouds flow past. He watched the current carry a red glass bottle covered with seashells and wondered where it had come from or where it would end up. And he sat quietly and thought about things he didn't normally think about. He'd been pondering a lot about his life in the past few weeks. Whether he acknowledged it or not, he had been questioning his life and changes that needed to be made for a couple years. There were thoughts that were quietly growing and creeping up on him and whispering in his ear. He couldn't decide whether change was coming or that he just felt the need for change. Either way, something was stirring and he couldn't shake the feeling.

"Did I ever tell you I had a kid a few years back?" Pellet asked without taking his eyes off the water or the island that sat a few hundred yards away. Avis looked at him and said nothing while he processed what Pellet had just said. He wondered what he meant by he "had" a kid. Did he mean it like he still had one, but he doesn't live with him? Or did the kid die?

"No. You never mentioned that," is how he left it and he looked back out towards his line in the water.

"Yup. A son. Justin Peter Pelletier. Called him JP. Hard to believe, huh? A little Pellet running around."

"I could see that. I could see you with a little guy hanging out with you," Avis answered without digging for more.

"A wife, too. She was damn good looking. Me and a wife and a kid. Just like an all-American family," he continued, still looking out over the water.

"How come I've never heard about any of this before?" Avis asked, maneuvering his way through a conversation that he had no idea of how it was going to end. "Seems like something you might have mentioned to me somewhere along the line in the past two years."

Pellet sat for a few more minutes without saying anything. Not that he didn't appear to be engaged in the conversation. It was more like he was considering how to respond and searching for words that carried the correct weight.

"When I left Waldoboro way back when I was lost, all I really knew for sure was I had to get out or I was going to shrivel up and die at the eraser factory. A few months after I landed in Florida I went out for a drink one night... I know, hard to believe, right?" Avis smiled, but he knew this wasn't that kind of conversation. Pellet wasn't the kind of guy who ever really bared his soul. For a guy who talked all the time, not many people really got to know him. Not even Avis. "I met a waitress at the bar and we hit it off from the first night. Sparks flew and all that stuff. Within a couple months we moved in together. Wasn't long before we eloped. A few months later there was a little Pellet."

"Damn, Pellet," was all Avis could muster for the moment.

"The day Justin was born was the happiest day of my life.

I had a beautiful wife and a fantastic kid. We were renting a cozy house in a cool neighborhood. Life was good." Avis listened without saying a word. There was no wife or son in the picture now. There was no possible way this story had a good ending. "One night when Zoe was at work, I had to run to the grocery store. I ran into a waitress friend that worked with her and we chatted for a few minutes. Justin was with me and she was being nice enough, smiled and cooed and played with his fingers and toes, but something was just a bit off. Couldn't put my finger on it. When I said good-bye and started to leave she took ahold of my arm. It was all weird. Thought she was hitting on me or something like that. Turned out I wish that was the case. You know how women can smile at you, but the smile pretty much screams "Oh, you poor baby." Well, she was giving one of those smiles on steroids. After a few seconds of staring at each other she just blurted out, "Pellet. You need to get Justin tested. You know... a paternity test."

"Damn, man," was all Avis could muster.

"I lived in denial for a few weeks, but you know how it is. Once a bell is rung, and all that stuff. Little signs I'd been ignoring started popping a bit clearer. Zoe would go to the store in the middle of the afternoon and be gone for a couple hours and come back with almost nothing. She wasn't quite as nice to me as she used to be. I just figured that things changed once we had a kid. Then again... I suppose I knew better. A few weeks after the grocery store thing I had Justin tested. When the results came in I was devastated. I called the waitress who had told me and we met up at a coffee shop. Turns out the bartender from work had been banging hips with Zoe. The only reason the girl told me was to get even. Some kind of soap opera shit going on at the bar." Pellet stopped talking and watched the water some more. The waves were kicking up and he thought if he could visualize how his emotions felt, they would have looked like the water crashing on the rocks.

"So how'd it all go down? In the end. What happened?"

"Nothing. I didn't say shit to her. Didn't tell her I knew

anything. Just let her keep treating me like an old, beaten dog. It took a couple months, but I made some calls, found a job here in the islands and made plans for my escape. One night she went to work and Justin was with his Grandma, I just got on a plane and never went back. Left a note on the counter and that was that."

"Must have been pretty rough I would think. Losing a son and a wife like that and keeping it all bottled in."

"Don't think I've really thought about it all that much since I left. I kind of buried it way deep. Softened the blow with a lot of rum, I suppose. Sometimes the only way to deal with something is to not deal with it."

"So why now? How come you didn't leave it buried?"

"She's here. In Anguilla," Pellet said. He finally looked up, and in a strange way Avis barely recognized the man sitting on the rocks in front of him.

"Who's here?" Avis snapped harsher than he had intended.

"Zoe. Desmund said some tourist woman came looking for me yesterday. Couldn't remember her name. A few minutes later he was on the other side of the bar and yelled, "Zoe. Dat was her name. The damn man is an idiot." All I could think was. holy shit! I almost fell off the stool."

"Why would she come here after all this time?"

"A divorce I suppose."

"You're still married?" It was a lot of information for a morning of fishing.

"Well… I left and never went back. Left my phone on the counter. Old beat up truck in the yard. Didn't bring anything but a duffle-bag of clothes. I'm guessing it took her a while to find me. She's probably ready to marry someone else. Poor bastard," he added with a halfhearted chuckle.

There was a small splash in the water and his heart raced at the thought of the shark returning. It was just a wave splashing on the rocks. In a way, the momentary panic wasn't all that different than the first few words of any real conversations he had had with women he met since getting to the islands. For the most part he kept everything superficial and shallow. No chance of having serious conversations like, "do you want to have kids someday," or anything that heavy. No chance of catching a shark when fishing at the shallow drunk end of a bar.

Avis lit a cigarette and kept an eye on his line. He was a thinker more than a talker. He wondered what was really going through Pellet's mind as he rehashed his failed marriage and dealt with the emotions of losing his son for perhaps the first time in years. He wondered if this was the first time that Pellet had ever dealt with it at all. Maybe he emotionally packed it away when he packed his duffle bag and left Florida. Maybe it had been packed away and never reopened for all this time.

Pellet stood up and looked out at the water where the shark had splashed down. He smiled at the irony that he'd almost caught a shark and Zoe had arrived on the same weekend. He lit a cigarette and decided he didn't care about either. His mind wasn't really on fishing. Surprisingly to him, it wasn't really on Zoe or Justin either. He was kicking thoughts of them around, but it wasn't like they were heavy on his mind. If Avis presumed Pellet was devastated by rehashing the past, he was mistaken. But her arrival fueled his already growing feelings of restlessness. Make no mistake, he was still Pellet which meant, well it meant he was still Pellet and that just about summed it up. With that said, things were changing.

He sat back down on the old scrap of cushion and made himself comfortable and looked out towards Scrub Island. He'd never been out there and wondered if there was anything worth seeing. Maybe one day, when he finally owned a boat, they would sail over and explore. Far off to the south he barely saw a spec of the sailboat that had cruised by a few minutes earlier. He turned and watched Avis fish for a few minutes and wondered what it was like to be like him. Avis had his shit together. He was even keeled and methodical. His wife was smart and beautiful. He was, for lack of a better word, solid. There was no emptiness in his life. He seemed to be at peace with himself and the world around him. Pellet wasn't any of those things, and he knew it.

"I want more," Pellet blurted out. Avis looked over at him without interrupting. "I want more out of life, Avis." That's all he said. He looked back towards the water. Neither of them spoke for a long time.

CHAPTER TWELVE

In the back of his mind, Pellet knew how he hoped it would go down. He hoped he would wander into Dez's for a typical Saturday afternoon beer and burger. Best case scenario? He'd plop down on his stool and Desmund would toss an envelope on the bar and say, "Dat Zoe woman left dis for you." Worst case scenario? She'd be sitting at the bar, sipping on a glass of wine, and waiting for him. Scenario he hadn't imagined. She'd be laughing and chatting with Desmund as if they were lifelong friends who hadn't seen each other for a while. And even worse than that, Helmut Brandt, who had sat no place other than at his corner table for the entire seven years Pellet had known him, was sitting beside the stunning and apparently quite charismatic, Mrs. Pelletier. Halfway between his truck and the front steps of the bar, Pellet stopped and hid behind a tall skinny palm tree and watched the three of them chatting and wondered why the universe was conspiring against him at his favorite bar. He momentarily considered running back to his truck and finding a place to hide until she left Anguilla, although he knew that hiding in Anguilla was about as easy as keeping a secret in Anguilla. The odds of success for either were absurdly low. Dez's elbows were planted on the bar and he leaned close enough to Zoe to make it clear to Pellet that they had somehow already become dear friends. Helmut was smirking and listening more than talking. Listening was what he did in life. Gloating was something he rarely did. Today he was doing both.

"You left dis one to come hang out in a bar wit us? What's wrong wit you, mon?" Dez blurted out as Pellet cautiously strolled up to the bar and took a seat five stools away from where Zoe was sitting.

"You know what they say," Pellet mumbled and motioned for a beer. "Devil's in the details. You probably haven't heard the details yet." He stopped talking and wished he hadn't said a thing. He slipped away in the night seven years ago precisely so he wouldn't have to take part in this exact conversation. He lit another cigarette and fell silent and tried to tune the three of them out.

The first week in Anguilla was rough way back then. The wounds were fresh, still bleeding, but he was comforted in knowing he'd caught her off guard and likely inflicted some sort of pain. It wasn't that he believed her to be heartbroken being she was screwing another guy, but his clean escape and her being stunned by his abrupt leaving was all he had to cling onto back then. Within a couple of weeks he was working and drinking, and he put Royal Palm Beach and Zoe far behind him. He locked it all in a closet. His wife. His son. Their home. Their life. All of it, neatly tucked away from his warm, blue, palm filled world. If they ever tried to creep to the surface and pay him a visit, it was nothing a bottle of rum or a dozen beers wouldn't take care of. Up until now the rum and beer had done the job. He was skeptical that it would do the job with her sitting only a few bar stools away.

"How'd you trick this woman into living with you?" Helmut asked as he swiveled on his stool and faced Pellet. No answer came. He didn't even look up. It turned out that years of bottled up pain and heartbreak didn't just magically slip away with time. Everything he hadn't dealt with since he found out she had cheated and since finding out Justin wasn't his son had quietly slept in some dark hidden place, but the feelings were all alive and awakened at this very moment. Pellet knew he had no desire to see her, but it never dawned on him that this flood of emotions would pour over him like boiling water. He reached into his pocket for a pack of cigarettes and pulled one out to light without realizing he had a lit one hanging from his mouth. Helmut's eyebrows raised and his forehead wrinkled as he watched his friend and thought he saw his hand shake when he clicked his lighter. Zoe was still smiling at Desmund and laughing at whatever he was saying, but she wasn't unaware of Pellet. She stole a quick glance out of the corner of her eye but hadn't yet worked up the nerve to look straight at him or say anything to him. Helmut was between the two of them and she couldn't see his face, but she could see Desmund. He slowly stood up and backed away from the bar. The smile was still on his face, but it was more polite and less embracing that it was moments ago. He had glanced at Pellet too. Over the years he had seen him lose fights, get shot down by more women than anyone he had ever known, and get flat out embarrassed by women who went above and beyond while rejecting his advances. He'd seen Pellet humbled and embarrassed and hung over and in physical pain. But he had never seen his spirit crushed. No matter how badly or how often he failed, he pressed forward towards the next disaster as if success was certainly just over the next hill or around the next corner. Pellet was like a boat adrift at sea, always confident that land would soon be on the horizon. But on this day, sitting on that stool, Pellet looked defeated. He drew hard on his cigarette and sat slouched over and stared at the bar. Helmut slid off his stool and eased back towards his table in the corner where his notebooks and satchel and pen waited for him. As he passed by his friend he reached out and squeezed his shoulder but didn't stop and didn't say anything. Helmut had a history too. He knew the kind of pain his friend was feeling. He recognized the wounds and the scars. There were no words from Helmut that were going to make anything better. Desmund wandered to the other side of the bar to wait on a customer he'd been ignoring for a while. Zoe sat uncomfortably alone and tried to figure out what to do or say. She looked his way a couple of times, but he was shutting everything out. Pellet sat and stewed and struggled with her being in his bar on what had become his island, as opposed to her island. He knew why she was here, or at least presumed he knew, but still couldn't wrap his head around why she hadn't just FedEx'd the damn thing. He made a clean break seven years ago and wanted to keep it that way. As far as he was concerned nothing good could come from her being here.

They sat in silence until it became unbearably awkward. When she couldn't take it any longer, Zoe took a sip of her wine and looked at Pellet who was still staring straight ahead.

"Hey, Pellet. Been a long time."

He didn't say a word. He didn't look at her. He just took a drink and tried to convince himself that she would disappear if he ignored her long enough.

"Nice place. Anguilla. Dez's Bar. Real nice too," she continued, trying to fill the silence and break the ice. "Desmund seems like a nice guy. Said you guys are good friends," she added.

"He's a dumb-ass," Pellet answered loud enough for his friend to hear.

"Seems nice," she whispered and looked into her empty glass. She held it up for Desmund to see. He wanted to pretend he hadn't seen her, but it was too late. They made eye contact and he meandered towards her with a wine bottle in his hand.

"Me too," Pellet snapped and pushed an empty Red Stripe towards him. Desmund set the new one in front of him and shrugged as if to say, "Hey. She seemed okay to me."

"The view of the Caribbean sure is beautiful. This is the first time I've ever seen it." She was floundering. In her mind this reunion was going to go better. A lot of time had passed since he left, and surely he had moved on by now. At least that is what she had thought. She figured he had probably found someone else. Maybe even had a family. She had no way of knowing that Pellet had completely and indefinitely postponed dealing with the crushing blow of his failed marriage. He postponed it until this very moment.

"What do you want, Zoe?" he blurted out with enough anger and hate to just about knock her off her seat. "What the hell are you doing here?" With each thought and each word he became angrier than he was the moment before. He didn't want to do this. Not seven years ago. Not now. Not ever. He did not want to have this conversation.

"I want to tell you how sorry I am Pellet. That's all," she said as if it was in fact all she wanted to say. Then she continued on. "I want to tell you how wrong I was. I want you to know I didn't mean to hurt you."

"You ruined me Zoe. You fucking destroyed me. We were in love. You gave me a son. Then you fucking destroyed me." He fought back the tears and he fought hard. No way in hell was he going to cry in front of this bitch.

"I know, and I know there's nothing I can say to defend myself. What I did was horrible. No excuses." She drew a deep breath and tried to gather her thoughts. Once she worked up the nerve, she slid off her stool and moved over next to Pellet. His teeth clinched when she sat down and he considered for a moment just getting up and walking out.

"If you were a guy I'd kick your ass just for having the gall to sit down beside me. Hell, I'd kick your ass just for showing up here and making me think about this shit again." He motioned to Desmund. "I need a shot of rum."

Desmund poured two shots into a glass and set it down. "Stay cool, mon. Don't do nothin you gonna regret. No ass kickin, right?"

"Look, Pellet," Zoe began. "I didn't come down here to hurt you or to start any trouble or anything like that. It's just that, you know, we're still married and I brought you something I presume you want."

"Married!?" Desmund blurted out. It was a kneejerk reaction and before the words finished coming out of his mouth he regretted jumping in.

"Oh. So, you don't really have all the details, huh? Guess she probably didn't…" Pellet stopped midsentence and drank his rum. Desmund didn't need the details. Didn't want the details. Pellet wished he didn't know the details himself. He knew the gift she brought was the divorce papers. There was nothing else left. Strangely enough, even though he left years ago and held her in the lowest regard possible, there was still a sting knowing that she was the one filing for divorce. She cheated on him. She lied to him about their son. Now, she was divorcing him. Pellet held his rum glass up to Desmund.

"Go easy, mon. Not a good time for too much of dat, you know?"

"Just pour." He finally stopped slouching over on the bar and sat up and looked at her. She was better looking than he remembered. She was good looking back then, but the years had served her well. Back then she was an attractive woman with a cute girlish quality. She was all grown up now and her girlishness was gone. He wondered if her childish inconsideration for other people's feelings had gone away, or had that just grown up too. He looked at her and shook his head. "How's Justin?" The words, the name, caused another swirl of emotions. He cherished him as his son for months, then he found out Justin was another man's kid. It wasn't the boy's fault, but it damn sure wasn't Pellet's either. The name stirred an internal battle between wanting to see a picture of him or give him a hug, and never wanting to see him again.

"He's good. He's with Mama this week."

"Not with Dad?" Pellet asked with a tone of sarcasm.

"No. He's not in the picture. Never has been."

"Well, he was for at least a few minutes," he snapped back and glared at her.

"Pellet. I didn't come here to do this. I know I deserve whatever you dish out, but we can end it better than this. There's no need to go down this road."

"You ever think that maybe I need to go down this road just a bit, Zoe?"

Zoe reached out and took the back of his hand in hers and squeezed. He was surprised that he didn't pull away. He was more surprised at how good it felt that she reached out and touched him. From that point on, the afternoon turned into night and with each passing hour, he simmered down ever so slightly. She kept apologizing. He for the most part continued to throw jabs and punches, but with each shot he threw, his aggression and hatred lessened. Hours later, after they talked about her life over the past seven years, Pellets life in Anguilla and his adventures with the Island Dogs, and after she filled him in on just about everything about Justin, it was time for the night to wind down.

"Well, I can either call a taxi, or you can drop me off at

the hotel. If you give me a ride, I'll give you the papers and I guess that will be that." It wasn't quite the reunion she'd been hoping for, but it was probably about as good as it was going to get.

Pellet shrugged and slid off the stool. He looked like he had aged about five years in one day. He nodded at Helmut and shrugged at Desmund. "See you tomorrow," he mumbled as he walked to his truck looking like a tired old man.

Ten minutes later he strolled to her room and leaned against the wall outside her door as she stepped inside. She stepped back out and looked at him. "You might as well come in for a minute. It's in my bag in the bathroom. He stepped inside and looked around the room. Big for one person, he thought.

"Nice room," he mumbled for no other reason than that it was a nice room and there was nothing else to say. He was in his hot looking, soon to be ex-wife's room in a really nice hotel to get served divorce papers. Strange night indeed. He heard her searching through her purse or something in the bathroom and he walked over to the window and looked out towards the lights of Saint Maarten. Zoe stepped back into the bedroom.

"We're still married, Pellet. We don't have to let it end the way it did before. We can rewrite this." Pellet turned and struggled with what to say without completely conceding defeat or stirring up his anger again. Her clothes, sundress, bra, and panties were dropped in a pile onto the bathroom floor and she had spritzed a bit more perfume behind her right ear.

"Oh shit," Pellet mumbled. She looked much better than he remembered.

CHAPTER THIRTEEN

Some things don't change with time. Pellet was always an early riser. Zoe never was and still wasn't. At six-thirty he opened his eyes and watched the ceiling fan slowly spin above his head. Not unlike Pellet, a half-dozen thoughts, relevant and irrelevant, whirled through his brain like dominos being knocked over on a coffee table. His mind went from "What a night," to "Man, this is the most comfortable bed I've ever slept in," to "What the hell was I thinking last night?" to "I wonder how they keep the dust off the fan. Mine always has dust bunnies on it," to "I'm hungry. Think I'll go get something to eat."

He sat up and stretched and looked down at her, amazed how he transitioned from hatred and loathing to hot sex in a seriously short span of time. He shrugged and smiled, amused by how simple he really was. Another thing that hadn't changed was that she was a sprawler when she slept. Covers kicked off, she laid flat on her back with one arm draped across her face, her mouth wide open and one foot sticking out over the edge of the bed. She was dead to the world. Pellet looked at and admired her naked body and shook his head as one more thought popped into his head. "Good gawd. She's twice as good looking than I remember." The muscles in her legs were toned. Her stomach was defined. Her breast were perfect. Her tanned skin was flawless and there were no tan lines. He presumed she must be into yoga or working out, or something along those lines. Her body was stronger and harder than it was seven years ago. One last thought came into his mind, but he decided it was a bad idea. With that brushed aside, he got up and slipped his shorts and shirt on, grabbed his flip-flops and quietly eased towards the door. He stopped and scribbled a note and left it on the desk.

"I'll be at Dez's tonight. Stop by if you like." He didn't

really know why he wrote it or why he would want to see her again, other than the sex. But he left the note anyway and slipped out the door.

Fourteen hours later Pellet pulled into the somewhat crowded dirt driveway and parked his truck between a new Land Rover and a new BMW. He paid no attention to either as he climbed out of his beat up, thirteen-year-old Dodge pickup.

Three catamarans and a couple sailboats were anchored a hundred or so yards from the beach in front of Dez's. There was a regatta or some other sailing event going on somewhere in Anguilla or Saint Maarten. Pellet had seen so many of them over the years he barely paid attention to them anymore, other than they sometimes made his bar uncomfortably crowded with boat owners and captains and crews and their drinking buddies. Modern day sailors were hardly the Cap'n Jack Sparrow type. Most of them were rich kids or knew rich kids with folks who could afford to sail around the Caribbean on expensive sailboats. They were typically good-looking adventurers who filled their youth with stories they could share with their business partners years down the line. What they often had in common with Cap'n Sparrow was when they were not sailing, they liked to drink and they were looking for fun. No place like an island bar to do both, if you have the time and money to pull it off.

Avis and Savannah sat at Helmut's table and watched the mix of locals and tourist and sailors mingle and talk and drink.

"So, that's her?" Savannah asked. Not that she didn't already know the answer.

"Yup, that's her," Helmut answered without so much as looking up from the paper he was scribbling notes on.

"Good looking," Avis added. Savannah wanted to disagree, at least a little bit. Truth was that Zoe was not only good looking, she was damn good looking.

"Hmm. She was married to Pellet, huh?" Savannah continued to watch her as if some key piece of information was about to be revealed.

"Still is, apparently," Helmut muttered.

"Well. She seems like a bit of a social butterfly," she added and looked at Avis. "Is it just me, or is she enjoying the attention they're giving her just a bit too much?"

"Been noticing that. Seems like she could at least finalize the divorce before showing up here and replacing him." Avis was impressed that Pellet's soon to be ex-wife was so good looking. On the other hand, a few years back he had first-hand experience with a hot looking crazy woman. The trade-off was usually not worth the pay-off. He watched as she said something to one of the crew members who was entertaining her for the moment. She laughed and took ahold of his arm and leaned in close. Her breast firmly pressed against his forearm and lingered there long enough to make it clear it was just a smidge more than incidental.

There is an almost endless list of addictions in this world. People are addicted to drugs and alcohol, power and money, sex, and gambling. Millions are addicted to cigarettes and video games. Millions more are addicted to church or their jobs or going to the gym. Avis knew a guy back in New Hampshire who was addicted to wool sweaters. He wore one every day of the year. In July and August he wore a white wool sleeveless V-neck. He was miserably hot, but it was better than wearing long sleeves, and he was addicted. Up until she was about sixteen, Zoe was a plain-Jane face in the crowd. She wasn't ugly or pretty. She wasn't smart or dumb. She wasn't athletic or out of shape. Most of the time she felt like a shadow. It wasn't like people couldn't see her. She was right there for everyone to see, but nobody noticed her. That's how her self-perception existed in her head. Then between sixteen and eighteen she made a metamorphosis of sorts. She transformed from plain to cute, and from cute to good looking, and finally from good looking to wow. And with each slight transformation came a slight increase in the amount of attention she received. And as the attention grew, her craving for more attention grew. When she and Pellet were together she was beautiful, but she had a sort of girlish quality about her and she absolutely loved all the attention men gave her. Seven years later she had become a full-blown physically beautiful woman. There was nothing girlish about her anymore. One thing that hadn't changed about her was as her beauty grew, the attention being showered on her grew exponentially. And as it grew, her craving for more, grew like a monster.

Pellet leaned against his truck for a few minutes and watched Zoe work the guys hanging around her. It stung a bit, but it all seemed to make more sense now than it did back then. Back then he pretty much ignored all the guys hitting on her and wrote it off as her being a waitress and a bartender. She was a grownup. He presumed she could take care of herself. In fact she had told him more than once to ignore them. Her exact words were, "I can take care of myself, Pellet. Don't worry so much." It was different watching her now. Now that he knew and understood who she really was. He leaned and smoked and watched for as long as it took to smoke his cigarette. He put it out on the side of his truck and tossed the butt into the rear bed and wandered towards the bar. He eased up the steps and across the floor and steered clear of Zoe and her suiters. Pellet sat himself down at Helmut's table and joined the rest of them watching his wife in curious amazement.

"Hola," he said as he plopped down and waved at the waitress for a beer. She waved back with no need to come to see what he wanted.

"How you doing, sweetie," Savannah asked with a look of sympathy on her face.

"Better than you think. Got laid, getting divorced, buying a boat. Life is good," he answered with a huge Pellet grin on his face. Avis smiled and nodded to him.

"Guess we need to find a boat then," Avis added.

"She had sex with you again?" Helmut asked as if he were amazed that it ever happened the first time.

"What can I say… I'm a chick magnet."

"Unbelievable," he mumbled and returned to jotting down notes. There was a fairly good chance he was writing something about an unbelievably attractive, and likely somewhat damaged woman who was willing to have sex with his knucklehead friend, Pellet…again.

"I'm serious, Pellet. Are you okay?" Savannah pressed for some sort of therapeutic response.

"Hey, last time I saw her I was getting screwed and not having sex. Heading in the right direction." His beer came and he raised it to his friends. "To getting a divorce," he toasted.

"To buying a sailboat," Avis responded.

The last thing she did before walking out of the bar with one of the sailors, was to give the waitress an envelope to deliver to Pellet along with a beer. When the beer and envelope were set on the table in front of him, he turned to glance at the sender, but she was gone. One more night in her luxury hotel, then back to Royal Palm Beach to do whomever or whatever she was doing before she waltzed back into Pellets life again. And just like that, the next part of Pellet's life was about to begin.

CHAPTER FOURTEEN

It turned out that if Pellet had about a half million dollars, there were quite a few sailboats to choose from in both Anguilla and Saint Maarten. He'd need about a couple hundred thousand more than that if he were to venture over to Saint Barths. Sadly for Pellet, he was about four hundred and fifty thousand or so short on the first half million, so his choices were pretty limited. Obviously he had increased from his initial limit of twenty thousand dollars. On the surface there appeared to be quite a few nice boats in his now, forty to fifty-thousand-dollar range, but "*on the surface*" were the key words.

His favorite boat so far, or at least the most interesting was a forty-one-foot Endeavour that had been completely refitted with everything, including fake leather leopard skin all over the walls, ceilings and cushions. The owner had even thought to add a glass top bar in the main cabin and a round bed in the rear birth with more fake leopard skin. Too bad he had overlooked rebuilding the diesel engine. It was an extremely sheik looking chick den that may or may not get him back home once he left the port. Then there was a fifty-foot Catalina that seemed to have good possibilities. The seller said the ports dripped a bit when it rained hard. Clearly, he hadn't expected a tropical downpour while Avis and Pellet were down below deck. The ports could not have leaked much more if they had simply been left open. Water dripped and puddled on the cushions, the table, the floor and anywhere else it happened to land. Half-a-dozen boats they saw had teak that hadn't been finished for so long that all the wood on the topside resembled driftwood. A few more potentials that were not old enough to require a complete renovation inside the cabin, had newish plywood replacing all of what was previously finished teak. It was safe to presume these boats had seen the bottom of the bay during one storm or another in the not so distant past. One guy had a fifty-foot Beneteau that was at least temporarily stocked with three long-legged, fit and skimpily bikini clad women he had hired from a Saint Maarten strip club. It was difficult for Pellet to focus on anything on the boat, other than the strippers. He presumed that was their purpose for being there. He also presumed he would have needed a couple grand a night if he hoped to keep them on the boat, not that strippers were his thing. To be honest, he found them a bit intimidating. He presumed, correctly or not, that he was somewhere around average under the sheets. Being compared to the couple hundred guys who had been there before him was too much for him to wrap his head around.

It was the last boat they had looked at on this particular day. He and Avis both decided they needed to take a few days off to regain their strength before looking at any more.

"Good gawd man," Pellet said as they wandered back towards the ferry to head back from Saint Maarten to Anguilla. "These guys make used car salesmen seem like the most honest people I've ever met."

"Car salesmen," Avis snapped back. "They make politicians look like saints." He shook his head and puffed his cigarette and started reciting the sales spiels they'd heard or read before actually seeing the boats. "Ports drip a little is what the guy said in his email. I guess he thinks Niagara Falls drips a little, too. Drips a little bit my ass."

"Hey. How about this one," Pellet chimed in. "Fully loaded with everything a sailor could want. It had three strippers and a liquor cabinet, no radar, the radio was shot, it needed the bottom painted, and I didn't even bother to look at the engine."

"Newly restored inside and out," Avis continued with the therapeutic venting. "It was five years old. Give me one damn reason you would restore a five-year-old boat, other than, as the dude put it, "Sunk? Well, it took on a lot of water. But I don't think it went all the way to the bottom." Jesus Christ!"

They bought their tickets for the ferry and cleared immigration. Pellet went up to the small bar that had some candy,

Cheetos, chips, three kinds of beer, Pepsi and Ting. He bought a couple Red Stripes and a snickers bar and plopped down in the chair next to Avis. "Sorry. No PBR in this place."

"So, what did you think of the strippers?" Avis asked with a grin.

"Kinda scary. I mean, they were hot looking and seemed nice enough and all that, but there's something about strippers that freaks me out."

"Well, they were paid to be nice to us. I'm guessing it's the dishonesty thing that throws you off kilter. You know... even if you're dumb as a rock and ugly as one of them hairless dogs, they still flirt with you and love on you until the cash runs out."

Pellet raised his beer to nothing at all, other than looking for boats had kicked his ass. They finished their beer and got in line to get onto the ferry. A couple local guys from Anguilla were tending the lines and one of them smiled and waved as Pellet walked towards him.

"Hey, mon. Heard you're looking for a boat."

"Yup," was all Pellet could manage.

"Come out to the house and see me. Got a good one for you to look at."

"What... that sailboat up on stands beside your garage?"

"Yah mon. Nice boat."

"It sat on the rocks on the east end for two years, Isaac. How do you figure it's a "nice boat?"

"Got it all fixed up, mon," he shot back with all the sincerity of the guy who owned the boat with the three strippers. "New inside. New paint outside. Engines rebuilt. You gonna be impressed," he said.

"Guess I'll have to pass on it for now Isaac. Tell your dad I said hello," he mumbled as he stepped up onto the boat and climbed the ladder so they could sit topside on the way back across the straight between Anguilla and Saint Maarten.

"Quite a day, huh?" Avis asked more as a statement than a question.

"Funny. It was kind of fun for the first few hours this

morning. But by the end of the day it felt like I was shopping for shoes for nine hours at the mall with a girlfriend." Avis gave him a funny look. He got the point about how the search was becoming frustrating, but wasn't sure how he appreciated being compared to a woman shopping for shoes.

"Well. There was one more thing I read, you know… when I was reading about buying a boat," Avis said without looking at him. He was looking straight ahead with the wind in his face. The warm Caribbean breeze filled with salt air and the sound of the boat's engines were washing away the frustrations of the day. Pellet looked at him and waited for him to continue.

"There's always another boat for sale. Be patient and don't force it. When buying a boat, let the right boat find you and you can't go wrong." Pellet almost zipped back a sarcastic response, but he caught himself. Avis had spent the better part of a month riding around Anguilla, making trips over to Saint Maarten to help him find a boat. They even considered taking a trip to Saba to look at one but decided against it. It was a wise decision. Saba was about a twenty-minute flight from Anguilla on one of the little island hoppers. In order to land, the pilots did a kamikaze routine over the top of the mountain that encompassed pretty much the whole island. The flight pattern was, fly to Saba, skim the top of the peak, bank hard and nosedive to the runway, then land as if it were all perfectly normal. To add insult to injury, they would have found a boat that made the stripper boat seem pristine. Besides, strangely enough, "Let the right boat find you," had a ring of truth to it. Maybe he was trying too hard. Maybe it was time to step back and let a boat find him. It wasn't likely the search would go any worse than it was already going.

Chapter Fifteen

Mardi Segal flew from Paris to Saint Maarten a half dozen times in her teens. The first time was with her mother. The next time it was with her cousins. By the third trip she had made friends on the French side of the island and at seventeen she found herself taking the trip to the Caribbean island by herself. The last time she made the flight was when she was twenty-one. Just under fourteen years ago.

A month after arriving to vacation with island friends, she headed back to the Princess Julianna International Airport to catch her flight back home. On the way there she stopped at a beach bar at the west end of the runway to have a rum punch. She was grabbing one more taste of her escape away from the real world while taking in the sea view and inhaling a final deep breath of salt air before catching her 3:45 PM flight back to Paris. Back to the city of lights, the city of ice and snow and the city of her mother, father and grandparents. Back to the demands of life and expectations put on her by a family who she felt knew nothing about who she really was. Back to the pressures of her mundane job. Back to reality. She sipped on her rum punch from eleven-thirty until twelve fifteen. Then she ordered a second one and watched a few planes land and take off. Then she watched a sailboat grow larger and larger as it neared the island. She watched tourist laughing and talking and giving no thought to any of the serious things in life that made up the majority of their lives. Sipping on the second punch lasted until almost one-thirty. At two o'clock on the nose, she took a deep breath, smiled at the girl tending the bar and said, "May as well have one last drink, you know… to whatever lies ahead." When the drink was slid across the bar in front of her, she picked it up and pondered for a few seconds. "Here's to the future," she said and tipped the glass towards the girl and her future, and then took another little sip. At three-forty-five she sat with her back turned towards the bar with Reggae music playing in the background and watched the Air France jet rev its engines. Less than thirty seconds later, the jumbo jet banked to the right and sailed up over the small mountain of the tropical Caribbean island.

Mardi didn't catch that flight, or the next, or the next, or any other. There was no plan or forethought to her staying in the Caribbean. In fact, when she had first sat down on the stool with her feet in the sand and her suitcase sitting on the ground beside her, she checked the time and thought she would just have one quick one and then she would hustle to the airport to catch her flight. When she ordered the second one, she still hadn't made any sort of commitment in her mind to stay. She knew her plan to go home was wavering, but she hadn't yet accepted that she was not going anywhere. It was near the end of the second drink when she mumbled to nobody in particular, "Oh shit! I'm going to live here, aren't I." And that was exactly what she did. Over the past fourteen years Saint Maarten had become her home and she had not returned to Paris, not even once. Family visited in the winters. She always talked about visiting them in the summer, but somewhere deep in the back of her mind she was afraid if she went back to visit, she might just sit in a café and sip coffee as her flight to the islands left without her.

Her first island job was a part-time bartender at the same bar she sat in on the day that she did not leave and return home. After that there were a series of bars and restaurants where she was a waitress or hostess or bartender. Sometimes she was all of them. A couple times she ended up being the cook. Somewhere along the line she worked as a desk clerk in the Marriot for a year or so. Then she worked as a hospitality rep at the ports where the cruise ships came in. Her job was to usher folks from the ships to various tours and taxi drivers. She worked on a dive boat for a season and then tried her hand at cutting men's hair for a while. During all those years and jobs, there were two husbands. Neither of them worked out. One she threw out. One she left. A few romances came and went. If she were honest about it, she had never been seriously committed to any of them, not even her husbands. Three years ago she finally found her calling and something to fall in love with. Mardi Segal it turned out, was a natural in sales. In particular, she was a natural at selling boats. She was a natural at selling them, sailing on them, living on them, studying them, and loving them. Mardi and boats went together as naturally as fish and water.

Through a conversation with an old friend who worked in a bar in Saint Maarten, Mardi heard about a guy named Pellet from Anguilla who was in need of a sailboat. Mardi loved boats and had herself become a seasoned sailor, and like any good sailor she knew there were boats to love and hopefully sail into the sunset. Then there were boats that were probably better suited for somebody else to sail into the sunset. Her job was to connect the *somebody else's boats* with the somebody else and get paid a commission to do it. Saturday seemed like a good day to catch the ferryboat from Marigot Bay to Blowing Point, Anguilla and head to the place she was told she would likely find the future boat owner.

Pellet wandered into Dez's and stepped over the old dog lying on the top step. It didn't so much as flinch, never mind consider moving out of the way. On the other hand, it was on the top step so often that most regulars just treated it as if it were that obscenely valuable carpet at their grandmother's house that nobody would ever dream of stepping on. It snored and continued to not move as Pellet pulled himself onto the barstool beside Lucy. Lucy sipped a glass of bubbly water through a tiny plastic straw and ignored him as he plopped down and started harassing her as if it were some sort of personal responsibility Pellet had assigned to himself.

"Weren't you just here like a month or two ago?" he grunted as if he mildly disapproved of her return. "Thought you were going to find a new job or something."

"I missed you too, Pellet. Thanks for the welcome back," she answered without looking up at him.

"You get fired from another one?"

"Nope. Just couldn't sleep at night, thinking of you down here all alone with me just lying in my big bed, sprawled out, naked and all alone. My imagination just kept thinking all kinds of thoughts. My dreams... I'd be too embarrassed to even share my dreams with you." She turned towards him and winked. Pellet looked at her with a straight face and raised one eyebrow while he processed what she was saying to him. He slowly nodded in approval. Then he rubbed the whiskers on his chin and leaned in and whispered in her ear.

"I think you're full of it, but it sounded good. Welcome back." He looked up at Dez who had been listening to the whole thing. "Where the hell is my beer? A good-looking woman starts talking dirty and the service just goes to shit around here," Pellet snapped and pulled out a cigarette and gazed around the bar before turning back to Lucy. "I'm going to have a couple of beers, then we can continue this conversation, if you'd like."

She shook her head and rolled her eyes up at him and let out a small laugh. Clearly this conversation was not going to continue, not that he thought it would. Then again, he had to be sure.

"Seriously, what brings you back?"

"Oh, I don't know. I've had a few job offers, but to be honest I think getting fired woke up something inside of me that I can't put back to sleep. I've been studying for the past twenty or so years. Then I went out and got that incredible job. And just like that, it all came crumbling down. I never gave much thought about one person or one company having the power to destroy a career in the blink of an eye."

"Welcome to the grown-up world, kid." He took a drink and thought for a few seconds. "You're not throwing away twenty years of school are you? Life is just life, Lucy. I've been kicked in the balls so many times that they practically became a hat. Just have a drink or two and get back up and give em hell again."

"Are those the Pellet magic words of wisdom?"

"That's what I got. And," he added and then nodded

towards Desmund, "And don't be hanging out with riffraff like this. Nothing good can come of that."

Desmund listened and was mildly impressed by Pellet's insight. He probably could have left out the part about his balls being a hat, but all in all he thought telling her she shouldn't throw away a life of education was pretty good advice. While that may be pretty standard advice coming out of most people, Pellet's normal advice would have typically sounded more like, "Screw them people. You don't want to do that kind of work anyway." After that he would buy another round so everyone would forget why they started drinking in the first place. But on this particular day Pellet was like a wise old man and Lucy was drinking water. He foolishly flirted with the thought that there just may be hope for Pellet.

A slender thirty something year old woman with a well-seasoned island tan strolled in and sat a few stools away from Pellet and Lucy. Dez eased over and she asked for a glass of wine. After a little bartender chatter he began to turn away. That's when Mardi asked the question.

"Aren't you the guy who was married to that crazy Caribbean Princess who moved to Paris?"

Desmund froze in his tracks. There were not enough years in all eternity to make him not cringe anytime a conversation about his ex-wife came up.

CHAPTER SIXTEEN

To Lucy's relief, whatever concerns Pellet had for her wellbeing and her reasons for returning to Anguilla were short lived. Much to Helmut's dismay, with his lack of desire to talk to Lucy, and Desmund being distracted by other customers, Pellet was looking for someone new to converse with. His eyes roamed the bar. There were no unsuspecting tourist women to bother other than the one Desmund was already in some sort of serious conversation with. There were no guys from his job to bitch about work with. Avis and Savannah were off running errands, and in the end, Helmut remained the sole winner of the who's going to get stuck with Pellet game. The only upside was that he brought a beer for his German friend as a payment of sorts for his listening services.

"Vie ghets, scheizer?" he blurted out and pushed the beer across the table. Helmut ignored him and waited for a more respectable greeting. "I can't believe you don't appreciate me taking the time to learn how to greet you in your native language.

"Well, I understand that, *How are you, shitter?* is likely an accepted greeting in the white trash neighborhood you come from, but in Germany we would say something like, "Good afternoon. Care to have a drink with me?"

"Humph…"

"So, I presume you're asking if I'd like to have a drink with you. What happened? Did Lucy threaten you with violence if you didn't go away?"

"Naw. She doesn't do it for me. Something about her. Can't put my finger on it, but there's just nothing there."

"Perhaps it's her complete lack of interest in you?"

"Oh, come on, man," Pellet answered with a grin. "You know better than anyone I don't pay attention to rejection. I chased Fatisha for two years before you stole her from me."

Helmut nodded in agreement about Pellet being immune to rejection. Both of them lit cigarettes and leaned back in their chairs and looked as though they were contemplating something meaningful, but neither of them spoke. Pellet was thinking the same thing he had been kicking around to one level or another for months. That being that there had to be more to life than this. It wasn't that he didn't have a pretty decent life in the islands, and it wasn't that he hadn't had a bunch of fun, but he seemed to be stuck in a loop where he was repeating the same chapter of a mildly bizarre book over and over. Helmut was actually pondering something serious that he wanted to discuss with Pellet for the past few weeks. He had two problems with the potential conversation. One being that he typically avoided serious conversations with Pellet at all costs since in Helmut's opinion, there was usually only one intelligent side to the conversation. The second being that the subject at hand was really none of his business and he wasn't the type of man to stick his nose into another man's business. But the truth was that whether he liked to admit it or not, Pellet was his friend. They'd been through a lot together over the past few years, and even Helmut knew that it was Pellet's relentless yet fruitless efforts to have sex with Fatisha that brought the two of them eventually together.

"So, let me ask you something," Helmut finally began with his slowly fading away German accent. "Your wife, or is she your ex-wife now? Anyway, that woman who devastated you a few years ago and then did it again when she showed up here unannounced, I've never seen you like that before. Not even with Fatisha. I understand how much things like that hurt. Don't get me wrong. I'm not sharing personal information with you because… well, because you'd probably get drunk and tell everyone."

"You never know, Helmut. I might be maturing," Pellet added with a grin, but in his heart he actually wondered if that was what was possibly happening. Helmut scoffed at the idea and took a drink.

"Anyway, she came in like a storm and I saw what she did to you. It took me years to get over what happened to me. I can't decide if I'm envious that you have such ability to handle that kind of pain, or am I concerned that you're just, you know... burying shit so deep that you're never going to deal with it."

"Ahhh... Dr. Freud, is it?" Pellet joked.

"Look Pellet. If you don't want to talk about it, just take your beer and go back and bother Lucy some more. Really. I won't be offended if you don't impose yourself at my table any longer."

"Damn, man. Kind of snippy today aren't we? First you're asking about my feelings and shit and then you want to get rid of me just because I'm not saying the right thing. Christ." Pellet thought for a minute and then added, "Wait. When have you ever worried about me?"

"Worried? No. I'm just being curious. To be honest, I don't really care about you one way or another. Well, I might be a bit worried that you think you're going to start sitting at my table on a regular basis, but other than that, just being nosey." Both men raised their beers and clinked them together and sat in another minute of silence.

"Look," Pellet finally said, "I spent half a decade hating her, wishing her dead, probably even considered helping her get there if the opportunity presented itself. Until I found out my kid wasn't my kid, I hadn't ever imagined that kind of pain. You know I love dogs and beer and all that shit, but kids, man that's a whole different level I never knew existed. Then throw in that I was actually in love with the devil woman. It was a pretty bad mind fuck. And you talk about burying it? I spent a couple months living with that woman after I found out and I just pretended things were normal. Sometimes I wonder how I pulled that off. Other times I just presumed I completely shut down. Then, as you might have noticed, I've drank a bit since coming to Anguilla. Just for the record, I've always liked a drink or two, or maybe a few more now and then, but never like I've done here. I did whatever it took to try to not give her so much as a passing thought. She barely existed even in my memories, but when she occasionally escaped from way inside my head, bad stuff went on inside my brain. Then when Dez told me she was here, all I thought was this is not going to end good. I had no idea what was going to go down. I was actually scared that things might get ugly. I mean… I don't know. I just don't have the words to describe how bad it all felt. So, with all that, you're wondering how the crash all came and went so fast. All I can figure is that by the time she got here, I only had a little hate left in me." Pellet took another drink and then looked straight at Helmut. "Damn, man. Hate is exhausting," Pellet added, as if any more explanation was required.

"How come you never told us?"

"Give you guys fuel to give me shit? I don't think so. Besides, I had a cure for the whole thing and you stole her." Pellet was of course referencing his undying love for Fatisha… again.

"Good god man. Get over it. That beautiful woman wouldn't have slept with you if you were the only man left to continue the human species."

"Ahh. So things are back to normal. It felt a little weird there for a few minutes."

"Won't happen again."

"You going to buy me a beer or what?"

"No. Go bother Lucy." Helmut opened his notebook and started writing something again. Pellet incorrectly presumed it was something about him.

CHAPTER SEVENTEEN

"Don't you be worrying bout dat woman?" Desmund snapped as he turned and faced Mardi.

"You seem a bit touchy about her," Mardi replied back to Dez, referring to his long-gone ex-wife.

"You a reporter? Got nothin to say about her. If dats all you got to chatta about, go find another bar." Desmund reached for her glass of wine.

"Calm down, please," she said with a heavy French accent that made Desmund even more suspicious than he already had been. "I'm looking for a guy named Pellet. They told me I'd find him at Dez's. So, I'm at Dez's. Okay?"

"What's he done now?" Desmund asked, switching straight from suspicion about this woman and his ex, to suspicion about this woman and what she wanted with Pellet. Mardi raised her eyebrows at him and reached into her shirt pocket and pulled out a business card. *Simpson Bay Boat Brokerage* was written in big blue letters on the face of the card.

"I heard he's looking for a sailboat. If so, I'm his woman."

Dez smiled. "Don't many women say "I'm his woman" when dey talkin bout Pellet. No *good lookin* women ever say it." He motioned to the guy who was just getting up from the table in the corner and wandering back to the bar. She gave him the once over and tried to size him up.

Other than just plain old rich people who looked like old rich people, there were different kinds of expats in the islands, financially speaking. There were people who looked as if they had money but in reality it was just a show. Then there were people with tons of money that looked like beach bums. And finally, there were all the people who fell somewhere in between the rich and the poor and who didn't pretend to be anyone. At first glance she presumed Pellet was one of the in-between people, although she couldn't be absolutely certain of it. The trick was to figure out which side of the *in between* he came from and then match him up with the most expensive boat he could pay for. She worked on commissions. Sometimes it was only two thousand dollars, Sometimes it was a lot more thousands. Sizing customers up was something she usually figured out in the first few minutes. With that said, the whole deal could be blown right out of the gate if she misjudged someone with a two-million-dollar budget or overwhelm someone who was scraping up the money for a cheap used boat. The best way to make sure that didn't happen was to treat everyone like they had money that they didn't want to spend. Mardi stood and stepped towards Pellet and extended her hand.

"Pardon. You are Mr. Pellet?" she asked with a heavy French accent.

He grinned wide and didn't respond to her, but instead turned to Desmund. "Did you hear that, Dez? "Mr. Pellet." You should refer to me as Mr. Pellet from now on."

"You lucky I refer to you at all," Desmund mumbled and turned away.

"You can just call me Pellet. No Mr. required. He reached out and took ahold of her hand and held it more than actually shaking it. Her fingers were long and soft and tan. A slight whiff of perfume floated in the air and once again Pellet thought this could be the one. "I take it from your accent you're from France?"

"Oui. Saint Maarten now, but originally from France."

"My last name is Pelletier. Most of my ancestors came from various parts of your country."

"Oui?" She feigned surprise and interest and continued to hold his hand. "Small world, no?"

"Oui," he responded with virtually the only French word he knew. "What can I do for you?" he asked, already presuming what she wanted. The unfortunate side of being the best friend and cousin with a guy who had money is that people foolishly and frequently presumed, or perhaps hoped, that Avis's money could be construed as Pellet's money. They were incorrect. What they didn't know was that Pellet would never ask Avis for money, nor would Avis likely give it to him. At least not for a boat. While Avis was supportive towards the boat idea, the reason was simply because his cousin wanted to buy a boat and Avis had nothing better to do than try to help him buy a good one. It wasn't his place to tell Pellet it was a bad idea, although he had mentioned the possibility of it not being the best idea he had ever had. On the other hand it was possible that it was a good idea. Didn't seem likely, but stranger things have happened. It also wasn't his responsibility to pay for it, good idea or not. Over the past couple months five other brokers had sought Pellet out and quickly lost interest when they realized that Pellet was not looking at half million-dollar sailboats. A couple others reached out directly to Avis who quickly shut down the conversations. In this particular case, Mardi knew nothing about Avis or the money he had. She was just following a lead and enjoying a Saturday afternoon trip to Anguilla to find a guy named Pellet and try to match him up with a boat.

"Oui. My name is Mardi Segal. I heard you are looking to buy a sailboat. I am hoping I can assist you."

"Yeah. Where'd you hear that?"

"A bartender. Gerry? Maybe you know him. White guy with the dreadlocks?" she continued in a French version of English.

"Ahh, yes." Pellet answered. He wondered for a moment what else Gerry might have shared. If Gerry had told her about the boat search, did she also know that some Israeli woman had kicked his ass and nearly killed him at the bar where Gerry worked? His momentary high that came from the slender tan French woman with nice perfume began to wane and he leaned towards not doing business with her. "What else did Gerry say?" he asked with a tone of skepticism in his voice.

"Uhmmm… nothing really. Just told me…. ahhh, he has met you a few times and you seem like a good guy. Oh. And you are looking for a boat. I ran into him and his wife at the market last week. She's from Paris and we, well, anyway, here I am." She smiled again and touched him on the shoulder. A tiny breeze blew another whiff of her perfume his way and all skepticism drifted off as quickly as her aroma drifted in. "So. You are looking for a boat? Oui?"

"As a matter of fact, I am looking for a boat, Oui. Are you the woman who can help me find one?" Pellet asked, this time with all skepticism replaced with unwarranted optimism.

"Well," she patted on the side of the satchel hanging from her shoulder. "I brought some brochures for you to look at. We can have a seat and go look at them?"

"Desmund. Two more drinks, please. We'll be at this table over here."

"No hope for dat idiot," Desmund mumbled as he reached into the cooler to get him another beer.

CHAPTER EIGHTEEN

The twelve-foot zodiac skimmed across the glass-like water after leaving sailboat number one. Mardi had the motor tiller in her hand and looked beyond Avis and Pellet while they cruised towards the next potential Pellet boat a few minutes away. Avis sat on the center bench just in front of her and Pellet sat on the inflated bow of the boat with growing mixed thoughts about Mardi. She was half long-lean and well-tanned French-Caribbean transplant and half full-of-shit used car saleswoman, who just happened to be selling used boats.

The first one they looked at was in a lot better condition than Pellet had hoped for. It was a forty-five foot, ten-year-old sloop that had been custom made for some guy from Dominica. A divorce or bankruptcy or some other life blunder that often plagued the sailing type was driving the hopefully quick sale. Halfway through the walk-through Mardi blurted out, "This is a great deal at seventy-five thousand dollars." Pellet cringed and froze in his tracks just as he entered the galley.

"So, when I said, "My budget is 30k, but I might go up to 40 or 45 for the perfect boat," you just said to yourself, what the hell. Let's waste some time and bump that up to 75k," he blurted at Mardi who was already turning and heading away from him. She'd been through the routine enough to read his reaction before he finished speaking. She wanted to find out if he really only had forty-five thousand to spend. Now she knew.

"So, this one's a no." she murmured and headed topside. Avis smiled and shrugged. Pellet pouted and began losing the optimism her perfume had given him. For the first time since they met a week ago it dawned on him that Mardi might not deliver on anything.

"Damn. I'm beginning to think she's not really interested

in me," he grumbled. Avis smiled and shrugged at him again.

Mardi kicked around the idea of working her way down to the preferred price by taking them to a fifty-thousand-dollar boat, then a forty-thousand-dollar boat, then a thirty thousand, and finally to a thirty-five-year-old Catalina. The owner was only asking nineteen thousand for it in, "as is" condition. With a little luck he would buy one of the others before he saw the "as is" boat.

Sales was a game to Mardi and it was a game she won more often than her counterparts did. Her looks didn't hurt the process any and her French accent only continued to tilt the scales in her favor. But more than anything, she had good instincts. She could read people and figure out what they really wanted, versus what they thought they wanted. And she also had the gift of figuring out what she could get them to spend versus what they thought they would spend. Off the starboard side of the zodiac, a powerboat was going faster than it should have been, and she turned towards the waves that were quickly rolling their way. Getting hit by a big wave from the side and tossing Pellet into the water would not likely help the sales process any. If she thought it would have helped, he would have been getting wet.

Pellet stopped feeling sorry for himself as they turned to the left and continued towards the next potential dreamboat turned to reality somewhere on the other side of the bay. They passed a couple of boats tied to mooring balls. One of them looked as though it had been tied there and abandoned somewhere around 1973 except that it looked as though someone was still living on it. Lines were strung around the deck with shirts and towels and men's underwear draped over them. Either fuel containers or water jugs, he couldn't tell which, were stacked on the bow. And beneath the tattered, faded green canvas that kept the seats drenched with shade, there looked to be a crusty looking Earnest Hemmingway type sitting with his feet kicked up and a newspaper in his hand. Pellet wondered if someone delivered the newspaper to him, or was he reading a month-old copy for the thirtieth time. Then he wondered how long the guy had lived there. Certainly ever since 1973 didn't seem likely, he didn't think. Finally, he wondered what it was like just hanging out on the deck of an old boat, in the quiet of a glassy bay, and hiding from the world. It was possible, he thought, that the old man read the paper as if it were a novel or a comic book that had no real effect on the tiny wood and fiberglass world he lived in. It didn't seem to Pellet that world politics would have all that much impact on a guy floating on an almost sinking, nearly ancient sloop that was anchored in a Caribbean bay. The boat and the old man quickly faded into the background and shrunk in the distance. Mist of water splashed into his face and cooled the midmorning heat enough to make the cruise enjoyable and stir the return of good boat thoughts.

They came up on another sloop about a hundred yards off the right side of the dinghy. It was in better condition than the old man's barely floating wreck, but it was nowhere near new. And instead of a crusty white bearded sailor who was reading a paper while manning the helm, there was a woman in black bikini bottoms and a t-shirt working on something on the mainsail. There's a joke in the boating world that every woman looks beautiful on the deck of a passing boat if you're looking at her from the shore. Pellet knew the saying but chose to ignore it. As far as he was concerned, every woman was beautiful on the deck of a sailboat no matter how close or far away she might be. So, as always he imagined she, with her lean tanned body and long hair, was possibly the most beautiful woman to ever stand on the deck of a boat. He watched as she tied a line off to a cleat and then he watched as she walked over and picked something up and tossed it into a bucket. She grabbed a scrub brush attached to a broom handle and dipped it into the bucket before she started scrubbing the deck. A long, lean tanned woman in a bikini scrubbing the deck and maintaining a boat. It was Pellet's dream come true, except of course that it was not his boat and as far as he knew it was not for sale. When they were as close as they were going to get to the boat, maybe fifty yards away, she stood up straight and shielded her eyes from the sun and looked at the three sailors in the zodiac. She nonchalantly waved in their general direction and Pellet felt his heart jump. Mardi had just been knocked off the top of his list.

The old man's boat they had passed a few minutes ago had shrunk in the background. The white boat with a blue waterline had just become his new dream boat. Of course, in his dream the woman on the deck came with the boat. They turned a bit more to the starboard and crossed behind the boat and headed across the bay towards the next boat that Mardi wanted to show them. That's when he saw the name of the boat, *Aqua Vita,* written on the back of the boat. "Son-of-a-bitch," he mumbled. The outboard motor drowned out his words and Avis and Mardi payed no attention to him. Five minutes later they were climbing aboard a Catalina that should have sunk a few years ago. In fact, as they rummaged through the roughly patched together interior, Pellet and Avis both wondered if perhaps it hadn't sunk at least once over the years. Nineteen thousand was about eighteen thousand more than it was worth.

"What do you think?" Avis asked, already knowing the answer. He gently tugged on a small cupboard door and it fell off into his hand. He just laid it on a shelf and left it setting on top of the dust and dirt that crumbled off the door.

"Did you see that boat on the way over here?" Pellet asked.

"The one with the guy reading the paper?" Avis wondered if Pellet was envisioning himself lounging about on a boat, drinking beer and reading the paper for the next thirty years.

"No man. The one with the bikini chick working on the deck."

"Guess I must have missed that one," Avis said, hoping that Pellet wasn't fixating on a boat that just happened to have a potential dream girl on the deck. He was aware of how Pellet's mind worked.

"We've got to go see that boat," he mumbled quiet enough that Mardi didn't hear.

"Didn't see a for sale sign on it," acknowledging that he did in fact see the boat and the bikini.

"Doesn't matter. Got to go see that boat."

CHAPTER NINETEEN

"You know, I still can't believe that... *woman*." It wasn't the word that came to mind, but Lucy had been besieged by an urge to use profanity far more often than her norm since the firing. Her mother told her she sounded like a construction worker and her father said he hadn't heard so much swearing since he left the Navy. All Lucy knew was that there was a lot of anger stewing around inside of her and Yoga and the stationary bike were not transporting her to some Zen like place in an imaginary beautiful universe. Since the denial stage of her situation, she had pretty much refused to move on towards all other phases except for anger. She decided that maybe it was getting close to moving on time, but the deciding and doing were not aligning. "That bitch," she added with a sense of relief, as if she had been holding in a secret burst of air that she had just let out. "I can't really explain why, but every time I call her that I feel just a smidge better."

"Maybe she is one," Desmund muttered as if he cared one way or another. "A bitch."

"The first couple of weeks I referred to her as," she stopped talking and looked around to see if anyone were listening, that fucking bitch, and it felt great," she said just above a whisper as if swearing was something that rarely happened in an island bar. She held her glass up to Desmund as a symbol of pride for having the nerve to call her those words.

"Cool," he said and held a plastic cup full of something in her general direction.

This was her third trip down to the island since the big day. Her first trip was a desperation trip. A place to cry and moan and bathe in self-pity without having friends around who would have tried to pick her up and brush her off and get her back into the game. She was over the game, at least for the time being. The game was overrated. The game was painful. The game was an illusion. The game was, she thought for a moment, shit. More swearing and more relief. The game was a make-believe pile of shit and she had spent eighteen of her first twenty-four years preparing for it. The game, she thought, did not string her along for enough time and did not flash glimpses of fulfilling her hopes and dreams enough times before kicking her in the head and screaming, "Fooled you!" So, for the third time in less than three months, she was sitting at a bar in the Caribbean, pondering how to recover from realizing that she may have wasted the better part of her first couple of decades studying and working and testing and stressing, and then doing it some more. She was also steadily draining the bank account that she had proudly been growing over the past year. Money, she thought, was much easier to make than what people had led her to believe. That, of course, was before she was railroaded out of a job and introduced to "life." The job was gone, the pile of money was shrinking, and the future looked like nothing other than... shit. She seemed stuck on that word for the moment.

"So, you're a bartender. Aren't you supposed to have all kinds of great life advice? Aren't you supposed to smile and make all my troubles go away?"

"Troubles. You ain't got no troubles. Hell, life hasn't even kissed you good morning yet," Desmund said and put his cup down and opened a beer.

"Ohhh, what do you know?" she mumbled and took a sip from the tiny plastic straw sticking out of her cup. "You own a beach bar in the Caribbean."

"I'll tell you about troubles. I was once married to the most evil, selfish, mean, black-hearted woman in all of the Caribbean. Took me years to shake loose from her and it almost ruined me. I was mashed up good before that witch flew away. You ain't seen problems yet. Better suck it up cause one day, dey'll be comin. You'll dream of da troubles you got now." With that, he downed whatever was in his glass.

"Not finding this all that inspirational," she snipped. "I'm guessing you probably got yourself into your own mess. All I did was work hard, sacrifice and got screwed," she said with the f'n bitch words lingering close to the end of her tongue again.

"Kinda mean when you pissed, huh?" he said and leaned back against the cooler. "You good looking, young, smart... hell. You got the world by da tail, Lucy. Could be worse, ya know. You could be dat guy," he said and nodded to the guy in the ragged shirt and faded baseball cap climbing over Schlomo who was, as always, dead to the world on the top step.

CHAPTER TWENTY

"Lucy?!" Pellet bellowed deeply, doing his best Ricky Riccardo imitation from the *I Love Lucy Show,* as he eased up to the bar. Lucy rolled her eyes and tilted her head in his general direction. "You know, I was thinking," he continued, "You're here just a bit too often without any good explanation. Don't you have a home in New Jersey or someplace up there?"

"Funny you should say that Pellet. People I talk to tell me you've been here way too long also without any good explanation." He took a quick glance around the bar. There were a few tourists, a couple of locals and Helmut sitting at his table in the corner. There was no doubt that Helmut would have been one of the "people I talk to" mentioned by Lucy. When he turned back around, Desmund was leaning against the beer cooler behind the bar with his arms folded across his chest and staring at Pellet as if he were waiting for an explanation.

"Oh, please," Pellet mumbled. "You'd probably go out of business if I left Anguilla. I'm like a walking billboard for this place. You know, I'm like free marketing. Hell. You should be giving me free drinks."

Desmund shook his head in the exact same way he had shaken his head at Pellet a few hundred times over the years. It wasn't so much the overall absurdity of Pellet's comment that puzzled him. It was more that Pellet believed so many of his own proclamations and he did it far too often. It was typical Pellet protocol to allow unfiltered and unprocessed thoughts to flow directly from some microscopic impulse in his head to the tip of his tongue, and then a bit further, with complete and unsubstantiated belief that his words were some sort of unquestionable gospel. The Gospel According to Pellet. A troubled gospel at best, and a gospel that was best ignored if possible. Certainly not a gospel to be pondered. His faithful listeners usually responded with back and forth shaking of their head in lieu of giving the sign of the cross.

"Ain't nothin free," Desmund mumbled. "Damn sure ain't bank-rollin your drinking."

"I'm here on business, if you must know," Lucy answered, and took a sip of her sparkling water and fruit punch. She had quickly learned that with people like Pellet, it was less trouble to look like she was drinking rum punch in lieu of explaining why she wasn't.

"What sort of business?"

"None of yours," she zipped back almost before he finished his question, with a tone that left Pellet wondering if she thought she was being funny, or if she was in fact telling him to mind his own business.

Pellet watched her in silence for ten seconds and fiddled with the unlit cigarette in his hand. "And I thought you said you were quitting those things," she added, glancing down at his hand before giving Desmund a wink. Lucy had not yet fully absorbed that those who befriended Pellet, almost always took on the role of looking out for his well-being sooner or later. Striking up conversations with him was easy. Getting rid of him was the challenge.

"Don't you have friends up in Boston you could be irritating?" Over the past couple months he had for unknown reasons, begun referring to a different city anytime he felt like urging her to go back home. So far he had correctly referred to New York City, and incorrectly referred to Buffalo, Detroit, Philadelphia, Atlanta, Los Angeles, Austin, New Jersey and now Boston.

"I have friends everywhere, Pellet. Even in Boston... and Anguilla," she added.

"Bartenders don't count. They're paid to be friendly," Pellet mumbled back without really thinking it through.

"So, Desmund is friendly to you because you pay him. Is that what you're saying?" This time she stared at him in silence awaiting his response.

"Easy now," Desmund interjected. "He pays me a lot to be his friend." He winked back at Lucy and they both smiled and shrugged.

"You know, I think I'll find someone else to sit with."

"Don't come over here," Helmut called out from his table in the corner without looking up from whatever it was he was working on.

"Any chance you're going to give me a beer today?" Pellet snapped without getting off the stool he was planted on or even feigning that he intended to go sit elsewhere. He lit his cigarette and fiddled with the empty coaster sitting in front of him. "So, Lucy. You're going to dinner with me tonight or what?" She rolled her eyes, dropped her head back and looked up at the ceiling in exasperation.

"You have asked me to dinner at least a dozen times. What don't you understand? I've been forewarned and we won't be going out for dinner, drinks, a walk, a talk, or anything else. Especially the anything else. Got it?"

"Well, I've got two responses to that. First, that sounded like a "maybe" to me. And second, if you've been forewarned then you're also aware that I am not easily discouraged."

"Ya, mon. He's like a fly on a dead dog. You can keep brushin him away, but he always comes back."

Lucy slowly turned from Pellet to Desmund and there was less of a smile on her face than she already didn't have on her face to start with. "Did you just compare me to a dead dog?"

"Oh shit," he stumbled on his own words. "No! You're not... I wasn't..." He turned from Lucy to Pellet. "Leave da woman alone, mon. Good lawd you can stir up a mess."

"Guess it's a good thing I pay you so well to be my friend." Pellet felt vindicated that the harassment had momentarily turned away from him and towards Desmund, who had somehow ended up on the defense.

"I'm going to sit with Helmut," Lucy said and slid off her stool. Helmut smiled a bit without looking up. He liked her. Lucy smiled at life in general despite her looming clouds. She strolled across the bar and looked out over the blue waters and Saint Maarten. Pellet smiled because he considered himself victorious. Desmund wasn't smiling as he watched Lucy walk away and then looked at Pellet smiling.

"You're an idiot, mon."

Pellet raised his beer towards the bartender in a gesture of solidarity. "To idiots."

CHAPTER TWENTY-ONE

Anyone watching Savannah and Avis casually strolling along the sandy white beach with their feet sometimes in the water and sometimes not would never have known that only three years earlier Avis had won nine-hundred and sixty-seven million dollars in a Powerball jackpot. Nor would they know that Savannah had ambitiously plotted out the tiny details of how to commit suicide and put an end to her bleak and pointless life. But that was then and time heals or at least changes all things big and small. In front of the backdrop of the Caribbean Sea the two of them looked like a normal couple; young and good looking, healthy and in shape, and mostly, like a couple in love. They looked happy. Content. Fate or God or the universe had brought them together in a perfect storm of strange circumstances. Love and tragedy had bound them together. And they were both good with that. *Good with that* was the exact kind of people they were.

Whether she was fully aware of the exact timing or not, Savannah completely scrapped her contemplative suicide idea the day she told Avis and his best friend Leo about it. Leo couldn't wrap his head around why she would do such a stupid thing and Avis thought it was unbelievably selfish and in no uncertain terms, told her so. Avis was a smart guy, much smarter than most. He knew his life had changed almost immediately after finding Savannah sitting on her broken-down car on the side of the road. He correctly understood that running into Savannah was a hundred times more significant than winning any amount of money.

So they walked and laughed and chatted and pondered the simpler things in life on the beach in Anguilla. Savannah picked up a shell here and there. Avis skipped a stone now and then. Savannah asked him when they were planning another trip back home to New Hampshire. Avis asked what they were having for dinner. Savannah asked how Alice Chen, his adoptive mother of sorts, was doing back up north. Avis asked whether or not they had any cold beer in the fridge or would he have to stop and get some on the way home. Savannah asked him if he was still considering working on one of the local conservation charities in Anguilla. Avis asked her if she wanted to go fishing tomorrow. Both of them just more or less shrugged and offered half-hearted answers to all the questions until Savannah asked, "How's Pellet's boat search going?"

"Mind blowing. How that man…," he hesitated and rephrased his words, "How that overgrown boy is still alive and well after all these years of being himself is a miracle. If he ever does buy a boat, I'm pretty sure it will sit anchored in Sandy Ground until it eventually drifts away in a storm. At least I hope that's where it stays. Until that day comes, he'll smoke and drink and talk about sailing around the globe on the high seas like some new and improved Captain Cook."

"Well anchored in the bay is probably better than venturing out to sea, right?"

"Better for him. Better for the boat. And better for whomever he might run into out in the middle of a great big sea that would seem big enough that he wouldn't run into anybody. But you know Pellet."

"So you really don't think he'll buy one?" she asked, a bit surprised. "He's been looking a lot and I think he's pretty excited about the whole thing."

"He gets excited about a lot of things that never happen."

"Yeah, but those things are women and he doesn't usually have any say in whether or not they "*are going to happen*" does he," Savannah said more as a statement than a question. She smiled and nudged him with her shoulder and then bent down and picked up a big shell. "It's a pretty one, right?" she said, holding it up for them both to take a better look at.

"Uh-huh," Avis said without giving it much of a look.

"You didn't even look at it!"

"Oooooh. It's beautiful," he said to pacify and mock her.

"By the way, you didn't answer. Do we have beer at the house?

"Uh-huh," she said without giving it a thought. Avis smiled and wondered if they needed to stop at the store or not. "But he's meeting us here, right?" she asked, nodding at Dez's Bar while small waves brushed against their feet.

"Yeah. He's all excited about some piece of..." He stopped talking and glanced towards Saint Maarten. Looking at old beat up boats was hard enough to do with a good attitude. He guessed there was no upside to deciding if it was a hopeless task before they even looked at the next boat. "Anyway, he's got some boat he's obsessed with and he hasn't even been on board yet. Maybe it's the one, right?" he said and smirked at Savannah as he raised his eyebrows. She reached and wrapped her arm around one of his and smiled that smile that always made him surrender and do whatever she suggested.

"Come on. You're his cousin and best friend. He's counting on your help. Besides, you'd never forgive yourself if you let him buy the wrong boat." Avis sighed a deep cleansing breath. It was a surrendering sigh and he allowed himself to be tugged up the beach by a woman who could convince him to jump into a fire if that was what was required of him.

"Lucy, your back," Savannah called out as she stepped over the old dog lying on the top step.

"Hey, Schlomo," Avis mumbled and reached down and scratched the back of the dog's head and gave a light tug on one of his ears. Schlomo did not flinch. Avis had mentioned to Dez more than once that the dog would be dead for a week before anyone knew it. He was probably right.

"Hey, Pellet," he said as they reached the bar. He reached over and rubbed Pellet's head and tugged at his ear. They'd all know the exact second Pellet died because the bar would have a newfound peacefulness. Pellet pushed his hand away and took a drink of his beer. "How goes the never-ending quest to find the perfect boat for an unrealistic cheap price? Any chance you have come to grips that a lot of things can go wrong out in the middle of the ocean?"

"You only live once," Pellet mumbled while lighting his cigarette.

"Only die once," Avis shot back.

"And I'll be dead, so what difference does it make?" was his defense. "Hey," he turned to Savannah who was giving Lucy a hug, "Tell your Debbie-downer husband to stop whining and start helping. If I want to listen to negative shit, I'll listen to him," he said nodding his head towards Desmund, "Or him," he nodded towards Helmut.

"I look forward to him getting a nice big sailboat," Helmut called out from his table. "If he ever gets it out of the bay, there's almost no chance of him making it back. Everyone wins."

"Pay your tab before you sail off, mon. You know… jus in case," Desmund instructed.

"Nice to know all my friends are supporting me."

It was a rare occasion that anyone could hurt Pellet's feelings. Generally speaking he was oblivious to judgement and opinions. And rarely did he consider the words of any naysayers. He didn't require emotional support to bolster his confidence as he took on yet one more dimwitted feat. But for the first time since taking the huge step and leaving his ex-wife back in Florida, he had a big plan and he wanted someone to believe in him. Up until this point in his life, Pellet had only done three big things. He left Waldoboro, Maine, with a few hundred bucks in his pocket, he married Zoe and number three, he moved to Anguilla. All those great adventures were done with no encouragement from anyone, no advice and most of all, with almost no plan of how he envisioned things working out. Success had been a presumption on each of those adventures. He was getting tired of feeling like a failure and it was time to take a huge step forward and whether he wanted to admit it or not, he was scared. He was tired of moving down the road and not moving ahead. He was tired of being the punchline to the jokes around the bar and mostly, he was tired of not having more. It was becoming clearer to him day by day that for the first time in his life, he wanted more. He wasn't sure what *more* was, but he knew he wanted it.

Savannah leaned against his back and wrapped her arms around him and squeezed. "Don't listen to these clowns Pellet. I think you'll find a great boat and I can't wait to see it." She hugged Pellet and glared angrily at Avis. "Have you found anything promising yet?"

"Man, I've looked at so many. A 78 Pilot House Catch, a 99 Dufour 38, an 84 Morgan 40, a 94 Pearson 36, and a 91 Irwin 38, but none of them matter. Why, you might ask?"

"I didn't," Avis answered. Savannah slapped him on the shoulder and glared at him once again.

"Because I've found her. I found the boat. Now all I've got to do is buy her."

"So, are you going to share this information or what? Because, you know… the anticipation is killing me," Avis asked in a flat monotone voice, making it clear to Pellet and everyone else he was not the least bit interested in his answer. He already knew which boat was *the* boat. It was the one with the black bikini woman scrubbing the deck. And Avis had not the least amount of faith that it was *the* boat or that Pellet was going to actually buy it.

"It's a 52-foot 1990 Endeavour Center Cockpit. I saw it in Saint Maarten when we were out looking at the other boats. Mardi wouldn't take me over to look at it. She said it wasn't appropriate to just pull up alongside a boat and ask to climb aboard and wander around. Not sure I agree. They looked pretty friendly to me."

"There was only a she," Avis said to Savannah clarifying the details of the story. "And she was long and skinny and wearing a black string bikini. And *she* is why homeboy here thinks this is the boat of his dreams."

"You know nothing." Pellet said with a half-cocked grin and one eyebrow raised suggesting there were definitely things Avis was not privy to.

CHAPTER TWENTY-TWO

It took a bit of asking around to eventually get her name and number. He started out at Lagoonies Bistro and Bar because it was the closest and the beer was always cold. Both were good enough reasons for him to stop there. Then he looped over to the Driftwood Bar, mostly because he liked it and the bartender was hot and always friendly. From there he made a quick stop to the Sunset Bar, less than a few hundred feet away. After only one beer at each, he was off to Snoopy's, and then to Skip Jacks. At each bar he ordered a beer and made his inquiry to see if anyone knew who the bikini woman on the Endeavor named Aqua Vita anchored in Simpson's Bay was. A few people at the different bars thought they knew who he was talking about, but they didn't have a name or a number. At The Saint Maarten Yacht Club there were a couple more people who knew who he was talking about but had no helpful information in contacting her. He stayed there long enough to chat for a while, have lunch, and of course a couple more beers. Between the trip over, driving his beat-up rental all around the island, and reaching the point that he figured he'd probably drank about all he could handle and still drive around, Pellet decided it was time to head back to the ferry and try again another day. He settled up his tab and was heading towards the door when one of the waiters stopped him and handed him a scrap of paper with a phone number on it.

"I don't remember her name, but I'm pretty sure that's her number," was all he said. Pellet took the number and put it in his wallet as if it were next week's winning lottery numbers. As far as he was concerned he'd just hit the jackpot and the day had become a success.

It took most of the week and quite a few calls to finally reach the black bikini woman he'd seen leaning on a broom on the deck on his presumed future boat. He had called her at least twice a day for five consecutive days before she finally picked up and answered. She sounded stoned when she began talking. At least that's what Pellet hoped she was. She was either stoned or she wasn't all there, and he didn't really like the idea of trying to buy a boat from someone who just wasn't all there. Years ago he'd bought an old car from a guy like that back in Waldoboro. It turned out the car he was selling belonged to his father who was on vacation and the son couldn't wrap his head around that selling stuff that didn't belong to him was wrong. In the end the father got his car back and Pellet got back one thousand of the fifteen hundred he'd paid for the car. The not all there guy got food and beer money while his dad was away. When it was all said and done, everyone but Pellet lived happily forever after. He was out five hundred dollars and still didn't have a car.

"Yeah…" she said in a long drawn out word as if she were spread out on her sheets and still half asleep. "I dropped my phone in the water a few days ago. Just got around to getting a new one. Had to scrape up some extra cash. You know how it is," she added, as if she presumed everyone knew what it was like to not work, live on a boat and have to scrape up enough cash to replace their old phone which now lived on the bottom of the Caribbean Sea."

"Cool. Glad you got a new phone," Pellet blurted out, not really knowing what else to say.

"Yeah…" she half-whispered again. "Do I know you or something? You called me a bunch of times. You're not the guy that I met at, ummm." He wondered if she were trying to remember the name of the bar or narrow down the list of guys she'd met there and given a phone number to. Or was she just waiting for him to fill in the blanks.

"No. We haven't met," he answered after waiting through an awkwardly long silence for her to finish what she was going to say.

"Ohhh. That's cool." He was leaning more towards her being stoned than slow. "Sooooo, you keep calling." She said adding nothing more and there was another odd uncomfortable silence before Pellet finally realized she was wanting for him to say why.

"Yes. My name is Wayne Pelletier, but everyone calls me Pellet."

"Pellet. I like that." Her voice sounded a bit strained, as if she were trying to hold smoke in her lungs while talking on the phone. There was a momentary silence again and Pellet presumed there was now smoke leaving her lungs. "What can I do for you, Pellet?" she asked in a more relaxed, almost suggestive sounding tone. Pellet being Pellet, his mind began to wander to things other than her selling the boat to him.

"Well the first thing is, I heard you might be interested in selling your boat."

"You did?" she said as she rolled over on her back and rubbed her hand on her face and wished she had a glass of water close enough that she didn't need to climb out of bed. She closed her eyes and licked her dry lips and listened to the water lap against the hull of the boat. The sound made her even more thirsty. She doubted he had heard she was selling her boat because she hadn't told anyone. On the other hand the long, lean black bikini woman enjoyed living on boats, but didn't particularly enjoy working on them. Scrubbing the deck was one thing. Sanding down teak, polishing stainless steel, cleaning the bilge, changing the oil, and the long list of other must-do task did not fall into the category of boat things she enjoyed doing. Tanning on the deck under the warm sun and having good sex under the stars was on the list of things she enjoyed. Riding on calm seas with full sails was something she not only loved, but she was quite skilled at. Reading books and having interesting conversations about the good things in life was on her enjoyable list, too. And getting stoned rated high on her list. But working on boats, hers or anyone else's, was not on any of her good lists. As it turned out, it was time to start working on her boat or time to sell it. If she didn't start do one or the other soon, the old girl was going to begin to fall apart around her.

"I was asking around about boats that might be for sale

and a guy in a bar told me you might be looking to sell."

"A guy in a bar, huh? Not sure I know any guys in bars who think I would want to sell my boat. I'm pretty sure I haven't told anyone I want to sell her?"

"Does that mean you're not interested?" he asked. For some reason he had a premonition that she would have been eager to sell. Now he wasn't sure. In fact, it suddenly dawned on him that there had been no reason for him to presume she would have been eager to sell in the first place.

"Well, Pellet. You know the saying. Everything is for sale. Or is it, everything's got a price? Anyway," she stopped and looked around one more time for something to drink. "My point is, that I'm not saying I would sell her, but it might be something I'd consider." She was still speaking soft and slow. Pellet wondered if it was better to bargain with her when she was stoned, or not stoned.

"Then it sounds like something we could at least discuss?" Pellet responded with his confidence returning.

"Sure. I like discussing things. You know where the Dinghy Dock Bar is?" she asked, already planning on getting a free drink and bite to eat out of their meet up. She slipped out of bed and eased towards the galley to get a drink and half listened to Pellet ramble on about something. "See you there at two o'clock," she said without letting him finish rambling on about whatever it was that did not interest her in the least. She pushed a button and ended the call. A couple hours later, she dove in for a swim and then climbed back aboard and got ready to head to shore.

He sat at a one of the outside tables on the back deck when she strolled in wearing cut-off jeans, flip-flops and her black bikini top that was sort of covered by an unbuttoned and open blue cotton shirt. From his view on the other side of the room she appeared to be a bit older, maybe a bit rougher than he had initially thought her to be. She saw who she presumed was the next owner of her boat and walked through the almost empty bar towards him.

"You must be Pellet," she said. He reached out to shake

her hand and she leaned in and kissed him on the cheek.

"And you must be Sheila," he answered and kissed her back.

"I am. Proud owner of the Sheila B," she proclaimed as she sat down.

"I thought it was Aqua Vita?" he asked, a bit confused. For just a moment he thought he might have the wrong black bikini woman.

"Yeah. Haven't got around to changing that yet. But I call her the Sheila B," she said and waved towards the only waitress in the room. "So, you want to buy her, huh?"

"I would like to talk about buying her." Pellet had pondered his negotiation technique for a few hours between their morning call and his ferry boat ride from Anguilla. It dawned on him that he should have had a better plan than calling up and saying, "Hey! You want to sell your boat?" if he had any hope of buying it for a reasonable price. It was a valid albeit late point that was not lost on Sheila. Her first foggy thought after she had strolled to the galley and gulped a glass of water was that he must really want to buy the *Sheila B* if he was willing to just call up randomly and ask, "Hey. You wanna sell your boat?"

"Buy me some chicken fingers and a Red Stripe and we'll talk," she suggested as the waitress walked up to the table.

She was almost immediately an enigma to Pellet. When he first saw her a week and a half ago she was simply the long, lean, hot looking, mysterious woman on the deck of his potential future sailboat. Of course that was from a hundred feet away. Once he started asking around, he decided she was the illusive woman who everyone in the Simpson Bay area knew of, but almost none actually knew. On the phone this morning she was either an erotic sounding stoned woman or someone who was dumber than a bag of sand. He wasn't sure if he went with the stoned version because that's what he believed or because he couldn't bear to have his dream woman of the day to be an imbecile. Now that she was sitting in front of him he could see she was attractive but not perhaps as attractive as he had once envisioned. She had long, thinnish blonde hair pulled back in a ponytail, high cheek bones, and a nice smile. The NY Yankees cap was a strike against her in Pellet's view, but she later told him she had stolen it from a guy in a bar who was harassing her. Stealing the cap from a Yankee fan weighed in her favor. Plus she was long and lean and had a nice figure. Pellet was typically forgiving of nearly all faults of good-looking women. Even a marginally good looking one. But there was something about her that he couldn't put his finger on. She was a bit unkept. Not dirty, but not clean. And she put off a criminal element vibe. Perhaps not an actual criminal herself, but for sure she associated with some questionable people. She just had that edge about her that let the world know that she could do bad if required. And perhaps even when not required.

He tried to downplay how much he wanted Sheila B or Aqua Vita or whatever the boat was currently called by explaining that he wasn't really looking for an Endeavor until the mysterious *guy in the bar* had mentioned her boat. He told her that he had sailed on one a couple times a few years back and kind of liked how it handled. That was his story of why he gave her a call or ten to see what the deal was. Sheila wasn't buying his version. She checked her phone after they talked and counted twelve missed calls before he eventually reached her. Not to mention that Sheila B wasn't for sale, so there had to be something more to his story. The truth was she didn't care what his story was. If they could work out a deal that worked in her favor, that's all that really mattered.

"*Sheila B*. What's the B stand for?" Pellet asked.

"Boat. Bold. Beautiful. Brandy," she answered with a shrug. "Boner," she added with a grin. "Whatever *B* makes me feel good at a given moment in time."

Pellet smiled back at her and picked up the beer that had just been set down in front of him. "To B's," he said and took a drink.

CHAPTER TWENTY-THREE

Pellet rolled over onto his back out of breath and covered with sweat. "I take it the a/c doesn't work?" he asked as he watched a bead of sweat run down the side of her breast.

"Don't know. I like the heat. I've never turned it on," she answered as if it had never dawned on her that she might be more comfortable with cool air streaming through the cabin. She reached up and wiped the sweat off the side of his face and then ran her fingers through his scraggly hair. "So, are we talking business or more pleasure?"

"Guess we should separate the two. I've got a feeling your negotiating skills are better than mine as long as we're in bed." Without realizing it, that was a pivotal moment in his life. It was possibly the first time that he put what he *should* do in front of what he *wanted* to do. Not that timing didn't play into it at least a little bit. If she had asked him the same question moments before they had had sex for the first time as opposed to moments after, the negotiations would have likely gone much more in her favor. This time it was Sheila who had stumbled in the negotiation process and she laughed at her own blunder. The two of them laid on the damp sheets and passed a joint back and forth. Pellet stared at the fiberglass tongue and groove ceiling and Sheila stared out into the abyss as she pondered what would come next after life on the Sheila B.

"How long have you owned the boat," Pellet asked between tokes.

"You don't really own a boat. It's kind of the other way around. Boats own us. We're just along for the ride." What she didn't say was that it was more often than not an expensive and frustrating ride, but she figured he'd learn that the same way everyone else does.

"Yeah. That's what people keep telling me. Guess time will tell."

"Come on," she said as she slid out of bed and slipped on the same black bikini he'd seen her in on the day he cruised by with Mardi. He watched her get dressed and then remembered how he felt when he realized he wasn't going to get anything from Mardi. Not a boat and not the perks he had hoped that would go along with it. He was pleased with himself on how well the negotiations had gone so far and he looked forward to closing the rest of the deal. On the way through the boat Sheila stopped in the galley and pulled two beers from the ice box and continued topside. Pellet pulled on his shorts and hat and followed not far behind. From an outside view one might have been led to believe that she was doing whatever it took to sell the Sheila B to Pellet for top dollar.

They sat across from each other and took in the view of the bay. Compared to down below the eighty-degree breeze felt cool and comfortable. They watched boats pass by off in the distance. They watched planes approach and leave Saint Maarten's Princess Julianna International Airport. They watched life in slow motion and it felt right. Neither of them spoke a word. They sipped and their thoughts drifted. The beer was cold. The air was comforting. The pot took off any rough edges of life, not that there were any at the moment. Pellet held his empty bottle without a care in the world. A few minutes later Sheila took the last swallow of her beer and set the bottle in a drink-holder. She took a long deep breath followed by a lingering stretch as if she were a graceful contented cat. Then with the same slinking movement she had come outside with, she stood up, took off her bikini top and tossed it at Pellet.

"Follow me," she whispered with a smile and a wink and headed back down towards the same bed they had just climbed out of an hour earlier. Pellet sat motionless with a look of mild stoned shock on his face. Moments later she tossed her bikini bottoms up at Pellet and added, "Don't take too long or I'll start without you." When the bikini bottoms landed at his feet Pellet snapped out of his daze and jumped up. "If you want a ride back to shore, you're going to have to work for it." She called out. Pellet slipped down below. Sheila had done most of the work in round one and he wasn't sure he really wanted a ride to shore. He wondered if buying the boat would cost more or cost less if he worked out a deal where Sheila would stay on board. It was completely lost on Pellet that he had only a few hours earlier thought her to look a bit old and slightly dirty with a criminal aura about her. Now he embraced her as the young attractive woman he'd seen from a hundred yards away. And the criminal underworld vibes she'd been emanating somehow turned into an adventurous free-spirited woman who pushed the boundaries. Sheila had become, like so many women before her, Pellet's dream woman.

Shortly after the sun had set over the Caribbean Sea, the two of them took the tiny zodiac to shore and he bought them another meal and more drinks before he headed back home. Pellet being Pellet, hadn't really planned out the day in detail and the last ferry to Anguilla had departed Marigot Bay an hour-and-a-half before they finished their final nightcap. He stood in front of the bar with his hands in his pockets and a slight look of bewilderment on his face while Sheila slowly strolled in the general direction of the water. He supposed he'd find a hotel or something, but that was about as much of a plan as he had formulated at that moment. He stood gazing up at the stars when she turned and looked at him, then looked up to take in the same view he was taking in.

"Pretty nice view, huh?" she said, gazing up at the glittering sky.

"Damn nice," he mumbled.

"Better from the deck of Sheila B. We'll throw some cushions down and sleep under the stars," she said as she turned and started walking again. Pellet broke his gaze from the stars and watched her linger towards the bay. He followed with his hands in his pockets and a grin on his face and beamed with confidence that he had found his boat.

CHAPTER TWENTY-FOUR

Endeavour sailboats in the 90's were sleek blue water cruising boats with a good reputation among those who had actually sailed the Caribbean waters and knew what they were doing. Pellet did not fall into that category. He had sailed almost no blue water, or any other water for that matter and didn't have a clue of what he was looking at or for. Endeavours were not massively spacious inside like some of the more modern boats that looked more like high-end, floating mobile homes than sailboats, but all-in-all they had most of the comforts of home and there was room to breathe inside the cabin. On the outside they had a nice deck with a narrow bow that cut smoothly through the water and a heavy enough keel to give her good balance. If she was being captained by a seasoned sailor, she would get you to any place you wanted to go.

"Looks cool, right?" Pellet asked Avis as he opened the door to the shower and glanced at the sink that sat atop a teak cabinet with a teak counter. He reached up and opened a couple small teak doors and re-latched them. Sheila stayed topside and smoked the joint she had offered to share with Avis and Pellet before they began wandering down below the Sheila B. Before Pellet had a chance to respond, Avis chimed in and made it clear that they would not be smoking, but she should feel free to do as she pleased.

It was her boat. She always did as she pleased.

"So, you're really going to buy a boat because there was a bikini chick scrubbing the deck?"

"This boat has history man," Pellet said as he opened and closed the teak cabinets in the galley. "Lots of history."

"Good history or bad?" Avis asked while sticking his head in the engine room. Avis was a whiz kid who knew a lot of stuff about a lot of stuff, but mechanics was his real area of expertise.

Back in Watermill, New Hampshire he'd been the best mechanic the town had ever had. As it turned out, a diesel boat engine wasn't much different than a diesel truck engine. The meter showed him the hours were low, below a thousand since the last rebuild. If they went out for a cruise and ran the engine for a while he'd have a pretty good idea of its condition.

"She's still floating isn't she?" Pellet retorted. In Pellet's mind, if an old boat was still floating, then it had good history. At least that was the standard he was clinging to for this boat. Typical Pellet logic. An hour and a half later, they had run the engine and worked their way out of Simpson Bay. When they hit open water the winds kicked up just enough to make the cruise fun for an experienced sailor and a bit nerve racking for a non-sailor. Sheila called out orders and showed her new crew what lines were what, and told them which to pull and which to crank. Within a few minutes the main sail was up and adjusted. The jib was full and the bow cut nicely through the water. Avis had read at least ten books on sailing and another ten about sailboats in general. He read everything about everything. And one common message that almost all the books on sailing shared was that there was reading and there was doing. The only way to learn about sailing was to leave the safe harbor and sail. Until that was done, everything else was just talk and theory. He stood beside Sheila at the helm and held onto the stainless-steel frame of the canvas Bimini that protected them from the sun.

Pellet stood on the deck halfway to the front of the boat and held onto rigging that ran from the deck to the top of the mast. The Sheila B tipped hard to the starboard side and he was oblivious to their speed or the wind or any other potential danger. In his mind, this was sailing. He hadn't yet begun to understand that sailing was checking water depths to watch out for reefs and rocks, updating charts, being vigilant of everything, on and off the boat, watching and adjusting the sails, watching the lines that he hadn't yet realized were all over the boat, looking out for other boats, and perhaps most important of all, making sure that he didn't fall overboard. The mistake of all mistakes when out to sea was to be swimming in the water and watching your boat sail away without you.

Sheila gave Avis a few pointers and answered his occasional question. It was not lost on her that Pellet was caught up in the fairy tale version of owning a sailboat. She thought that Avis would make a good sailor. He had focus and seemed to have a curiosity to learn whatever there was to learn. Above all things, he seemed to be at least a smidge scared of the sea and that was a good thing. Any sailor who didn't have the appropriate respect for the power of the sea was flirting with disaster. The sea was not cruel or vicious or hateful. She was eternally and completely indifferent to all things. She rose and sank and splashed and stormed with no malice or compassion or reverence for anyone or anything. As far as she was concerned, a boat on the top of the sea was no different than a boat on the bottom of the sea. Anyone who counted on dumb luck to survive while far from land was stacking the odds of survival against themselves. Pellet took his ball cap off and stuck it in his back pocket when it started lifting off his head. His scraggly hair blew in the wind and he howled a long, loud howl. Avis shook his head. Sheila smiled. The price just went up ten thousand dollars.

A week and fifty-five thousand dollars later his boat sat anchored in Sandy Ground in Anguilla. The boat survey was done by some crusty old sea urchin in Saint Maarten and all went well with only minor items identified. Nothing that couldn't be fixed with lots and lots and lots of elbow grease. Pellet hadn't yet learned about the last two "lots" yet. The negotiations between the clueless beer drinker and the stoned bikini woman were comical to watch. Avis was surprised that Pellet managed to get the boat in the neighborhood of the right price. He was also absolutely certain that if he had not been there Pellet would have gotten laid again and the boat would have cost him another twenty thousand dollars.

A few days after closing the deal, Pellet, Avis and Lucy dropped anchor off the shores of Anguilla and came to shore in the little dinghy. Lucy had been sailing with her father since she was a baby and she was the only reason they sailed the short journey from Saint Maarten to Anguilla without hiring someone to bring them over. The current negotiations going on was Pellet trying to convince Lucy to stay on the island for a while to teach him how to sail. She was tougher than Sheila and she was making it clear that if by some unlikely chance they reached an agreement there would be no sex involved. But she was not seriously considering staying in Anguilla or teaching Pellet to sail. Pellet agreed to her guidelines, but he was Pellet. He still held out hope.

Lucy and Savannah stood on the beach and looked out at the boat. Both were mildly surprised that Pellet had bought her and were even more surprised that he had actually picked out a pretty decent boat.

"She's beautiful, Pellet," Savannah complimented as she looped her arm through Pellet's and gave him a reassuring squeeze.

"Pretty damn cool, huh?" he grinned from ear to ear.

"What's her name?"

"Bella Vita," Pellet proudly announced. Again, they were all impressed. He bought a beautiful boat and gave her a beautiful name. In the back of their mind they were all expecting something like, "Rum Runner or Happy Hour."

CHAPTER TWENTY-FIVE

Two days after helping Pellet sail Bella Vita from Saint Maarten to Anguilla, Lucy rode the ferry back across the straight between the two islands. From there she caught a cab to the airport to journey back to New York and pick up the pieces of her life that somehow felt as though they were lingering somewhere between what the hell happened and no big deal. She was healthy, educated, still had some money in the bank and there were opportunities in front of her. But no matter how hard she tried to use her logic and drive to convince herself that this was all just a bump in the road, a setback on her journey, wind in her face, or as she kept repeating to herself, no big deal, it just never felt right. While she was sitting in the airport watching tourist come and go with vacations either just in front of them or just behind them, she recalled something Avis had said one evening when they were standing at the porch railing of the bar and looking out to the glittering reflection of the setting sun on the Caribbean Sea.

"What we think or what we believe doesn't really alter our reality Lucy. It only alters our perception of reality. But as they say, perception is everything. What do you perceive?" Before she had time to respond or even ponder over a response, Pellet chimed in. "I perceive I need another beer." And just like that, her perception of the conversation was immediately changed. Sitting in the airport and recalling it brought a smile to her face. The thoughtfulness of Avis, a man she barely knew to befriend her and care about her was touching. And Pellet, well, he was just Pellet.

But she wasn't in the bar now and it was time to embrace a grownup version of reality. A reality where a company in New York City, another in Boston and a third in Hartford were all interested in interviewing her. Those were just the ones in the northeast. She was confident she could get decent offers from any of those companies and more. She thought about heading out to Seattle or San Francisco to continue running away from her recent failure, but she had always been an East Coaster. She had never felt any draw to go out West. She scrolled through her calendar and looked at the interview dates and times for no particular reason. Mentally, Lucy was moving on. She had endured a great tragedy of sorts and spent her time crying and ranting and resting and hanging out in the Caribbean. It was still overwhelming to her that such a small bump in the road, relatively speaking, could have been so devastating. She knew it wasn't good that she was pondering something that Pellet had said the same night that Avis talked to her at the bar, but his words had a ring of truth to them. "Shit! That's the worst thing that's ever happened to you? You live a damn charmed life, baby. Try waking up and finding out your kid isn't yours. Can't replace that with a new job." Only Avis saw the irony that both of them, polar opposites, each had their lives turned upside down and ended up in the same bar in the Caribbean comparing life notes. Then he realized that he wasn't all that much different than the two of them, sort of.

There's a big difference between mentally devastated and emotionally devastated. There's a logical path to recovery from mental devastation. But the road to recovery from emotional devastation did not necessarily follow such a logical path as the mental side. No matter how hard Lucy tried to move past what had happened, there was a lingering thought that she could not escape. *Everything had changed.* Those words echoed in her head over and over. Everything had changed. Mentally she could plan, scheme, schedule and work her way back to success. One step at a time, one problem at a time, one solution at a time. It was the same process she had been repeating since grade school. But emotionally she was stuck and couldn't find the motivation to move forward. Every time she reviewed the list of how and why to move forward she hit a wall. Everything had changed and there was no undoing it. She had in a way, reached the end of her innocence. Childhood was over.

Thirteen days, three interviews, and three job offers later,

Lucy sat in a NYC coffee shop talking to Pellet on the phone while he was sitting on the deck of his boat in Anguilla drinking a beer. She shook her head back and forth in disbelief that she was going to return to the islands to teach him how to sail Bella Vita. She laid out her employment terms and he was amicable to all the terms, less one.

"Pellet, I swear to God, if you try anything funny or out of line I will cut it off and use it for fish bait. Do you understand me?" she scolded and took another sip of her mint/mocha flavored cappuccino and watched the hustle of customers coming and going from the coffee shop. The two women at the next table stopped talking and looked over in her direction. Pellet cringed and unconsciously dropped his hand into his lap as if she had an app that would take care of business even from NYC to Anguilla. "So, agree to those terms and I'll come down for a couple of months and teach you how to sail. Deal or no deal?"

"Well, we should at least agree that there's a possibility to renegotiate the terms at a later date, if we feel the need." Pellet flattered himself and tried sounding as if he could negotiate with Lucy at somewhere in the vicinity of her business abilities.

"Fish bait, Pellet." The women glanced again and whispered something to each other. She made no effort to have a civilized negotiation that could leave room for any miscommunication or misunderstanding. And the two women at the next table, she could not care less about them. She was talking loud and clear at Pellet level. "Deal or no deal?"

"You know, you're really putting a damper on having any chance to date me down the road. I'm really just looking out for you, Lucy. I'd hate for you to come to your senses and have no option to…"

"Clocks ticking on this offer, Pellet. Sooner or later I'm going to come to my senses and accept one of the far more generous offers from someone up here who has a lot more money than Wayne Pelletier will ever see. So, I'll stay on the boat when you're staying on land, and I'll stay at your apartment when you're staying on the boat. You'll pay me five hundred bucks a week, plus you'll supply food and drinks. I'll take you out sailing as often as you want to go out, or not at all if you just want to pay me to be on vacation," she repeated the details for the third time just to make sure he was clear on the terms. "And any funny business, it will be fish bait."

"Well," Pellet paused and searched for an appropriate response. "Since you're in a jam and you need the work, I'll help you out." He grinned with satisfaction that he'd got the last shot in. Lucy took the phone away from her ear and looked at it as if she were searching for a reason to not just hang up on him.

"Oh, and you have to pay for my flights," she added as payback for his last comment. "You might want to stop negotiating and either accept the deal or walk away. I promise you, the more you talk, the more you're going to pay. My advice, just say okay and be done with it."

"Okay," he mumbled after a long pause.

"Excellent," she answered. "See you in a couple days." After hanging up Lucy sat and sipped her coffee and wondered what the hell she was doing. The corporate world was waiting with arms wide open. There was little doubt that a promising career was lying right in front of her. All she had to do was walk through the door, settle down at a desk and begin a twenty- or thirty-year journey to corporate success. But instead of doing that, she stood up and turned to the women at the next table and snapped, "Fish bait," just to leave them with something to talk about.

For the time being, Lucy knew there was no going back to the corporate world. Not like this. Things had changed. Lucy had changed. Whether she liked it or not, Allison Lanahan changed the course of her life. When she first got fired she was blown away. A few weeks later she embraced the anger that she presumed would fuel her ambition for the foreseeable future. When Allison first stuck the corporate knife deep into Lucy's back there was an internal struggle of how to move forward. After her first trip to Anguilla, Lucy returned to NYC and the internal battle continued. Years of conditioning and competing to be the best of the best left her far more disillusioned than she could have imagined. One voice pushed her to become a success and then find a way to crush Allison, making sure she knew exactly how it felt to be left in ruins. Another voice told her to be positive and move on. Focus on her future and let this experience be a learning and growing experience. And yet one more voice whispered ever so quietly that she should just go home, eat ice cream and bathe herself in self-pity until the she forgot the feeling of being crushed. A couple weeks later she found herself sitting on a stool in front of Desmund once again hiding away for a bit longer before making a decision about life back in the real world. After bringing Bella Vita to Anguilla, she had accepted that it was time to go home and get her life back on track.

It was during the third interview when it hit her. The anger and bitterness seemed to slip away and her perception of her future changed directions. Her hunger to conquer the corporate world eased away like a leaf on the wind in Central Park. It wasn't a revenge thing or a giving up thing. It was like she was walking in the park and when she reached the fork in the path where she had always turned to the left, she stopped and looked and then started walking down the trail on the right just to see where it would end up. For the first time in her life, Lucy Lapuenta acted impulsively. She took a chance and threw caution to the wind and tried to not think about the possible consequences. She caught a train from Boston to NYC, walked out of the station to a coffee shop, and set in action a plan to return to Anguilla.

CHAPTER TWENTY-SIX

At 6:30 in the morning the sun crested above the bay in Sandy Ground and Lucy sat and sipped on her hot cup of coffee, appreciating the simplicity of boating life. She waited for Pellet to work his way out of bed and ride the dinghy to the boat for his second lesson, and she gave absolutely no thought to NYC, her career or to Allison Lanahan.

His first lesson yesterday afternoon went about as well as she had anticipated it going. She intentionally made lesson-one informal as she presumed the only thing she could hope to accomplish was to get his attention.

"All right. Lesson one. Safety first. Safety last. Safety always," she snapped like a drill sergeant welcoming new recruits to basic training. Pellet nodded and sipped his beer. "So, with that in mind," she continued, "No drinking beer during sailing classes." Pellet looked at her with an almost blank confused look and took another sip of his beer.

"Sounds good," he mumbled with a shrug and took another sip and waited for more instructions. Lucy sat motionless in front of him and waited for him to connect the dots. There was a long silence and no dot connecting.

"So, that means the beer in your hand needs to go away, and I don't mean you should chug it down. We do sailing lessons correctly or not at all."

"Okay, I get it. You want us to be safe, but let's not be unreasonable. I mean, we're just sitting at the table. Nobody's getting hurt while the anchors still down."

"Beer or sailing lessons Pellet. Your call. I get five hundred bucks a week either way."

"Hey, I'm paying the tab. I think I get a little say so in how we do this."

"If that's what you're thinking then you're thinking incorrectly. Safety first. Once you've become Captain Morgan and start sailing all over the world without me, you can drink all you want. While I'm teaching there's no drinking. And it's not open for discussion." He took a deep breath and slouched and pouted like an eight-year boy old who just had his video game taken away. Lucy casually leaned over and picked up his beer and dumped it into the sink. Pellet slouched further down and pouted even more.

"Safety first. Safety last. That's the rule of every good sailor. Just remember, it's easier to go out to sea than it is to return."

"Seems a bit extreme" he mumbled. Lucy waited another few seconds before saying anything just to see if he was going to start crying.

"Clearly you have no idea of how extreme sailing can be," she said, and tossed the empty into the sink. "Let me ask you a question. If you're sailing by yourself and you do something as simple as slip or trip over something and fall overboard, do you know what happens?" He looked up at her with another clueless look and provided no answer to a question that should have had an obvious answer. "You watch your boat sail away," she answered herself and continued, "Because whether you know it or not, Bella Vita will sail just fine with you splashing about in the water and screaming for her to come back. She does not need you. You do need her." She watched him to see if the lights even started to come on. They flickered ever so dimly but did not burn brightly. "Then you drown," she added. His forehead wrinkled and the lights seemed to flicker just a tad brighter. She spent the next hour explaining the difference between a close haul and a close reach and a beam reach or broad reach. Then she explained the difference between the mainsail and the jib. The final lesson for the day was meant to intentionally overfill his mental toolbox, so she explained aerodynamics of wind on sails. Pellet's brain swirled with information he was not processing, and as she was well aware that he understood almost none of it. It was too much to take in on the first lesson, but the lessons had to start somewhere. All she really wanted to do was to give him a wakeup call. The only thing she insisted that he learn on day one was that he wouldn't be drinking beer while learning to sail. When he looked sufficiently confused and overwhelmed and mentally beaten up, she stood up and reached into the icebox and pulled out a cold Red Stripe. "Congratulations. You made it through day one," she said and opened the beer and handed it to him. "Six more weeks and who knows, maybe you'll learn something."

"Damn. My head hurts and we haven't lifted the anchor yet."

"It'll hurt more before we're done. There's a lot to learn Pellet. But if you want to have fun sailing, then you need to learn to do it right."

"Damn," he mumbled again and took a gulp and tried to shake the fuzz from his brain.

That was day one and day two was about to begin. She presumed the beer thing would go better today considering they were starting before breakfast. Five minutes later, Pellet tied the dinghy to the back of the boat and climbed up the ladder. The first words out of his mouth were, "Good morning. I suppose I can't have a beer this morning either?" Lucy ignored his question and asked one of her own.

"Which side is starboard?"

"Need coffee first," was all he said and headed below deck.

"Already made. Grab a cup and come back up."

"You're awfully bossy first thing in the morning," he said as he brushed past her and climbed down the steps.

"First lesson for today. There is only one captain on a boat. Always! I'll be waiting for you up here."

"You know I'm not really into bossy women. Doesn't really work for me," he yelled while he poured his cup of coffee.

"Good. Sounds like we're on the same page. You coming back up today or what?" Pellet slowed down his already slow pace and stood in the galley and sipped his coffee. Bella Vita rocked gently on a small rolling wave that worked its way from the sea to the shore. Lucy was still barking out orders from topside, but he tuned her out and looked around his boat. *His boat*. He smiled. A small lantern swayed back and forth on a hook in the ceiling, and the door to the rear birth creaked as it swung halfway closed. The smell of coffee filled the cabin and for a moment in time he felt like only good things laid in his path.

"Pellet!" she snapped as she stuck her head through the doorway without climbing down. His vision of an untainted path to the future disappeared and he was mildly irritated that Lucy had ruined his moment.

"You know I'm beginning to regret hiring you."

"Don't feel special. I regretted it the moment we made the deal, but my father taught me that you finish things you start in life. You're my burden to carry for the next six weeks," she answered, and left him trying to figure out whether or not she was joking. She sat back down and waited for him and tried to figure out the same thing.

Pellet took two months off work and he and Lucy spent several hours on Bella Vita every day. It was on the thirteenth day of learning to tie knots, familiarizing himself with lines, rigging and sails and knowing what a windless was and how to use the manual bilge pump and how to change filters and how to raise and lower and fold sails and how to use the radar and how to read a compass and how to read charts and track a route and more things than most people would learn in six months. That's when he blew up and couldn't take any more.

"Jesus Christ!" he snapped and threw down a piece of line he'd been practicing tying knots on. "Are we ever going to sail or what?"

"I thought you'd never ask," she answered as if he had not asked every day since day two. There were a few reasons she waited so long before taking him out to sea. She wanted to make sure he had a pretty good idea of what he was doing and what she was talking about when she said things like, "Coming about." She also wanted him to be hungry for sailing before they raised anchor for the first time. She didn't want this to be something that came easy or was taken for granted by Pellet. He was the king of taking important things for granted. In fact, he was nearly a god at taking important things for granted. And perhaps most importantly, she wanted to see how long it was going to take before he finally blew his top. With the answer of thirteen days being revealed, she supposed it was time to let him live a little. "Let's go tomorrow. Be here around seven and we'll have some fun." She reached in the icebox and handed him a Red Stripe. "Don't go out drinking tonight. Not taking you out with a hangover."

CHAPTER TWENTY-SEVEN

His first couple of weeks of actual sailing came and went with Pellet being a lot more capable than Lucy would have thought. She stood at Dez's Bar and tried to explain something that she just couldn't wrap her head around or put her finger on.

"I remember when I was a little girl there was a song that said something about there's going to be a day of reckoning," Lucy said to Avis and Savannah and shook her head back and forth.

"He seems to think he's getting the hang of it. At least that's the impression I've gotten from him," Savannah answered. "He stops by at least a couple times a week for dinner and tells us about the boat and your lessons and sailing and everything he's learned. We were both looking forward to going out with him." She argued as if she were telling Lucy she was wrong about Pellet.

Avis sipped on his beer and didn't say much, but he listened to both sides of the story. He'd known Pellet off and on for years, and over the past two they had become pretty close. While Pellet didn't seem to pay all that much attention to Avis's idiosyncrasies, Avis had paid attention to Pellet's. He had watched enough to know that Pellet was not a stupid guy and he wasn't as inept as everyone thought him to be. On the other hand he was well aware that the overall group opinion of Pellet, while largely incorrect, wasn't without merit. He reached up and repositioned his ball cap and took another drink.

"It's not that he's not learning. He is absorbing everything I teach him," Lucy continued. "And it's not that he can't sail. He can. It's just that," she hesitated and searched for the words that would accurately describe the issue she was having with Pellet's sailing.

"It's just that," Avis interrupted, "you can teach a kid to

not play in the street and if he's a smart kid, he'll understand how dangerous playing in the traffic could be. But if that smart kid is Pellet, well he just might play in the traffic anyway."

"How do you figure playing in the traffic is smart?" Savannah shot back in a confused attempt to defend her friend.

"Oh, it's not. I'm just saying that Pellet's not stupid. He knows right from wrong, and he knows the hazards of doing wrong." Avis answered.

"But he does it anyway," Lucy finished. "And that's the problem. I'll teach him things and he understands and learns them, but when he's in charge, I can actually see it on his face. He knows what he is doing. It's not like he's trying to figure out what the right decision is. It's more like he's trying to decide whether or not he wants to do the right thing."

"Really?" Savannah asked, as if she'd never seen that side of Pellet.

"Oh, come on Savannah. We've seen him do the exact same thing right here on these bar stools. Would you like me to remind you of some of the stories?" Avis shot back.

"I know, but," was all she managed to say before the wheels began turning and the memories began running through her head.

"Hell, I saw him get dead drunk one night and challenge Herbie Walker to a fight." Lucy looked and waited for him to explain who Herbie Walker was. "He's a fisherman from the east end of the island. Almost seven feet tall and weighs about three hundred and fifty pounds. Pellet ran his mouth and took a swing at him. Herbie put him under his arm and carried him to the shore like he was a loaf of bread. Then he flung him almost thirty feet into the sea. Flung him like a sack of potatoes. Pellet spun around like a frisbee until he hit the water."

"Oh my god. Was he alright?" Lucy began to wonder if teaching Pellet to sail wasn't irresponsible on her part.

"Still alive isn't he. I mean, that's really Pellet's talent isn't it. After all these years of being Pellet, he's still alive."

"What happened after, you know, he got tossed?" Lucy

asked.

"He sloshed back into the bar and told everyone that he had to pee anyway so getting thrown into the water saved him a trip to the can. Then he plopped himself back onto a stool and bought Herbie a drink and asked him how the fishing was going lately." Avis finished his story and Lucy wondered if she might want to stand and not sit on her stool anymore.

"So how do you figure this means Pellet isn't stupid then?" Savannah questioned as her loyalty to Pellet began to waiver.

"Because even wasted Pellet knew he couldn't possibly have an outside prayer in hell of winning a fight with Herbie Walker, but you know what? He started one anyway, just for the fun of it. Just because he decided to," Avis answered and took another drink of his beer. "And he pretty much knew how it was going to end," he added.

"He's right," Desmund chimed in. "Da boy almost always knows how tings gonna turn out. Does em anyway. Jus da way he is."

"Sounds stupid to me," Savannah mumbled.

"Reckless," Lucy answered. "He's not stupid. He's reckless. It's not like he thinks he's invincible. He just wants to see how irresponsible he can act before life catches up with him."

"And den he acts surprised bout da way tings turn out," Desmund added.

"Yes!" Lucy almost yelled. "That is the most infuriating part of the whole thing. It would just be frustrating if he wasn't getting it and kept making mistakes. But he's impulsive and always acts surprised when the predictable things go wrong. And you're right," she said to Avis. "He's smart, or at least not stupid. Last week, I went below for a bit to make lunch when we were out sailing. Before going down we looked at the charts and depths and everything was all good. Then when I came back up I saw he had changed course and had sailed right between to reefs that were less than a couple hundred feet apart. And he acted like it was no big deal, like there was no chance of hitting one of them if a gust of wind or a current had hit us. If he hit one of those reefs we could have been screwed six ways from Sunday." That was the phrase her father always used when he was teaching her back in her childhood sailing days. "If you do this or don't do that, we'll be screwed six ways from Sunday." But when she blew up and used the phrase on Pellet, he shrugged and just said, "But we didn't hit it and we're not screwed." It was a rare occasion that Lucy drank anything other than a fruit drink with sparkling water but there were days when Pellet could push her over the edge. She finished telling the reef story and said, "Heineken, please Dez. With a glass." She was possibly the only person who ever came to Dez's and drank beer from a glass. Another week of sailing with Pellet and she would likely graduate her drinking habit to drinking straight from the bottle. And possibly something stronger than beer.

"Da boy can drive you to drinking," Dez said as he slid the glass across the bar. She laughed and picked up her glass and held it up to her friends.

"To Cap'n Pellet," she said and they all raised their glasses and laughed. Helmut had listened to the entire conversation in silence until they raised their glasses.

"Point him out to sea and wish him well. With a little luck…" he stopped talking and shrugged. He let them fill in the rest of the sentence.

"Day of reckoning," Lucy added and drank her beer.

CHAPTER TWENTY-EIGHT

It had been years since that evening when Yossi Eliat leaned over and brushed the hair out of his daughters face and sat down on the edge of her bed. It was something he had done more often since his wife, Shira's mother, had abruptly left them seven years earlier. After she was gone, Shira had aunts and uncles and cousins, but mostly she had Papa. He was her hero and for the most part, her world. He made no secret that Shira was the center of his universe and there was almost nothing he would not do for his little girl.

"I'm going away for a couple days. Aunt Hila is coming by in the morning to get you to school," he said and adjusted her blankets. This was a normal way of life for the two of them. Yossi owned a small travel agency. It wasn't unusual for him to go away for a day or two every few weeks. Occasionally for a bit longer. Shira didn't like it, but she was used to it.

"Where are you going Papa?"

"I need to fly to our office in Kuwait and meet with some people. Just business stuff. I'll be back in two days."

"Will you bring me back something?" she asked, as if there were any chance that he would not.

"Aahh. I thought you might miss me," he teased. "But as long as I return home bearing gifts, then all is forgiven." Shira giggled and sat up and gave Papa a hug and held on until he patted her on the back and told her good night. "Behave yourself in school and learn something new to share with me."

"Will you take me out for dinner on Friday?"

"Sleep young lady. Friday is a long time away. And don't forget to look at the stars." With those final words he stood up and turned off the light and walked out of her bedroom. Those were the last words he would ever say to her. "Don't forget to look at the stars."

On Thursday afternoon she came home from school and set her bookbag on the bench in the entryway. When she walked into the living room her aunt and uncle were waiting for her. Her uncle was sitting in the chair at the end of the couch. It was Papa's chair. Her aunt was sitting on the couch with a space next to her for Shira to sit. Before either of them said so much as a word, Shira asked the question.

"What happened to Papa?" And before either had a chance to answer, the blood began to drain from her face and a knot tightened in the pit of her stomach. She didn't know how she knew that something had happened. She walked in and looked at them and her universe just didn't feel right. The air was heavy and the colors were bland. Her uncle didn't have the far-off disconnected look that was almost always pasted on his face. Her aunt who was typically aloof and unconcerned, looked anxious. She was one of those Zenlike yoga women who lived a sheltered life and pretended the world was a wonderful place. Her world, for the most part, was a wonderful place. She usually left the dirty work and the ugly details of life for other people to handle. Just as often as not, Yossi was the other people. But on that day, Yossi was not in the room and there was nobody else to handle it. Shira's mother was long gone and Yossi was in trouble. She could sense it. When Shira walked into the house, the looks on her aunt and uncle's faces were unfamiliar. They were serious and focused and concerned for someone other than themselves. The truth was that they loved Shira and would do anything for her, but up until this moment, all they ever had to do was to be her loving aunt and uncle. They never had to do the dirty work or heavy lifting of being a parent. On their very first day of parenting, they were given the heaviest of loads.

"Sit," was all Aunt Hila said, and patted the couch cushion one time indicating where she was to be seated.

"Your father's been in an accident Shira," her uncle announced. There was no soft selling this kind of news. There was no sense in torturing her by searching for words that were not

147

going to cut into her heart.

"How bad?" were the only words she could manage to whisper.

"We don't know yet," Hila said with no confidence in her own words. "All we know is that it is serious."

"When are we leaving?" Shira demanded, as if she were the one to decide that they would be flying to Kuwait to go and save Papa. Her aunt and uncle looked at her with no answers. "We are going, right?" she demanded. "He would come if it were one of us." The blood was back in her face and she turned from pale white to bright red. Her skin was burning as if she was going to explode at any moment. "We've got to go," she said through a choked whisper. "It's Papa. If he's hurt, he will need me." Shira looked at her uncle and saw no sign that they were going to see Papa. "Aunt Hila, we've got to go."

"Shira," she stood and reached out and took her hand. "I know you want to go, but we need to wait. They will call us with news soon. Then we will decide what to do."

And then they waited. The afternoon sun burnt away and dinnertime came and went. Hila busied herself in the kitchen preparing food that they would not eat. Shira sat on the couch and waited for the phone to ring. Her uncle paced back and forth and tried to look as though he knew what to do with himself. Daylight faded into night and the sun was replaced by stars that neither Shira nor Papa saw. Papa always told her to look up at the stars when they weren't together. He said the universe made the world a smaller place. And if the world was smaller, then they were closer to each other than it seemed. She waited on the couch in an immense universe and the phone did not ring and the world did not seem small. Hila tried to put her into bed at midnight, but Shira would not budge. She would rest when she heard Papa's voice.

She woke up on the couch the next morning to the sound of whispering voices in the kitchen. Her first thought was that it was all a bad dream, not real, but she knew better. She wanted it to be a bad dream and she wanted it to be not real, but it was more real than she could have ever dreamed.

When she walked into the small kitchen her aunt and uncle were sitting at the table and they both stopped talking at the same time. And Shira knew. She could see the emptiness on their faces. She could hear it in their silence. She fell to her knees and closed her eyes and the entire world disappeared. She knew at that very moment that her world would never return. Everything she thought to be real in her life was gone. She knelt on the floor and saw empty blackness that reached into eternity and listened to thunder explode from somewhere deep inside.

Over the next few days the details were spoon fed to her. Papa had been in a bad car accident and was taken to a hospital in Kuwait. He died sometime in the night. The body was flown back to Tel-Aviv. There was a funeral but he was too badly destroyed for his little girl to see. Relatives came and cried and ate and talked. They all hugged her and kissed the top of her head and on her cheeks and told her how much they all loved her and Yossi. The world around her was bustling like they do when someone who is loved by all passes away. Then they were gone. And then, even though she lived with her aunt and uncle who were wonderful people, Shira was alone and would remain alone.

Seven years later she had already done her three years of Israeli military and she was nearing the end of her first year at the university. Her aunt sent a text and asked that she come to visit for dinner. There was something she wanted to discuss. When Shira arrived, there was a man standing on the back porch with a drink in his hand. She didn't recognize him but supposed there was no reason she would. He wasn't anyone she had ever met, so she gave him little thought other than to shake his hand and be pleasant when they were introduced. Hila handed her a glass of wine and gently squeezed her arm. "I'll let you and Amit talk for a few minutes. I'll be in the kitchen if you want me." Before Shira could say a word, Hila turned and walked inside and closed the door.

"Please, sit," Amit gestured towards a chair. She sat and waited. "There are things that are best heard from someone who knows what happened, rather than through some rumor." He stopped speaking and sipped the bourbon in his glass. Her forehead wrinkled. She hadn't the slightest idea of what he was referring to. He took a deep breath, signaling that this was not going to be good news he was sharing. "Shira, I knew your father. In fact we grew up together and we were close right up until," he hesitated and searched for the right words, then said nothing.

"I don't remember you," she challenged. "I remember a lot of the people who came to our house or that he talked about. I have an excellent memory," she added as if she were questioning just how close they may have been.

"I need to explain something to you, Shira. About when Yossi, about when your father died."

She sat up and stared at him and tried to decide if this was a conversation she wanted to have, or why they were even having it. She wanted to know who was this man that was talking to her about a knife she felt stabbed deep into her heart each and every day for longer than she cared to recall. But she froze and said nothing as he began to speak. "When your father died, it was not in a car accident in Kuwait," he blurted out. "Yossi and I were in Mossad together. I can share some of the details with you, but probably not as much as you will want to know." He stopped talking and looked at her. She sat motionless without saying a word. "Your father was in another country handling some business we were involved with. Somehow the people we were dealing with found out who he was. They killed him almost as soon as he arrived."

"I thought he was in Kuwait?"

"It was just his cover story. He had a lot of them."

"Where was he?"

Amit just shook his head. This was one of the details he could not share.

"And," she stopped and pondered the words "cover story" and then her mind began racing. "And the travel agency?"

"Well," he said and nonchalantly moved his head back and forth, "Much of his life was part of his job."

"Did his job have anything to do with my mother leaving?" That question caught her by surprise as the words came out of her mouth.

"It's complicated, Shira. All of it." This was another one of those details. The short version was that their marriage was not going well and during one of their rough spots, his wife threatened to expose him as a Mossad agent. They quickly reached an agreement of sorts and she went back to Paris forever. Part of the agreement was that Shira would remain with Yossi and there would be no future contact. Sadly, it was a detail that they were both in favor of. Amit shared none of those details with her. He left it at "It's complicated."

"How did he die," she instinctively asked. She wanted to know that he did not suffer. This question, of all questions was one she hoped he gave the right answer for. This was a question that required the correct response, even if it was a lie.

"He was shot. It was quick. And that's about all I can tell you."

She sat in silence for several minutes. Twice he began to speak and she held up her hand and silenced him. Long after his drink was finished, she looked up and looked back down and thought in silence for a while longer. She was a young woman, who, like her father, spoke with a sense of authority. When she silenced Amit, he obeyed. He began to stand up as if he were going to leave and allow her to try to wrap her mind around the information he had just dropped on her.

"Sit," was all she said without looking at him. When her mind finally stopped racing and analyzing and conjecturing, she asked one question. "How can I find out more?"

"I suppose you could join Mossad, but that's not why I came here. It's just that Yossi and I were good friends and I think he would want you to know." This time he sat and searched for words. "Perhaps I was wrong in telling you, I don't know. But it's been weighing on me lately, so… here I am."

Shira sat up straight, as if new life had been breathed into her lungs. Amit was caught off guard when she raised the glass of wine to her lips and drank the half full glass in one tip. "How do I join?"

Two months later, Shira was employed by the Israeli Mossad and for the first time in seven years, she felt close to her Papa again.

CHAPTER TWENTY-NINE

Fatisha casually strolled into the bar with the soft warmth of a Caribbean breeze and gave Lucy a light kiss on her cheek. She followed that greeting by leaning over the bar and giving Desmund the same. Without a word he poured her a glass of white wine and slid it in front of her.

"Pellet, you still here?" she called out with a tone of sarcastic surprise. There was no gentle kiss on the cheek or tender hug or even a handshake.

"Still waiting for you Fatisha."

"Gonna be a long wait, Pellet," was all she said before she turned and gave him a wink and strolled over to Helmut's table where she eased into the seat beside him. Helmut received a warm kiss on the lips from Fatisha and a dirty look from Pellet. He lost the battle almost three years ago and didn't really see an upside of not holding a grudge. Lucy watched the whole episode with a sense of amusement. Watching the Pellet & Fatisha routine was like watching a comedic spin on groundhog day. A day where he never gives up and she never gives in. He always loses and she always wins. But they play it over and over and over.

"Why do you torture yourself?" Lucy asked, as he continued to cast a disapproving look towards Fatisha.

"Aw. No torture felt on my end. I just can't bring myself to let Helmut think I've given up. Besides, I've got nobody else to chase at the moment. Unless," he added as he looked Lucy up and down.

"Fish bait," was all she said before he turned back to look at Fatisha.

"Well, we'll be done sailing in a couple days. Once that's done, we'll see if you can resist my charms." Pellet picked up his beer and drained it to the bottom and then stood up to leave. "Until then, I've got to go get some sleep before we go sailing tomorrow." Lucy shook her head but wasn't sure if she was acknowledging the absurdity of him not being able to receive a clear message of rejection or amazement of how Pellet simply did not know how to give up. She had thought more than once, that if he ever endeavored on something worthy of pursuing he would be unstoppable. On the other hand, she had also considered the unlikelihood that he would ever focus his unstoppable energy towards something worthwhile, with one exception. Sailing.

At sunrise Lucy stirred around the cabin and made coffee. Before she poured the first cup, she heard the motor of the dinghy pulling up and then Pellet climbing aboard Bella Vita. She wasn't surprised when he didn't come down to get a cup. Even though she occasionally questioned his decisions, she didn't question his sailing ability, confidence, or determination. Perhaps sailing really was his calling. It all seemed to come natural to him and there was no doubt that he looked at home on the water. As she mentioned to Avis and Savannah, her concern was that he did not fear it. On the other hand, perhaps it was not recklessness. Maybe it was simply a deep true love for the sea. She'd seen it before in a few prolific sailors. Pellet often reminisced about his sailing ancestors and he talked about other sailors he had read about. The fact that he was even reading, according to those who knew him well, was something of a shock. The first time she mentioned it to Desmund, his response was, "Pellet? A book? You kiddin, right? Didn't know he could read." When she told Avis about Pellet reading, he smiled like a proud father who had somehow convinced his lost son to embrace the power of books. Whatever the motivator was, Pellet embraced everything about sailing even more than drinking beer or pursuing hopeless relationships with women whom he stood no chance with. The truth was Pellet wanted more out of life, and sailing was more. The sea was more. Leaving land, leaving Anguilla in search of something, anything, was more than sitting at a bar and drinking his life away. Maybe it was his ancestry, maybe sailing was in his DNA, or maybe just wanting more was his true motivation. Maybe it was just time to make a move. Whatever it was, no matter how much Lucy harassed him and shot him down, and no matter how much she shook her head at him, there was one thing she was certain of. Pellet was a natural at sailing and she was proud of what she had taught and what he had learned. Her only concern was whether or not the sea bearing Pellet could remain separated from the Pellet that hung out in Dez's Bar.

He steadily and purposely walked the deck to the bow and checked to make sure the anchor lines and chains weren't tangled. Then he checked the two forward hatches to make sure they were secured. After that he turned off the gas tank that fed the stove and presumed that one way or another, Lucy was done making coffee. He checked the rigging, checked the sails, connected a couple lines to this or that, pulled up the ladder, and removed the covers from the radar equipment at the helm. All that was done before heading down below to see Lucy.

"Morning. I'm going to run the engine for a few minutes, but I don't think we'll need it. There's a nice breeze blowing out and nobody's anchored close. We should be able to let the jib out a bit and slip out of the bay until we're far enough to raise the main." He stepped into the galley and poured himself a cup of coffee.

"Sounds good," Lucy answered without looking up from the chart she was studying. They had sailed almost every day for over a month. They'd been hit by two or three small thunderstorms and one pretty strong one along with the winds and waves that went with them. Some days were calm seas and mild breezes. Other days were choppy seas with gust. When they began, Lucy was fully in control, even when she let him take the helm. Over the past three weeks, she had become the crew and he had become the captain. For the first time since he married Zoe and becoming a father, he was stepping up to the plate. Sailing in the open sea was a big deal. This wasn't the lazy river raft or a houseboat on the lake. This was blue water sailing and Pellet either had the grasp of the basics by now or he didn't. It was her opinion that he did.

Within an hour they were out of the bay with the sails full

of wind and the bow cutting through the water. The plan was to sail to Saint Barths and drop anchor for the night and return the following day. Pellet plotted the voyage, estimated the sailing time there and back and checked and double checked everything. From Sandy Ground in Anguilla, he figured that even with a conservative estimate they would arrive in nine and a half hours. Eight hours and seventeen minutes later they dropped anchor in Anse a Colombier, an uncrowded inlet near almost nothing in Saint Barths. As soon as they anchored, Pellet checked and double checked everything above deck to make sure nothing had come loose, no lines undone and nothing that would be a problem on tomorrow's sail back home. Then he checked to make sure the dinghy was tied off and secured the mainsail. One last meticulous journey around the deck to check and double check, then he stood and inhaled a deep breath of salt air and looked across the bay towards land. After taking in the view he returned to the cockpit. Lucy sat with sandwiches on the table and beers, cold and open.

"So, you feeling like a captain yet?"

"Shit. I felt like a captain before you taught me anything. I just didn't know how to sail," he answered with his usual grin. For the next five hours they sat and drank and talked, mostly about sailing. Lucy had three beers. Pellet had more, but not a lot more.

"You understand Pellet, that you haven't seen a real storm at sea yet? Those little thirty-minute things that tossed us around like we were nothing, let me tell you something, they were nothing." She stopped talking and opened her third beer which officially put her into what she would define as a wild night. She was celebrating what she believed to be a successful indoctrination of Pellet into the sailing world. "The biggest waves we saw were less than ten feet. I'm certain of it. In fact, probably not even nine feet."

"I get it Lucy. Safety first. Safety always. Waves can be big. The sea is dangerous. Blah, blah, blah. Damn. I can't spend my whole life waiting for doom and gloom."

"Ohhhh. Pellet, Pellet, Pellet. I wish the best for you and Bella Vita," she said with a tiny bit of a slur.

"Just wish it for Bella Vita. I'm just along for the ride. She just needs to stay on top of the water," he said and raised his beer to her. Nine hours later she woke up under the covers in the v-birth. The first thing she did was to lift the blanket to make sure she was still dressed. She breathed a sigh of relief when she saw she was not only wearing her windbreaker and shorts from last night, but she was also still wearing her deck shoes. The fog began to clear from her head and she smelled the coffee Pellet had already made. He was on his second cup and planned on pulling up the anchor in twenty minutes. Ten hours later they walked into Dez's to celebrate his graduation of sorts with Avis, Savannah, Dez, and of course, Helmut who sat at his table in the corner. Fatisha arrived late just in time to act shocked that he hadn't sunk the boat yet. Pellet ordered the first round. He clinked his Red Stripe to Lucy's fruit punch, and of course, he suggested what everyone knew he would.

"So, we're at least going to kiss to seal the deal, right?"

"Fish bait, Pellet. Try anything and it will still be fish bait."

CHAPTER THIRTY

It wasn't a named storm. Not even an identified pressure system that had little hope of becoming a named storm. It wasn't even a front or two fronts that the weather gurus were keeping their eyes on with the outside chance that it might become a pressure system of one degree or another. There were no hazardous weather warnings or rough sea notifications. There was absolutely nothing to lead anyone to believe the seas were going to be anything but average seas that come and go nearly every day of the year. All was calm in the Western Atlantic.

Unfortunately, mother nature does not get the weather reports and apparently she doesn't watch the Weather Channel or keep an eye on what's coming off the coast of Africa or what fronts are colliding from Canada and the US. She was unaware that there were no notable air currents or systems or anything else. When all weather things look good, when all fronts and systems and seas are calm and storm free, good ole Mother Nature still has the power to rain hell down onto the face of the earth and onto the surface of the seas and the oceans. And she does it without malice or compassion or even the least bit of consideration for who or what may be affected.

The Ebony Z was a big cargo ship by any standard, and she was on her way from Lisbon, Portugal, to Los Angeles, California, via the Panama Canal. It was a trip the crew had done so many times that it was only slightly more challenging than a long drive to and from work. By all accounts it was a relatively easy trek with less hazards than nearly any long sea voyage on the face of the Earth. There were no narrow straights to maneuver through, other than the canal itself. There were no hazardous capes to sail around. No strong unpredictable currents. No reefs right where you wouldn't expect to find one. Other than normal Atlantic and Gulf of Mexico sea traffic there was little for the ocean freighter to be concerned about. As far as ocean traffic, the large ships were well mapped and easily seen by the naked eye and on radar. And smaller ships like sailboats, it was their job to get out of the way of the Ebony Z. If they failed to do so the paint on the Ebony Z would get scratched and the people in the sailboat would likely die. Story finished. The captain and crew were experienced and reputable. And when it happened, the captain was on the bridge performing his duties and not drinking scotch or napping in his cabin. The senior crew were all sober and doing their jobs just as they were supposed to be doing. But it was Mother Nature. None of this mattered to her.

The first thing to be noted was a sizeable thunderstorm forming to the north west, heading south towards their path. It appeared they would probably be sailing through it in a couple hours if it didn't break up first. Other than simply noting it and being aware of it, it was not a flag raising event. This was the Atlantic. Storms came and went so often that it was just part of their daily routine. A half hour later another storm popped up on the radar. This one was southwest and heading north. This was perhaps a bit more noteworthy, but still nothing to create panic or large concern. The crew and ship had been through hundreds of storms over the past several years. Wind, rain, waves, it was what they did for a living. Another half hour went by and a third storm formed. This one was dead ahead and barely moving in any direction. None of the storms were particularly threatening on their own. But it became obvious that within the next hour, none of the storms would be on their own. In fact, it became hopelessly obvious that all three were going to merge into what was likely to be a sizeable storm that would create a lively ride.

"Sonofabitch," the captain mumbled. "Notify the crew. Tell them to be prepared to be bounced about." The notification didn't panic anyone. Being told that there was an impending thunderstorm and rough seas ahead set the crew into a flurry of activity, but most of it was cargo ship preventive activity. It's easier to batten everything down in the galley than it is to clean it all up afterwards. And the Ebony Z was a big ship. She was a Panamax that was the size of a football field and had a dead weight of over 52 tons. Simply put, she was big and heavy and not easily intimidated by wind and rain and waves. Ten to twelve-foot seas were barely more than ripples in the water as she headed across the Atlantic towards the Gulf of Mexico. Once the seas got up around fifteen or twenty feet, the ride would get bouncy, but bouncy wasn't the end of the world.

Almost an hour to the minute, the Ebony Z began to rock. The rain was pounding down so heavily that the front of the boat was barely visible from the ships tower. Twenty to twenty-five-foot waves were crashing one after another over the bow of the boat. But she was strong and the hundreds of containers on her deck were secure. From what they could see on the radar there would be an hour or so of this weather and then they would come out on the other side of the storm. After that they'd be back into blue skies. And that's almost how it went. Lightening cracked, thunder boomed, rain drove down, and wave after wave came over her bow. With ten minutes or so remaining before they broke out of the worst of it, one of the officers looked out a window on the north side of the bridge. That's when he saw it.

"Monster wave!" he called out with absolute certainty that there was nothing anyone could do other than to hold on and perhaps say a very short and quick prayer. Less than ten seconds later a fifty-foot wave slammed into the starboard side of the Ebony Z. The entire front deck of the boat disappeared and at least twenty containers were washed overboard as if they were little sticks being tossed into the sea. She listed heavily to the port and for just a moment it was unavoidable for the crew to wonder as to whether or not she was going to capsize. If she did, their chances of survival were slim to none. If she flipped she would likely be yet one more boat that disappeared on the fringes of the Bermuda Triangle. And they would be one more crew who would not be able to tell their version of what had happened. But, with the exception of the giant wave that had just struck them from the north, most of the waves from the storm were slamming into them from the south. As the boat leaned further and further to the portside and almost reached the point of no return, a twenty-foot wave slammed into her from the south. The boat froze in place for what seemed to be an eternity. They waited to see if she were going to continue her roll towards flipping or not. Slowly, the Ebony Z eased back to the starboard side and righted herself. Then she did what she was designed to do, she continued on her journey with twenty or thirty less containers than she had when she first entered the storms.

Chapter Thirty-One

"You know, sometimes I'm shocked you actually pulled this off."
Avis looked out to the sea when he spoke, as if he were speaking
to the horizon and not actually speaking to Pellet. It turned out that
Pellet's aptitude for sailing was uncanny and it felt like there was
at least a small chance that he may have been correct when he said
sailing was in his DNA. He was horrible at relationships. You
couldn't depend on him for almost anything. If he said he'd be
there at seven, chances were good he would show up at eight or
not at all. If he said he would drop something in the mail for you,
you'd probably find it on the seat of his truck a week later. If he
fixed a faucet for you, it would probably work, but it would have
a constant drip. And if he painted your living room, it would get
done, but it would need to be redone after he left. But sailing it
seemed had been a trait handed down through eternity from some
French guy to the next over and over again until it finally landed
in Pellet's lap. Sailing came as natural to him as fishing for brook
trout in New Hampshire came to Avis. On the other hand, Pellet
was still Pellet and gracefully accepting a compliment was not
something that was handed down from generation to generation.
In fact, it seemed more than likely that much of the
multigenerational failures by most of the Pelletier's throughout
history, could be directly or indirectly linked to allowing a little
success to go to their heads.

So, Avis hesitated before complimenting and questioned
the wisdom of actually doing so. But he had to admit that Pellet's
sailing abilities were impressive. He had listened to Lucy's
instructions and he had learned quickly. Once she got the ball
rolling he grasped the mechanics of the sails and lines and
understood the aerodynamics of the wind and the sails. He could
factor in the currents of the water and he had the ability, if not

always the inclination, to make sound decisions required of a captain sailing a vessel that was not within sight of land. Pellet took the compliment in stride and sipped on a Red Stripe. Just one. That was another thing that impressed Avis. While Pellet almost always drank far too much, he drank almost nothing to speak of when he was out sailing. One beer, perhaps two. He took his captain responsibilities seriously. When he was on the water he absorbed the vast beauty of the sea and horizon and occasionally thanked God for all that was created. And he was sober when he did it.

"Can't believe you ever doubted me," Pellet answered as he pretended he had never given anyone a reason that they should be anxious and stressed about climbing aboard a boat with him as the captain and sailing off to the horizon. Avis smiled and didn't give the needless response.

"Heard from Lucy lately?"

"Yeah. Guess she turned down a couple more job offers. Still trying to figure out her life. Think the corporate bitch who screwed her over made her grow up a bit too much too fast. Still trying to wrap her head around it all." Pellet took another drink and a stupid grin began to crack. "Plus, I thinks she's torn between staying there and getting a job and coming back down here to hang out in a skimpy bikini on Cap'n Pellet's boat."

"Yeah, that's probably it," Avis laughed shaking his head back and forth. "I can see how a Pellet conundrum could cause her to be at a crossroads."

The truth was that Lucy was indeed at a crossroad in her life, and whether she realized it or not, Pellet was helping her choose her life direction. She had been sailing almost since birth. Her grandfather was an ex-Navy man and he had a boat on a lake up in New York since before she was born. Her father was also ex-Navy and spent much of his adult life and a fair part of her childhood on boats. Lucy took her first lake cruise at three months old and spent as much time on the lake or on a boat in the Atlantic, as most of her childhood friends spent on social media or in malls. Her sailing time lessened once she went off to college and almost disappeared while she was in grad school. She hadn't so much as given a thought to sailing after she began climbing the corporate ladder.

Then along came Pellet. An irresponsible obsessive shit-talking drinker who was as hard to shake off as a bad cold. And fate or God or the universe or whatever great power that controls such things, took ahold of her well planned out life path and twisted and turned it and her until she found herself on the deck of his boat trying to teach a supposedly ancestral sailor how to not sink his boat or anyone else's. And perhaps more importantly, she was trying to right her course across the great sea of life.

Somewhere along the line she had charted a path that was based on information she presumed to be solid. It was information provided by good meaning people who based their advice on what they were taught by other good meaning people or by life itself. As it turned out, playing the percentages and odds in life will only get you so far. She was on the fence as to whether she was glad to find out at such a young age that you can still lose even when the odds appear to weigh heavy in your favor. So, she cast away years of advice and all the odds, good and bad, and decided that she had to find her own path and only she could truly answer what the right course for her to follow was. On that first short sail from Saint Maarten to Anguilla to help Pellet bring his boat home Lucy began to realize that she had lost her way somewhere along the line. Of course realizing she was lost, was not the same as realizing how to get unlost, any more than realizing that you are drowning is the same as not drowning. But it was a start. She was pretty sure that teaching Pellet to sail was more beneficial to her than it was to him. In fact, she was certain of it. And while she was confident that he was a fast learner and he absorbed everything about sailing like a sponge, he was still Pellet. That was always a concern to just about everyone who knew him. "But he's still Pellet," was a line that would seem vague to someone who didn't know him, but crystal clear to all who did.

He had sailed at least two or three times a week since Lucy had left the island and gone back to New York. Sometimes it was just an hour or two jaunt all by himself. Other times he would bring someone along and they'd go out for a few hours. Desmund was the only member of the gang who hadn't gone out with him yet. As Desmund put it, "Oh hell no. Known Pellet lots longer den da rest of you. He's gonna have to sail for more den a couple months before he drowns me."

Even Pellet was surprised when Helmut and Fatisha went out with him for an afternoon sail. Fatisha spent the afternoon easing her way around the boat in cargo shorts and a skimpy tank-top with a brilliant pink marijuana leaf on the front of it. Her dreads hung long down to the small of her back and Pellet thought she looked like a Caribbean angel lingering about the deck of *his* Bella Vita. Helmut sat in the cockpit sipping a glass of wine and silently taking it all in and pondered what he was witnessing. It was though Pellet morphed from, for lack of a better description, Pellet, into a responsible sea-bearing adult. In the fifty-foot walk from the beach to the dinghy he transformed into an actual grown-up. As they cut through the waters with the sails full and Bella Vita steadily riding over small rolling waves, it was obvious that Pellet was knowledgeable and aware of his surroundings. He was home. From all the signs, it appeared that he was concerned for his boat and his guest. Helmut found the entire afternoon to be inspiring. Pellet split his sailing time in small conversations with both of them while attending to the sailing tasks. He pondered once the possibility of Fatisha finally falling in love with him if Helmut accidentally fell overboard, but decided the chances of the plans success were slim to none so he abandoned the idea. For the most part, he focused on the sea and Bella Vita. His new love.

His dear friends, Oscar and Iggy and their two small children took a short Saturday cruise. Iggy was comfortable with going out as long as they stayed within sight of land. What neither Oscar nor Pellet knew was that she had a local fisherman watching them through binoculars from the shore. If anything happened, he was to jump on his boat and come to the rescue. As it turned out, like Helmut, she and Oscar were amazed by the Pellet transformation. Once they pulled up anchor, he was like a born-again sea captain who cast away his wicked ways and became a *saved* man. They had known Pellet since his early days in Anguilla. Back in those days, all of the gang with the exception of Iggy and Fatisha drank like fish. In fact, most of them probably drank more than most fish. So to see Captain Pellet pulling on lines and cranking handles and trimming sails and monitoring the compass and depth finder was all quite amazing. The adults stayed up top and took in the stunning afternoon while the toddlers ran around the cabin and tried to find out what was hidden behind every tiny door on the boat.

Savannah and Avis sailed with him at least once a week during the month after Lucy had gone home. They were both cautiously happy for him, but their skepticism shrunk bit by bit each time they went out. Other than taking a ferry or sea taxi back and forth from Anguilla to Saint Maarten, Savannah had never set foot on a boat. The first time he lifted the anchor, she had a life vest strapped on tightly. She was keenly aware of how to get onto the lifeboat and she spent almost the entire time out to sea turning from one direction to the next constantly scanning the water and the horizon in search of some unseen things that they were surely going to collide with. When he dropped the anchor a hundred yards from the Sandy Ground pier a few hours later, her stress level sank as quickly as the anchor. On their next cruise she did a bit better, and a week later they repeated and she improved until she had made a transformation almost as dramatic as Pellet's. On their last trip out Avis was caught by surprise when she blurted out, "Maybe we should look for a boat. You know, one of our own."

"Don't need one," Avis shrugged. "Got this one. Right?" and looked at Pellet.

"Hell no, you don't got this one. Bella Vita is my baby. Sink your own boat," he scolded, as if Avis had no knowledge of boats or sailing. It was true Avis didn't have the sailing experience. But knowledge, there wasn't likely anyone in Anguilla as knowledgeable about most things, including sailing, than Avis Humphrey. He had read hundreds of books and retained most of the knowledge inside each one. In fact, he had read a stack of books on sailing and more books on the Endeavour model that Pellet had purchased, including the boat's technical manual. Two of the things that had struck Avis about boats is that they are referred to as *a hole in the sea to throw money into,* and if even just a few things go wrong, they can sink. Avis liked to find his adventures in books and he liked to try a lot of new things. For instance, he climbed Mt Washington in Northern New Hampshire and he liked it. With that said, once he'd done it his desire to climb mountains was fulfilled. After that, he could read a book about climbing Everest and Fuji or a hundred others and feel like he had context, but there was no driving force compelling him to go and climb them. Likewise, he sailed with Pellet and watched him deal with tons of boat stuff. He now had context to put with what he read. No need to go buy a boat.

Four months, almost to the day, after Lucy climbed off his boat for the last time, Pellet and Avis climbed aboard to make their first overnight sail on their own. Pellet had sailed over to Saint Maarten and spent the night a couple of times, but he didn't really count the ten-mile sail as anything monumental. But this was different. This time they were going to leave land behind and spend time where there was no land in sight, or where the land was nothing more than a dot on the horizon. It wasn't as if he were pulling out of the bay and heading across the Atlantic or anything on that grand scale, but they were still going to be out on the open sea on their own. The "on your own" thing was a first for Pellet. Lucy was with him the last time. Being out of sight of land for more than an hour or so was also a first for Avis. He was more aware than he wanted to be that he was putting his life in Pellet's hands. Pellet was proving to be a competent sailor and Bella Vita was a great boat, but Pellet was still Pellet.

She leaned hard to the west and then cut through the straight between tiny Scrub Island and the east end of Anguilla. In no time at all they'd be passing the east end of Saint Maarten. It was midmorning, the breezes were brisk enough to push them along. The seas were rolling, but nothing to be concerned about.

Avis smiled and looked at Pellet behind the helm.

"You've done good, Pellet."

"I know," was all he said back.

The plan was to spend one day sailing from Anguilla to Saint Barths. The second day they were to sail from Saint Barths to Saint Eustatius, and the third day they would take the long sail home. Pellet was excited. Avis was uncharacteristically nervous. Bella Vita was solid and indifferent to it all. She was built for the blue water and the blue water loved her. From lifting anchor in Sandy Ground to dropping anchor in Saint Barths took just under ten hours. They could have gone faster, but they weren't in a hurry. It was a good sail. A memorable sail. There was no rush to wrap it up. The forty-plus mile journey ended with them anchored in the same bay as Pellet had stayed at with Lucy. Once they settled in, he fired up the small grill and dropped a couple steaks over the flame. They ate, drank a few beers and looked up at the stars. Life was good.

From Saint Barths to Saint Eustatius was a bit shorter than Anguilla to Saint Barths. The day was somewhat of a repeat of the day before. The weather was perfect, the breeze was brisk, the seas were friendly and for the second day in a row, life was pretty damn good.

CHAPTER THIRTY-TWO

It was the third day of their journey when everything went to shit. The storms that had hammered the Ebony Z a couple hundred miles to the east had come and gone more than a week ago. Those particular black clouds that had slammed boat eating waves across her decks had dissipated and drifted off to wherever the winds blew them. Storms come and storms blow away and then they fade. Blue skies and star filled nights that seem to go on forever return until new clouds and storms fill the skies once again.

They spent the night in Oranjestad Bay on the south side of Saint Eustatius. The seas were calm, the winds were almost non-existent and the stars went on for an eternity. Pellet climbed out of bed at five in the morning and put on a pot of coffee. While the coffee was brewing, he dove into the water to wake up and get the day going. By the time he climbed back on deck, Avis was pouring the coffee and looking at the radar next to the plotting station. There was a small storm about an hour to the west but it didn't appear to be anything worth worrying about. Pellet thought it would pass behind them if they pulled up anchor in the next few minutes and that is precisely what they did. With the anchor up and the sails filled, the winds quickly carried them around the east end of the island. Once they rounded the point, Pellet pointed Bella Vita's bow straight north and they headed home. Other than monitoring their direction and keeping the chart updated, there really wasn't much to do for the next several hours except to sit back and enjoy the ride. At some point they'd see Saint Barths to the east. A few hours later they'd see Saint Maarten to the north. Once they skirted around Saint Maarten they'd be on the home stretch.

An hour north of Saint Eustatius there was really no need to look at the radar, but they both looked anyway. The storm that

Pellet presumed would pass south, behind them, did not do as it was instructed. The reason there was no need to look at the radar was because all they needed to do was to look towards the sky to see the dark black clouds to the west that were quickly closing in on them. The sea had only begun to kick up, but Pellet had been through a couple of these storms with Lucy. In those cases Lucy intentionally sailed straight towards them when she saw them on the radar. She wanted to make sure Pellet experienced a couple of good storms while she was with him so he would know what it felt like to be pounded by wind and rain and waves. In this instance, she would have advised him to stay put in the bay until it passed. But she was not with him and he took a calculated risk that they would skip out past the storm before it arrived. He was wrong. Lucy was right. Pellet knew what to do, but he didn't do it. "He was wrong" were words that you might not mind hearing when someone makes a mistake on dry land. They are never the words that should be uttered by the captain while out to sea.

They trimmed the jib and reefed the mainsail before the strong gusts started pounding them. With the sails adjusted and everything above and below secured and ready for a bit of a blow, Avis looked over at Pellet and wondered if he were up to the task. That's all it looked like on the radar. Just a bit of a blow. The first waves were rollers, but it wasn't long before the rollers became whitecaps. And the first winds were notable gust, but that didn't last either. Bella Vita pounded the waves for about two or three minutes and then a huge squall blasted from the west and she tipped so far that her sail almost touched the water. She immediately righted herself while Avis flailed around down below deck trying to figure out just what the hell would have possessed him to come on this trip. He'd read books about sailing and he had sailed. That should have been enough. Whatever loyalty had pushed him towards sailing with Pellet disappeared along with the blue skies. Five or six more waves slammed against the hull and then another mighty gust pushed her over again. Avis swore some more and cursed Pellet for buying the damn boat. Meanwhile, Pellet was at the helm with his harness attached to a tether that was secured to the boat. He had it tied off short enough so he didn't get tossed overboard each time she laid on her side. If it hadn't been raining so hard, he still wouldn't have been able to tell where the clouds ended as there was no blue sky within sight in any direction. The rain was coming down so hard that he could barely see the bow each time it dove under a wave and then came back up and readied to do it again. Unlike the gusts of wind that came and went, the fury of the rain came down in a wall of water and just kept coming. For over half an hour the waves pounded, the wind slammed, and the rain nearly drowned him. Then an hour passed. Then an hour and a half. Pellet was stuck in the storm and couldn't get out. He had turned almost straight into the waves so they didn't swamp them each time they slammed over the bow and over the deck, but the dark grey skies, the winds and the thrashing sea kept ahold of Bella Vita. Wherever the storm went, they went.

"Avis," he yelled below. "Look at the radar. Are we close to getting out of this?"

"Still right in the middle of it. Moving east pretty fast."

"I'm starting the engine. Going to try to motor to the west and break free." With that, Pellet slammed the door closed and turned the key and the diesel engine roared. He gave it less than a minute to warm up before he began to push the throttle forward until it was pushing the boat through the storm as fast as it was going to go. The rain continued to come down so hard that he still couldn't tell whether he was being hit by the rain or the waves. As she ran faster and faster, her bow buried further under the relentless waves she was heading straight into. Two more massive gusts of wind grabbed her and pitched her over. As the boat got pounded and bounced, he could hear the propeller coming out of the water searching for something to push against. After another fifteen minutes, that seemed like hours, Avis yelled up from below.

"You're making headway, Pellet. We're heading towards the edge of the storm." The words were reassuring, but for the moment they were just words. It wasn't that Pellet didn't believe him, it was just that all he could still see were dark skies and waves and rain and feel the wind pounding on the reefed sail. He pushed on the throttle in hopes that it would go a bit faster but she was giving all she had to give. Another pounding wave, another slamming gust, then there was more rain. And then, just like that, it began to die down. In less than two minutes they sailed from what felt like hell on top of the sea to calming seas and easing winds with light rain. Off in the distance there was a tinge of blue sky. He pulled back on the throttle about halfway and for the first time in almost two hours, Pellet drew a sigh of relief. Avis, white with nausea and fear, poked his head up from below. "We gonna live?" he asked, hoping for a bit of humorous reassurance.

"Seems so," Pellet answered with a stupid grin. He reached into his pocket and put a soaking wet cigarette in his lips. There was no chance it was going to light, but he put it there anyway. Avis stepped outside and the rain continued to lighten as they looked at each other. They both waited for the other to say something that a seasoned sailor might say after riding through what they were certain was something comparable to riding out a hurricane. It wasn't.

"Well, that was fun," Pellet started to say, but he didn't get the chance to finish. The two things the storm had lacked for the entire adventure, up to that point in time, was thunder and lightning. And even then when it finally did explode, there was only one single strike. One measly crack of thunder and one lonely lightning strike in an entire two-hour storm. And that single strike flashed from the top of the mast out into eternity and back. Pellet and Avis were momentarily stunned and struggled to figure out what had just happened. The storm had appeared to be over. Then there was a blinding and deafening explosion. A few seconds later the smell of smoke began to waft through the air. For a second, maybe two, they both stood like statues staring at the surprised looks on each other's faces. Then almost simultaneously they both said, "Oh shit!"

Pellet spun in circles looking up at the mast and around the deck to see if anything was on fire. Avis jumped below to look for flames. The first thing he did was to grab the fire extinguisher and pull the pin and readied it to aim and spray. All the electrical devices at the plotting station were smoking, but none seemed to be on fire. The radar, the depth finder, the radio, the battery monitor, the handheld radio in the charger, the phone plugged into the charger, they were all smoking to one degree or another. The phone cord was completely melted into what looked like a black piece of spaghetti. The screen of the phone had turned to some sort of odd glowing greenish color. The engine died the moment the lightning struck. Pellet climbed down and opened the door to the engine room. It was the same as the electronics. A lot of smoke. If he had inspected the room thoroughly he would have found miles of melted black spaghetti wires. But the good news was that there were no flames. Lightening it seemed had done its damage and gone along its way along with the rest of the storm.

Above deck, beyond the slightly chard mast and the hobbled boat that was left adrift in the Caribbean Sea, the skies were blue and the seas were calm. The contrast between the sound of the howling wind, waves and rain and the roar of the engine being suddenly replaced with almost nothing but the sound of small waves lapping against the side of the boat and the sail flapping in the gentle breeze, left both of them in an eerie state of mild shock. Mother nature had spun a tiny bit of excitement and then moved along on her way with complete indifference. All was quiet and good and right with the world once again. Except of course that their engine and all their navigational equipment, other than their compass, were burnt up and useless, and they had no way to reach anyone on land.

"Do you remember more or less where we were on the radar the last time you looked at it?" Pellet asked Avis as he reached in the ice box and pulled out two beers.

"No. Not really. I was focused on the storm on the screen and trying to figure out if we were ever coming out of it and wondering whether or not we were going to die," Avis answered. He was still a bit more rattled than he thought he would be if a storm kicked up. "Hell man. That shit was real."

"Yes it was," Pellet answered and passed him a beer. "We were heading north before the storm. Got pushed east, but I'm not really sure how far. I don't think we made any headway west when I ran the engine. At best, we stayed in place as the storm passed. We'll point it to the northwest for a bit and keep our eyes open for land. If we screw up and go too far west, well sooner or later we'll hit Puerto Ricco. If we go too far east, it's a long damn way to Canada," he said as if sailing to Canada was far away, but a possibility.

Avis plopped down and looked down at the table in silence and tried to piece things together. He finally looked up at Pellet and said, "I think I need a shot of rum. Need something to calm the nerves. Don't think a Red Stripe is going to do the job." Pellet laughed at him and reached into the cupboard and grabbed the bottle of Appleton Rum and tossed it to him.

"Got to go and point us in the right direction. Think we're heading the wrong way."

Pellet was still holding it together. The lightning rattled him for a bit, but only for a bit. He quickly regained his composure and stepped up and began to act like the Captain of Bella Vita. It was time to continue their voyage home.

CHAPTER THIRTY-THREE

It was quite a few hours later when things got worse.

"What the hell was that?" Avis yelled as he scurried up the stairs and out of the cabin. He half ran and half crawled to the rear of the boat where Pellet stood looking down at the water.

"Double Slug Bug," was his three-word response. Avis glared at him and waited for more information that did not come.

"What?"

"A Double Slug Bug. You know, a Volkswagen bus. Double Slug Bug." He smoked his cigarette and calmly looked at the water behind the boat like he was waiting for a dolphin to come back up to the surface. He said nothing more as he presumed Avis was fully up to speed.

"What the hell are you talking about?" Avis yelled. They were sailing in over a thousand feet of water, miles from any dry land. Avis was sitting at the chart table wondering if Pellet had any idea where they were heading or was he just taking a wild guess when he set their course for north/northwest and let the sails out. He had almost convinced him that Captain Pellet had things under control when something slammed into the bottom of the boat. The impact was jolting enough and the crash was loud enough to be a car accident, but that seemed highly unlikely fifteen or twenty miles or more from the nearest land. Whether an auto accident was unlikely, or perhaps better stated, impossible, Pellet claimed they were hit by a VW bus while they were sailing in the Caribbean Sea. Avis was convinced that his beloved captain was delusional and he was confident that they were not just involved in a hit and run.

"Have you lost your mind?" he snapped.

"It was two toned. You know, red on the bottom and white on the top. Pretty typical of how they painted the old ones." Pellet took a puff on his cigarette and continued to look at the water. Avis looked too and saw nothing but water. "It had flowers painted all over it. You know, like the flower power stuff from the 60's. And a big blue peace sign on the front of it. I saw the peace sign just before it went under," he said it all matter-of-factly as if he were describing a cool bus that had just driven past. Avis stopped staring at the water and began staring at Pellet. After what seemed to be an eternity, he glanced back down at the sea and then back at Pellet again.

"Pellet, there's no bus in the water. I mean... a bus? What are you even talking about, man?" he mumbled again. Avis had spent the last few hours trying to regroup after the lightning strike. He suddenly thought it might be possible that perhaps Pellet hadn't handled the stress as calmly as he had appeared to. On the other hand, they had definitely just been run into by something.

"Hey. I saw what I saw. I was standing at the helm and felt something hit us. I ran back here and saw the big white roof all covered with flower power shit. Then the back of the bus sunk and the front popped up like a bottle that was filling up with water. It had a big peace sign stuck up into the air for a few seconds before it went under. Then... gone. It sunk and didn't come back up."

"A VW bus floating around the Caribbean? I mean," he paused and searched for the right words. "A fucking VW bus Pellet?" he yelled again.

"Slug Bug. It's a game we played whenever the family took trips when I was a kid. A VW Beetle was a slug bug and a bus was a double slug bug. One point or two, you know, depending which it was. Whoever called it out first got the points." Pellet told his story as calmly as if he were describing a seagull that had just landed on the bow of the boat. "Double Slug Bug, by the way. Two points for me."

Avis slowly took a three-hundred-and-sixty-degree panoramic view of nothing but water. "Where the hell would a Double Slug Bug come from out here?" he asked without realizing he had just more or less accepted Pellet's version of hitting the bus. Just as the question flowed from his mouth he saw something shiny float to the surface. It looked like a sun reflector that goes in a windshield. Then a Styrofoam cooler popped up. The lid was still on it. "Sonofabitch," he mumbled in acknowledgement that they were probably just hit by a VW bus.

"Maybe they got stoned and went for a drive to the sea," Pellet answered with a stupid grin on his face.

The red and white 1967 VW bus tattooed with flowers all over and a bright blue peace sign on the nose, with dozens of stickers on the back that Pellet did not see, had come from a lot of places. Its journey began in Topeka, Kansas, in 1967 when Seth Cohen's grandparents gave it to him to go travel for a while before heading off to college. His first journey took him to San Francisco to experience the epicenter of the Peace, Love and Rock n' Roll religion that swept across America in the 60's. From there he spent over a year traveling from California to Chicago and Detroit and down to Miami and eventually up to New England before working his way back down to New York. In August of 1969 the van took eight of them to Woodstock New York for a long, memorable weekend. He held onto it through the college years and beyond, and in those early years the bus had been a part of almost every memorable piece of his life. At some point in time when he was teaching at Syracuse University, he came to realize that the VW would be with him forever.

Shortly before retiring three years ago, Seth had the van restored to its original glory, with the exception that the memorabilia such as the flower stickers and the giant peace sign had to stay. A year after he retired he shipped it to England and spent almost two years touring Europe. In over five decades, Seth and the Double Slug Bug had gone from the heartland of America to the Pacific, to the Gulf of Mexico and then over to the east coast and up the Atlantic coastline. They had been to New York City. They'd traveled to London, Paris and a hundred other places. From California deserts to the Grand Canyon to the Swiss mountain tops. They'd traveled from epic concerts in Hamburg to a Jewish concentration camp in Austria to Puerta del Sol in

Madrid. Seth and the bus had seen and done more than he had ever dreamed possible way back when it all began. After two years of traveling throughout Europe, he decided that it was time to head home and get some rest. His plan was that he would fly to LA to pick up the flower powered VW and make one final grand trip driving down to Mexico and then from Veracruz, to Anchorage, Alaska. The Gulf of Mexico, to the Gulf of Alaska. From there he would journey back to Syracuse, where he would drive it only when he needed to get groceries. For over half a century he travelled and kept detailed logs of where he had traveled to, when he had gone to the places and who his companions had been. Sometimes the logs were almost poetic and meticulously detailed. Sometimes they looked like a sea captains log on a Navy ship. Other times they were nothing more than scribbled notes that said things like, "January something, 1968. Hanging out with group of cool people I met at Cocoa Beach for a few more days, then heading up the coast."

But that was a long time ago and it was all, including Europe, behind Seth and the van now. A few weeks before it ran into Bella Vita, Seth turned his beloved VW over to a shipping company who carefully loaded the van into an almost full shipping container. In fact, it was the last thing to go in and get secured before the heavy steel doors were closed, latched, locked and sealed. A few days later the container was loaded onto the Ebony Z and set a course heading directly into the intersecting point of three thunderstorms in the southwestern waters of the Atlantic Ocean.

As fate would have it, the container carrying the VW was not the first or last to be swept off the deck. It crashed onto containers already in the water, and others crashed on top of it. Only the doors of one single container blew wide open in the cold dark waters on that day. When they did, a red and white VW bus with brilliantly colored flowers and a blue peace sign painted on the front of it and dozens of stickers stuck to its back window floated to the surface and began to methodically drift in the waters of the Caribbean Sea. Even though Seth would never know what happened to his bus, he would have been inspired to find out that it's final journey after running into a beautiful sailboat, was to drift to the bottom of the Caribbean Sea and become a sanctuary for sea life.

And as much as Seth didn't know about the end of the story, Pellet and Avis had no knowledge of the beginnings of its story. But a few minutes later, while standing back at the helm and laughing about what had just happened, Pellet realized that the VW might not be the only thing that sunk to the bottom of the sea. Bella Vita was beginning to veer slightly off course and he turned to bring her nose slightly to the west.

"Sonofabitch," he mumbled.

"What's the matter now?"

"I think the rudder is gone. She's not turning," Pellet answered. Avis ran his fingers through his hair and tried to get a grip on everything that was happening. He climbed below into the cabin to pull himself together and fight off any impending panic.

"We're taking on water," he screamed. "Fuck. Pellet, we're taking on water!"

"Well... that's not good," was Pellet's monotone response.

CHAPTER THIRTY-FOUR

Not all news was bad news. The good news was that Avis had pretty much memorized the maintenance and owner's manuals for the Endeavour. He knew where the rudder came into the boat, what it was connected to, how its mechanics worked, and most importantly, he knew where the water was probably coming into the boat. The other good news was that it didn't bother Pellet one bit that he was going to have to dive overboard in water over a thousand feet deep and so far from land that they couldn't even see it. He was perfectly fine trying to plug the hole that was draining the ocean and filling his boat. He snapped on his harness, tied a fifty-foot rope to it and tied the other end off to one of the cleats on the deck. Then overboard he went. Less than thirty seconds later he popped back up above the surface.

"Props gone too," he called up from the water.

"What?" Avis answered, not really grasping what he was being told.

"The propeller and shaft. Both gone."

"And the rudder?"

"Gone."

"Shit. You see any holes in the bottom?"

"Just the two where there's supposed to be a propeller and a rudder." Pellet was still as composed as he was after running into the red and white VW bus in the middle of the Caribbean Sea. Avis couldn't decide if he was the bravest man he'd ever known, or maybe he just didn't grasp the danger that they were in. "You might want to put the dinghy down in the water. You know. Just in case," he called out just before diving back under the water. And with that comment, Avis watched with amazement as Pellet's feet popped into the air and he began kicking to push himself back under the boat.

Pellet drank too much on a regular basis. He overreacted to just about every stressful situation that ever came up. He put his foot in his mouth nearly every time he attempted to talk to a woman. But when he was on the sea, he was as cool as a cucumber and as calm as a sloth. Nothing seemed to fluster him. Once again Avis found himself curious as to whether or not there might actually be a sailing gene that was handed down through the centuries. He was nothing short of amazed by Pellet's composure.

His head popped up above the surface and he grabbed a few breaths and dove back under to do whatever he was doing. Avis, the guy who was usually the go to guy when things were going to shit, patiently fiddled with the lines on the dinghy and readied it to be lowered while he waited for Pellet to diagnose the boat issues and get out of the way so he could drop the dinghy down.

"Hey. Go down below and grab those rolls of Rescue Tech tape in the cabinet next to the door of the engine room." Before Avis could ask why, Pellet was gone under again. For the next half hour he had Avis break off pieces of the putty-like tape and roll it into balls and hand it down to him. One piece at a time Pellet took the golf balls size chunks of putty and stuffed them into holes that previously had other pieces of the boat filling them. And with each piece he stuffed in, the water slowed from a full flowing hole, to a trickle, to a drip, and then to nothing at all, at least for the moment.

That of course was just issue number one. The second issue was that the boat had a bilge pump and a pretty hardy one at that. Unfortunately, it was an electric pump, meaning Bella Vita no longer had a hardy bilge working pump to pump the water out of the inside of the boat. What it did have was a much smaller manually operating pump with a handle that attached to a socket in the cockpit. If the putty held up, and the *"if"* was a very real word, it would take a few hours of non-stop pumping to get rid of the water that had already flowed in through the holes into the cabin. If the putty didn't hold up, well, then they were screwed.

They had dropped the front sail again and lowered the

mainsail halfway while they worked on the leaks. Now that they were ready to move again, they raised the sails, corrected their course as best as they could without a rudder and headed to what they hoped was home.

"After you let the dinghy down and tie it off, get me a beer and I'll take the first shift," Pellet said and sat down and started pumping. "I think we should switch off every fifteen minutes or so. We're going to have to keep up a pretty good pace of pumping for quite a while if we want to make any headway." Avis just nodded in obedience and dropped the boat into the water and tied it off to the back of the boat. Then he hopped into it and put the drain plug in so it wouldn't fill with water and climbed back up onto the boat with Pellet. A few seconds later he trudged through six inches of water in the cabin and climbed back up into the cockpit and handed Pellet a beer.

"I gotta tell you, seeing water inside the boat freaks me out."

"Well," Pellet pondered how to answer. "It's not a good thing," was all he had.

For the next two hours they sailed and pumped and sailed and pumped. Pellet uncharacteristically had three beers but justified it as replenishing his stamina as they continued to take turns at their fifteen-minute workouts. With all the water she was carrying, Bella Vita sat low in the water and sailed unusually slow. Neither of them mentioned it, but they were both concerned that they saw almost no difference in the water level since they began pumping. At just about the time Pellet considered diving back under the boat to see if the plugs were still holding, the water began to show its first signs of receding.

"Your turn," Pellet said and stood up and walked over and began to pee over the side of the boat. "Guess we won't forget this trip any time soon."

"Jesus Christ. Superman wouldn't forget this trip, Pellet." Avis shook his head back and forth and once again tried to figure out how he ended up out here with the most unreliable guy he knew. Then he laughed and shook his head again. "I wouldn't have missed this for the world. I mean, let's be honest. We're probably the only two guys in the universe who have ever been out sailing and got hit by a Double Slug Bug."

"Go big or stay at home. That's my motto." Pellet laughed and added a disclaimer. "Of course I should mention that I've crashed and burned a bunch of times, but this one may have taken first prize."

"Let's go home Pellet." Avis said as he picked up the pace of pumping and thought about being on dryland sometime soon.

CHAPTER THIRTY-FIVE

Depending on how they looked at it, the first problem they had was to get the water out of the cabin. The second was they had no rudder to steer with. On the other hand, the no rudder thing might be a bigger issue than the water since there was a solution to the water problem. The only thing they could do about not having a rudder was to try to sail north by using the sails as best as they could. It was something that an experienced sailor would have probably been pretty good at. Too bad they didn't have one of them on board with them.

After another hour the water inside the cabin was pretty much gone. There was no doubt that plenty still sloshed around under the floorboards, but they were both worn out and decided to go with the idea of out of sight, out of mind. The pumping had slowed down to just a tad more than a standstill. Avis sat for a half hour and pumped once every ten or fifteen seconds. They were both too tired to even make small talk. Neither of them cared to ponder what had happened over the past few hours. Pellet sat and watched and slowly dragged on a cigarette that looked heavy hanging from his lips. Eventually he took a final puff and tossed it overboard.

"My turn," Pellet mumbled and slid over to take over the weak pumping duties. "Go get some rest. It'll be dark in an hour or two and I'm guessing we're not sleeping much tonight." Avis just nodded and stumbled down the steps and wandered into the berth where he collapsed onto the bed. One of the hatches was open and a breeze blew through the cabin from the bow all the way out the back door. He lazily dozed half awake and half asleep and dreamt about better days. He dreamt of fishing for brook trout in New Hampshire with his friend Leo. He dreamt of sitting by a campfire in New Hampshire with Leo and Savannah and tossing empty PBR cans into the flames. He dreamt of kissing and making love to Savannah at the lake in New Hampshire. He dreamt of...

"What the hell was that!" he screamed and jumped up so fast he slammed his head on the ceiling. The VW sounded like something big had crashed against the boat but this... this made the VW hit and run seem like a fender bender. This felt like they had just been broadsided by a train or a cruise ship. The VW had sounded and felt like someone had wound up and beat the hull with a sledgehammer but this crash jolted the boat so hard that he felt them change course and he immediately thought whatever it was must have punctured the bottom of the boat. Avis ignored the fact that he had slammed his head on the ceiling and began running through the cabin towards the stairs. Halfway to the back everything began to spin and he stumbled and landed on the polished teak tabletop. Whatever they had run into took an eternity to go by as the horrific crashing sound started at the bow and seemingly crashed against every inch of the hull, bow to stern. He laid on the table and listened and waited for the sound of water to come gushing into the cabin. The room stopped spinning almost as fast as it began and he felt a trickle of blood run down his forehead.

For a moment he grasped the idea that they might have hit land but then wondered just how long he had been sleeping. Then he wondered if they had struck a reef or some other sort of rock formation that was nothing more than a cruel joke from mother nature just to remind sailors that she did not care who lived or died out in the middle of one of her big beautiful seas. Avis struggled to his feet and continued his journey above deck and found Pellet standing in the same spot he had found him when he was looking at the VW. It turned out that he hadn't slept for more than fifteen or twenty minutes. It would be dark in an hour or so, but not yet.

"Don't tell me we hit another car," he yelled out, literally meaning, don't tell me we hit another car.

"Nah. Container," Pellet said and motioned to something floating behind Bella Vita. The faded yellow shipping container covered with rust and barnacles, floated by with the same grand indifference that fueled mother nature. The container meant no harm and held no malice towards their vessel any more than mother nature did. They just happened to be traveling on the same path in the same universe at the same moment in time in opposite directions. These things happen. It had lagged behind the VW almost ever since they washed off the deck of the Ebony Z. As it turned out, they both bumped into and said hello to Bella Vita and then continued on their way. The container already looked as if it were struggling to stay afloat. It probably wouldn't be long before it joined its Double Slug Bug friend.

"What the..." was all Avis could muster. It seemed impossible that they had run into a bus. The possibility that they would run into a bus and a container would seem less likely than winning the lottery. While he watched the yellow container drift away as Bella Vita eased forward through the blue water, a thought popped into his head.

"Shit!" he blurted out and sprinted towards the bow of the boat. He stepped around the front edge of the sail and grabbed ahold of the steel cable that ran to the top of the mast and scanned the water for anything that was not water or a fish. First he started looking at the water directly in front of the bow. Not that it would have done any good other than to yell, "Hold on!" if there was something just a few feet in front of them. His eyes scanned back and forth and with each scan he worked further and further from the boat. Once he felt momentarily safe, he climbed back around the jib sail, ran back to the cockpit, climbed down into the cabin and grabbed the binoculars that were hanging on a hook next to the smoke charred plotting station. A couple seconds later he was back up the stairs, down the deck, around the sail, and searching for any more sea hazards that may be floating their way. He was mentally tired and physically exhausted. The little rest he got while sleeping was pretty much expended by waking up. Avis Humphrey, the guy who was always steady and always calm was fraying around the edges. He wasn't a guy filled with regrets. He didn't have time for them. He wasn't a guy who prayed for help. He didn't feel the need for it. But standing on the bow of Bella

Vita scanning the horizon for more sea litter that could literally be the difference between life and death, he began to regret coming on the voyage. And he caught himself saying a small prayer to the god he didn't believe in. "Please God. If you get me back to dry land, I'll never sail with this idiot again."

He hung the binoculars around his neck by its nylon strap and slowly began working his way to the cockpit to rejoin Pellet. His posture was slouched and his steps were small and slow. His feet barely lifted off the deck as he meandered towards the back with the look of a beaten man. The thirty-foot journey felt like a mile walk down a hot dusty dirt road. Avis slid onto the cushioned seat and set the binoculars down beside him.

"Well, that went well," Pellet grumbled. It was a desperate attempt at lighthearted sarcasm. Neither of them thought it was funny. Avis reached into the pocket of his cargo shorts and pulled out a pack of cigarettes and lit one. Pellet reached out and Avis tossed the pack in his general direction. They both sat and silently smoked as the wind carried them north-ish. Then there was a new noise.

The sound was a loud pop, but not like they had hit something. This was not a crashing sound. It was clearly one very loud pop that came from inside the boat. They looked at each other both half expecting the other to have the answer. Then they both leaned forward without standing up and looked down into the cabin to see if perhaps somebody was down below who they had forgotten about. Moments later there was another similar but a bit quieter popping noise that again came from inside the cabin. Right after that there was a loud taring noise that sounded as if the boat was being torn in two by some force that was strong enough to actually tear a boat in half. Immediately after that sound there was a whooshing sound and Bella Vita went from sitting about five feet deep in the water to about one foot deep, and she began to slowly tip.

"Ohhhhh, fuuuuck," Avis said in a speed that matched the slow tipping boat.

"What's happening?" Pellet asked. It was the first time he

had shown the least sign of panic.

"Your 14,500-pound keel is probably about halfway to the bottom of the sea right now."

"What do you mean?"

"The keel broke off, Pellet. It's no longer attached to the boat. It's gone to join the VW. It's…"

"Yeah. I get it," he snapped back. "Now what?" he asked as if Avis had just become the captain.

"Now the boat tips over and sinks and we climb into the lifeboat and watch it sink."

"Are you sure?" Pellet asked, hoping there was a shred of hope.

"The keel is the great big heavy piece of lead that was connected to the bottom of the boat. Its job was to keep the boat from tipping over. Once it's gone, the mast that's sticking fifty feet up into the air becomes the big heavy thing. The biggest, heaviest thing always determines the bottom of the boat. So in answer to your question, the top of the boat just became heavier than the bottom. In a few minutes, the mainsail is going to become the new keel. Yeah. I'm sure."

"A simple yes would have been enough, dickhead," Pellet snapped back. Avis shrugged.

They sat in shock for about five seconds. The boat stopped slowly leaning further and further to the starboard side and began to rapidly tip further and further to the starboard side. Then, as if they had been struck by lightning again, they both kicked into gear and prepared for what was coming. Bella Vita was going down.

"Untie the dinghy and stay right next to the boat," Pellet yelled and headed down into the cabin. Ten seconds later he scurried up the stairs that were leaning over far enough that they were going to start taking on water at any moment. He tossed a small orange bag that said "First-Aid" on the side to Avis. Right after that he tossed one that said, "Emergency Kit." By the time Avis caught them and tucked them away, Pellet was back down below. Seconds later he came back up with a case of water and tossed it like it was the one pound first aid kit. Avis tried to catch it but it had been thrown too hard and too far away from him. He barely laid a finger on it before it hit the water. As it turned out, a case of water sinks as soon as it hits water. He whipped back around and Pellet cringed at what he had just done, then headed back into the cabin. Water was pouring through the doorway.

There were several cases of water on the boat but only one that was easily accessible. He just threw that one into the sea. The others were stowed in a closet towards the front of the boat. Bella Vita was laying completely on her side and taking on water. Pellet glanced towards the doorway but he knew they needed drinking water. If they had nothing else, they needed water. He grabbed the closet door handle, but it wouldn't open. With all the twisting and turning and pieces breaking off the boat it had jammed closed. He gave it a ferocious yank and then stood waist deep in water with a knob in his hand that was no longer connected to the door. Bella Vita had passed the point of laying on its side. The mainsail was beginning to go under and Pellet envisioned what Avis had only moments ago described. The mast was about to become the keel.

Avis was still outside trying to hold onto the boat, but she was sinking. In a few more seconds he was going to have to push off or go down with her.

"Pellet! Get out here!" he yelled. "She's going down!" He waited for three more seconds and let go of the line in his hand but stayed as close as he could. The cabin door was completely submerged and there was still no sign of Pellet. "Jesus Christ," he whispered, either to nobody in particular or to Jesus Christ himself. This couldn't be happening. Pellet couldn't go down with the ship. He couldn't be alone on a twelve-foot Zodiac all by himself in the middle of the Caribbean.

Pellet was frantic. He had no intention of going down with the ship, but he couldn't believe he carried a case of water out and tossed it into the sea. He was trying desperately to fix his screw up. Sometimes he felt like his entire life was a series of screw ups that he just never got right. Jobs, relationships, drinking. You name it and he'd screwed it up and had never fixed any of them. This one fucking time he wanted to make it right. Bella Vita was nearly full of water and he knew time had run out. With no knob in place he wasn't able to pull on the closet door. He grabbed something floating right in front of him and stuck it in his shirt and headed for the exit, but he had pushed it just a bit too far. The back of the boat began going down which meant he had to swim down to get out and he had to get out to swim back up. He was astonished how quickly the inside of the boat got so dark that he could barely see where he was going. He swam almost straight down and grabbed onto things along the way to help work his way to the doorway. He was almost there when he realized he was out of air and he wasn't sure he was going to make it. With one last lunge, he pushed himself outside and grabbed onto the first thing he reached. He yanked with all his might and pulled himself towards the surface. Ten feet later his forehead slammed dead center into the steel mast and split a deep two-inch gash into his forehead. Out of breath and disoriented he fought the urge to breath, but it was too late. Water began to pour into his lungs and he floated not aware if he was going up or down. Everything became quiet and his energy was gone. It was done, and he knew it. This screw up was his last screw up. There was no more fight. No more smartass comments or stupid grins or double shots of rum that were going to make this a distant memory. He thought he would have been more scared or more confused or more something. But he wasn't. He was just done with it all, and he wasn't sure if that was good or bad. Everything had gone hazy and quiet. A strange sort of stillness began to consume him. Then something happened. Something, or someone grabbed his hair and pulled him straight up until he was above the water. Avis leaned over the edge of the dinghy as far as he could without falling overboard and pulled Pellet to the surface.

"Jesus Christ," he said again, either to Pellet or to Jesus Christ. "Who the hell stops swimming two feet from the surface?"

Pellet looked up at him with blood streaming into his eyes and down his face. He was coughing water and choking, but Avis knew that was a good sign. "Am I going to live?" Pellet asked. He had momentarily made peace with the end and he was a little confused that the end hadn't come.

"What is wrong with you? Who goes back into a sinking boat?"

"Wanted to get some water. You know. Since I threw the first case overboard."

"Ohhh. How'd that work out?"

"Pellet held the rope on the side of the Zodiac and reached into his shirt and pulled out a bottle. "Got some rum," he said with a stupid grin on his bloody face. He was not dead. He was still Pellet. And they still didn't have any water.

Avis reached down and grabbed him by the back of his shirt and pulled him in. Pellet laid on the bottom of the dinghy looking straight into the sky. "You might want to see this," Avis said. Pellet struggled to sit up and watched the nose of Bella Vita point straight to the sky and slip away to the abyss. They both sat and looked at the empty sea without saying a word for a long time.

"You know," Pellet began. "On TV there's always a bunch of shit floating around and they say things like "there was debris scattered where the boat went down." There's not shit here. Nothing floating around. No debris. What's up with that?"

Avis looked at him and tilted his head while he searched for a response. He put his hand to his face and rubbed his chin and then eventually ran his fingers through his hair. "What is wrong with you, man?" he finally asked.

"What?" was all Pellet could come up with.

Pellet laid back down on the bottom of the boat and pressed on his gash and tried to stop the bleeding. Avis looked around. As far as he could see in every direction was nothing but water, water, and more water. He looked down at Pellet and then picked up the first aid kit and pulled out a four-inch piece of gauze and handed it to him.

"We're adrift at sea, Pellet."

"What do you mean?"

"You know, like in the movies or books when a ship goes down and only two guys survive. We're in deep shit Pellet. That's what I mean. We're adrift at sea."

"You're kind of a downer, man. We're in a boat in the Caribbean and have a bottle of rum. That's how I look at it," he said and glanced at the bloody piece of gauze in his hand before he pressed it harder against his head.

Avis looked at him and searched for the right response. After a momentary struggle, he simply shook his head back and forth and said nothing. Pellet, unfazed by nearly everything other than throwing the water overboard and the gash in his head continued to press the bandage against the bloody cut. Then, as if a light had just come on in his typically dark attic, he sat up and looked at Avis. Then he looked towards the spot where his boat was sitting a few minutes earlier. Avis watched as Pellet continued to hold the bandage on his head and his mouth began to hang open. It appeared their situation was beginning to sink in. "You okay, Pellet?"

"Fifty-five fucking thousand dollars. Do you know how long it took me to save that much money? Seven years. That's how long," he answered without waiting for a response. Avis shook his head again. Pellet still didn't seem to realize that they might die out here. "I've got like three thousand dollars left. And an old piece of shit truck."

"Well. We're still alive," Avis responded. "For the time being," he added.

"Wonder if any of my ancestors did anything like this?"

"I don't suppose any of them were hit by a Double Slug Bug."

"Man," Pellet said as he continued to stare at the empty boat spot. "That was a lot of money to send to the bottom of the sea." They both stopped talking and watched the empty boat spot, as if there were a slim chance that it might come bouncing back. It didn't. "You interested in buying me a new boat?" It was a bold question that Pellet would have never asked under normal circumstances, but he was in mild shock over the realization that his life savings was gone. It being gone was magnified by yet another fact, which was it was the first time in his life that he had ever had a life savings, or any savings at all.

"That's like asking me to buy you another bullet to play Russian Roulette because the first one misfired," Avis answered.

"That a yes or a no?"

"How in God's name did I ever let you talk me into going to sea with you?"

"I'm a natural born leader. People follow me," Pellet said, as if he almost believed his own words, while he continued to watch the empty fifty-five-thousand-dollar spot in the sea. "So, you going to buy me another boat, or what?" he asked and looked straight at Avis.

Avis, in a rare loss of words simply drew a long deep breath, reached down and unscrewed the cap on the bottle of rum and took a drink before handing it to Pellet.

He held the bottle but didn't take a drink for a long time. For one of the few times in his life he was aware of things around him and he didn't like it. Somehow being in the dark was better than facing reality. The reality was that while he made plenty of his own misery when it came to his day to day malfunctions, the big ones where the deep scars were permanently burned into his soul were somehow outside of his control. Zoe wrecked him in ways that he still could not fully comprehend and for the most part all he had done was to fall in love and marry her. That was the first deep wound. And this time, he had done almost everything correctly. He made sure he bought a decent boat and had Avis verify it before he made the move. Then he learned how to sail. He studied and practiced skills and hired a professional to make sure he did everything right. But Mother Nature and some floating sea litter unleashed themselves on the Bella Vita. Once again, Pellet was broke and discouraged and wondering what he had ever done to the universe to be treated like this. Finally, he broke his gaze from the empty spot, sat up straight and took a sip of rum. "Well, Lucy said that the sea could be randomly vicious. Seems like a hell of a lot of random kicked our ass today."

CHAPTER THIRTY-SIX

Being Mossad was like being in the CIA or MI-6 but it was nothing like being James Bond. The planning stage for most missions dwarf their actual execution. And the execution of the plan almost never goes exactly as it is supposed to. All in all, Shira found that being a spy was quite boring. Once the planning was done, the actual preparation of the mission often took weeks of putting people in place where they did mundane jobs that gave them access to the alleged bad people who were being spied on, or set up, or simply harassed. If there was an actual execution stage, she didn't ever see it happen.

She had been trained in Mossad for a little more than a year and then planted in a couple different offices for a few weeks at different times to gather intelligence and report back to the more important people. It was safe work for the most part, and she had no idea if the information she provided was helpful or not. Her intel included intriguing tidbits like, "Ali leaves the office at 12:00 every day for lunch and returns at 12:45." There were other people she watched and other information she shared, but it was all the same. She was not Angelina Jolie or Charlize Theron kicking down doors and shooting people with guns that had silencers and never-ending ammo. Her job was to type on her laptop, do office work, be friendly, take mental notes and pass those notes on to her superiors in a preset process that was dictated by higher ups who had a job as boring as hers. With almost no exceptions, if anything exciting ever happened that was related to her spy work, she never heard about it. Information she gathered was put into peoples "permanent files" and kept in some big electronic vault, likely to never be seen again.

Early in her second disappointing year as a female James Bond wannabe, Shira was assigned to yet one more office job performing more unremarkable tasks. She was the head office girl at a strawberry farm close to the Israeli-Palestinian border. The owner was Jewish, but the bulk of the workforce was Palestinian. With few exceptions the workers were of no interest to the Israeli government. There were, however, two men who had caught the eye of somebody who reported them to somebody else who filled out forms that put them on a list that got the ball rolling. Two more possible enemies of the state were now officially in the game, whether they knew it or not.

Yasser and Rashid were cousins who worked in the office and helped manage the fieldworker's schedules, pay and any other administrative stuff that needed to be handled. Ghalia was a young Palestinian woman who answered the phone and ran errands and was mostly in the office because the Jewish owner insisted that a young woman from Palestine work along with a young woman from Israel. Shira handled calls and interactions with most of the Israelis, and Ghalia did the same for the Palestinians. The two women not only filled administrative duties, but they also acted as ambassadors of sorts. Tensions between the Jewish owner and the two Palestinian men were often heightened, but Shira and Ghalia both shared a gift for lightening the mood and snuffing out any harmful sparks that could lead to flames. And just like the previous jobs where she had been assigned, Shira was to monitor and report back on Yasser and Rashid. For good measure, whomever did the original paperwork added Ghalia's name to the list, but Shira presumed that her name was simply added because she happened to be there and for no other good reason. She would likely never know that she now had her own "permanent record."

This particular morning was no different than any other. Jacob Friedman came in grumbling a nonstop slur of words that nobody could really hear, but they all understood. *The workers were coming in late. They were working slow. He was going to go bankrupt if things kept on like this. How could these workers be so ungrateful while he was being so generous to them?* And on and on. The list was repeated each and every day. The next step in the routine was for Yasser and Rashid to grumble indiscernible words back to him that nobody could really hear, but they all knew that the two of them were outraged by the workers behavior and they would immediately handle it. All three men shuffled out the door one behind the other. All three simultaneously grumbled. And none of the three listened to the other two. Shira and Ghalia looked at each other and laughed.

"This is how war should be, you know," Shira said to her new friend. They'd been working together for four months and bonded almost immediately.

"Yes. Can you imagine it. Fifty thousand soldiers on both sides scratching their heads and grumbling about all things. That would be a nice change." They both smiled a warm but painful smile. This was something that would never happen and they both knew it.

There were Mossad protocols in place on how to handle a lot of different situations. Shira was schooled on all of them and used almost none of them. Her only job was to be a regular office worker, listen and watch and report back on a regularly scheduled basis. But she was taught that if a particular number was texted to her, she was to excuse herself and find a private place to call her handler. That particular number was never texted to her. She knew that if a different number was texted to her, she was to return to the Mossad office at the end of the day. That had happened twice so far. Both times it signaled that the current assignment was finished and she would not be returning to work there. And most importantly she knew that if she received a text from someone named Eli that said, "Your aunt has been in an accident. Come to the hospital," it meant, get out now. "Get out now" would seem like a self-explanatory action, but it wasn't quite that simple. It did not mean drop what you're doing and run out of the office. "Get out now," signaled that something was about to go down and they didn't want anyone tipped off, but they wanted her to leave for her own safety. On the other hand, it also didn't mean to take an hour to finish up what she was doing before slipping out. So in actuality, what it really meant was to slip the phone back into her pocket and nonchalantly step outside as if she needed to grab some fresh air or perhaps smoke a cigarette. Cool, calm, collective and pronto were the keys to *get out now*.

The two women were still chatting and laughing when the three men returned. Jacob was still ranting and mumbling. The other two remained momentarily outside the door while they continued nodding and ignoring. All was normal. With one parting grumble, Jacob walked towards his car. Yasser and Rashid walked through the door acting just as they had been when they had left. Everyone was content that the daily catastrophe had once again been averted, until tomorrow morning.

Shira's phone buzzed and she glanced down and saw the message from Eli. "Your aunt has been in an accident..." She stared at the message for only a moment and then smiled as if she had just received a joke from a friend. Without so much as a glitch in her motions, she put the phone into her back pocket, and stuck the papers in her left hand into a folder and slipped them between other folders in the top drawer of the file cabinet. Once that was done, she turned to Ghalia who was sitting in front of her computer.

"Come with me, please." Shira spoke in a soft friendly voice, but she was instructing more than asking.

"Where are we going?" Ghalia asked without looking up from her computer.

"I have something to show you. Come," she continued and walked towards the door.

"Just a couple minutes. I'm almost done with this," she answered, again without looking up. Shira was in an uncomfortable dilemma. She knew her priority was the mission, but Ghalia was just a side character with nothing to do with any of whatever may or may not be going down. She was a twenty-two-year-old girl with a pretty face, a good heart, a sharp mind, and a hard life. She had dreams just like women of Israel and America and India and any other woman anywhere in the world. She had only a mild interest in religion and no interest in politics. She loathed war of any kind, for any reason. She wanted more out of life. Not too many mornings ago the two of them were sipping coffee and Shira asked her point blank, "What do you want in life, Ghalia?" Her one-word answer was "More." It was all she said. She didn't embellish. Nor did she seem particular what *more* was. Whatever was out there in the world in Ghalia's mind, had to be more than the life she was living.

The two men were already back to work at their desk and paid no attention to the two women who they considered to be nothing more than office girls who spent their days chatting with people.

"Come on," Shira urged as if she were a small child trying to drag her father to the ice cream stand.

Ghalia looked up and rolled her eyes. "The last time you did this all you showed me was you smoking a cigarette." Shira laughed and waved her cigarettes and lighter towards her friend. Ghalia threw her hands in the air signaling her surrender and got up to follow. They stepped out the door and strolled across the yard. Shira lit her cigarette and Ghalia rolled her eyes one more time just to remind her friend that she was lured out on false pretenses once again.

"Come. I'll buy you a dessert today," Shira motioned towards the bakery that was owned by the same family who owned the strawberry farm.

"You've lowered yourself to bribing me to hang out with you," Ghalia responded, knowing that the pastry was an acceptable bribe. She stuck her hand in her pocket and stopped walking. "Ugh. I forgot my phone. Wait here. I'll be right back," she said as she turned and started jogging back towards the door.

"You don't need your phone. Let's go eat," Shira called out, but it was too late. Ghalia was already nearing the door. Twenty seconds later she would be back out with the phone in her hand. But time stood still as Shira watched Ghalia stop dead in her tracks when she reached the door. It was a crushing moment. It was that microscopic slither in time that perpetually sat right between all things good and all things bad, and Shira knew it.

Time is a strange phenomenon. A wonderful day can go past so quickly that it seems barely more than an hour. And a horrific moment in time can stand still for near eternity. That moment in time came just before the shooting began. It was like Shira was looking at a photograph. The world stopped spinning. Time stopped passing. Her heart stopped beating. The entire incident lasted less than a few seconds, but Shira was on the outside and it seemed like an hour. The only thing that she witnessed was Ghalia freezing in the doorway and time standing still. All sounds became so deafening that she heard nothing. She said something that Shira did not hear. The shooting started and stopped almost immediately. Ghalia stumbled backwards in slow motion for several steps and crumbled to the ground. The front of her white cotton blouse had a single red dot in the center of her left breast. The dot grew and grew until her white blouse turned red. The photograph was gone and the world was spinning again. She couldn't stop the passing of time now, even if she wanted to.

What Shira had not seen was the men who slipped through the back door when Ghalia arrived in the front doorway. It wasn't as if Ghalia hadn't seen Israeli soldiers nearly every day for her entire life, but she still asked the question even though she knew the answer. "Who are you?" Those were her only words.

Then as if by magic, Yasser and Rashid both had guns in their hands and were firing towards the intruders. Yasser went down immediately with a bullet in his forehead. Rashid fired two shots before going to the ground. He was still alive, but he was finished. Ghalia looked down at the red dot in her left breast and looked back up with a confused look on her face. Why were the soldiers shooting? Why did her friends have guns and why were they shooting? Why was blood oozing onto her white cotton shirt? She stumbled backwards away from the doorway and collapsed on her back in the yard where she and her friend were speaking only moments before. "Shira!" she called out. Shira's entire world disappeared except for Ghalia. She ran to her and cradled her in her lap.

"I don't understand what's happening," she sobbed.

"It's okay, Ghalia. You're going to be okay." She brushed hair out of her friends' eyes and kissed her on the side of her face.

"We're going to get you help. Just hold on."

"Why did this happen? They shot me, Shira. Everyone had guns. I don't understand."

"Shhhh. Hold on, Ghalia. Everthing will be okay."

"Will it?" she asked. She wanted an answer. "Will everything be okay?" she added. Did Shira believe that all the fighting and killing would stop? Did she really believe the hatred that flowed in the streets everyday would go away? Did she think that her friend was going to stop bleeding and get up and walk with her to go get a pastry?

"You're going to be okay. Just hold on to me," was the only answer Shira could give.

"I'm tired of all this Shira. I want to run away from all of this stupidity." The entire front of her blouse was crimson red. Shira pressed down hard against the blood-soaked fabric to slow the bleeding, but it had little effect. "Can't we just go away?" Her eyes were glassing over and she struggled to breathe.

"Shhh. Don't talk, Ghalia. There will be an ambulance in just a minute."

"Shira. I don't want to go. There's supposed to be so much more," she whispered.

"Hold on Ghalia. You're going to be okay, baby. There's going to be more. You and me… we're going to leave here and go see the world. No more Palestine. No more Israel. You'll see, Ghalia. Just hold on." She kissed her again on the side of her face and held her tighter, as if to keep her from leaving.

"Do you promise we can go?" she asked with the slightest sound of hope in her words.

"When you get better, we'll run away together, okay?"

Ghalia smiled a weak smile and struggled hard to keep her eyes open. A quiet wheezing sound came from underneath Shira's hand.

"Where will we go? Where will we run away to, Shira?"

"To a tropical island," she said, and tried to convince herself that they would go there together. "There will be white beaches and turquoise water and waves at our ankles."

"Ahhh. That sounds wonderful," she whispered.

"I'll hold your hand and nobody will care that you're an Arab or I'm a Jew. We won't even tell them. And we will be nice to everyone and they'll be nice back to us."

"I don't know how to swim," she whispered barely loud enough for Shira to hear.

"I'll teach you to swim. And we will get paddle boards and go out and look for turtles and dolphins."

The smile left Ghalia's face. "Why did this happen, Shira? Why did the soldiers come? Why did Yasser and Rashid have guns? I don't understand," she whispered once more.

"I don't know, Ghalia. I don't know." She lied to her only friend. She did know. They came because Shira told them stupid meaningless shit that they put together with other stupid meaningless shit, that all added up to something that meant something to someone who had the power to send soldiers with guns to find the Arab men with guns. And with only a moments warning, they told Shira that they were coming and she failed to get her friend out of harm's way. Then they shot Ghalia. They shot her only friend.

A soldier's hand touched Shira on the shoulder. "Come Shira. We'll take care of this. Time for you to leave." She slapped his arm away and screamed at him.

"Get away from me. Stay away from me and my friend," she snapped. She drew Ghalia closer to her own body and held her tightly. "You'll be okay soon, sweetie. The ambulance will be here soon." The soldiers stepped back and made sure the workers and others left them alone.

"I don't have any money, Shira. How will I pay to go away? How will I survive?" She was growing weaker with each passing second, with each passing word, with each passing breath, but she clung to Shira's promise. They were going to a tropical island together.

"I will pay. I have money, my friend. My sister," she sobbed. "We will take care of each other. How's that sound?" Shira asked with tears streaming down her face.

"Beautiful. It sounds beautiful... my sister," she whispered so quietly that Shira knew she was slipping away. One last breath eased from her lips and a tear slid from the corner of her eye. Those were her last words. *My sister*. Then she was gone. Shira sobbed and kissed her softly on her cheek and rocked her like a baby whom she were protecting from danger, but she had already failed. Years of grief burst from deep inside as she clung tightly to her friend. Shira had only known Ghalia for a few months, and though she had not realized it, Ghalia was the best friend she had ever had. Since Papa had died all those years ago, Shira lived a safe life. She lived in a protective shell where people could get near her, but not close to her. Ghalia was different. She was kind and good. It was that simple. Her friend Ghalia was all things good combined with nothing bad. And all she wanted from life was a little more. A little more happiness. A little more love. A little more kindness. A little more laughing. A little more peace. A little more forgiveness, A little more of the universe. And she was always willing and able to return in kind. In fact, she gave all those things and more to others and usually got nothing in return. Shira was overwhelmed with the pain. A river of tears flowed. She refused to let go.

An hour later Ghalia was gone and Shira was in the back of someone's car heading to meet with people who dealt with this sort of thing. As the car turned corners and zipped down straightaways, she began to feel more clarity than she had ever felt. For the first time in her life, everything was coming into focus. She told Ghalia they would move to a tropical island. That is what she would do. Papa, Israel, Mossad, Palestine, the world as she knew it were about to become her past.

For the next few weeks, she met with counselors and people higher up the chain of command. They helped her and advised her. They told her all this would pass. They explained that there was paperwork and a process to be followed to leave Mossad. This wasn't, they explained to her, like quitting her job at the Café Mersand. After getting all the advice and run around that she cared to tolerate, she packed one suitcase and grabbed her passport and called a cab. Four hours later she was on a plane that would eventually take her to the tropical island of Saint Maarten in the Caribbean. It was all behind her now. At least that's what she kept telling herself.

CHAPTER THIRTY-SEVEN

Pellet dabbed his fingers in the water and gently wiped at the patch of dried blood on his face, bitching and complaining the whole time.

"Ouch. Damn, that hurts," he winced and whined each time his fingers touched his face.

"Serves you right for climbing back into a sinking boat. I think that might have been one of those questionable judgement calls that Lucy was concerned about."

"What the hell does she know? She's back in the states turning down two-hundred thousand-dollar jobs because some evil shrew screwed her over. Welcome to the world, baby," Pellet added as if she were listening to him. "Gawd! That hurts," he said again as he continued to dab saltwater on his open wound. Truth was that she had listened to him say those very words more than once. "Try working in an eraser factory for a couple years," he told her in one conversation. "In case you've never experienced it, eight bucks an hour barely pays rent on a crappy trailer. And trust me, my boss screwed everyone over on a daily basis. Most of the time my plan B was a twelve pack."

"She probably has reasons for turning down the jobs," Avis defended for no other reason than he felt like being contrary towards Pellet.

"Probably still pondering the idea of coming back down here to go sailing with me," he said and continued to dab at the gash on his face. Avis looked up at him and wondered if he was going to think about what he had just said. A few seconds later, the "Ouches" resumed with no epiphany.

"You know you don't have a boat anymore, right?"

Pellet shrugged. "I've got one. It's just at the bottom of the sea. Ouch. Man, this hurts."

"Well then leave it alone dumbass. There's nobody out here to see you anyway," Avis snapped as he watched the sun setting to the west. "Gonna be dark soon," he mentioned with a tinge of concern in his voice.

Pellet turned and looked over his shoulder to where Avis was looking. "Man. Nice sunset," was all he said.

"I think my point was that we're out here in the middle of the sea in a twelve-foot blow-up boat and it's going to be pitch black soon. No moon tonight." He shook his head at Pellet again. "But I suppose you're right. Nice sunset." He was being sarcastic.

"I wonder if we'll see a green flash when it goes down? Have you ever seen it? I've seen it a couple times. Only last for a split second, but it's cool." He sat and watched just as he had done dozens of times and not once had he wondered what caused the green flash. Tonight was no different.

Avis looked at him and wrinkled his forehead. The DNA thing kept kicking around in his head. It was more than obvious that Pellet had absolutely no fear of the sea. None. And up until they had been struck by lightning, hit by a VW bus, lost the propeller and rudder and then finally lost the keel to a passing shipping container, he was actually a good sailor. Maybe sailing was in his DNA. But the sailing DNA wasn't an exclusive strand. There were other threads. Brown hair, blue eyes, big feet, drinking booze, they all appeared to be part of his DNA, too. And Avis was beginning to come to the conclusion that there was a *stupid* strand in his DNA. Or perhaps better stated, an *oblivious* strand. A talk and act without thinking strand. A good god, what is wrong with you strand.

"Well, flash or not, it's going to be pitch black in about twenty minutes. And it's going to be a long night."

"We should have a drink of rum. You know, to celebrate surviving," Pellet suggested to Avis who had tucked the bottle behind him, out of Pellet's reach.

"Alcohol dehydrates the system. That's why the morning after a good drunk you feel like drinking a gallon of water."

"Good to know," Pellet answered. "A toast?" he added,

not persuaded in the least by the trivia that had just been shared with him.

Avis hesitated and pondered and finally reached down and picked up the bottle and twisted off the cap. He took a swig and savored the warm, sweet rum that ran down his throat and then handed it to Pellet. It dawned on him that there was only about a 50/50 chance they'd be found, meaning there was the same 50/50 chance they would die at sea. Now probably wasn't the time to become a Nagging Nelly. To Avis's surprise, Pellet took one strong chug and handed the bottle back to him. "I'm good," he said and turned to watch the sun disappear. "Bummer. No green flash," he mumbled when the lights went out. Then he laid down against one of the inflated sides of the zodiac and watched the stars for what seemed to be a long time. In reality it was difficult for Pellet to estimate the time with nothing to mark it against. It's not like he could say I drank three beers, so that's probably about an hour. Or I've been bugging Helmut so that was probably about a half hour. They were in the middle of the quiet sea and even though there was plenty of beer on the boat, it was on the other boat. The one sitting in the sand and coral deep below the surface. And neither of them owned a watch. Like most of the western world, they depended on their cell phones for things like telling the time. Unfortunately both phones were now comfortably resting somewhere within a few feet of their beer.

Avis slept a bit here and there and tossed and turned and fought off the night chill. The air was warm, but the water that the boat was sitting on was cold. The thin layer of rubber and fiberglass between them and the water provided no warmth. He guessed it was somewhere around midnight when he climbed to his knees and peed over the side of the boat. Pellet sat up and rustled his hair and dipped his hand into the water on the opposite side of the boat and rinsed his face.

"Sun should be coming up soon," he said and looked around at the endless blackness. Avis laughed.

"Naw. It's going to be five or six hours before the sun comes up. Better get some sleep or it'll be a long night."

"Man. It feels a lot later than that. Could be later than that, you know. It's hard to tell without... Holy shit! Look at that?" Pellet exclaimed, pointing to the east.

"What?" Avis asked and semi-frantically looked around thinking maybe there was another VW or container or something along those lines.

"Right there," he said and pointed again. "It's a boat." He stopped pointing and frantically grabbed the emergency kit and began digging out the flares.

"Pellet. You gotta be kidding me. That thing is at least six miles away and has no chance of seeing us."

"I'm firing a flare. We've got to at least try."

"Hey. We've only got three flares and that's presuming all three work. We need to save them for a boat that's in the same hemisphere as us."

"They'll see the flare, Avis. They're damn bright," he said a split second before a bright white flare shot into the sky and slowly drifted back down.

They both sat and silently watched the spec of a boat on the horizon.

"Oh, look. They're turning," Avis sniped.

"You think so?" Pellet asked as he continued to peer in its direction.

"No I don't think so," Avis snapped. "It's three hundred feet long, five stories tall and has hundreds of lights on it. And guess what? It looks like a speck of a light so small that you could fit ten of them on a pinhead. No, Pellet. Nobody except me and you saw the flare."

That was when he realized that even though there was only a light breeze, Pellet had shot the flare at an angle that allowed it to drift ever so slowly back down to pretty much where it started. While it was no longer burning as brightly as it was a few seconds ago, it was still burning and they were in a rubber raft. Both of them watched it draw nearer and nearer before it hit the water and hissed less than ten feet away. Avis looked at Pellet in silence. Pellet grinned.

"That would have been a hell of a way to go," he said and laughed and looked where the flare had landed. Avis slowly shook his head and reached down and picked up the bottle and twisted the cap again.

CHAPTER THIRTY-EIGHT

In Pellet's mind yesterday was the first day even though they didn't get into the life raft until sometime in the late afternoon or early evening, depending how one looked at it. In fact, as Avis pointed out to him, it was almost night when Bella Vita slipped beneath the surface. He figured since they ate breakfast and lunch, or at least munched on some chips and had a couple of beers before the bottom dropped off the boat, it didn't really count as their first day in the Zodiac. Last night was the first night. This was day one. It was an argument they would have several times before it was all said and done. Either way they both woke with the sun's rays brightly shining in their faces.

"This first day won't be too bad. You know, we'll be thirsty and we'll get hungry, but nothing too serious. Believe it or not, it will be worse when the sun goes down." Avis thought it would be best if Pellet knew what to expect if they didn't get rescued soon."

"Yesterday was the first day."

"No. We were on Bella Vita yesterday. Today is day one."

"I don't know what you're talking about. I'm already hungry and thirsty. I'm pretty sure this is day two."

"Once the sun goes down the problem will be that since we didn't eat or drink all day, we're going to be dehydrated from the sun, we're going to get cold pretty easily."

"Again, has anyone ever told you that you can be a bit of a downer?"

"We're probably going to have to curl up with each other to keep warm tonight and conserve body heat," he continued and paid no attention to Pellet's comments. "The second day will be worse than the first."

"Tomorrow will be the third day. And how do you know

all this shit," Pellet asked not seeing how knowing any of this was helpful.

"Books, Pellet. I've read a lot of books. You should try it. There's a bunch of good information in them."

"You might kick around the idea of reading less. You know, ignorance is bliss and all that shit."

"This is the one time that being fat would be a good thing," Avis blurted out as another fun-fact in his seemingly endless stream of knowledge that continued to flow.

"Is that so," Pellet answered, more or less dreading the lesson he was about to get. After all, what difference would it make? He was skinny as a beanpole.

"Once we go two or three days without food and water, the body more or less starts feeding on itself. Fat people do better at surviving starvation."

"Hey, Google boy. I don't see that this is really all that much help."

"No. I don't do the Google thing too often. I like books. Much better info," he said wishing he had a book. He wished Pellet had thrown a book at him before Bella Vita went down.

They sat in near silence for a long time. Both of them scanning the horizon and both of them wishing they had hats and sunglasses and the case of water Pellet had tossed into the sea. There was no place to hide from the sun and it was brutal. Mid-eighties and not a cloud to be found. No food. No water. And no rescue anywhere on the horizon.

"You ever think you'd wish for shade this much?" Pellet blurted out.

"Nope."

Neither said anything else for another long time. Both of them knew how much the other was suffering. Shorts and t-shirts were no defense for the sun. They found themselves trying to cover their faces with their hands or turning to be facing away from the sun. But once they turned, their necks were exposed and baked.

"How far you think we can go on this little tank of gas?"

Avis asked Pellet.

"Not far. Maybe a couple miles. I thought about starting it and you know, just seeing how far we'd get. Didn't see much sense in it."

"Guess we'd better save it. I'd hate to see a boat a mile away and not have a way to get to it."

Another hour of silence.

"What's it like to be rich, Avis?"

"Just like being poor, but with more money."

"I'm serious man. What's it like?"

"I'm serious too. It didn't change me all that much. Still like reading. Still like fishing. Still like beer. Still love Savannah. I've just got more money."

"All good in Avis-ville, huh?"

Avis laughed and took a deep breath. "Pellet, I live in the same screwed up world you live in. Deal with the same screwed up people you have to deal with. Get judged by the same society that judges you every day. No free rides in this world, buddy. Even if you have money."

"I suppose. But still…"

"Well, look at it this way if it makes you feel better. I'm stuck in the same lifeboat as you. The money isn't doing shit for me right now." Strangely enough, it made Pellet feel good enough that they laid on opposite ends of the boat in silence for two more hours.

"What's your favorite song?" Avis blurted out and startled Pellet.

"What?"

"Your favorite song? Name it."

Pellet unconsciously reached up and rubbed his face and instantly regretted it. His burned skin wasn't blistering yet but if it didn't happen today, then tomorrow for sure. And then of course there was the deep gash on his forehead.

"Holy shit, that hurts," he moaned.

"Favorite song?" Avis insisted.

"Can't say there's just one song," he said while he

mentally scanned a song list in his head. "Sometimes I'll hear a song and think it's the greatest song ever. Then the next time I think, eh, it's good, but nothing special."

"Come on. There's got to be a song or two that ranks at the top of your list."

"Well, Samba Pa Ti by Santana is pretty epic. It's an "everything" song."

"What's that mean?"

"You ever listen to it? You could sit and get stoned and it would be a great chill song. Or if you're with a woman, it's a great put her in the mood song. It's just got a vibe and I'd have to say it's in my top ten list. You?"

"I'd say I'm torn between What A Wonderful World by Louis Armstrong and just about anything by Beyoncé."

"Really? Beyoncé? You're shitting me?" Pellet asked with a surprised voice.

Avis laughed. "Yeah. Just kidding. I like Armstrong, but not a Beyoncé kind of guy. I'd say my taste is more with old school rock and roll. Growing up I always liked the stuff from the sixties and seventies. Duran Duran and Pat Benatar never really did it for me. Early Springsteen, Bob Seger, Pink Floyd."

"So, name one song that you consider great at this moment in time."

"Ohhh. Riders on the Storm by The Doors," Avis responded. "Pretty deep stuff. I think most of the music was a lot more honest back then. And you've got to admit, it's a pretty appropriate song for our current situation, right?"

Pellet laughed as much as he was able. "Yeah. I guess we're a couple of riders on the storm now, huh."

"So far so good."

Another few more hours of silence.

"I wonder what was in the shipping container?" Pellet said and sat up and looked around as if there might be something to see.

"I wonder what the hell a VW bus was doing in the middle of the ocean," Avis answered. "Jesus Christ. What are the odds of being hit by a bus while sailing?" They both laughed. "You know what else I wonder? Is someone more likely to win the Powerball Jackpot or get hit by a VW bus while sailing in the Caribbean."

"You know what that might mean, right?" Pellet asked and then answered his own question. "It means that you might be the luckiest guy on earth, but it isn't necessarily good luck. You beat the odds both times. And that might just mean that your luck caused all of this. I just happened to be along for the ride."

"Hmmm," was all Avis responded with.

They both turned and watched for the green flash. It didn't come. The lights went out. Day two, or one, was over depending which one of them you asked.

CHAPTER THIRTY-NINE

The sun rose again. It was day two or three depending on who was talking. Pellet was still laying on his back with his arm shielding his face from the sun. He started singing an old Marley song, *No Woman No Cry*. He didn't really grasp the meaning of the lyrics, but the hook line had become his unofficial anthem. He rarely had a woman in his life. And if he did, he was never able to keep her there. Few and far between but quick to exit once they did come along. Given the choice of moping and feeling sorry for himself or embracing the premise that he wasn't fazed by the situation, Pellet chose to adopt *No Woman No Cry* as his motto. Avis laughed a hoarse parched laugh at the absurdity that these words were what popped into Pellets mind at a time like this.

"You are actually thinking about women at a time like this?"

"Can you think of anything better?" Pellet asked without flinching a muscle.

"Some water to drink. A boat to get us home. A hat. A phone." He rattled off the list and then conceded, "Savannah." He drew a deep breath and grunted as he sat up. The cold boat stiffened his bones and made him miss his bed. "If you hold them in such high regard, why don't you find a good one and settle down?"

"I'm picky. Haven't found the right one yet," Pellet answered. He had said something similar to Desmund a couple years back. Desmund responded, "Haven't found a deaf, blind woman yet?" Avis was thinking similar thoughts.

"Thought you were interested in Lucy?"

"Naw. Don't think she's right for me," Pellet rationalized.

"Young. Good looking. Good hearted. Educated. Probably going to have a successful career making decent money

214

one day. Knows how to sail a boat. I can see why she wouldn't be a keeper," Avis mumbled and scanned the horizon to see if there was anything other than water. There wasn't.

"Guess you see my dilemma," was all Pellet added before going silent again and trying to not think about all the things Avis had mentioned. Water. A boat. A hat. A phone. What he would give for any one of them.

There was basic worrying and then there was high levels of stressing out, and finally there were complete extreme panic attacks. Savannah was bouncing back and forth between all three. She was trying to stick with the basic worrying mode but the other two constantly grabbed at her. Avis had phoned her once they dropped anchor and got settled down for the night in the harbor in Saint Barths. He did the same in Saint Eustatius. Then he went silent. They were due back yesterday. That's when her persistent mental battle began.

On one hand she was filled with a dark feeling of desperation. On the other she could envision them sailing, fishing, laughing and drinking beer. But it wasn't like Avis to be inconsiderate. Then again he was with Pellet. Her internal battle continued. She had mentioned her concerns to Desmund, Oscar, Iggy, Fatisha and Helmut. Without exception, they each shrugged and said, "He's with Pellet." Helmut actually added, "You should be worried for all the other sailors on the sea in this part of the Caribbean," implying that Pellet was more danger to them than he was to Avis.

She stood on the beach in Anguilla and looked towards Saint Maarten and beyond for a sailboat that she somehow felt was not returning. To add insult to an already painful injury, there were other sailboats pushing through the waves and currents between the two islands. None of them carried the man she was waiting for. They served as a taunting reminder that his boat was missing.

Avis sat on the back seat of the Zodiac and felt the first tinge of the mental and emotional struggle that he knew would consume them if they were not mindful that panic and bad decisions could be deadly. Too much sun, no food and water were perhaps less deadly than the onset of panic. Bad decisions killed more people in these situations more often than the elements themselves. That information was straight from a survival book he had read a few years ago. He tried to lick his lips but his mouth was dry. His tongue roughly rubbed over his cracked and blistering bottom lip. His gaze turned north and he tried hard to focus, as if he thought if he looked hard enough, he could see her. She faced south on her long empty white beach and did the same in his direction.

"Hey man," Pellet blurted out and broke the silence. As if their communication link had been broken, Savannah turned and walked up the beach and sat at the bar in front of Desmund. He set a bottle of Ting down in front of her and waited for her to speak.

"I'm worried Dez."

"No need to worry. Can't kill Pellet. He's stupid all day, every day. Always standing when da storm is over."

"What about people around him?" she asked, as if Pellet lived a charmed life at the expense of others.

"Come out of it even better. You'll see," he continued, but even Dez had a bad feeling about this one. Poetic justice, he thought to himself. Pellet finally got good at something other than drinking, and it possibly killed him. "Anyway," he added, trying to convince himself as much as convincing Savannah, "Probably just being Pellet. Soon come." He slid a bowl of beer nuts across towards Savannah and then grabbed himself a beer.

Avis looked at Pellet and waited to follow up on his, "Hey, man," but he looked like he was thinking about something, so Avis waited.

"Why do you think it feels like time stands still when you're waiting for something good to happen or something bad to end?"

"No such thing as time," Avis answered matter-of-factly. "Not really, anyway."

"No such thing as what?" Pellet asked, removing his arm from across his face.

"Time."

"What the hell are you talking about? This is only our third day out here. You'd better get a grip."

"It's our second, but back to the subject at hand, the past and future are just illusions. The past is like a meal you ate yesterday. You don't refer to a meal that you already ate as something that is still around. It's gone. The past isn't some sort of old version of the present. It doesn't exist anymore. You cannot go back to it."

"No leftovers, huh? Could use some right now."

"And the future is a myth. It does not exist until it arrives. Never has. Never will."

"So, then what is tomorrow?"

"Tomorrow? Well, today it is nothing. It's a make-believe day that has not been born yet. And it may never come. If it doesn't arrive, then it never was. It's just a theory of what might or might not happen."

"And what will it be tomorrow?"

"Tomorrow it will be today. And it will only exist for a microsecond at a time. Then it will disappear and will never exist again."

"I dunno," Pellet said as he reached into his pocket for a cigarette that did not exist. "Sounds like you're just making shit up to me."

"All that ever matters Pellet, is today. Now. This minute. The present time. Yesterday is a memory. You can't touch it any more than you can touch tomorrow. And tomorrow is just a dream. We don't even know if we'll see tomorrow. Nobody does. So all we really have is now. Today."

Pellet pondered his theory for a couple minutes. "So what do you think about today?"

"I think today would be better if our boat hadn't sunk. You know, in the past." And after all that, Avis closed his eyes and dreamed of a few days ago when he kissed Savannah's lips and tasted the flavor of her lipstick in his mouth. He remembered the precise feeling of her tongue against his. He felt her hair as it brushed against his face and felt the softness of the curves in his hands and against his body. He heard a seductive sigh as she breathed out and opened her eyes and looked at him. Her windows. Her deep blue windows that captured him the first day they met. He could ramble on to Pellet about time and reality and the past and the future all he wanted to. But as he sat in the hot sun dying of thirst and hunger, standing on the beach and kissing her goodbye seemed more real to him than the unbearable present he found himself in. The future? His suspicion was growing that his earthly future may be drawing to a close. He shut his eyes again and tried to return to Savannah.

Another hour or so passed before Pellet spoke up again.

"Do you know what just hit me?" he blurted out in his dry, parched voice.

"Nope," was all Avis said without looking over in his direction.

"I keep beating myself up and struggling with this whole screwed up ancestor thing and I just realized that you're my cousin."

"You didn't know we were cousins," Avis flatly answered as if he didn't already know where this was going.

"I'm just saying that half of those screwed up assholes are your ancestors too. You've got the same shit history as me," he gloated as best as he could muster.

"You're just getting that, huh?" Avis said and smiled. His cracked lip started to bleed just a bit and the smile disappeared. The shared ancestral debacle seemed obvious to Avis the first time Pellet cried to him about his bleak family history. He had wondered how long it would take Pellet to figure out that they had both fallen from more or less the same diseased tree.

"Looks like your ancestors stole candy from a baby, too." Pellet somehow felt vindicated.

Avis knew Pellet, even being Pellet, must be considering how this trip was going to end. Given their painful state of burntness and dehydration it was difficult to not at least consider the worst-case scenario. He also knew from what he had read in more than one survival book, survival is in many ways, a state of mind. Step one is to commit to surviving. No matter what. Step two was committing to not considering the alternative to step one. They had to fight it off, no matter how difficult.

"Louis Zamperini," was all he said and waited for a response.

"There's no Louis in the boat, Avis. Don't know who you're talking to," Pellet mumbled without moving.

"Louis Zamperini and Russell Allen Phillips survived in a blow-up raft for forty-seven days during World War II. No food. No water. They were in the South Pacific, so the weather was similar to ours. Just thought I'd share that with you."

"Only forty-three more days to go," Pellet flatly responded.

"Forty-four, but you're missing the point. We'll need to stop waiting to be rescued pretty soon and start working on surviving."

"That's all you've got?" Pellet asked and waited a few seconds for a response that didn't come. "Just wondering if maybe there's a more inspirational speech coming."

"Well, back in the 1970's there was a Rugby team from Uruguay that crashed in the Andes. They were up in the snow-capped mountains for seventy-two days. And in 1847 the Donner Party got stuck in the mountains in a winter storm," Avis answered. "But people ate each other in both of those survival stories. I don't want to encourage anything."

"No worries, Avis. Unless you've got a beer for me to wash things down, I'm not eating you."

"In the 1890's Stephen Callahan survived for seventy-six days in a rubber raft, but he had a few bottles of water and some other things. I figured you'd just complain that we don't have water if I shared that story."

"Yet you shared it anyway," Pellet said unable to resist complaining.

"The point is that whether it was those folks, or Robert Peary going to the North Pole, or Tenzing Norgay climbing Everest, they all had the same attitude. Failure was not an option."

"You've got to stop reading books, Avis," was Pellet's weak response.

"You should start reading," Avis responded.

"Maybe I will eat you."

There was no talking for the next few hours.

CHAPTER FORTY

Day three, or day four, depending which of them was correct. Both of them had been awake for a couple of hours, though there was little difference between being awake and being asleep. They were physically drained. Both had awoken more than once in the middle of the night with muscle spasms and cramps. The signs of dehydration were beginning to show and Avis knew what to expect. Hot flashes followed by chills. Headaches. General pain throughout their bodies. Especially their joints. And the most dangerous symptom of all, hallucinations. If one of them climbed overboard to retrieve a cooler that wasn't actually there or to go to a rescue boat that wasn't there, well... that would be the end. All they could do for the time being was to preserve as much energy as possible and chat with each other now and then. There was nothing else.

"You never told me what was so special about Bella Vita. I know there was the bikini chick but you said it had history. What else didn't you tell me?" Avis sounded like even the simple task of talking was exhausting, but he thought they should keep talking to remind themselves that they were not yet dead.

"What do you mean?" Pellet whispered through his dry, hoarse throat.

"That night when we were all at Dez's, a few weeks before you bought her, I made a crack about you just wanting to buy the boat because there was a woman in a bikini on the deck. You said, "You know nothing," and I got the feeling that you knew something I didn't." He stopped talking and waited without knowing if Pellet would answer. He wasn't even sure Pellet had the energy to answer. But he did answer. In fact, he somehow worked up the energy to chuckle a little before telling the story.

"I sailed on her, you know, before seeing her in the bay in

Saint Maarten. Me and Oscar and my friend Maddie, you've heard me talk about her before, we took an overnight cruise with a guy named Julio. He owned the boat." He stopped talking as he mustered up enough energy to force more words through his parched throat. "We went on a weekend party cruise from Anguilla up to Tortola. At least, that was the plan." He stopped again and a smile came to his face as he thought about that weekend on a boat with a guy they hardly knew. It didn't go as planned," he added, and raised his eyebrows towards Avis and then cringed when his wrinkled forehead pulled on his cut. "Long story short, it turned out Julio wasn't actually Julio. Seems he was just a guy who screwed over some drug runners and they came and killed him while we were sailing with him."

"What do you mean, killed him?"

"Made him dead. Not much more to it than that. Shot him," Pellet answered without the energy to embellish or fill in the blanks.

"Why didn't they kill all of you?"

"Don't know. Lucky I guess. It certainly wasn't a conversation I was going to have with the guys with the guns. They told us to keep quiet. We nodded in agreement. They left."

Avis presumed Pellet was beginning to hallucinate or he was just plain hearing things. Or he was completely missing the point. The story was supposed to be about why he bought the boat. His burned and blistered face grimaced in pain as he tried to make sense of the story.

"Anyway," Pellet continued, "I'd never sailed before, but somehow I managed to sail her for twelve or fifteen hours. And then I somehow found Anguilla and anchored her in the water in front of Dez's bar. We swam to shore and Dez called someone to get rid of the boat. Never saw it again until I saw her anchored in Simpson Bay. I thought it was karma or destiny or some kind of shit like that."

"Let me get this straight. The first time you went out on the sailboat, the captain was killed. And when you saw it again, you said, "Hey! That's the boat I was on when the captain got murdered. It's my lucky boat. Then, since it was so damn overflowing with luck, you ran out and bought it. And then you talked me into going out on your *lucky boat* and it got caught in a storm, then struck by lightning, followed by being hit by a bus, and finally sunk by a shipping container. Oh. In the middle of all of that, it lost its propeller, the rudder and the keel. Now we're probably going to die in the middle of nowhere while your *lucky boat* is sitting on a coral bed a thousand feet below the surface of the Caribbean Sea. Still think it's your fucking lucky boat?" he snapped with the tiny bit of energy he had left. Avis was not prone to anger. In fact, he wasn't even that prone to much conversation. As he tried to wrap some sort of logic, even Pellet logic, around the story, he couldn't believe what he was hearing. "Christ. It's like a million drunken Pellet stars aligned to put us right here in this boat in the middle of nowhere." He regretted the last statement before the words reached Pellet's ears.

"When you put such a negative spin on it, it does sound a lot worse," he answered with typical Pellet optimism. "You've got to admit though, I sailed her pretty good." The million stars insult was completely ignored.

Avis would have shaken his head in disbelief if he had the energy to shake his head. They laid in their spots and were kept company by only their own thoughts for the next few hours.

Pellet eventually struggled and sat up and was surprised to see that Avis was already sitting up and blankly looking off into the distance. He reached over the side and dipped his fingers and gently wet his face. The cool saltwater reminded him that it was a bad idea and he immediately cringed in pain from the burning salt washing through the blisters and cracks that covered his face and lips.

"Need to be careful about reaching over like that," Avis said, barely louder than a whisper. When Pellet looked at him, he made out little more than a hazy version of his first mate. Avis nodded towards the water on the other side of the boat. Ten or fifteen feet away something was sticking out of the water. Pellet squinted hard and tried to focus on whatever it was.

"Dolphin?" he asked hopefully, already presuming it wasn't.

"Shark. Hammerhead I think. Eight or ten feet long."

"Oooh. Hammerhead. They're not the friendly kind, are they," Pellet stated more than asked.

"No. Not friendly," he chuckled. "I believe they're the kind of folks who eat their dinner guest."

"Not very hospitable. Don't believe I'm interested in having dinner with them." Pellet stared for another couple seconds and then slid to the center of the small seat, away from either side of the boat. He stayed there for as long as he could, before eventually laying back down. He didn't let his feet hang over the side of the boat anymore. The shark didn't come any closer for the moment, but it didn't swim away either.

"Got a question for you," Pellet mumbled.

"Hmmm," was the slight response.

"You're a pretty smart guy, but you don't usually have much to say. Why is that?" Pellet asked, still lying with his arm draped over his face. There was a long silence before Avis answered. Pellet didn't know if he was thinking, or just wasn't interested in talking. Either way, he had asked and that was that.

"Most people don't want to hear what they don't want to hear. I don't feel burdened to fight with them, and I don't like lying. So, I just don't say much.

"Hmmm," was Pellet's response this time.

CHAPTER FORTY-ONE

Lucy caught the next flight from NYC to Saint Maarten a couple hours after Savannah had called her. While everyone else was confident that Pellet was just being Pellet and Avis was just along for the ride and they would likely ease in and drop anchor at any time soon, Lucy understood the gravity of the situation. She had the good fortune of having three generations of sailing under her belt. She knew the sea would not be forgiving just because he was Pellet. This wasn't getting drunk and hitting on somebody's wife or insulting a tourist or passing out on the beach. This wasn't being a never-ending thorn-like friend to Desmund, Helmut and the rest of them. It was nothing like waking up with a hangover that made him pray for death. And it was nothing like making a mistake on dry land. Pellet had left the world he had known for his entire life and gone to sea. The sea consumed people who made careless mistakes like a lion consumes weak prey. The sea like the lion, could be ruthless and unforgiving as easily as it could be harmlessly docile. More importantly, it could change from docile to violent faster than an inexperienced sailor could imagine.

At just about the same time that Avis and Pellet were discussing whether or not to have dinner with a hammerhead, Lucy walked off her flight from New York into the Princess Juliana International Airport. She hurried through immigration as fast as she could and ran to comfort her friend. When Savannah first saw her coming through the gate, she finally broke down and began to cry for the first time since Avis and Pellet had not returned home. They were almost four days late and until Lucy arrived, there had been nobody who shared her concerns. She threw her arms around her neck and buried her face in her hair and sobbed. Lucy held her tightly and consoled her and insisted that everything would be alright. She told her that she had taught Pellet well. She reminded her that his boat was stocked with supplies and emergency equipment. They had a good lifeboat. And he had Avis with him. Avis was a thinking man who knew how to stay composed when he had to. Between the two of them, she was certain that they would be alright. Those were the things she told Savannah and she was convincing, even if she was not being completely honest. They were four days late and nobody knew if they were lost, stranded, drifting or worse. She and Savannah went outside and sat on a bench in the shade of a palm tree and began discussing what information they were sure of and what the rescue plan was going to be.

Savannah sat up and inhaled a huge breath and then blew air out as if she were trying to blow up a balloon. The breath was repeated three times before she composed herself enough to start talking without crying. Lucy listened to every word as if someone's life depended on how they handled the situation.

"The last I heard from them was five nights ago. Avis called me from the bay in Saint Eustatius. I made some calls and a couple boaters who were anchored there told the police that they remembered seeing them, and they remembered them leaving in the morning."

"That's good information, Savannah. At least we know they were heading home," she answered, trying to be encouraging with every response.

"There's more. The weather reports showed a thunderstorm blew through that morning and it would have probably hit them if they were following a course straight towards Saint Maarten." She looked at Lucy in hopes of getting some sort of conclusion that she knew in truth Lucy could not give.

"Pellet's been through thunderstorms with me. They suck, but they're not particularly dangerous," she lied. Of course there was no way for her to know the size and intensity of the storm, the strength of its winds, the size of its waves or whether or not they were caught off guard. Any one of those things could have led to disaster. For now, all they could presume was they were out there somewhere and they needed help. The only thing Lucy and

Savannah could do was find that help and put a plan in action. Savannah had already begun.

"I checked around and found the name of a small island hopper charter company. They have a plane available and I hired them to start a search mission. They'll be leaving within the hour."

"Can we go, too?"

"No. I asked and offered to even pay extra if they let us go, but they said it was their experience that things can get too emotional with family and friends along. Besides, I want to be around if they come back."

"What about the authorities? You know. Marine Patrol? Navy? Coast Guard?"

"I've spoken with the French and Dutch Navy dispatchers on the island. They both sent out word to their ships that are out to sea to be on the lookout. But it sounds as if this is almost a weekly thing for them to get word of a missing sailboat. They both said the boats and crews almost always return late due to some detour they decided to take without notifying family or friends. I tried to explain to them that that wasn't the case, but they insisted that I just give them a couple more days."

"I know a lot of sailors, Savannah, and I understand their point of view. It probably won't do any good to argue with them. I'm sure the people on their ships will keep an eye out for them. The best bet is the search plane anyway." Again, Lucy lied. The Caribbean Sea is more than a million square miles and a sailboat is less than a speck on its surface. The likelihood of flying out into the abyss and finding a single boat, especially if they were in a dinghy, was so astronomically low that it wasn't worth mentioning. "Did you and the pilot go over the route that Bella Vita was supposed to be following?"

"Yes. Well, no. I talked to a manager in the office. I told them they were heading straight from there to here and I told them when they headed out. Then we discussed the storm and I gave them some weather charts a guy in the French Naval office gave me that showed the wind speeds and directions of the storm and the time and location where it hit. I don't know if they were of any help or not, but I gave them to the guy in the office and he was going to go over all of it as soon as the pilot arrived."

"How far is their office? Let's go and see if we can talk to the pilot before he leaves," Lucy said, hoping she could talk her way onto the plane.

"Fifteen minutes to walk. Five by taxi."

Lucy stood up and waved for a taxi. Five minutes later they into the front door.

"Savannah," an elderly man with scraggly gray hair said as she walked in. He was standing next to a twenty something year old woman with long hair pulled back in a ponytail. She was wearing a loose-fitting Columbia fishing shirt and cargo shorts. Savannah presumed the woman was a client and while she didn't want to be rude, the search for her husband was more important.

"Excuse me for interrupting," she said to the woman he was speaking with, "but this is urgent, Arnie. This is Lucy. We need to speak with you."

"Savannah, this is Shira. She's the pilot I was telling you about. Very experienced. Second generation Israeli Air Force." He took the liberty to exaggerate the truth in order to reassure his newest client. Shira was never actually in the Air Force. "We're just going over all the information you gave me. She's leaving in about ten minutes."

"I'd like to go with you," Lucy said to Shira before the introduction was even finished.

"No," was her one-word answer. "I'll be on the radio Arnie. I'll keep you posted. Let me know if they come back in." With that she headed out the door.

"If they're in danger and you rescue them, I'll pay a hundred thousand dollars above the rate I'm already paying," Savannah blurted out. Everyone froze.

"Savannah. This is a stressful time, I don't..."

"A hundred thousand," Savannah repeated.

"Are you sure about this," Lucy asked. "I mean, do you have that kind of money?"

"A hundred thousand cash if you rescue him."

"And what if he's drunk on the deck with a fishing rod?" Shira asked.

"He's not. Bring him home, please."

Shira hadn't meant to be short with them, but the last thing she wanted was loved ones sobbing and pleading with her when she said that the fuel was running low and they had to turn back. Savannah wasn't trying to play the money card or come off like a rich bitch. She just wanted Avis back and she didn't care what it cost. She would have paid more. A half hour later, the flight checks were done. Arnie called in the flight plan to the tower. Shira was cleared for take-off and headed south to look for a tiny piece of driftwood afloat at sea.

CHAPTER FORTY-TWO

"Do you ever think about dying?" Pellet asked. It was something they couldn't help thinking about, but neither of them wanted to say it out loud. Pellet figured if they waited much longer they'd actually die while pretending that the end was not rapidly moving in on them.

"Thinking about it more than usual, now that you mention it." Avis replied in a scratched whisper.

"Me too." Somehow Pellet felt better now that the ice had been broken.

"I suppose everyone does at times like this but we're not dying yet?" Avis said to reassure Pellet that he hadn't thrown in the towel quite yet.

"I think about it sometimes and it kind of freaks me out. Not times like now, but when I'm lying in bed at night or sitting on the porch at three in the morning smoking a cigarette. I think shit like, damn man. I don't ever want to die. Then I think well, unless it's cool. You know. In the next life. If it's like a thousand times better than it is here I'll be wondering what the hell I was waiting for. Confusing stuff."

"Well, here's some good news. There's a relatively good chance that you'll have your answer in two or three days," Avis said with a faint tone of sarcasm.

"Cool. Unless it sucks on the other side. That'll be very uncool," Pellet answered and continued to waffle between the cool and uncool versions of the land of the dead.

Avis smiled as much as his painfilled face would allow. It struck him as a bit of irony that he was just now realizing that his cousin Pellet was a pretty amazing guy. Nothing ever seemed to get him down.

"You have any big regrets in life?" Pellet asked, almost

as if they may need to clean their slates and get prepared for the worst.

"Kinda regret going on this trip," Avis answered, more as a joke than anything else.

"Yeah. Sorry about that."

"Not your fault man. Shit happens."

"Is that how you come to terms with all of this?" Pellet asked seriously, looking for final hour answers. "Shit happens?"

"Well," Avis pondered. "You know me, Pellet. I've read just about everything I could get my hands on for the past twenty years. I've read more about religion than probably any ten religious people I know could have read in three lifetimes. I've read stuff written by philosophers and scientist who have made their case for the existence of a higher power somewhere out in the great unknown who is overseeing all this mess. And not one time was I ever really convinced enough to say, "Yeah. There's probably a god." I've always been a strong believer in the chaos theory. That pretty much says that in this great big universe we live in, shit happens."

"Not sure how I feel about all that," Pellet answered not fully convinced that he wanted the end of his life summed up by the words, "Shit happens."

"But," Avis continued, "In less than a twenty-four hour window I was sailing on a boat in the middle of the Caribbean Sea and it was caught in a storm, struck by lightning, got hit by a Volkswagen bus, lost its propeller and rudder and ran into a shipping container that broke off its keel and sunk the boat. Can't really help but think that it was somehow pre-ordained. That's a lot of pretty specific chaos for one boat in one day. I suppose that's a whole bunch of shit happens."

Pellet unintentionally cracked a painful smile of relief hearing that the smartest guy he knew, might believe in an afterlife after all. It was reassuring to believe that this might be the journey to the next life as opposed to lights out. "Sort of like the finger of God controlling things, huh?"

"Or the finger of the devil himself. Whoever it was, one

of them dudes trashed your boat and left us lying here like cookies in an Easy Bake Oven."

"Fuckers," Pellet added "Any of that rum left?"

"Probably not a good idea," Avis mumbled. Then just as he had done more than once, he realized the absurdity of choosing this as the time to be concerned about drinking rum. He reached down, picked up the bottle and twisted the cap and took a sip. It burned his lips, his tongue, his throat and then it burned all the way down. He took one more small sip and then handed the bottle to his cousin, his friend, Pellet. A last drink together probably wasn't the worst idea in the world. Being that Pellet was the king of doing things that were labeled, *probably not a good idea*, he took a big swig and then immediately started bitching about it hurting his lips, and his throat and his stomach. Then he took a second one.

"So," Pellet said as he tried to power through the pain of the rum, "On a scale of one to ten, how would you rate your life?"

Avis thought for only a second before blurting out his answer. "A fucking hundred, man. My life has been spectacular. My life is spectacular. How did you describe it a few days ago? "We're just two guys in a boat with a bottle of rum." Probably not the worst way to go." It dawned on Avis that they were turning a corner. Up until now they had been waiting for someone to come along and rescue them. Now, it seemed like they were waiting for something else. He screwed the lid back on the bottle and they both laid back and stopped talking.

They were both more or less unconscious when the faint buzzing sound began to grow. At first they were too exhausted to even recognize that the sound of the sea was changing. It was like a mosquito buzzing around their ear and it took a bit to realize that the sound didn't belong there. The plane was almost over them when Pellet opened his eyes and looked up at it. Even then it didn't immediately register. Avis followed suit a couple seconds later and they both laid there and watched the plane fly past. Then, it hit them both at the same time and they tried to get up. It was like a moment from a movie. It didn't seem real.

"Aaauuugggg," was all that came out when Pellet tried to yell. Nothing came out of Avis's mouth, but as the little adrenaline they had left kicked in, both of them sat up and watched the plane bank to the left. Avis started waving, and laughing a loud hoarse sounding laugh as he watched the small plane take a wide swooping turn. Pellet dumped the entire contents of the emergency kit on the bottom of the boat and rummaged through the small pile until he found the flare gun that he had loaded three days ago. Avis's arms were frantically waving in the air for no other reason than to say thank you and to celebrate to whomever it was that was circling around. Pellet was oblivious to him or the plane. All he knew was that there was no way they were going to be unnoticed.

"No need for that," Avis whispered and grinned ear to ear with not a care in the world about his pain. The small white plane had passed over them, taken a wide turn and was coming in to buzz close enough that they would know help was on its way. He tried to stand up and raise his arms in victory but couldn't muster the strength to balance himself. Tears of joy would have come to his eyes if he had any tears left to shed. His arms dropped into his lap and he continued to whoop and holler as much as he could. The pilot dipped the plane's wings back and forth a couple times to acknowledge to the castaways that help was on the way. Pellet continued to clumsily rummage in the nylon bag in search of the flare that was obviously not needed. Avis closed his eyes and tried to wrap his head around knowing he was going to hold Savannah again. He was going to kiss her and be with her again. Such a simple thing, yet only moments ago it had seemed like an impossibility. His eyes reopened and he looked towards Pellet and the smile dropped from his face. "NO!" he screamed. But it was too late.

Pellet scrounged around and eventually grabbed the gun, pointed it straight into the air, and squeezed the trigger. There was a small explosion from the end of the orange gun and the flare zipped into the air. The normal sequence of events would be the small explosion followed by a few seconds of the flare shooting upwards towards the sky. Then a bright glowing flame would slowly drift back down to the sea, just as it had a done few nights ago when Pellet foolishly fired the gun in hopes of getting the attention of people on a ship that was too far away. But the plane was not too far away. In fact, it was too close. So when he pulled the trigger, the gun popped, and the flare zipped into the air for a single second and then exploded again. He had fired a flare directly into the bottom of the wing of the small plane as it passed just a few feet over their heads. Their entire world stopped for a few moments and they watched in disbelief.

Shira saw what was about to happen, albeit too late. She dipped the wings a couple of times and a smile came to her face. One of the guys was waving and one of the guys had something in his hand. "Oh, shit!" she said and banked the plane hard to the right, but she knew it was too late. The flare hit the plane with a loud thud.

Given her demeanor and training, Shira was not prone to panic, but as her plane continued to turn she took no emergency actions. She simply looked at the small flame and large amount of smoke billowing from her wing and wondered why the guy she was rescuing would shoot her down. It seemed like she watched the wing deteriorate for five minutes, but it was less than five seconds when she began preparing to crash into the water before the plane exploded in mid-air. The small flame quickly ignited into a large flame and she knew she only had seconds to do what needed to be done. She took a deep breath and braced herself and pushed the yoke of the plane forward. A couple seconds later the nose and propeller slammed into a wall of dark blue water. The flame died out instantly and the smoke turned into steam as it mixed with the sea. Between the seatbelt and sheer strength, Shira kept herself from slamming forward and being knocked out. She quickly undid her seatbelt and prepared to open the doorway. The second it opened, water would gush in and the plane would sink in moments. With one more deep breath she forced the door open and water came in so fast that it was impossible for her to get out. But Shira remained calm and waited for the cockpit to fill with water and then she slid out and swam up to the surface.

"Ohhhh. That is not good," Pellet whispered as the plane began to disappear out of site. Avis slouched in a moment of self-pity but then remembered there might be someone who needed to be saved, or maybe not. He pulled the cord and started the motor and the Zodiac slowly cut through the glassy water towards the wreckage. At first all they could see was the top of the plane with the right side, the nearly wingless side, a bit more out of the water than the left. Then the plane began to sink faster than they would have expected. A few moments later, a head popped up above the water and looked around for their boat and then began swimming hard towards them. Avis slowed the boat to a crawl then put it in reverse to bring it to a full stop. He weakly reached down to help the pilot, but the woman who was clearly in better shape than either of the two of them, grabbed the rope on the top edge of the inflated side of the Zodiac and pulled herself up and over with such ease that they were both surprised.

"Who shot the flare?" she snapped.

Avis didn't mean to rat anybody out but his momentary glance at Pellet may as well have been him screaming, "Pellet did it!" while pointing his finger at him. Pellet didn't get so much as a peep out of his mouth before her fist shot out and slammed into the end of his nose. He fell backwards and crumpled down in the bow of the boat with blood gushing from his newly broken nose. If he hadn't gone down, she would have hit him again. He moaned in pain. His head was split open a few days ago. Every inch of his skin that wasn't covered by his shorts and shirt was burned and blistered and cracked. He was dehydrated and starving to death. And now he had a broken nose. His eyes were glassed over and he half consciously looked at the beautiful angel of death that hovered over him.

Avis looked down at what was left of Pellet and then looked over at the woman who had just climbed into their boat. It took him a few seconds to realize that he recognized her from a bar in Saint Maarten a couple months earlier. "Hey. I know you," he said with a look of amazement. "You kicked the shit out of him a couple of months ago," he said and gestured towards Pellet. She looked back down at him and tried to picture him without all the recent damage.

"Good god. I should have killed him when I had the chance."

Pellet didn't move. He just moaned, "Any of that rum left?" Avis unscrewed the lid and handed Pellet the bottle. It didn't seem like a scene from a movie any longer.

CHAPTER FORTY-THREE

Almost four hours after Shira's plane took off from Saint Maarten the fuel was running low and she needed to turn around and head home. Plus fuel or not, the sun was about to go down and it was time to suspend the search until the morning. It was difficult enough to search in the daylight and pointless at night. Just as she readied to turn back to the north her voice came over the radio at the Saint Maarten airport tower and onto the radio on Arnie's desk. Against all odds she had spotted a small Zodiac adrift at sea. There were two men in it and one of them was waving to her. It appeared that Avis had won the lottery one more time. She read out the coordinates and said she was circling around to try to signal and reassure them that help was on the way. Right after that her radio went silent and that was the last they heard from her. For the next six hours they, Shira, Avis and the guy who shot her and her plane out of the sky drifted in silence. The few times either of them tried to speak she sharply snapped, "Shut-up," and they did. It was almost midnight when they first spotted the lights of the Navy cutter. Shira picked up the gun and fired a flare high into the air and looked at Pellet.

"Did you notice that I didn't aim it at the ship?"

He was too beaten down to even look up, never mind respond. His only saving grace was that he was barely coherent and was more or less numb to all physical feelings, including pain. Her words did not faze him. Twenty minutes later the small Navy ship pulled up and dispatched a lifeboat to drag the three of them to safety. The two beaten down men were put on stretchers and lifted over the side. Shira climbed up under her own power with the assistance of what seemed to be half the crew. Once on deck two French sailors tended to Pellet and Avis enough to keep them from dying. At the same time, sailors being sailors and the French being French, a half dozen focused a considerable amount of time and energy trying to save the beautiful young pilot from whatever tragedy she had just survived. She leaned against the steel outer wall of the cabin without responding while they barraged her with questions like, "Are you sure you're okay? Can we get anything for you? Would you like to come inside and we'll get something dry to put on?" Meanwhile, the two men she was hired to retrieve, one of which was worth a hundred thousand dollars if he was alive, barely clung to life with each of them hardly being tended to.

"Who's the highest-ranking man here?" Shira asked in a pleasant voice as if being the highest-ranking sailor in a group of sailors who were not doing their jobs was a good thing.

"I am," one of them spoke up with a slightly puffed out chest.

She leaned in close as if she were going to say something to him but she was as unpredictable as the Caribbean weather. A storm of sorts blindsided the poor guy before he knew what happened. As she leaned in, he did the same in return. He saw her hand moving but thought nothing of it until she had a tight grip on his left ear and twisted it nearly hard enough to tear it off. Her forearm of her free hand pushed two others out of the way and she marched the proud owner of the highest rank over to where the injured sailors lay, on what might be their death beds.

"These men have not eaten or drank anything for four or five days. They were nearly cooked to death by the sun and basically, they look like shit. You're not getting laid," she emphasized first to the guy whose ear was still in her grip, and then to the others. "None of you. Now, get these men medical help," she said, and pushed his head away and gave one last tug before letting go. There was something about her that commanded respect and perhaps fear. She was five foot seven inches tall and weighed no more than a hundred and ten pounds. Her build was slender and everything else, her legs, her arms, her fingers, all of her, was long and strong. Her face was distinct with a defined jaw line and slightly high cheek bones. Her eyes were dark hazel, with just a tinge of smoky mystery to them. Her lashes and brows were naturally full. Her sandy blonde hair that was still pulled into a ponytail flowed two-thirds of the way down her back. She was good looking enough to be a model but there was something more. She oozed utter physical and emotional confidence. When she took Pellet down in the bar she hadn't gotten into a fight she hoped to win. She had won before it started. The same thing happened when she broke his nose. And once again, when she grabbed the sailor's ear and told him to do his job. The others did not dare to question her. A few seconds later, Avis and Pellet were being carried inside and their journey back to life began.

Shira followed them inside and watched as IV's were slipped into their arms and fluids began to drip into them. As soon as that was done, they started dabbing some sort of salve on their wounds. As if they didn't already look bad enough, the degree of their wounds was amplified as a sailor cut open Pellet's t-shirt in order to remove it without disturbing his injuries. To see the smooth tanned skin on his chest in contrast to the blisters and cracks and dried blood on his neck and face was shocking. For just a moment she felt a little bad for breaking his nose. Then she recalled that he shot down her plane while she was trying to save them and her guilt disappeared.

The ship's Captain came through the doors and the men continued scurrying around and taking care of their patients. Shira stood off to one side like an angelic overlord ready to strike down anyone who dared to not do their job. He came in and nodded to her and began talking to his men in French. When he finished he turned to Shira and stuck his hand out to shake hers. He had watched her brutalize his men through the window of the bridge. He was torn somewhere between amused, impressed, slightly aroused and mildly offended by the whole incident. In the end he decided his men got what they deserved.

"I am Captain Gerard. You are the one who called this in?"

"Yes," was all she said.

"And your plane?"

Her jaw clenched and a vein popped in her forehead. She nodded towards Pellet. "That delirious idiot shot it down with his flare gun. Caught fire and crashed into the sea."

He looked down at Pellet as if he were trying to imagine the incident. "Impressive. I would think it would be difficult to hit a plane with a flare," he answered, as if she had been successfully shot down.

"I was almost on their boat. Hard to miss," she scoffed and pushed her way past him and went back out onto the deck.

CHAPTER FORTY-FOUR

Arnie got excited when he first heard from Shira. Finding the lost sailors on the first day was a miracle in itself. Finding them still alive in their lifeboat he presumed qualified his company for the hundred-thousand-dollar bonus. It was a double whammy. Then after he lost contact with her he wasn't sure whether he should call Savannah or not. He didn't know if he had good news or bad. He didn't know if he just made a chunk of money or not. In his mind the whole thing was more stressful for him than it was for Savannah. She and Lucy were staying in a hotel not far from the airport and waiting for a call from anybody. After an hour of waffling back and forth on what to do, he finally picked up the phone and made the call. Twenty minutes later they were sitting with him in his small office and it quickly became apparent that they were not going anywhere until they got word that everyone was okay. Arnie was a bit agitated that the two women didn't care that they weren't the only ones who were worried. He had a missing plane and a missing pilot, but mostly a missing plane. He couldn't afford to lose either, never mind both. Losing the hundred thousand would just be salt in his wound.

"Is it usual that you would lose radio contact with her?" Savannah asked.

"No. Not really." He sounded as if he wanted to lie to her, but he couldn't bring himself to do it.

"Then why wouldn't she radio in? I mean, what do you think happened?" she pressed.

"Could be something as simple as the radio stopped working," he answered and he left it at that. He didn't bother following that comment up with, "If it was simply a radio issue, Shira would have landed at the airport a few hours ago.

So, they sat and waited. They paced around the office and

waited. Then they sat some more. Just after midnight, Savanah and Lucy continued to impatiently stir in Arnie's office, wide eyed and waiting for news. Arnie drank his fourth cup of coffee and fought the urge to let his head tilt forward and drift off to sleep. He didn't see how going without sleep would help the situation. Savanah's cell phone rang at 12:18 A.M. She looked down at it and froze. One way or another, life as she knew it hung in the balance. It was as if she had been on trial for a murder that she did not commit and there was no reason to think the jury would see anything other than the truth and find her not guilty… unless they saw it differently and convicted her. In her mind, she was at that moment standing in front of the courtroom waiting to hear if her life was over or was she free to keep on living. If Avis was not alright, if he was gone, her life was over. There was no other way for her to look at it. The phone rang three times before she hit the answer button and even then she just stared at the phone until Lucy nudged her to put it up to her ear and say "Hello."

"Yes. Is this Ms. Humphrey? Savannah Humphrey?" a woman's voice asked with a strong, French accent.

"Yes," her voice barely squeaked out. She felt as though the point of a dull knife was pressed firmly against her chest, ready to be thrust in by the power of just one or two words. The conversation had played through her head all night long. She tried to silence it, but it was in a loop that just would not stop. There was no doubt in her mind that if the first two words were, "I'm sorry," then the knife would be driven deeper into her flesh and her chest would explode, blood would pour from her heart, and she would die. She stopped breathing or thinking. The looping conversation had stopped and there was absolute silence in her head. The verdict was about to be read. Pressure on the knife increased and the pain increased with it.

"Wonderful," the woman responded. "I have some good news for you."

"Oh, thank you. Thank you so much. Thank you, thank you, thank you, thank you," she kept repeating but each time was less and less understandable as Savannah began to sob harder and harder.

The woman on the other end continued to try to provide more information, but Savannah had held her emotions in for as long as she could. When the phone call came, she was going to shatter in pain, or shatter in joy. "Thank you," she continued to say but by now the phone was nowhere near her face. Lucy gave her a big hug and then reached down and took the phone from her hand. A few minutes later, she hung up and shared the details with Arnie and Savannah.

"They're both in rough shape, but conscious. The Navy boat will be in Marigot in three or four hours and they'll be going straight to the hospital."

"And what about the plane?"

Lucy looked at Arnie and pretended he had misspoke. "The pilot is okay, too," she said and turned back to Savannah and gave her another hug.

"Ahh, yes. The pilot is okay. That's good. And the plane," he asked again. Lucy looked at him again and thought he could not be this stupid but she would explain anyway.

"Well Arnie, they're all on a boat a few hours from shore. Unless it's an aircraft carrier..." She allowed him to fill in the blanks. He looked as though he was going to cry.

"I want to go to Marigot," Savannah said as she stood up and stepped towards the door.

"Let's wait for a few minutes Savannah. There's plenty of time. How about we just step out for some fresh air and let this sink in for just a bit." Lucy took her by the hand and led her out to the parking lot and they stood and felt like they had just come out of a pressure chamber. The air seemed fresher than it had for days. Perhaps fresher than ever before. The world seemed better. The stars were brighter. Savannah tried to tell Lucy something. She wanted to explain how much it meant that Lucy had flown back down for her. She wanted to somehow express her gratitude. But when she opened her mouth, nothing came out. When they looked at each other all she could do was smile and give her friend a crushing hug. It took a few minutes but Savannah felt herself coming back to earth. That was when the logical questions began to pop into her head.

"Did they say what happened?"

"No details to speak of. When the Navy arrived, the three of them were in the lifeboat. I guess the guys are pretty rough. Cuts and bruises. Both of them have third degree burns all over. Whatever happened, they didn't get much time to prepare for it. Doesn't sound like they had a chance to grab any supplies."

"And how did the pilot end up in the boat?"

Lucy just raised her eyebrows and shrugged. "Dunno. All I know is that the guys are coming home and we're going to be there to meet them." She squeezed Savannah's arm and a thought came to her. "You know, Savannah, if you didn't come here and hire the plane they wouldn't have made it. They sound pretty rough. You saved their lives." Savannah started crying again.

CHAPTER FORTY-FIVE

Other than the first couple of sailors who ran to help tie off the vessel, Shira was the first to walk down the gangway when they pulled up to the dock.

"I think you'll be buying us a plane," was all she mumbled when she eased past Savannah. Her attitude was one of cool indifference. If tonight had been stressful or exciting for the woman who had saved her husband's life, she showed no sign of it. She glanced at Lucy as she walked by them and added, "Good luck with everything," and said nothing more. The truth was that she had begun internalizing most of her emotions when Papa died. Once she started training and working for Mossad, she further mastered compartmentalizing pretty much anything that couldn't help her with whatever task was at hand. After Ghalia died in her arms, she began to break down those walls for a little while as a tribute to *her sister*, but the walls began growing again over the past several months. She was putting her life behind the safe walls again. Behind the walls was simple and nearly problem free, with the exception of occasionally beating up Pellet, which was more of a problem for him than for her. Despite the lonely isolation, it was where she chose to stay. Solitude was an almost certain antidote that prevented her from being hurt by anyone.

She waved to one of the taxi drivers playing dominos at the taxi stand and he slowly motioned towards his van and walked over and met her there. She mumbled her address to him and they both climbed in. Seconds later they drove away and the day ended for her. Mission accomplished. Complete. Go home and decompress. Tomorrow is another day. That's the way she had been wired or programmed or perhaps that's the way she had programmed herself. Perhaps she was not going to live the carefree love filled life she had promised to Ghalia as her young friend drew her final breaths on the blood-stained dirt in Israel. Maybe she found the need to compromise and step back not only from the bad world, but from the entire world. It wasn't the sweet dream that she and Ghalia shared on that last dark day, but there wouldn't be any more emotional scars. Not in Shira's life. That was that. Besides, Ghalia was gone. If Shira hadn't allowed herself to get close to her, she wouldn't be dealing with the painful memories now. She was slowly slipping back to the place of numb indifference.

The ambulance crews had been waiting when the ship arrived and the medics rushed the gurneys onto the deck and in through a large metal door. A sailor on the dock stayed with Savannah and Lucy and wouldn't allow them to climb aboard. He repeatedly reassured them that their men would be brought out at any moment, but a lot of moments came and went and nobody came off the boat. Joyful anticipation began to turn back into stressful worry. An officer appeared on deck and walked down the gangway towards the two of them. Savannah began to become rattled again and Lucy held things together enough for both of them.

"I'm Captain Gerard," he said and reached for Lucy's hand.

"Lucy," she answered and squeezed his hand. "This is Savannah. Her husband is one of the men you rescued."

"How are they?" Savannah blurted out.

"They're both in rough shape. One of them is a bit worse than the other. Looks like he might have had an accident or something. Cuts on his face and a broken nose." He didn't want to paint a pretty picture just to have the two women be shocked when the medical team brought them out.

"Do you know which is the injured one?"

"Mmmm. I think the one that's doing better is called Avis," he said and nodded. "He was talking and joking with a couple of the crew, but I think they'll both be okay. Is the other one with you?" he asked Lucy.

She cringed at the question and felt ashamed at the

answer. "God no. I taught him how to sail."

"Ouch," he joked with a smile that melted Lucy just enough that it caught her slightly off guard. "Don't worry. It's probably not your fault," he added and winked at her before he got serious again and looked back to Savannah. "They're just trying to make them a bit more comfortable and preparing to bring them out to the ambulance," he said, turning back and forth to both of them. "You should prepare yourselves. They look a lot worse than they probably are. The sun burned them badly."

"Okay," Lucy answered and Savannah just nodded.

"Oh," he added just before turning and walking away, "And I know it's going to be difficult, but please don't hug or touch them. As I said, their burns are extensive. I'm sure they'd love a hug, but…" he trailed off and turned and strolled back up the gangway. Lucy watched him walk the whole way. Whether she was aware of it or not, she was waiting to see if he glanced back at her. After walking onto the boat and then walking halfway down the deck, he reached a door and grabbed the knob and turned it. He pulled the door open and started to step inside. Just before disappearing, he glanced back over his shoulder. Both of their hearts jumped ever so slightly.

As soon as the Captain disappeared, the first gurney wheeled through the door with a medic at each end. Seconds later the other one appeared. Both men had IV's in their arms with a bag of fluid laying on their chest. Pellet was on the first one. As he was wheeled off the boat, Lucy and Savannah couldn't tell if he had been medicated or if he was just delirious.

"We got hit by a bus," he whispered with a shadow of the ever-present Pellet grin. They both smiled and Lucy leaned over and almost kissed him. "We'll see you at the hospital?" she whispered. He was spent and said nothing more.

Savannah stood with her hands up to her face and watched Avis being wheeled down. She wanted to jump on top of him and hold him forever, but she just leaned close to him and whispered, "I love you so much."

Avis smiled as best as he could and whispered the same

back to her. "I love you too, beautiful," and then he cracked a small grin. "We got hit by a bus," he added, and they wheeled him away. Savannah looked at him with a puzzled look on her face and noticed that Lucy had the same look. They both momentarily tried to envision any possible way that Bella Vita could have been hit by a bus while out at sea. They both failed.

CHAPTER FORTY-SIX

Pellet sat at the bar with Dez leaning against the beer cooler.

"Do you know that the three days we were on the sailboat, it rained for at least a few minutes every damned day. And the five days in the dinghy, not a drop."

"So you told me... twenty times." Dez shot back.

He and Avis had spent the first ten days in the hospital and the next three weeks nursing themselves back to health at home. They'd been up and out of the house for a couple weeks and life was slowly returning to normal. Avis was fishing a lot from the rocks along the shore on the east end of the island. Savannah went with him more than usual and read or listened to music or just chatted with him. He was grateful to be alive and in love and just happy to have her around. She was awestruck at how overwhelmed she had been by the thought of losing him.

Oscar and Iggy had come around to see Pellet more than usual during his recovery. It was almost like old times except Oscar and Pellet were both sober. Iggy was still beautiful and gracious. Helmut wrote a short story about their great sailing adventure that almost immediately got picked up by a major sailing magazine. He named the story, *Double Slug Bug* and everyone loved it. Lucy stayed around to help Pellet with his recovery. She slept on his couch for a few nights until he began to recover. After that she moved into Savannah's guestroom and slept there at night and went to tend to him during the day. For reasons that could have only existed in Pellet's head, he once again clung to the idea that he could somehow coax or perhaps guilt her into having a relationship with him. If not a relationship, he'd settle for sex. Surely after all that he'd been through she would reconsider. He was a bit disappointed when he asked for a sponge bath and her response was, "Still fish bait, Pellet." As the days went by she came by less and less. She stopped by in the morning, spent an hour or so with him and then came back in the evening and did the same. When he asked what she did to kill the time during the day, she shrugged and rambled on about the beach or Dez or vaguely mentioned taking day trips to Saint Maarten to do this or that. Then came the day when she didn't show up in the morning. When he called her phone there was no answer. He called Desmund to inquire if his nurse was hanging around the bar.

"Hey. You seen Lucy?"

"Tink she mentioned going to Saint Maarten for the night when I saw her yesterday afternoon," he said while sipping a cup of bush tea at the bar and looking out at the sea.

"For the night. For what?"

"Guesin she stayed with dat French sailor dude she been seein," he said, not realizing that Pellet had not yet been given the bad news that his current fixation had moved on without him.

"Sonofabitch," he mumbled. "She's cheating on me."

Desmund laughed. "She probably don't know you guys are a couple. You try telling her?"

"Yeah," he said in a long drawn out word. "She threatened to use my penis for fish bait again."

"Okay den. Guess everyting is clear, huh?"

Pellet hung up the phone and pouted. "The French dude? Why would she pick him over me?" He asked both questions out loud even though he was the only person in the house. They were rhetorical questions that even he knew the answer to. Asking why a young, educated, attractive and successful woman who loved to sail would have a relationship with a young, attractive, successful Naval Officer from France was a question that pretty much answered itself. But Pellet was stubborn and indignant and convinced himself that he was hurt. It seemed, at least for the moment, that there was little that he could do other than go to Dez's and feel sorry for himself. So, that's what he did with as much energy as he could muster.

"Guess who's comin to visit?" Dez blurted out as he

handed Pellet a beer. Pellet shrugged. "Maddie."

"Get the hell out of here." Maddie was part of the original Island Dogs gang shortly after Pellet arrived in Anguilla. A few years back she, Pellet, Oscar, Clive and Desmund were all partners in crime who somehow survived a couple years of hanging out together, with Helmut sitting in the same corner as he always did. Maddie and Oscar were on Bella Vita with Pellet on that first tragic sail, back when it was still named Aqua Vita and floating about the surface of the sea. She and Pellet stayed in touch after she left and always planned on getting together, but she had a life back in the US and Pellet never got around to going to visit her. They were about as much of a couple as Pellet and Lucy, but Maddie always loved Pellet for who he was. Like so many other good women, she was never going to sleep with him, but he was like a helpless little island dog that she couldn't help but fall in love with. Since leaving Anguilla she got married, dashing any delusional hope that Pellet might have once had. Pellet loved her, too, even if there was no hope of ever being with her. Desmund had called her when Pellet went missing and she was about to fly down when she got the call that he was found. Now that he was back up and around and since none of them had died yet, she thought it would be nice to see them again. "When's she coming?"

"Be a month or two still. Said she'd let me know the date as soon as they booked a flight." Pellet felt a tinge of jealousy or maybe disappointment when he heard "they." But he'd survive. He always did.

Two weeks later, almost nine weeks to the day of being rescued by Shira, Pellet bounced into the bar like a new man, grinning from ear to ear.

"Wha choo smilin bout?" Dez asked and slid him a beer to him.

"Got a plan," he said, oozing the same confidence that he oozed for all his plans.

"Oh, shit!" Helmut chimed in from his table. "That has never ended well for you. Why don't you just sit there and drink and resist the urge to plan anything." But Helmut and Desmund both knew it was already too late. Once Pellet began putting *a plan* together in his head, the only thing to stop him was the imminent pain he'd feel when he eventually crashed and burned. Bella Vita was the perfect and most recent example.

CHAPTER FORTY-SEVEN

There are some hard and fast rules that hold true in the spy world. One is that full disclosure is counterproductive to the spy business. Just about everything is a secret to the point that even how they decide what is going to be a secret is kept a secret. Another is that rarely do the key players know anywhere near as much as they pretend to know. Reliable information is often unreliable. Complete information is more often than not, partial information. And when they are one hundred percent certain about the details of a mission at hand, they are often fifty percent incorrect.

What his colleagues at Mossad did know in relationship to what happened to Yossi "Papa" Eilat, is that about ten years ago three Israelis went on a mission in an undisclosed city, in an undisclosed country, neither of which were in Israel. All three were caught off guard when they met up with the people that they were supposed to be catching off guard and all three Israeli's were shot. None of the bodies could be recovered for the simple reason that they were doing things in a place where they were not supposed to be. As they say in the movies, "If you get caught, you're on your own. The government will deny any knowledge of your actions or even of your existence." But Mossad had absolute confirmation from two reliable sources that the three men were dead. On the upside, it turned out that the killers shared a similar disavowing view since those who were nearly infiltrated by Israeli spies did not want the world or their superiors to know of how close they came to being exposed. After the disastrous mission for all involved, the killers discreetly disposed of the bodies out in the desert and that was the end of the story. There were no survivors. No interrogations took place. And just as importantly, there was no backlash for either side as there would have been if the world found out what both sides had actually been up to. The spy story ended for almost everyone when the men were buried in the sand.

For Shira of course, that was not the end of the story. She lived day in and day out, year in and year out with the void left by her long-deceased Papa. After years of dealing with his memory as best as she could, there were still nights when she bolted awake from a deep sleep where she had been dreaming that Papa had just kissed her goodbye again and told her to get some sleep. Sometimes it still felt as though she had seen him just a few days ago. Other times, late at night in her dark room, it felt like only minutes ago. More than once she awoke and for just a moment, she could smell his cologne and feel where he had just kissed her on the side of her cheek. When the fog lifted, reality would set back in. It puzzled her that after losing her mother, it was painful at first, but with the passing of time her memory faded. Slowly but surely her voice became unfamiliar. She began to forget what her perfume smelled like. She didn't really remember what it was like to get a hug from her or to play a game with her. Even when she occasionally thought about walking with her or talking to her, she didn't recall what it felt like. It was as if she could recall eating dessert, but without recalling its delicious flavor. Memories of dinner conversations or bedtime stories slipped away like small boats drifting out to sea. First they were there. Then they were a bit further away. And eventually they became tiny specs that simply disappeared beyond the horizon. But it was different with Papa. For the first few years, none of it made sense to her. She presumed, even as a young woman, that tragic deaths of people you love never made sense. One moment they're with you and the next they're gone. No reason. No explanation. Then she got the new version of what really happened to him and she thought if she joined Mossad she would find out the details that would help to make the pain go away. If she knew more, she thought, then she could finally have some peace. The void he left would be filled with something that would allow her to sleep again. Perhaps, she thought, becoming a spy like Papa would in a way bring him back to life. Whatever she had thought, she was wrong. In due time she read reports that included sketchy details of what had happened to him and how it ended, but it was all for naught. Her pain did not ease up and her loneliness did not subside. Sleep did not return and just as it always had been, it made no sense to her why Papa had gone away. The walls that surrounded her only grew bigger and taller and stronger than they were before. Memories of him and the wound he left behind remained fresh and never healed. There were times when she could force the memories and pain away, but sooner or later she would bump into someone, or find herself in a place or a situation that brought him back to the front and center of her pain. All these years later, he remained the ghost in her life that would not rest and would not allow her to rest.

Things began to change for her bit by bit after an irresponsible, disoriented sailor she was trying to rescue from the clutches of death shot her plane out of the sky with a flare gun and she crashed into the Caribbean Sea. There was nothing she could put her finger on and there was no reason to believe it had anything to do with the flare gun guy, other than she was certain it was a turning point in her life. It struck her as being a little odd that she didn't find the events of that night or the crash itself at least a bit traumatizing. She was cool and composed by nature, but even Shira realized that it was odd that her anxiety didn't so much as twitch or spike as her plane dove towards the water. But she could feel the shift in her universe. She sensed an ever so slight deterioration in the walls that surrounded her as she watched in slow motion as she and the plane slammed into a sea of water that engulfed her world. For a single moment in time, she felt at peace with the universe.

Even though the walls just barely began to crumble at that very moment, something told her that the walls were not as impenetrable as they had once been. A few nights later as she slept in her bed and the fresh air blew into her window, she dreamt she heard Ghalia's voice calling her to go for a walk on the beach. Shira saw her standing ankle deep in the blue water. There were flowers in her hair and she looked happy. "Shira, come in the water," she called out. "It's wonderful, *my sister*." Then the dream faded away. The scent of tropical flowers blew through Shira's window and she drifted in and out of sleep. There was a smile on her face. She tried to look back into the dream she had just left to see if she could find Ghalia again. She was nowhere to be found, but she had left something behind, Shira was certain of it. As she faded back to sleep the smile remained.

In the morning, she strolled down to the water where Ghalia had been standing in her dream. There was a small pile of coral and rocks that someone had stacked up beside a single set of footprints. Change was coming. She could feel it.

CHAPTER FORTY-EIGHT

The whole thing sounded like a great idea. As he sat on the lounge chair on his porch, it sounded like a terrific idea bouncing around in his overly optimistic head. When he was drinking a beer at Dez's Bar the idea kept running through his slightly buzzed brain and no matter how he looked at it, there was no real downside. The worst that could happen was that he'd end up exactly in the same place as always. Dez's Bar. On the ferry boat ride to Saint Maarten he still thought he had a good idea and a great plan. He had a good feeling about this one. Then again, he always had good feelings about his plans. When he bought Bella Vita he was so certain it was a good idea he referred to it as his lucky boat. So, as he was walking across the parking lot towards the front door he had a few butterflies, but nothing to be concerned about. Just a few nerves sparking to life. It was a good plan. He was almost certain of it. When he reached for the door he was more or less still confident that this was a good idea. It was when he turned the knob and pushed the door open and saw her standing there that the idea of what might happen if things did not go well went off like another flash of lightening.

It had been about a week since the revelation that Lucy had run off with another man had hit home. He moped for a couple of days until this brilliant idea came to him in a moment of divine inspiration. It dawned on him that he had never properly thanked the pilot lady from Saint Maarten for saving his life. In fact he hadn't seen her since they were on the boat together. Considering his castaway condition and her beating him up again, he didn't really see that much of her in the lifeboat. He did however recall what she looked like the first time they met at the bar. So in a moment of creative genius, he decided that going over to Saint Maarten and personally thanking her would present the perfect opportunity to take her out for a drink as a token of his appreciation. "What's the worst thing that could happen?", he asked himself. She turns me down. No big deal. Nothing ventured, nothing gained. Those were all the thoughts he had before opening the door and looking at her straight in the eyes. Then it all came back to him. The first time they met she knocked him out, choked him, and almost killed him. The second time they met, she broke his nose and almost killed him. So when he quickly reviewed the possible answers to his question, "What's the worst thing that could happen?" It suddenly seemed like, "She turns me down," didn't come anywhere near to the worst thing that could possibly happen. In that moment he realized he had inadequately answered the question.

Pellet stood in the open doorway with a blank look on his face as if he wanted to say something, but nothing came out. The blood felt as if it were draining from his head and his mouth went dry. He just looked at her and stood like a lost child who didn't dare talk to strangers. Shira looked back at him and surprisingly, smiled and waited for him to speak. It was the first time he had seen her when she wasn't violent towards him the moment they met.

"Hi," he eventually blurted out.

"Hi," she answered and said nothing more.

"I thought, ahhh," he struggled to find the words he wanted to say. As with most of Pellet's plans, he forgot to include the small details like, what to say to her when they met. "I came over on the ferry and ahhh." Shira stood in front of the counter with some papers in her hand and continued to watch him struggle for words. She thought it was cute in a mildly pathetic sort of way. "Anyway. Look. We kind of got off to a pretty bad start. You know, you and me. You kicked my ass in the bar and then you kicked my ass in the lifeboat," he struggled to get the words out.

"If I recall correctly, you grabbed me in the bar and you shot me out of the sky before I climbed into the boat," she answered in a polite tone with a warm smile still on her face.

"Yeah," he began, "Probably shouldn't have grabbed

your arm. Definitely shouldn't have shot your plane down. In my defense, the second one was an accident." He was back on his heels. The conversation wasn't going as well as he had hoped. And coming to the realization that if things went badly again, he could end up back in the hospital, didn't lower his stress.

"I don't think we've ever actually been introduced. I'm Shira," she said as she stepped towards him and extended her hand. He flinched when she reached for his hand and she smiled a bit broader. "It's okay. Don't do anything stupid and I won't hurt you," she joked.

"I do a lot of stupid stuff. I'd appreciate it if you don't hurt me again even if I do or say something inappropriate," he said, not joking. "I'm Pellet," he added and reached out and took her hand in his. It felt good. It felt right.

"Pellet?" she repeated. "I've never heard that name before."

"My real name is Wayne. Wayne Pelletier, but everyone calls me Pellet."

"Wayne," she said just to hear the name roll off her tongue. "Wayne Pelletier. That's a nice name. Do you mind if I call you Wayne instead of Pellet?"

Time stood still and the world seemed to disappear except for her and the sound of her voice. He hadn't really known what to expect. Rejection was the most likely result. To hear the most beautiful woman he had ever met say, "Wayne Pelletier. That's a nice name," was beyond his comprehension. Until that moment in time, he hadn't even realized that he didn't really care for the name Pellet. It was cool when he was twelve and unique when he was sixteen. He was almost thirty-five now and in the briefest span of time, Shira made him want to be called Wayne for the rest of his life.

"Not at all," he answered and smiled back at while the blood began to flow back into his face. It felt good to hear someone say his name. It felt good to hear *her* say his name. Friends and family had been calling him Pellet for as long as he could remember. He'd always been okay with it and never given it any thought one way or the other. But to hear Shira call him Wayne, he suddenly felt grown up. He somehow felt like a man who could have a real, live grownup conversation with a beautiful, mature grownup woman. "First, let me say thank you for saving my life. There are no words…"

"It was my pleasure, Wayne. Except for the getting shot down thing," she added.

"And also, I'd like to apologize for grabbing you in the bar. I'm not the kind of guy who does things like that. And again, I can't tell you how bad I feel about shooting down your plane."

"We're good, Wayne. I'm all in one piece. Besides, the plane belonged to Arnie and I'm sure between the insurance and what your friends paid him, he came out ahead on the deal. Arnie always comes out ahead."

He stood in front of her and nodded, as if there was something more to be said. Shira stood in front of him and waited for him to say it. There was a long awkward silence.

"Anyway, I was wondering if I could take you for a cup of coffee or a drink or something like that. You know, as a small token of my appreciation."

"A cup of coffee for your life. I don't know, doesn't seem to me that that would even things up.

"Okay. How about dinner? Do you have plans for tonight?" The question was more a reflex than thought out. If he had taken the time to inflict Pellet logic, he would have likely screwed it up. But Wayne responded with the logical invitation. The Pellet side of him had a slight sense of relief that he wasn't bleeding.

"Dinner it is," was how she sealed the deal and made Wayne Pelletier the happiest man he had been in a long, long time.

"Where and when?"

Shira scribbled her name, the name of the restaurant, the time and her phone number on a note pad and handed him the page she tore off. Just like the handshake, Pellet flinched just a little before reaching out to take it. Shira handed him the paper with one hand and touched him on the shoulder with the other before she walked away. "See you tonight, Wayne," she said without looking back as she went back into a back office.

He flagged down a taxi and headed to the restaurant to see how fancy it was. Then he found a hotel room for the night so he wouldn't be stranded at Marigot Bay waiting for a ferry that wouldn't be there until tomorrow morning. And after seeing the restaurant and getting his room he went and bought a pair of pants, a new shirt and a pair of shoes so he wouldn't be taking Shira to a nice place to eat with her all dressed up and him in cargo shorts, a golf shirt and flip-flops.

At eight PM he walked into the dining room and Shira was sitting at the bar waiting for him. She was dressed in cargo shorts, a tank-top and flip-flops. She pulled it off far more elegantly than he could ever have hoped to. He eased towards her and reached out to shake her hand. Shira leaned in and kissed him on the cheek. "You clean up very nice, Wayne."

"You're beautiful," he answered before he could even process the words in his head. She smiled and took him by the hand and led him to a table beneath the stars. He was relieved they had made it this far and he hadn't been assaulted.

CHAPTER FORTY-NINE

"You're really going to ask the woman who beat the hell out of you if she'll go on a date with you?" Avis asked before Pellet took his first drink.

"Twice," Dez added. "She beat em down twice,"

"Hey, you got Savannah. Anything's possible," Pellet shot back.

"Well to be honest, he was rich. That kinda turned me on," Savannah said and winked at Avis.

"And Hitler, sitting over there in his corner got Fatisha. If that doesn't qualify as a true miracle, then nothing does," Pellet continued.

"Amen to that," Helmut muttered and surprised Pellet by agreeing with him. It was a rare occasion when they agreed on anything.

"And chubby, pasty-white Oscar got Iggy. There's no way in hell that anyone could come up with a good reason why that sweet-hearted beauty should have ever fallen for someone like him." Pellet continued to plead his case only because he enjoyed giving his friends shit. He didn't really care what they said or thought about his new plan. The joke was on them. He'd already been out with Shira seven times and each date was more unbelievable than the time before. Even Pellet was shocked by how well their relationship was working out. "Besides, I've got a plan," he repeated once again, just to taunt them.

"So what's da plan?" Dez asked. "You gonna send her an email or something safe like dat?"

"Well, I thought since the sailing thing didn't work out all that well..." he didn't get a chance to finish.

"All that well! It was a gawd damn disaster," Avis said and almost choked on his beer. "If that's "not all that well," what's it like when it goes really bad?"

"I suppose we'd be dead," Pellet answered with a shrug and took a drink of his beer. "Anyway, I was thinking, since our first two dates were…" He didn't get a chance to finish his sentence when Avis interrupted again.

"Those weren't dates, Pellet. She kicked your ass in a bar and then she kicked your ass in a boat."

"You're always so negative. How do you put up with this attitude?" he said to Savannah and returned her smile and wink.

"So, da plan?" Dez asked again.

"Well, like I was saying before Avis threw his little hissy, I was thinking that I'm going to stick with that ancestry thing. Sailing wasn't the only thing my forefathers did."

"Oh, lawd," Dez muttered and wondered what he'd come up with now.

"Did I tell you that I had a distant great uncle or fifth cousin or something like that who was a pilot in WWII?"

"For which side," Helmut asked.

"Bit foggy on those details. Some seem to say he was a French pilot, but there is at least one version that says he might have been executed after the war for being a Nazi. Either way, he was a pilot. That's my point."

"Oh no, Pellet," Savannah sighed shaking her head. "A crash landing in a plane is not a good idea." She was serious.

"Besides. There's the karma thing to consider," Avis added. Pellet looked at him and waited for clarification. "You shot down her plane," he added, as if it should not have required an explanation.

"You guys worry way too much," Pellet said and lit a cigarette. "Besides. I've only got to fly long enough for her to fall in love with me."

"Angels in heaven don't fly that long," Helmut chimed in again. Pellet turned and gave him a dirty look but didn't respond. For the next two hours they sat and drank and harassed him. Pellet drank and defended and instigated. When it was all said and done it had been a fun and relaxing night with friends and the only thing none of them knew was that Shira was already in the early stages of falling in love with Wayne Pelletier. Of course, he had already fallen in love with her when she proclaimed *Wayne Pelletier* to be a nice name. He was taking the ferry back over to see her again tomorrow.

The last time he had gone over, she met him at the ferry at Marigot Bay and they walked arm in arm down an old street on the French side. She had taken him to a local waterfront restaurant where she had been a few times. They ordered dinner and a bottle of wine and talked and laughed more than Shira had laughed in years. She felt comfortable around Wayne. He had a good heart and wasn't as dumb as he had gotten in the habit of pretending he was. He was lighthearted and funny, but he was also smart and quick witted. Somewhere along the line in the distant past he had lost himself. It had never dawned on him that while he had never been a raving success, nobody ever considered him to be a clown until he started spending too much time drinking too much beer in a Caribbean bar. Somehow, the moment they began talking, Shira sensed what a good heart he had. She saw the kindness in his eyes and felt the warmth of his smile. She had no need or desire to see the part of Wayne Pelletier who had been a long, funny, train wreck on the wrong side of a bar. Pellet was not who he was. Not really. So she forgave Pellet for his earlier blunders and then began falling in love with Wayne.

"It will take me awhile but I was thinking about maybe getting another boat. Any thoughts?" Pellet asked as he poured her a glass of wine.

"You're asking me to chime in on a life decision? A bit early in our relationship for that don't you think?" she teased.

"I suppose your right," he answered. "Probably should have sex at least once before taking such a big step." He raised his eyebrows signaling he expected a response.

"Dream on Pellet," she shot back. It was a cruel shot given in good humor.

"Damn. Just like that. Wayne is destroyed," he laughed and looked down at the table for a few seconds. "So, seriously.

What do you think about me getting a new boat?"

"I'm flattered that you ask, but you need to understand that I can either answer honestly or not at all. Your choice."

"Go ahead."

"I think it's a horrible idea. The seas aren't safe. Between the weather and boat problems in general, and the stories of pirates in the islands these days, it doesn't seem like a good idea to me."

"Then I'd like to learn to fly," he responded without hesitation.

"What are you going to name your new boat?" was her straight-faced response.

An hour later the taxi dropped them off in front of her house. She took him by the hand and they strolled up the sidewalk to the front porch. She motioned for him to sit on the lounge chair while she went inside. A few minutes later she returned wearing a pair of cotton boxers and a t-shirt with two glasses of wine. That night, when Wayne Pelletier drifted off to sleep, it was the happiest he had ever felt. The next morning when he awoke and rolled over and watched her sleep, he was more content than he was the night before. Life had finally dealt him a winning hand. Fate had finally been kind to him. The universe had finally spun its chaos in his favor. God had mercy on him and sent an angel to save him not only from the harsh grips of mother nature, but more importantly, from himself.

CHAPTER FIFTY

The first three weeks of their relationship had gone incredibly smooth. Not only had he avoided any bodily harm, which was a trait unique to Shira, but he had also avoided doing or saying anything tasteless or stupid. Both traits uniquely and commonly held by Pellet. He had found a nice balance in life. Pellet by day, Wayne by night, except on weekends. On Saturdays when he was with Shira, Pellet stayed in Anguilla while Wayne enjoyed her company.

"So, when are you going to take me over to Anguilla to meet your friends?" Shira asked for at least the third time in the past few days.

"Well, you've already met Avis and Savannah. There's not really any hurry in meeting the rest." By *the rest* he was referring to Dez and Helmut. "

"Met them? I nodded at Savannah the night I walked off the rescue boat and Avis, well he was barely even aware he was on a boat the night you shot me down."

"I thought we weren't going to talk about that night anymore," he begged, referring to the unfortunate incident.

"You know, I think it would be great if we could make the image in my head disappear, but you did fire a flare into my wing. Pssssssshhhh!" she said shooting her hand up and into the air as if she were reenacting the flare hitting the wing. "Anyway the point is, I don't think you'll ever hear the end of it. It'll probably be something that comes up every time we have a fight. Plus, you're the one who brought it up."

"We don't have fights," he defended.

"Wayne. Sooner or later we're going to have a fight and when we do, I'm definitely going to remind you that you shot my plane down."

"The good news is that you're such a wonderful woman that you went out with me in spite of what I did, and…" then he added, "On top of all that, you're going to teach me how to fly."

"Anyway, back to my question, when am I going to meet your friends?"

"Soon Shira. Soon," he mumbled as they continued their walk towards the plane. He was keenly aware that Shira had only had a couple of brief encounters with *Pellet* over the last number of weeks. After she turned him into Wayne he had transformed into a more civilized and responsible version of who he had previously been in Anguilla for almost a decade. It was his justifiable fear that the gang and any others who happened to be hanging around at the bar when he took her to meet them, would feel the certain need to provide a full disclosure of his typical antics. What he did not know was that when the stories eventually did begin to pour out, Shira would shut them down with Shira like authority. She would tolerate no mocking of the man she was in love with, even from the people who were his closest friends.

"I can't believe you've talked me into giving you a flying lesson." Shira said' still confused and trying to figure out how he had managed it. She had been one-hundred percent clear that him learning to fly was out of the question.

"You said I shouldn't get another boat, so you really left me no choice," he said and playfully nudged her with his shoulder as they strolled across the tarmac towards one of Arnie's planes. They weren't going on an actual lesson. It was more like a test lesson to see if Shira was going to have the patience to give real flying lessons to Wayne.

"Do you understand how unforgiving mistakes are when you're flying a plane? It takes a split second for everything to go wrong."

"I understand that you can't get hit by a VW bus when you're flying a plane," was his defense of why it was safer to fly than to sail. He reached into his pocket and pulled out a pack of cigarettes and she stopped in her tracks.

"Wayne. First, you need to quit smoking. I don't like it,

But beyond that, you cannot smoke on the flight line. There are fuel trucks and planes everywhere. The airport authorities discourage blowing them up. And second, you can't ever smoke when we're flying. Period."

"Man. The next thing you're going to say is I can't drink when I'm flying either," he said with a big grin. She did not grin back.

"Not funny, Wayne. Flying is fun, but it's serious fun. Not clowning around fun."

"You've got to meet Lucy. She sucked so much joy out of sailing while teaching me I almost sold my boat. The two of you would get along perfectly. I kind of get the same feeling with you and planes."

"Good," she answered. This time she nudged him with her shoulder and smiled.

They did a walk around ritual at the plane and Shira gave him enough information about flaps and rudders, cables and screws, fuel and hydraulic fluid, and tires and propellers and a dozen other things that they had to check before they even climbed into the plane that it made his head spin. It was Lucy and sailing lessons all over again. Only this time Shira wasn't trying to inspire Wayne to pay attention and take it seriously. She was trying to overwhelm him and get him to lose interest in taking flying lessons.

Once they climbed into the cockpit and got situated, she got worse. She explained every button and lever and gauge to him. Even the ones that were virtually never touched or looked at. She piled on information on top of information on top of information. Once he looked completely lost and slightly dizzy, she handed him a headset and let him listen as she requested clearance and received the go ahead from the tower.

The plane was a brand-new twin-engine Cessna, compliments of Avis Humphrey and the insurance company. They taxied about halfway down the runway with Shira and the tower chatting back and forth. The guy in the tower said something about the runway being clear to enter and take-off. Shira turned onto the runway. Without slowing down she pushed the throttle forward and headed toward the mountain directly in front of them. Long before they reached the end of the pavement the plane gently lifted off and easily flew over the mountain top. It was the first time he had flown with her without other passengers being on board. He slowly cleared his head of the thick fog of details Shira had filled it with and sat back and took in the view.

First they flew north to Anguilla where she pointed out familiar landmarks. After that they circled back around and went past Saint Maarten and flew over Saint Barths. From there she turned the plane to the southwest towards the tiny island of Saba. It consisted of little more than a mountain and a runway with a few houses. After that, they headed back towards the Princess Julianna Airport. As they flew, he surprised her by the number of logical questions he asked about the plane and how many details he retained about the navigation buttons, levers and gauges. Instead of being completely lost, he asked about when would you use this lever, or what would she do if the pressure went down on that gauge. In fact, she was so impressed she asked, "Do you want to fly it for a few minutes."

"Hell, yeah," he answered in more of a Pellet voice in his head than a Wayne voice. Shira didn't detect the difference.

"So, like I said, this is the yoke. You do everything in slow motion. Slowly push if forward to go down." She emphasized s-l-o-w-l-y. "Slowly pull back to climb. And slowly turn it to go left or right. That's it."

"What about the throttle?" he asked as he rubbed his hands together as if he were warming up to drive a race car. She looked at him in a way that momentarily made him think that he might be assaulted. "Okay. No throttle," he added and calmly took ahold of the yoke.

"Just keep it level and keep us going straight ahead," she instructed. For the next ten minutes he did surprisingly well. He didn't bounce it up and down. He didn't drift to the left or right. And most importantly, he didn't lose focus. Wayne paying attention to what he was doing didn't surprise Shira in the least.

She had no way of knowing that Pellet was considering making a surprise visit.

"You're going to let me turn a couple times, aren't you? I mean, I've got to do something other than just sit here and go straight." He gave her a quick glance but before giving her a chance to respond he turned over so slightly to the north. She gave him a look without saying a word and he turned it ever so slightly to put them back on course. A few minutes later he did it again but turned a little further than the last time and he didn't look to her for approval, or the opposite. Less than five seconds later he righted their course once again.

"Please behave or give the controls back to me," was all she said.

"This is pretty damn cool. Everything on the sailboat was a delayed reaction. There was no turning on a dime, but this, man. I like it."

Shira looked at him again but he pretended to not notice and behaved himself for another five minutes. Then Pellet made his full arrival in the cockpit and tossed Wayne aside. In a moment of divine inspiration he banked hard to the left and pushed the yoke a bit further forward than he intended to. Not only did the plane turn sharply to the left, it began a descent much faster than he anticipated. He quickly straightened the yoke and started to pull it back up, but the engines began to sputter. He pushed it back forward momentarily and the engines began running smoothly again. Unfortunately, they were still on a downward trek and picking up speed. Pellet felt the adrenaline begin to flow and his heart was racing. He looked at Shira with a look of panic on his face.

"Hey, you're the pilot. Better fix your screw up," was all she said with a shrug.

He took a deep breath and began to slowly pull back on the yoke. By now they were in a steep dive and even though he was correcting it to a small degree, it was only enough to delay the impending crash, not prevent it. They had been flying at about nine thousand feet when he started pretending he was a pilot. He glanced at the altimeter and saw that they were just reaching five thousand with forty-five hundred not far behind.

"I think I need help…. please!" he said with his eyes glued on the water that was nearing fast.

"You *think* you need help? You mean that you're not sure you need help? Is there some possibility that you don't need help?"

He glanced again and saw they were just passing four thousand feet and picking up speed.

"Help, please!"

Shira took a deep breath and put her hands on the yoke in front of her. "Let go of yours and sit back. Just be a passenger and stop pretending you're a pilot." Then she reached down and pushed the throttle forward and the plane accelerated even more. She immediately pulled up on the yoke and the angle of descent began to plane out from steep to slanted to almost level, to level at less than five hundred feet over the water. Pellet was as white as a ghost and looked as though he might get sick. Shira, as always, was cool and calm. "That was fun, don't you think?"

"Jesus Christ," he whispered. "That happened fast."

"Yes, Wayne. Everything happens fast on a plane. We were flying at over two hundred and fifty knots when you decided to pull your little stunt. That means that everything you did happened at the same speed. And there's a cause and effect thing going on. Nose diving and crash landing is easy. Anyone can do it. Getting out of a dive can be a little trickier."

He just kept looking straight ahead and said nothing more.

"And in case it hasn't dawned on you yet, " she continued "I won't ever be giving you pilot lessons. Any questions?"

Pellet rubbed his chin and quietly thought for twenty or thirty seconds before responding. Finally his eyebrows raised as a question popped into his head.

"Have you ever seen any turtle hatchlings crawl out to sea?" he asked as if it were a logical question to be thrown into their conversation.

She looked over at him and thought about his question.

His bar friends probably would have thought it was a stupid Pellet question, but she didn't. As far as she was concerned, it was a brilliant question to ask. The flying conversation was done. There was nothing left to be said. She had begrudgingly taken him flying. He almost killed them. They both silently agreed there was no need to discuss it any further.

"I've seen the trail of a sea turtle's track to shore to lay her nest, but I've never seen the baby turtles come out of the sand." She smiled at him. He reached out and brushed the side of her face with his hand as the plane climbed back into the sky where it belonged.

Once they landed in Saint Maarten they stopped at a café for a quick bite to eat and then they spent the remainder of the afternoon doing things that were much more enjoyable than dying in a plane crash.

That night as he sat at the bar at Dez's he only half listened to their harassment about him becoming a pilot. His thoughts and heart were eight miles away across the bay in Shira's arms.

"Jus don't see me ever gettin in any plane dat you're flyin, How bout you?" Desmund asked Avis, who just shook his head back and forth.

"He almost killed me in his boat."

"Hey, I think I'm a natural born pilot," Pellet said to both of them. "What could go wrong?" he asked, just to add fuel to the fire.

CHAPTER FIFTY-ONE

"I was wondering," Pellet began. "Will our anniversary date be when we first met in the bar?"

Shira thought for a few seconds. He deferred to her, despite the fact that she didn't care in the least bit about unimportant things like anniversary dates. "I suppose it would be nicer to say it would be the day you came to the office and asked me out." But then she smiled a wicked little smile, "Although it might be more entertaining to say I knocked you out and choked you on our first official date wouldn't it?"

He smiled and leaned in and kissed her. "That's what I like about you. Sweet and tender and thoughtful."

"How about we do this," she suggested. "How about we celebrate our one-day anniversary every day. Just think of all the celebrating we'd be doing." This time she leaned in and gave him a long kiss.

He had caught an early afternoon ferry over and they had spent the afternoon in bed. As far as the Anguilla gang was concerned, he was still taking flying lessons and making the sky a less safe place. Clearly, that was not happening. If the thought of him being a pilot was discomforting when they talked about it last week, all was good now that it had been settled. After their afternoon nap they went out and grabbed a bite to eat. Then they strolled along the waterfront and watched tourist buy things that only tourist buy. She held his arm for a while. He walked with his arm around her shoulder for a while. They stopped and had gelato and then stopped and had a café and then strolled hand in hand some more. An hour or so before the last ferry departed, he walked her to the corner market where she grabbed a loaf of bread, a can of coffee, and a half dozen bananas.

"Need anything else?" he asked.

"No. Just you," she said as she laid her stuff on the counter. "You sure you don't want to spend the night?" she asked as she counted out the money to the clerk. "We could celebrate our anniversary," she added with a wink.

"I'd love to but I told Avis I'd help him fix the fence around his house."

"You'd abandon me for Avis?" she accused.

"No. But Savannah's pretty good to me, so I try to keep my commitments... to her."

Shira raised her eyebrow. "Another woman?" she asked half-jokingly.

"Jealous?" he asked with a puffed ego. There were times she made his head swirl. She was the real deal and every single part of her was kind and strong and beautiful inside and out. She had told him about her father and warned him that she was a broken woman. He told her that if this was the broken version of Shira, he hoped he lived long enough to see the put back together version. They were lying naked in bed a few nights earlier and she leaned up on her elbows and said to him, "Describe me in one word." He turned his head and looked at her long flowing hair. Her dark eyes. Her gorgeous smile. Her flawless skin. He thought about her sense of adventure of being a pilot and an ex-spy. Then he thought about shooting her down and she still chose him.

"Magnificent. You are magnificent, Shira." He wanted to add the words, "And I love you," but he was too scared to say them. He was scared on his own behalf because he hadn't said those words since Zoe and that hadn't worked out all that well. And he was scared on her behalf. He was afraid that it might be too much too fast. So, he thought it and he felt it and he had the urge to say it, but he backed off and laid his head back down on the pillow.

"I love you," she whispered and laid her head on his shoulder. He pulled her tight. "I love you too, Shira." It was the happiest moment in his life.

Shira walked him back to the ferry terminal after they left the market and she gave him a long, deep kiss to hold him over for the night. "See you tomorrow?" she smiled and said as the sun began to set in the background.

"I'll try. I'll call you either way."

"See you tomorrow," she repeated without the question mark. He nodded in agreement and watched her walk away and waited until she got into the taxi. When she was out of site, he turned and walked into the terminal wishing he had climbed into the taxi with her.

The ride to her house was not long. She sat quietly in the back seat and watched the buildings, the trees and the other cars whizzing past. Now and then there were women walking along the road carrying grocery bags or men playing dominos outside local bars. The sun was gone and the stars shone as brightly as they could through the yellowed streetlights. The taxi stopped in front of her house and she paid the driver who sped away. The past few weeks had been the best of her life. She thought about the other night when they had been talking in bed and thought to herself that it was the first time she had felt whole for a long, long time. As she walked along the sidewalk towards her house, she realized it was the first time she had ever felt whole. It was as if Wayne was her missing piece.

The grocery bag hung from her left hand and her right hand was stuffed into the pocket of her jeans when she reached the first step of her front porch. That's when she first noticed someone sitting in one of the wicker chairs. She momentarily hesitated and then slowly climbed the four steps and kept her eye on the man in the chair waiting for him to say something. The light was dim and was on the other end of the porch. He was in the shadows and Saint Maarten wasn't known for being a completely safe island. She climbed the last step and stood on the porch and stared at him, waiting for him to make a move. He slowly stood up and spoke to her.

"Shira," was all he whispered.

She dropped the groceries and grabbed at the railing.

"Papa?"

CHAPTER FIFTY-TWO

The next month was a blur for all involved. Yossi "Papa" Eilat shared only enough information to tell the story without breaking her heart. Most of the details were mercifully omitted. He told Shira he had been on a Mossad mission, but he couldn't say where or why, even though she more or less knew those details. Or at least she thought she did. He told her he had been shot but downplayed the seriousness of his wounds. He did not tell her he had been shot four times and presumed he was going to die. He told her that they nursed him back to health and put him in a prison. He did not tell her that they threw him in a dark damp basement and let the wounds heal on their own with no medical attention. If he died, he died. His captors did not care. He did not tell her about the years of torture or that when he was finally rescued he looked like a Jew coming out of Auschwitz. He told her that when he returned to Tel Aviv he was put into a military hospital and given good medical treatment and he was feeling pretty good now. He did not tell her that he was at the hospital for almost three months before he gained enough strength and could manage to get up and walk around. During his last few weeks in captivity, his body had finally given out and only by the grace of God had he lasted as long as he did. The timing of his rescue was nothing short of divine intervention. But he did not tell her any of that and he did not tell her that he demanded that none of his family was to be notified about his rescue before he regained his health. He would not be seen like that by the people he loved. Two days after his family was finally brought in to see him, Yossi was on a plane heading to Saint Maarten.

Shira cried tears of sorrow, tears of joy and tears of overwhelming emotion. Her father was alive and was in Saint Maarten sitting on her couch. After years of having a hole in her heart so vast that it felt like a vacuum eternally sucking every ounce of joy from her life, she was now so full that it was overflowing. First, Wayne had come into her life and healed wounds she thought unhealable. They laughed and loved and walked and talked and for the first time in her young life, Shira was a woman in love. For the first time since Papa had died, she was new again. There had been other men before him. Some were smarter. Some were better looking. Some were better in bed. But none loved her like this sailor who had almost killed her. And none were loved by her the way she loved him. As far as she was concerned, their love was destiny that could not be denied. And now this. Papa was resurrected and her joy was unmeasurable. As far as she was concerned, it was eternal. In a thousand years she would not have dreamt that life could ever be this full of love and happiness. For the first time she understood the meaning of the words, love conquers all.

The day after Papa had returned to her world, Pellet strolled up the walkway and took a deep breath and prepared himself to meet the legend Shira had told him about. It was hard enough to meet *the parents* under normal conditions, but this was almost more than he could deal with. Papa was a former Israeli Military Officer who became a deceased Mossad legend, and single parent who had risen from the dead. His girlfriend understandably held her father in godlike status. Pellet was an American construction guy who was quite obviously the winner of the dating game. There was no doubt in his mind that Shira was so far out of his league that he couldn't begin to understand how the universe worked when people like the two of them ended up together. It wasn't a question he pondered too much. He just thanked whatever god was responsible and tried to not screw it up.

Yossi was warm and welcoming. Pellet reached out to shake his hand and Yossi wrapped his arms around him and gave him a crushing hug. Shira had told him all about Wayne and if she was happy, then Papa was happy. Pellet didn't know what to say or what to ask. What was he supposed to say? "So, I hear you've been locked up in a dungeon for the last decade or so. What was that like?" There was a few minutes of awkward tension and Shira kept filling in little tidbits of what he'd been through. Yossi finally decided that it was a subject he wasn't going to be able to hide from and he repeated his story almost word for word. As he repeated the details, Pellet was speechless and Shira sat awestruck as she hung on to his every word, again. She sat on the couch beside her father with a glass of wine in her hand and a smile on her face. Pellet had a beer and Yossi drank coffee. He said he found it curious how much he missed coffee while he was locked up.

Shira could not contain her joy. She was radiant and Pellet was happy for her. After all these years her father had returned and his little girl came back to life. It was an afternoon that none of them would ever forget. It was a flawless day for her, but Pellet was already considering the repercussions. There was always a ripple effect. Hell, he was the king of ripple effects. Sometimes there was a tidal wave effect. He was already hoping it was just going to be a small ripple. A few days later his questions were starting to be answered. They had talked for hours the night before but she more or less ignored nearly everything he said. She had everything worked out and her plan was being put into motion and that was that.

"Wayne, you will love Tel Aviv. It's beautiful. And you'll love my family," she insisted.

"I don't know Shira," he said and shook his head back and forth. But he did know, and he had tried to tell her but she refused to hear. He couldn't move to Israel. He wasn't really sure why, but he knew he couldn't do it. The islands were about as far as he could stretch his journey from Waldoboro, Maine.

"Oh, you worry too much," she continued. "Everything will be good. You'll see." And she continued to make plans with absolute certainty that Wayne was going with her. They held hands and walked back from the market and Shira was full of life as she continued to plan their future. Pellet listened and savored every moment. Deep in his heart he knew these moments were numbered and running out fast. Although he hadn't put his foot down yet, it was only because he was well aware that when he did, they were finished. Shira would be heartbroken and he would be crushed, but he couldn't go. He didn't know if it was just too much geography and too far away from the people he loved, or was it just that he knew he didn't belong on the other side of the world. Or perhaps he knew that he would live every day in the shadows of Papa until the day he died. Even then he would likely live in the shadow of the legend of Papa. It wasn't something he thought he could do for the rest of his life. And he certainly didn't want to go to Israel for just long enough to talk Shira into leaving her loved ones behind on his behalf. He wouldn't do that to her. If he was going to break her heart, he would do it now. If she had asked him to go there a couple of weeks ago, he would have probably followed her to the ends of the earth, but everything had changed. For just a few weeks in his life, Wayne Pelletier's life had been perfect. Perfect by any definition that could be conjured up.

"I dunno," he mumbled again and squeezed her hand.

"Nonsense. We belong together," she scolded. She was persistent and in love. With these two men in her life, there was nothing she could not accomplish.

CHAPTER FIFTY-THREE

It had been five weeks since he gave her one last hug and kiss and they both cried. She said she would see him soon and somewhere deep inside she truly believed it. He knew it was a lie. He said he couldn't wait, but knew he'd be waiting forever. Their moment in time was finished. It was the legendary love that poems and songs and books were written about, but it was finished. She turned and walked to the plane. Pellet sat down in a chair in the airport and cried.

Sitting at Dez's Bar he thought the saying, "Time heals all wounds" was pure bullshit. The only thing that had softened the pain lately was alcohol and hangovers. And he had plenty of both. He sat lost in thought and looked at his half empty beer bottle. He shook his head at the magnitude of the epic failure this time. Another plan crashed and burned. But this plan had gone so catastrophically wrong that it would affect him for longer than he cared to consider. Probably forever. He wouldn't be bouncing back this time. The more or less famous *Pellet resilience* was not going to allow a stupid grin to be placed on his face and enable him to simply move on to the next one. This one was going to leave permanent scars. It was three o'clock Saturday afternoon and he was on his fourth beer. Dez had made an effort to give him slow service, but Pellet wasn't having it. Desmund just shook his head and slid another to him.

"Easy, mon," he mumbled. Pellet shrugged.

A fifty-foot catamaran dropped anchor not too far offshore and the two people on board climbed into their dinghy and motored to the beached in front of the bar. Lucy and Captain Jules Gerard of the French Navy walked in and said hello to Helmut and eased over to the bar.

"Christ. Can't you find someplace else to hang out," Pellet

snapped.

"You'd miss me?" Lucy shot back at him. She wasn't having any of his nonsense. As far as she was concerned he should have gone to Israel with Shira. "One plane ticket will solve your problems," she added. Then before he had a chance to bite her head off Helmut chimed in. He had heard enough of Pellet's pity party, too.

"Good god, man. I'll pay for the first-class ticket if I don't have to listen to you cry and moan anymore." The truth was that Helmut knew the pain of losing true love and thought it inexcusable that Pellet hadn't followed Shira to the ends of the earth.

"And where'd the Catamaran come from?" Pellet asked, nodding at the sailboat in the bay and more importantly changing the subject. He still didn't know why he didn't go with Shira, but the discussion was over.

"Bought it."

"You bought it?" he asked surprised. "Where the hell did you get money for that?" He was on a roll. He got up and walked to the railing and looked out at the catamaran floating a few yards offshore. "What'd it cost, three hundred? Four hundred?" He left no time to answer the questions before he moved onto the next. Over the past few weeks he had decided that meeting Lucy had been a bad thing. She wasn't like Shira. She hadn't crushed him with one mighty blow. With Lucy it was more like she was beating him to death with a small stick. First, she taught him to sail, which almost cost him his life and life-savings. Then she met the French dude and their relationship was serious and they were even discussing getting married. Pellet was convinced she was just doing it to piss him off, as if he could somehow be that significant in her life. Now this. She bought a sailboat. His was at the bottom of the sea and her big shiny and expensive one was sitting in front of the bar taunting him. "Where the hell did you get money to buy that?" he asked again. This time he waited for an answer.

"We bought it together," she nodded towards Jules. "My father helped me finance my half."

"Of course he did," Pellet ranted. He glanced at Jules with a look of contempt. Jules raised his beer in a halfhearted toast and winked at Lucy. Pellet just stood there staring at the boat as he puffed on his cigarette. Lucy couldn't quite tell if he was dreaming of sailing on it or drilling a hole in the bottom of it. He snubbed the end of his smoke out in the ashtray and finished the last drink of his beer.

"Well?" he snapped at Lucy, as if she knew what he wanted.

"Well, what?" she snapped back.

"Are we going out to take the nickel tour or what?"

"What am I? A mind reader?" she shot back. "Good lord. Why do you guys keep him around?"

"Tried giving him to you. You brought him back," Dez answered.

"And the little Jewish girl tried to take him off our hands, but he was too stubborn to go," Helmut added and then began mumbling in German.

"Are you coming or what?" Lucy barked and they continued going back and forth like bickering siblings all the way down to the dinghy and then all the way out to the boat.

"You not goin?" Dez asked Jules.

"Noooo. Never heard two people bicker as much as those two. I'll let them handle it."

On the boat Pellet looked like someone who was used to Hotel 8 but found himself wandering around the Ritz Carlton. His hands were neatly folded behind his back as he walked through the main cabin into the bow of the boat. He returned and went below on the starboard side and repeated, "Not too shabby," every time he opened a door and saw a new bedroom or storage room or bathroom. When he eventually reached the galley he reverted back to being Pellet. "Hey. A refrigerator," he said already opening it and reaching inside.

"Hey. That's not your galley, you know," Lucy scolded.

"Oh don't get all snooty on me," he said, but hesitated getting his beer. "Lucy, may I have a beer?" he snipped.

"You may." She looked around, pleased with herself and proud of her new boat. "You know, you should get another one."

"I haven't drank this one yet. Damn."

"A boat, Pellet. A new boat."

"Turns out that my daddy won't be buying me a boat. And you know, Jules is taken." She looked at him and they were both speechless for a minute. Then, for the first time in weeks, he stopped being an ass. "You did good Lucy. Nice boat. I'm really happy for you."

"I'm really sorry about Shira, Pellet." It was the first time she found a way to bring the subject up in a compassionate way. It hurt her to say the words. She could only imagine how hard it was on him. He looked around the cabin and tried to think of something to take his mind away from the topic. He didn't want to feel that pain in his chest again, but the reality was that there was no way to ignore the constant jagged edges of life being driven deep into his heart.

"Can you believe I got hit by a VW bus in the middle of the Caribbean Sea?" They both laughed and she walked over to him and wrapped her arms around him and gave him a big Lucy hug. Pellet reciprocated and took in the moment. Then, just like that, he was Pellet again. Had sex on this thing yet?" It was a suggestion more than a question. She punched him on the arm and turned to walk back to the dinghy. He stepped into the galley and grabbed another beer for the trip to shore.

"Help yourself," she scolded. He did.

CHAPTER FIFTY-FOUR

By the time Maddie called and cancelled, Pellet was acting indifferent to most situations that would have typically sent him off the deep end. He had pretty much given up on everything in life since Shira had gone away, but the Maddie thing got under his skin. Maybe even more so than Lucy buying the damn boat with the French dude. When he first heard she was coming for a visit he was pretty stoked. Not all that long ago they were close. Seeing her would have brought back some good memories. Then everything went to shit with Shira and they continued to go downhill from there. Maddie was just one more in the ever-growing list of beautiful women who had broken off relationships with Pellet and then found another man to take his place. The fact that none of them considered themselves to be in a relationship with him in the first place was lost on Pellet. Or in the very least, it was a detail he chose to ignore.

He knew Maddie wasn't a *what happens in the islands, stays in the island's* kind of woman. She was beautiful and good and intelligent and more to the point she was not the cheating type. With that being said, her not being the cheating type wouldn't have hindered Pellet's attempts in the least, as long as the other half of "they" was not around. If she had come alone to visit, he would have tried and failed just like old times. Pellet was a lost soul in need of being rescued more than he had ever needed to be rescued at any point in his life. The thought of Maddie rescuing him was an appealing one.

He strolled into the bar and sat on a stool and waved for a beer that was already being delivered. There was a woman sitting a couple stools down and he would likely bother her in time, but for the moment, "Beer."

"Whatchu tink I'm given you?" Desmund scolded and

then meandered back to the other side of the bar and puttered around. He organized one of the beer coolers, then he straightened a line of liquor bottles and then he finally moved onto organizing the straws and napkins. All the while he watched Pellet out of the corner of his eye. If Pellet had not been so self-obsessed with feeling sorry for himself, he would have noticed that for perhaps the first time in history Desmund was cleaning and organizing the bar. But as it turned out, Pellet was still self-obsessed and in an all-out self-pity mode going on two plus months. He didn't notice the abnormal cleaning. He didn't notice Dez making occasional eye contact with the woman at the bar. And perhaps more importantly, even though everyone had become accustomed to Pellet doing or saying inappropriate or just plain stupid things, he didn't notice that just about everyone's tolerance level, which had always seemed begrudgingly never ending, was in fact ending. His perpetual public display of poor me-ism had run its course and everyone involved was pretty damn sick of it. It was a unanimous opinion that Pellet was a lot more likeable when he was bothering perfectly innocent and more often than not beautiful strangers than he was when he just moped around like a miserable whiner who always seemed to muster up enough self-pity to feel sorry for himself.

Halfway through his first beer he glanced up at the woman a couple seats down the bar. She smiled at him as if she knew him but didn't say anything before looking back down at her half full glass of rum punch. He looked away, drew a deep breath and let out a deep sigh and took a drink of his beer. Then he repeated looking at her, and she repeated smiling and saying nothing before looking away again. They sat for a few minutes, then he repeated and she repeated and they sat some more. Again, repeat, repeat, sat. Halfway through his second beer, he lit a cigarette and looked at her one more time. She looked at him and smiled and he finally decided to take an ever so brief respite from his self-pity fest and talk to the complete stranger.

"Welcome to Anguilla."

"Thanks," she said, and kind of nodded her head up and

down without saying anything more.

"Been here before?"

"No." She took another sip.

"Enjoying yourself?"

"Yes," was all she said. He was a tad confused because her smile said to him that she was quite friendly, but her answers were all one word and weren't really encouraging him to talk with her.

"What brought you to this beautiful island?"

"Vacation," she answered and wondered how long they would keep this up.

If there was anything in this world that could motivate Pellet to do something, it was to tell him that he was probably going to fail at doing the something. And there were a lot of ways to tell him. With women, a sure way to encourage him to stick around and bother them was to politely not encourage him to stay. One-word answers or a cold shoulder were not hints that he missed. He simply did not accept them. The most effective way to get Pellet to go away was to say, "Go away." And that only worked about half the time.

"You look sort of familiar. You're not from Maine are you?"

"No."

"Florida?"

"No."

"There are a lot of states. Could be doing this for a while."

"Okay," was all she said. While most men would have thought "Guess she doesn't want to talk," Pellet thought, "Guess she wants me to do this forty-eight more times."

"New Hampshire?" he threw out there for no particular reason other than Avis was from New Hampshire. She smiled at him again while taking a sip from her little twizzle straw, and then shook her head back and forth without saying even one word.

He took another drink and a long drag on his cigarette and sort of squinted at her like he was thinking excessively hard while trying to figure out why she looked like someone he should know.

He decided that she looked sort of vaguely familiar in a mildly unfamiliar way. It wasn't like he was certain that they'd met before, but on the other hand she just had a look that he could almost, but not quite, place.

"Are you famous? You know, a celebrity or something."

"Afraid not," she answered and was immediately disappointed in herself for giving him a two word answer instead of only one. It was a slip up.

"A criminal? You know, like there's a wanted poster for you or maybe you're one of those people on America's Most Wanted?"

She inhaled a deep breath and gave him a sad look as she shook her head. "No," she said on the exhale and acted just a bit bored that he was headed in the wrong direction.

"Saint Maarten!" he blurted out like something had just popped into his head. Before she had a chance to answer, he already knew she wasn't from there. Not tanned enough. Didn't have that island vibe.

"No."

"I swear it seems like we've met before," he said. She just shrugged and said nothing. Then Pellet smiled and wondered to himself how many times he had used that line before. But this time he meant it. "So, we've never met?"

"No."

Desmund kept eyeing them from a distance. By now, Helmut was watching Pellet try to place where he knew the woman from. Avis and Savannah had walked into the bar, but Helmut flagged them down and motioned for them to sit with him and watch. All they needed was some popcorn and soda and the Pellet Show would be in full swing.

"So to be clear, I've never offended you, never hit on you, or done any other embarrassing or offensive thing to you or with you, anywhere?"

"Never," she answered, slightly proud of herself that she was back to her one-word answers.

"And you're not trying to pay me back for something I've

done? Cause I've done shit to more than a few folks over the years."

"Nope," was all she said.

"Wouldn't it be easier if you just told me where you were from?"

"Probably." She smiled and swirled her straw and nonchalantly gave little thought of curing his curiosity.

"So are you going to tell me where you're from?" At first he was just being sociable. She was good looking and sitting at the same bar as him. Now the whole not being able to figure it out, was beginning to frustrate him.

Her mouth opened as if she were going to say something, but then it closed again while she pondered his question. "No."

Pellet racked his self-pitying brain and tried to place where he knew this woman from. He took her word for it when she said they hadn't met but then he wondered if she was lying. If she were getting even for something then she probably wouldn't be too motivated to be honest about it.

Over the past year or so he'd had an epiphany of sorts and thought that it was time to pick up the pieces of his life, perhaps for the first time ever, and do something meaningful. He'd repeatedly told Avis and Savannah and Desmund that there had to be something more for him. Maybe it was because his sister did that damn ancestry search thing and unearthed so much unflattering information about his ancestors that he would have just as soon never found out. It also dawned on him that it didn't appear that he had turned out all that much better than a lot of the distant relatives that hung from the family tree. Or maybe it was because his crazy ex-wife came and went like a storm. Or maybe against all odds, he was simply growing up and he just wanted more. Whatever the reason, it motivated him into action. Since then he bought a boat, sunk a boat, almost died, shot down Shira's plane, fell in love with her, got her to fall in love with him and then lost the new love of his life to her resurrected dead father. He felt like he had been run over by a truck and the driver took the time to put it in reverse a couple of times to go back and forth just to ensure a substantial amount of damage had been done to his already nearly worthless life. In all the years before the recent hellstorm, he had come to the bar to socialize, to drink, to hit on beautiful women and to simply have a good time and forget all that needed forgetting. These days he came to sit and sip or perhaps chug alcohol and to ponder his misery while contemplating what, if anything, to do next. Today was not all that different, except for this one minor distraction.

"Never met, even for a few minutes. Never sat beside each other on a plane or on the ferry?"

"Never." She smiled and casually raised her drink and flashed a brief smile in his direction before glancing at Desmund and then back down at her glass.

Pellet slowly sat up straight and stared at the woman. His face went blank with the wheels in his head spinning full speed.

"And I've never kissed your husband, or anything like that?"

"Husband?" she snapped back, as if having a husband was almost an accusation of her doing something wrong.

Pellet was all in now. It started innocently enough. There was a woman who was obviously to anyone who could see, two or three times too good looking for him to have any grand expectations, but Pellet always had grand expectations. If he didn't, it was just because he hadn't worked his way there yet. And it was kind of her fault that he was pestering her, he promptly told himself. She kept smiling and being polite. Why would she do that if she didn't want him to stick around? The final straw? She scoffed at the idea of having a husband. Everything was a go.

He looked down and stared at his beer bottle and tried to place her face again. There was something about her. Her hair. No, not her hair. Just something. Her eyes, maybe. Then he thought for a minute more and looked over at her. It was her eyes. Maybe her whole face, but especially her eyes. His head tilted to the left and he rubbed the his face. Then he slowly wagged his finger in her direction for a few seconds without saying the words that were working their way from his head to his mouth.

"Stodgy, Arkansas!" he blurted out.

"What?"

"You're from Stodgy, Arkansas?"

She smiled and raised her eyebrows and shrugged.

"You're related to Maddie?" he finally blurted it out. "You look like Maddie."

"Cousins," she nonchalantly responded, proudly continuing the one-word answer for the moment.

"Are you who was coming down with her?"

"Yes." She watched him try to process what was going on with a look on his face like a kid on Christmas morning.

"H-o-l-y shit. Maddie's cousin. What the hell are you doing here?" he asked, getting up and extending his hand to shake hers. She slid off her stool and ignored his hand and wrapped her arms around his neck and gave him a big hug and a kiss on the cheek. As quickly as she had stood and hugged him, she stepped back away and sat back down on her stool.

"Maddie always calls me her lucky angel. Still tells people that I'm like a good luck charm. Nice things happen when I'm around."

"Is that so?" Pellet asked. The old Pellet would have taken that statement and run with it in his mind, but the new beaten down, heartbroken and pathetic Pellet simply asked the question and left it at that.

"That's what she says."

Pellet looked at Desmund who had watched the two of them and then he thought about the crazy times they had had when Maddie was around. He thought about all the stupid things they did together and then he thought about the day that she left. Pellet and Maddie were like a hurricane back then, but it was a long time ago.

"She said you're funny when you're drunk, but you're a good guy when you're sober. In fact she said that you're a great guy when you're sober." Then she sat back and waited to see how he was going to respond to it all. "Desmund said she wouldn't know what you were like sober," she said with a smile and a wink towards Desmund.

"Desmund knows nothing."

"He said that you'd say that, too," she shot back.

"So what brings you to Anguilla?" he asked as he turned and reached for his beer.

"I'm here to save you, Pellet," she answered matter-of-factly. "I'm here to take you out to dinner." Then her beautiful smile stretched across her face. "And maybe cook you breakfast," she added and jolted Pellet into wondering if she were a mind reader. She took another sip on the tiny straw in her drink. "Maddie said you deserve some good luck more than anyone she's ever met."

"Really? She said that?" He froze with his beer in his hand halfway to his mouth when a thought popped into his head. "Helmut didn't put you up to this did he?" he asked and threw a scowl towards the corner table. Helmut shook his head and mumbled something in German which everyone presumed was an insult. When he glanced over, it was the first time he noticed Avis and Savannah sitting there watching everything unfold.

"Have you met everyone else?" he asked and motioned towards the table.

"Yes. I think you're the last."

"Really," he sarcastically snapped and gave them each a dirty look.

"My name is Samantha, but you can just call me Sam."

"Sam," he whispered and slouched back onto his stool.

If he didn't know better it felt like Sam was flirting with him. It dawned on him that it was too soon and Shira was still too fresh on his mind. He could still smell her perfume on his pillows when he went to bed at night, but that was mostly because he hadn't washed the pillows she slept on since she had left. He couldn't bring himself to do it. And he had pretty much formed the habit of feeling sorry for himself. Sam could throw a wrench into his whole new persona. Plus if he was really honest about it, Shira had destroyed him three times. First in the bar, then in the boat and finally when she went away. He had a lot to recover from.

Then he recalled the sunbaked philosophy lesson from Avis when they were back in the dinghy floating near death. He had said something to the effect that there was no such thing as time and the past and the future were nothing more than myths. The past was gone and the future would always be in the future. The only thing that mattered is now. Now was the only time that truly existed. And Sam was here now. Everything seemed to make sense just as it always did when he decided that things were going his way. He raised his eyebrows and shook his head back and forth while he reasoned everything out in silence as his friends and Sam watched him having the silent conversation with himself. He slid down a couple of stools and sat beside her. And as if the chaos theory suddenly began to work in his favor, Samba Pa Ti began playing over Dez's speakers and Santana's guitar began to sing.

"You know Lucy says I should buy another sailboat. You like sailing?"

"Who's Lucy?"

"She's the woman who wanted to sleep with me on my last sailboat."

"You have a sailboat?" Sam asked, as if she wasn't aware that it had sunk.

"Gone."

"What happened to it?"

"Got hit by a VW bus when me and Avis were out sailing. Sunk."

"Avis. I believe we met this afternoon," she continued.

"He's my protégé. Taught him everything he knows," he said and raised his beer first to Avis and then to Dez.

"Good lawd," Dez chimed in. "He never stops."

"You going to get me another beer or what?" Pellet asked and then added, "Used to be a nicer bar not far from here. Gone now."

Sam shrugged. Dez tried to figure out what this poor girl did to Maddie to deserve this.

Pellet smiled while Santana jammed in the background.

CHAPTER FIFTY-FIVE

One Year Later

The bar was made from an old wooden boat hull they had bought from some local fisherman who couldn't believe someone would actually pay money for it. He was quite certain no amount of work would ever make her seaworthy again, but if they were paying, he was selling. After it was hauled it to its new home the bottom was cut out and what remained of the hull was set down on top of a sandy floor with Bob Marley and Mishka music playing quietly in the background. A lacquered wooden bar top was attached to the top edge the hull and bar stools were placed all the way around, bow to stern. A canvas canopy made from an old sail stretched ten feet beyond the full length and width of the bar to keep the sun or rain off the customers, or more importantly, off the bartender. At least half the islands in the Caribbean had a bar like this, but as Pellet stood behind his bar, he was a long way from the waters of the Caribbean. Tel Aviv was too big for him, but after they opened *Bella Vita, with the words "An Island Dogs Bar"* written under its name on the sign, he and Shira more or less pretended most of Tel Aviv ceased to exist.

Sam, as it turned out, did save his life. They went to Blanchard's Restaurant for a dinner and a couple of drinks. Then they took a long stroll on the beach in Meads Bay and finally they dropped down on the sand and watched the waves roll in and splash onto the shore. They talked until the sun came up the next morning. The longer they talked the more he thought she was wonderful. She was just like Maddie. She was smart and beautiful and honest to her core. And the longer they talked the more she thought that Maddie was right. Behind his bullshit facade of being a clueless drunk, Pellet was kind and considerate and, if not brilliant, at least not particularly as dimwitted as he pretended to be. Beneath his shallow surface was a man of character and depth and a man that almost nobody really knew. After the sun came up they headed back to his truck and he drove her back to her hotel. They parked in the gravel driveway and then walked along the stone path surrounded by bougainvillea and frangipani almost all the way to her room. At the door she gave him a long lingering hug and softly kissed him on his cheek.

"Go call her Pellet. You're in love. I promise you it will be the smartest decision you've ever made." And with that instruction she said goodbye and disappeared into her room and out of his life. She had done what she said she had come to do. She saved him. Pellet turned and looked around and took in what she had told him. He didn't fully understand what had taken place over the past few hours, but he felt more at peace than he had felt in weeks. For once in his life he had a simple plan and it was a good plan. Call Shira.

Pellet stood behind the bar in Israel with his arms folded and listened as one of his customers complained about trivial life problems. When the opportunity finally presented itself and the guy stopped talking, Pellet slid a beer across the bar and gave typical bartender advice.

"Give it time man. Life has a way of working out. Probably better than you think." It was nothing advice but it was good advice. It wasn't so much that the guys life was going to get better or worse. It was probably just better than he thought it was when he first sat down. There was a good chance that a cold beer, some good conversation and some passing of time would change his perspective. Shira sat at a table off to the side with a couple of friends. They were laughing and talking about something that Pellet couldn't hear. He didn't know or care what they were so happy about, as long as she was happy. That was all that mattered to him.

The bar was small and it was miles from the beach. They didn't have the kind of money to buy waterfront real estate, but neither of them cared. A small bar/restaurant on a side street in a middle-class section of Tel Aviv suited them both just fine. Business was good, but not so good that it was stressing. They served cheeseburgers, fish sandwiches and french-fries. With Pellet's help, Shira created a specialty cocktail and named it *The Ghalia*. It was a Caribbean blue drink with a pink umbrella served in a tall glass that had palm trees and flowers all over it. She was certain that Ghalia would have loved it. Pellet created a drink and called it *The Helmut*. It was a tall glass of water that he charged ten dollars for in honor of his friend/nemesis who drank more glasses of water in a bar than any man in history. He never actually charged anyone for it, but it made for good conversations.

Pellet took Helmut up on his offer and made him pay for the first-class ticket to Israel. Helmut claimed to the very end that it was simply to fulfill his dream of getting rid of Pellet. He said it was his contribution towards the betterment of Dez's Bar and Anguilla in general. But the truth was that he had witnessed a miracle the few times he saw Shira and Pellet together. Shira took a defeated man and a broken soul and breathed life back into his nearly meaningless life. Helmut knew that kind of love twice in his life and he knew the weight of losing it once. It was more weight than any man should ever have to carry. When he saw Pellet with Shira, it became clear that perhaps none of the gang at Dez's Bar really knew the real Wayne "Pellet" Pelletier quite as well as they believed. They knew the guy who hid behind sarcasm and stupidity and alcohol. They knew the first layer of a deeper person. They knew what he allowed them to get to know and nothing more. They knew the empty vessel that had needed a good woman to breathe life into his broken soul. When Shira arrived he was reborn. A new man rose from the beer-soaked ashes and Wayne Pelletier was resurrected.

Only Avis and Savannah went to the wedding. There was no way Desmund was ever going to leave his precious bar for more than a day or two. And for Helmut to go, he would have had to admit that he cared about Pellet. Since he was still clinging to the claim that he paid to get rid of him, flying halfway across the globe to see him get married simply would not do. Oscar, Iggy,

Maddie and the rest of them sent gifts and wished them a life of happiness. While Pellet wished they could have come, he understood why they didn't. Besides, he had Shira. That was all that mattered.

After their night on the beach, Sam returned to her office in Little Rock just a couple hours north of her childhood home in Stodgy, Arkansas. There, she continued with her successful practice as a marriage and relationship counselor. That little piece of information was never shared with Pellet. Nor had she shared that it was Helmut who employed her to come down after he told Maddie about Pellet blowing it with Shira. Maddie was originally still coming to Anguilla with her husband but knew Sam had to go first. Pellet needed to be saved and he didn't need to know any of the little details. In the end, Maddie finally saved Pellet's life, just like she tried to do all those years ago.

The baby was due in a couple of months. A girl. She would be named Ghalia after the most beautiful woman Shira had ever known. Pellet was all for it. In fact, he was all for anything Shira wanted. She was his heart and soul and his reason for getting out of bed each and every day. She was the energy that made him whole. She was everything to him, and he had no understanding of the joy that would come into his life in just a few weeks when a little angel named Ghalia became the living embodiment of their love. He would love her more than he ever imagined possible.

Shira tore down the walls that she had imprisoned herself in for most of her life. She had convinced herself that the walls were to protect her from the kind of pain she felt when she lost Papa. Then Pellet landed at her feet and it was a turning point in both their lives. Neither of them had known it at the time. There were two things the walls could not keep out. One was anything that fate or God or the universe decided to send in. You cannot stop what is meant to be. The other was Wayne Pelletier. Much like the universe, he operated on his own set of rules. Little things like almost killing him or breaking his nose did not deter him from asking her out for a date. Even Shira, who was miles out of his league with her mighty walls built high enough to reach the sky, could not say no to a man with that kind of determination.

Yossi liked Pellet from the first moment they met in Saint Maarten. Then he watched his little girl get crushed when she lost the man who she was certain was the love of her life. As much as she rejoiced the return of her Papa, suddenly a new hole had been created. Once again, there was an emptiness and sadness in her heart. Yossi was overcome with joy when he received the news that Wayne was on his way to save and be saved. Reunited with his daughter, a new son-in-law, and soon little Ghalia was more than he thought possible less than a year ago.

And Pellet? His sprit was alive and well and more or less grown up. The customers all called him Pellet. Only family referred to him as Wayne. He stood behind his bar and told stories about the time his boat was hit by a VW bus while sailing in the Caribbean Sea and how he almost died when his boat sank. Everyone's favorite part of the story was always when he hammed it up and told in minute detail about shooting down the plane that had come to rescue him. When the audience of *The Pellet Show* found out the pilot was Shira, the guys laughed and the women all got sappy. Pellet would look around and find her and give her a wink. Then he'd tell them about the bar fight and the broken nose in the life raft. Everyone loved his stories and he loved telling them. Shira loved that he was happy. And he was happy.

Wayne "Pellet" Pelletier had told his friends he wanted more out of life, and then he found it. Now all he had to do was not screw it up.

CHEERS TO ISLAND DOGS EVERYWHERE

ABOUT THE AUTHOR

Standing in front of Hemmingway's home in Cuba

B.M. SIMPSON was born in rural Maine. He joined the Air Force at 18 and lived and moved across the U.S. and Europe. After retiring from the military, he spent many years living and working in the Caribbean. On the islands of Anguilla, St. Kitts and Grand Cayman, he discovered a passion for island life and formed friendships second to none. After 30 years of writing poems, songs and short stories, he wrote his first novel ***Island Dogs*** in 2015. His second novel ***Avis Humphrey*** was released in 2018.

Today Simpson calls West Bay Grand Cayman home. He continues to enjoy the peaceful vibe, sun, sea and warm breezes of the Caribbean islands. And of course, a good rum punch made perfect by a local.

He is currently writing his next novel, ***The Package***.

www.bmsimpson.com
www.facebook.com/*BMSimpson.author*

Made in the USA
Monee, IL
12 October 2020

44794688R00180